ACCRETION

ERIC MILTNER

Printed in the United States of America
First Printed October, 2023

Published by:
Between Friends Publishing,
1080 GA Hwy 96, Suite #100,
Warner Robins, Georgia 31088

ISBN: 978-1-956544-60-2

Between Friends
PUBLISHING

To my wife Catherine for putting up with countless nights of my inane rambling and my daughters for understanding why I spent so much time in front of a computer.

PART 1

CHAPTER 1

Runa a'tah Shyena sits whistling at the stern of her family ship, gazing out at the viridescent reflection on the chattering sea. Through the cloudless night sky, a glittering halo trails behind the verdant moon, imperceptible on all but the darkest of nights. Ignoring the familiar sight of the flotilla rising and falling, she trills a doleful melody which skips over the waves and far into the night. To Runa, her people's adoration of the moon Fengari has never seemed entirely reciprocal. After all, Fengari thrashes them, the Janamudra, as surely as it pulls the tide. She glances down to the sea, letting her whistles trail off into silence. The wake of the boat scatters the reflection of the Fengari into a thousand shimmering wisps as her eyes grow wide to devour the spectacle. She ponders her place among her people as the motion of the Shena cradles her like a doting mother. "Tomorrow's just another day," she says into the wind as it catches a few of her unruly copper locks and carries them to her lips. She sputters and turns to see her younger brother Amil approaching from the rear. He playfully greets her with a gentle jab at her as he joins her. His sharp features are muddled in the pallid green moonlight, but Runa need only wait for him to speak his mind. The siblings admire the night sky for a time, drawing out their reunion into a poignant silence. "She's beautiful this low in the sky," he says, disturbing their reverie, "it's a shame what they are doing to Her." Runa rolls her eyes, ignoring the gravity etched in Amil's young features. He continues without regarding her, "I mean those lights to the south. Father says they've been sending men up there." Runa lets out a sardonic trill. "Men flying to Fengari? Their arms must be tired," she says, overly pleased with herself. Amil's anger radiates from him, her attempt at humor missing its mark. She cranes her head to the south. The shoulder star of The Heretic hangs defiantly above the horizon. "Aye, the stars agree with you," she muses, "but going up there must be a little something like sailing." Amil scoffs as he turns his back to the railing. The pall of an impending sibling squabble rises between them for a moment, but Runa leans back and meets her brother's sidelong glance through the dark. She crosses her eyes to defuse her brother's temper. Amil lets out a muted chuckle. "It's just the boot dusters, you know they get to me," he says, "They think they're so much better than us." A bit of sea spray kicks up as Runa turns to straddle the railing. She licks her lips, tasting the briny mist. "Do you think father will let me go ashore next time?" she asks. Amil averts his gaze. "I think you shouldn't press his patience—" he replies, "but maybe." Runa fidgets with a flake of loose paint on the railing and sighs. "I'm not content to stay here forever. I want to contribute more, like Mom," she says. Amil tilts his head back to look at her. "I think you're the only person that can keep this ship afloat. If you ever left it wouldn't be the same," he says, with typical stiffness. Runa flicks the loosened paint chip into the sea. "That is true," she says, holding her chin high. Without a pause, swings her leg over the railing and plants her bare feet on the deck. "Last one to bed is a faulty sump!" she shouts, before darting in the direction of the lower deck. Not one to shy from competition, Amil chases her. They race noisily through the belly of the Shyena tugging and shoving each other. A man's voice, their father, shouts something indistinct as they bump down the corridor to their quarters. Laughing and gasping, Runa stumbles into their room with Amil trailing closely behind. Then she flops into her bunk giggling. Brushing aside the unruly mass of curly hair that clings to the sweat on her forehead she says, "So! One, you get to clean the de-sal tomorrow while I'm work—" "Oh come on!" Amil whines as he places his hand on the ladder which leads to his bunk. "Like you said, I keep this ship afloat, the least you could do is help while I'm away. Mom will be so impressed." "Fine," Amil says as he rests his head on a ladder rung. "I hope she's well," he says in a reverent tone as he climbs into his bunk. Runa replies with a grunt as she shimmies under her blanket. Their mother is a Kasapna, a herald, a woman of honied water. She, like all the others, carries the history and culture of the Janamudra to the people ashore, and in return she gains something more valuable than metals or money; Favor.

As Runa stares up at the motionless cot above, she mutters a vain, habitual prayer. "O Fengari, as your consort swells beneath me, I shall abide him in my time," she drones and yawns, "as he delights in your union, so too shall I relish my return to The Deep." She recites the words, but with little affect. She supposes her ancestors told tales of things they saw on the sea to explain the unfathomable. The tales she enjoys, but the whimsy of gods seems a poor explanation for existence. Her credence corroded over the past few years. She looks up at her brother's bunk. Amil's fervent belief perturbs her. At times, she wishes that she was still so enamored. Rolling restlessly on her side, she regards the narrow alcove beside her cot. The crimson biolume light of the cabin illuminates the shelf of worn codices. The volumes of world languages, maintenance manuals, and histories of the Janamudra are all crammed so tight into the alcove that they remain unmoving as she runs her fingers along the bindings. She closes her eyes and runs her knuckles slowly across them. With each successive thump she imagines footfall somewhere ashore, somewhere her steps won't anticipate the tide. Amil groans in protest of the noise. He had always been quick to fall asleep. Rolling onto her stomach, Runa sighs into her pillow. She imagines the unseen depths that sprawl below her. The inky abyss above which she has lived her entire life. She imagines herself sinking into the dark until sleep enshrouds her.

Runa startles awake, her body tense and drenched in sweat. Her hands are reluctant to let go of the blanket wrung tightly between them. Through the window the sun peeks over the horizon, just beginning to banish the sea-clinging fog. Her father, Sasa, braces himself against the door frame of the cabin, concern painted across his wind-worn face. As Runa shakes off sleep and her eyes fall upon him, his features harden. "Unlike you to be late," he says as he turns away into the corridor. In a panic, Runa launches out of her cot, scrambling to change while avoiding the clutter Amil had left on the floor. Moments later she is pulling her deck shoes on with several hair ties in her mouth. She flips her waist length titian hair over her head, the tips of which fade into a sea-bleached blonde, and begins amassing a semblance of a bun. In her hurry she trips over a misplaced shoe and stumbles into the corridor; One final insult from Amil. "Fengari's tears!" she yelps as she bounces off the opposite wall. "Don't blaspheme," Sasa says sternly. Runa shambles onto the deck proper, the sun kissing her copper skin. Off the starboard side, Amil waits for her in the dinghy to take her to her work detail. "Did you load my stuff?" Runa shouts down at him as he presents a cheeky smile. He nods and beckons for her to get in the boat. She hops down to the boat, forgoing the ladder, then undoes the tumble hitch with a hasty motion before Amil whistles to their father. Then they are off, skimming over the deep sapphire sea in silence. Runa checks her satchel for a number of tools as they draw closer to the center of the flotilla. Several ships have fallen in close to the massive, refurbished and repurposed Esoptrian warship affectionately known as 'the Sabby.' The Sabitum's culture farms are the lifeblood of the flotilla, providing power and sustenance to the mercantile fleet. Runa waves to another straggling dinghy. They pass the two young women, the smell of hot metal on the wind. "They'll be fine," Runa says, "no better teacher than the unexpected." Minutes later they pass into the shadow of one of the massive skyward cylinders atop the Sabby. Cylinders which have propelled the massive ship since before she was born. "The Takma," Runa says as she points to one of the ships off the port quarter of the behemoth Sabitum. As they come around to the sunward side, a crescent-shaped boat abuts the Takma as several young women bob in the water in between. Above them hangs a hoist which sticks unmoving against the surface of the larger ship. One of the girls waves as Amil brings the dinghy alongside the maintenance craft. To Runa, all these young women are girls, each two or three years her junior. There are three in total in the water, and one on the boat. All of them share the same distinctive Jana traits; rust colored skin in varying hues, deep copper hair, often kinked or curly to the point of unruliness, and a spry limberness which comes from a life on the sea. As Runa unloads her pack, the girls conversing in the water resemble a vermilion algae bloom against the cobalt depths below. They giggle and sneak coy glances at Amil before he putters away. "Sorry I'm late. What's the consensus?" Runa says as she sheds her shoes and checks a piece of equipment. One of the girls blows bubbles. Another says between swells, "Shipfather says she's slowly taking on water. We are shirring up the plate welding forward of this section." The other girls vehemently nod in agreement. Turning to List, Runa says, "You concur? It's your home, not ours." List's eyes flit between Runa and the girls bobbing lazily in the waves. After a moment she nods hesitantly. "Let's see what we've got," Runa says as she slips into the water. Under the waves a panel has already been temporarily affixed just above the keel. An electromagnet holds it fast to the hull, but it has yet to be tacked in place. There is evidence that similar repairs have been completed in the past. Runa resurfaces with a sputter. "What is the leak like?" she says as she wipes the saltwater from her eyes, "Is it a trickle?" List waggles her hand in an uncertain manner. Runa sighs. "Like a cold sweat," List blurts at last. "Hand me the needle scaler... and the probe-scan," Runa says holding her hand out. The uncertain young woman hesitates before moving to find the tools. As she hands off the first piece of equipment, their hands touch, sending a sharp, unfamiliar spark shooting up Runa's arm. Her body resonates like an instrument's strings haphazardly struck. "She doesn't have to be so bossy," a voice says in Runa's mind, followed by the acrid taste of bile. She regards List curiously, wicking seawater from her brow. Perhaps it was her imagination. She shakes off the distraction as she attaches the belt and tools about her waist. The other girls murmur to each other nearby.

Moments later, Runa plops beneath the waves and passes under the keel of the Takama to the opposite side of the ship. One of the chatty girls follows her. Runa gives her an indistinct hand gesture as she inspects the life laden hull, then with the scaler she removes a section of barnacles near an old repair. Several minutes pass as she affixes the scanner against the bare metal. The girl who followed her flounders before surfacing for air and returns before the scan is complete. The clicking sound signifying that the five-minute scan has finished stirs Runa from her daydreaming. Then, with a kick off of the hull, she surfaces on the port side and takes in great gulps of air. For some time, in the portside shadow of the ship, Runa fidgets with the crude display of the scanner. She taps the screen anxiously awaiting the biopixels in stasis, before sighing and beginning a leisurely swim around the bow. With a hand from List she boards the maintenance craft. She begins shedding equipment onto the grated metal surface. "I need to speak to your father," Runa whispers to List, her mouth forming in a grim line.

ACCRETION

CHAPTER 2

On the deck of the Takma, List converses with her father. Presently, Runa watches the sun evaporate the damp footprints on the deck's surface. There is a sense of propriety for occasions such as this. It isn't Runa's family ship so she must be invited aboard, and to speak with the shipfather. List's father is a thin, hunch of a man with dark, deep-set eyes. List's mother must be beautiful to compensate for her father's homely appearance, Runa thinks from a distance. From her brief glance at him, she doesn't like him much. "Come, speak," List's father says, shooing his daughter away, "she says you refuse to repair my vessel?" The man wears a long smock of raw linen which hangs awkwardly from his wiry frame. Runa is certain now that doesn't like him. "No, Shipfather, never," she says stepping closer, "I refuse to assist in these particular repairs. Your home needs weeks of overhaul, not more patches. You'll have to lift her." The man scoffs. "We're sitting high in the water, unladen," he says as he fidgets with a Pauk-bone necklace which hangs low on his exposed chest. "Your mother is Kasapna?" he asks, rolling his sleeves up above his elbow. The mass of scars across his thin forearms flash in the morning sun against his deep bronze skin. Runa nods. "Then by all rights you can miss a haul, but we cannot," he says with a forceful, dismissive hand wave. On Runa's periphery List flinches. The indirect jibe toward a Kasapna catches Runa off guard. Even if no offense was intended, she is quick to reply, "Sometime in the past, a Kasapna established the indenture that feeds your family." The man furrows his brow, heavily shading his narrow eyes. List injects herself back into the conversation saying, "Father's sharp with numbers," she says, "the fastest in the flotilla. If it pleases him, we may extrapolate." Her father grunts. "It may convince me more than the assertions of a shipmaiden past her prime," he says with a crooked grin. As she turns away, Runa's face burns at the slight.

Runa and List confer for a time as they look over the results on the scanner. With one last look and measure of the micro-fractures on the display, they sit beside the bulwark and set to work. "Do we have to combine the factors for dynamic—" List says, uncertain. Runa nods, trying to let go of the anger. She knows she is rather old for a shipmaiden by Jana standards, but she is still a teenager. As she watches List scribble equations on the stark, white paneling with a grease pen, she feels the stare of List's father. He paces about the fore deck, muttering to himself. List makes a mistake. "Can't use this, material thickness is unknown in that section," Runa says, pointing out the error. The two young women share a knowing glance, then Runa pats List on the back. The sensation from before returns, sending nauseating static arcing through her.

Synesthetic tangles of thoughts bounce around her mind, like unparsed data. She tastes a breakfast she didn't eat. She feels a warm palm resting against her back. She remembers a limerick to approximate the base of natural logarithms. Then in confusion, thoughts of fear paint her mind with violent hues. She watches hopelessly as Father strikes Mother in a rage. This isn't Runa's father. These aren't her memories.

List leans forward with a hum to peer closer at the numbers, pulling away from Runa's touch.. "Am I hypoxic?" Runa thinks to herself as she checks her pulse. She had only spent seven minutes under, and that was a while ago. The sickening aftereffects of the peculiar sensation fade and she eventually relaxes. After several minutes, the truth is writ plain in grease by List's own hand. "The Takama is a disaster waiting to happen," Runa says, feeling vindicated as she hops to her feet. List's father strolls over, chewing at his nails. List, bows her head, saying, "She's right. New welds will only embrittle the steel further. I'm sorry, Father," He looks over the figures, occasionally flashing his eyes at Runa. Then he turns away from the math. "A moment please," he says as he beckons to List with a crooked finger. In the end, this is a family matter and Runa takes the cue. She strolls over to the starboard bulwark, leaving the List and her father to speak in private. She rests her elbows against the rail covered in thick layers of paint and gazes off over the flotilla. With her chin perched on her hands, she watches boats zip around and between the dozens of nearby ships. The sight of the three-hundred paces long Sabitum coaxes memories and a smile from her. As if she can see through the bulkhead, she imagines the thousands of people moving throughout the ship. She ruminates on her numerous assignments aboard the gargantuan vessel and lets her mind wander.

List taps Runa on the shoulder, pulling her out of her reverie. "Shipfather agrees, reluctantly," she says with a short-lived smile. The tension in Runa's shoulders yields to the news. "Aye, it's safer this way," she says with a nod, "I'll tell the girls, then radio—" "I'll tell them," List says hurriedly. Runa cocks an eyebrow. "Of course," she says with a smile, "it's your home." As she moves to give List an affirming pat on the shoulder, the visceral pangs from earlier stop her. Instead, Runa makes an awkward shuffle past her and says, "May I use your cabin radio while you take care of that?" List nods before making her way to the ladder. Sometime later, the five young women sit aboard the maintenance vessel watching the bustling boat traffic. Runa remains mostly silent, not joining in the gossip about the flotilla. She perks up when she recognizes the dinghy with Amil approaching. As he comes along side, she turns to the others and says, "Amil is fast, I'm sure your rides will be here soon." The girls call out to Amil, ignoring her sentiment. A sense of unease settles over her as she transfers her things to the dinghy. As Runa turns to speak, List says, "Be well, Runa," with her arm extended. They clasp arms. The sensation returns for a third time.

The cool spittle from Father's subdued shouting sprinkles her face. She apologizes, feeling the hot tears playing at the corners of her eyes. "Alright, I'll send her away," she says, trembling. The words come from her mouth, but the voice is not Runa's. "Don't you dare cry. Your mother cries enough for the both of you," father says before the physical unease becomes too much to bear and she pulls away...

"Don't do it, List," Runa slurs as she returns and retches violently. Her abdominal muscles tie in knots as her vision blurs. Gravity shifts its inexorable pull sideways. The dancing stars which skip through Runa's vision play about the view of List and Amil, their features marred with fear. Muffled shouting is the last thing she hears before ringing drowns out the world.

"Runa, can you hear me?" a soothing voice says as Runa returns to consciousness. She recognizes the voice as her mother. Once, twice, Runa blinks the sleep away from her eyes. "Mom?" she rasps, as the world swims into focus. She is back aboard the Shyena and she glances about to see Amil as well. He is perched on the fold-down storage door which serves as table, or now, a seat. Their mother, Usha, sits on the edge of Runa's cot leaning over her. "How do you feel?" she says, her face a mask of painted elegance. It's a face Runa has seen countless times, done up with alluring accents of turquoise and ruddy foundation to obscure any imperfection. Her hair is pinned and shaped in an ornate updo studded with gems in an imitation of the splendor of the stars. "You just got home?" Runa asks as she rolls onto her side. "Aye, but do you feel alright?" "Hard to say... Wait!" Runa says, snapping her fingers, "They're going to do the repairs. I have to tell Dad. That man is a danger to his family." Usha shushes her. "It may be hard to hear, but your wellbeing is more important. Now, are you okay?" "Answer the question, Sis," Amil says with a sigh. After a moment of patting about her body, Runa sits upright and says, "I guess. I felt, saw, terrible things. It was unlike anything I've felt." Usha narrows her eyes, drawing creases in the makeup around the corners of her eyes. "I wouldn't be so sure," she says, turning to Amil, "Please go help your father inventory the power cells until I call for you." He recoils and says, "That's bog water, Mom. I—" she cuts him off with a stern glance. Amil dismounts the table and leaves hurriedly, but he still takes a moment to slide closed the door. "What do you mean by 'you wouldn't be so sure'?" Runa says. "They called a physician from the Sabbitum to check on you. I sorely wish he had found something wrong with you," Usha says, bowing her head. Tingles travel up Runa's arms and neck. She doesn't know what, but something is amiss. "Why would you say that if they found nothing? Is this about List and her father? I didn't mean to cause trouble," she says with a manic tinge to her voice. Usha tuts in an attempt to calm her before saying, "This has nothing to do with that poor girl or her detestable father. It has to do with the Elder that accompanied the physician. When you were young, you sent the Elders into a panic, and again today."

She pauses to glance at Runa.

"You were always quick, but you'd know things, improbable things. The type of things that caused problems. You'd wake from a fitful dream knowing that someone was injured from a bight before the call was even made. Or another time when you were only five, you were being held by a ship maid at the festival of coruscating lights. From your mouth came the most intimate details about the girl and the father of her husband-to-be." "I'm sorry, I don't remember," Runa says, shaking her head. Usha sighs and says, "I suppose they were more patient with you because of me but you were never far from their gaze." Runa scoffs, suddenly having a certain clarity to her treatment among the flotilla. "Is this why I've never been paired?" she says, raising her voice. Usha averts her gaze, but the shame is plain for Runa to see. "Ah..." "The things you experience, such things disrupt the harmony of the flotilla," Usha says, her voice flat, as if she doesn't believe what she is saying. "I don't understand. What would the Elders have me do? Leave?" Runa says. Usha lets out a grief-stricken breath then says, "I've only seen it once, but their fear and superstition would see you dealt with in the old ways." Placing a hand over her mouth, Usha hides the tremble in her lip. Runa isn't sure what that means, but she understands her life is about to change. Tightness creeps in and clenches Runa's throat. "Mama, I…" she says, hot tears welling in her eyes. Usha shushes her gently as she pulls her to her breast and cradles her. There in her mother's embrace, Runa lets out great, gasping sobs. Between the fits of tears, grief turns to anger. Five years have passed since her Assay which bound her to the covenant of the Janamudra. She had been only twelve, but she had drunk the seawater without fear. Fear had come though. It came in the spasmodic moments as her body rejected the brine and she vomited, writhing on the deck. She recalls turning to see Amil, still with the face of a child. His face had been fixed somewhere between awe and fear. She ponders how much she has given to the flotilla as an ember of hate smolders within her. They would cast her away for something she cannot control. "Can't you do something?" Runa says, wiping her face with her hand. "Aye, I can, and I will," Usha says as she caresses Runa's head. "You said you'd seen it before?" Runa says. "Not since before you were born. But, aye. I've prepared for this day, but hoped it would never come," Usha says. Runa stiffens and pulls away from her mother, saying, "So I'm to leave the only life I've even known? How can you expect me—" "I'm waiting," Usha says calmly, "to hear back from a patron. He's willing to help but he doesn't possess the skills to assess your condition." "Assess my condition? Do you agree? Is something wrong with me?" Runa says, beside herself. "No, but life is often unfair, my sapphire star. The patron I spoke of, where he lives others like you are regarded as… more. Revered and afforded more than exile and shame. Runa, please know that no matter what, you will always be my daughter and I'll do anything to keep you safe." The earnest love of her mother clashes with the overwhelming hate of rejection and a piece of Runa fractures. The community she had always known is casting her away and she is powerless to stop it. "And what if I choose to stay?" she says, throwing her hands up. The natural serenity of her mother slips away as rage hardens her features. "They would send you back to the Deepfather with chains around your ankles. And that, I cannot abide," she says, setting her jaw. Dread grips Runa in its steely talons as she comes to understand what she meant by 'the old ways.' She sees her mother in a new light. The

Janamudra have many fabled stories of the Kasapna. Stories that claim they feel more strongly due to their embodiment of reserved grace, or ultimate giving. A superhuman calm and a capacity for forgiveness are their reverential propensities. But as Runa watches the tension in her mother's neck, she can't be so sure. She reaches out and touches her mother, but no sickening wave washes over her, only a stark silence mingled with the sway of the sea. Glancing to the porthole, Runa pines for a distraction, some detachment. She yearns for unfeeling, like air to a drowning man, but she can't escape. Outside the sun kisses the horizon. Tears sting her eyes again as she watches the sun ignites the sea and sky with myriad shades of violet and orange. It's a most beautiful and welcome sight on her darkest of days. And so, full of unease, Runa shudders as she watches the waves capped in vibrant glory. She feels so terribly small.

CHAPTER 3

Runa's night is fitful and full of terrors. She tosses and turns struggling to contend with the world-shattering changes and their suddenness. Thoughts mound upon her delirious mind like untended vines. When she drifts off to sleep, her dreams are chaotic. Great storms wrack the Shyena, sending wave after wave crashing over the deck. She sees Amil standing on the foredeck as another volley of waves bears down on the tiny vessel. Runa's muffled shouts falter as the torrent of water sweeps her brother overboard. As the ship lists heavily to port, she braces herself against the gunnel and holds out her hand for her brother. The angle is so steep Runa can nearly touch the surface of the sea. As they clasp arms the flesh of her arm falls away, crumbling like unfired clay. Helpless, Amil smiles as he slips beneath the waves. She cries out, the visceral pain lingering in her limb as she wakes in a sweat.

It is some time after dawn as Runa emerges topside. Be it from sweat or humidity, her sleeveless nightshirt and baggy pants cling to her as she stretches in the briny breeze. She runs her fingers through her unkempt hair, catching several times before she leaves the tangle of orange to its own accord. Glancing off to the west, a chill runs down her spine. The flotilla can't be seen. She hops over to the railing then glances off to the north. Still the flotilla is absent. "They went on to port Cardis," the deep baritone of her father crackles from behind her, "We'll rendezvous when they turn back northward." Runa turns to him unsure of which side of him she'll see, the shrewd merchant, the firm shipfather, or the loving husband. He gives her a crooked grin and crosses his arms. Runa returns a half-hearted grin then sighs. "Come with me," he says as he turns on his heel. He lets out three sharp whistles before heading below deck. Amil, unseen, answers with a single sharp trill from the helm as Runa follows Sasa below. "Today you'll see if I missed my calling as a linguist," he says as they pass into the main cabin, her parent's quarters. "How do you mean?" Runa says as her father pulls the chair away from the desk that abuts the aftmost wall. "Well, you have books, and us, but this will be your first chance to speak in Esopt with an Esoptrian," he says as he kicks his feet up onto the desk. It's true that she and her father practice conversing in the languages of his trade, but Runa never considered that she hasn't spoken with a native speaker. Sasa takes out an arm length copper pipe and a leather sack from a drawer. He undoes the string and lets the clump of lodestones held within thump on the stable. Runa sits on the chest of drawers not far away, the seeming disregard of her circumstance fanning the flames of isolation and resentment. Pondering how he can be so unconcerned that she faces exile, she watches him pull a lodestone from the clump then read the engraving with a loop. Then he drops the magnet through the pipe. Runa counts the seconds until the magnet falls out the other end. Sasa checks the engraving again then places the currency aside. "How long has it been since you really needed to check?" Runa says, watching her father drop another stone in. Sasa grunts. "Haven't seen a counterfeit in twenty years," he says. "So why still do it?" Runa says, placing her elbows on her knees in a hunched posture. "The same reason I'm continuing my life as if yours isn't changing," he says, setting down the pipe and looking to her. "I do it because it is familiar. Everyone grasps for control in the face of uncertainty, but how they do it says more than the practice itself." Runa stiffens, the direct answer catching her off guard. In the past her father has sought to teach lessons with allegory or metaphor, if he sought to teach at all. She sees that the circumstances are affecting Sasa as well, despite his hard demeanor. "Mother said she has been preparing for this. Have you?" Runa says. Sasa drops another magnet through the pipe. "We are of the same mind on this. Honestly, I'm not worried about you, Runa," he says as he sighs and toward the desk, "you are clever and skilled, so I know you will adapt, but I worry about Amil." Runa's face pinches in discomfort. She hasn't considered how anyone else feels about the situation. Realizing that she may not get the chance to ask again, she says, "Does Mom talk to you about her patrons?" "No," Sasa says. Runa mulls over a different question, seeing her father is in a more receptive mood. "Then do you know about this person coming to meet me?" Runa says. "Yes," Sasa folds his hands and rests them in his lap. "So, he's not a patron?" Runa says. "That stands to reason," Sasa says pinching the bridge of his nose. "Don't you ever wonder what kind of people they are?" Runa says. "I don't burden your mother with the finer details of captaining a vessel and she doesn't burden me with the details of her trade. It's that simple," Sasa says sharply with a tense brow. Runa shrinks. "I—" she stammers before falling silent. Standing and bowing her head, she says, "May I go?" "You may," Sasa says, turning the chair away from her. She clasps her wrist in front of herself and walks away. As she passes into the corridor Sasa says, "Find a thing within your power, then dedicate yourself to it. That's all anyone can do." Runa is not sure how he had known what she was thinking, but in this time of trepidation she is glad to have him. Then she remembers that her circumstances are changing. That the constancy of her parents will not remain. In a daze she closes the door behind her, then makes her way down into the engine room of the Shyena. Her eyes flare wide, acclimating to the low crimson biolume within. She touches the panel as she shuts the heavy hatch, and the light rises to a soothing seafoam green. As she runs her fingers along the port-most of the two motors, strands of her hair stand on end. This is her space, the space she feels the most herself. At a certain speed, the props make the Shyena sing. She ponders how much she will miss that as she pulls her hand away and sits beside the droning machine. The simplicity of the mechanical is a space she can lose herself. Often, if something breaks, she can figure out how to fix it. But how can she fix this, she wonders. Closing her eyes, Runa begins to hum along with the persistent droning. She doesn't feel the fresh tears as she loses herself among the sound.

The crunch of the hatch opening jolts Runa awake. She stammers as the sight of Usha looms in the access. "It's nearly time," she says as Runa wipes the crumbs of sleep from her eyes. She hops up and heads topside. The sun hangs low behind a blanket of fog, diffusing the celestial light. Unease settles over Runa in the eerie, liminal quality of this time and place. Roughly a mille away, off the Shyena's starboard bow, several lights pierce the fog. The mystery ship is passing them green-to-green, heading out into the open ocean. As it passes, the size is difficult for Runa to gauge, but the armored gun batteries standing proud of the main deck imply the ship's function. "Esoptrian warship," Usha says, resting her hand on Runa's shoulder. Runa shrugs her off and strolls to the foredeck. Massive pylons wider than any vessel jut out of the sea in seeming defiance of the deep. The lights marking the large concrete structures strobe through the haze, betraying the duplicate structures running southward, out of Runa's sight. Sasa's raised voice stirs her from her wonderment as they pass beyond the floodgates and into the lagoon beyond. He argues with someone over the radio for a time before going quiet again. As the light dies over the misty lagoon, Runa shambles to the cabin she and Amil share. She packs a bag filled with a few days with of clothes and a book, then puts the book back.

She lets out a small chuckle. "I did want to go ashore," she says to herself as she runs her fingers along the books beside her cot one last time and turns away.

The drop of the anchor greets her as she returns to the deck to see her mother and father watching a boat approach. Sasa holds Usha from behind in a loose embrace, resting his chin on the top of her head, speaking words only they can hear. Runa looks about but Amil for a moment, but he is absent. The boat maneuvers alongside the Shyena then comes to a crawl as a man calls out in Esopt, "May I come aboard Captain?" "Aye," Sasa replies with a belt as Usha tosses down a ladder. Moments later, a man heaves himself onto the deck. He is tall and fairer than the Jana but not by much. Even under the light pouring down from the foremast to the deck, his dark coat blends in with the dark of night. "I'm sorry we are later than planned," Sasa says with a nod to the man. "It's alright Captain, considering the circumstances. Ah—" the man says as he surveys the deck before stopping on Runa, "is this our prospective charge?" "She is," Usha says in a cordial tone as she ushers the man and Sasa below deck. Before falling in step with the rest, Runa glances down at the boat. A flaxen haired woman in similar dress to the man stands on the boat muttering to herself. She is short and thin, with fairer skin that the man, but as she glances up at Runa, she has a fierceness to her gaze. It reminds Runa of the shorebirds that are nothing but feathers, beaks, and claws. The woman looks away to tend to something and Runa heads below. Laughter emanates from the galley as she rounds the corner to the dining area. Her parents and the man are sat around the table which they use for communal meals. An apparent gift of spirits has found its way from the man's coat and onto the table. Upon seeing Runa, the man stands and in mediocre Jana says, "Good wind, good waves," as he extends his hand in greeting. His hazel eyes and full dark hair flash in the amber light. Runa reaches out to take the man's arm, but Usha stops her. Confused, Runa moves around and sits between her parents. The man, unmoved by the gesture smiles with his eyes and returns to his seat. "Your mother is wise to the ways of the world. She meant no disrespect," he says as he places his hands on the table, "My name is Adanon Chlorosa, and you have a wonderful home." Before the words have left his mouth, he decants the bottle into three glasses, starting with Usha's. Runa watches the man carefully. His gestures and speech convey a practiced confidence, but his eyes. His eyes are inscrutable and dark, not of color but of luster. Sasa and Usha savor the libation as the man spins the glass slowly between his fingers. Adanon gazes into the umber liquid as it turns, seeming to mull over his words. "I won't deceive you," he says as he looks past his brow at Runa, "You're in the unenviable position of leaving behind everything you know to live among strangers. It will take bravery, but the alternative..." Runa casts her gaze down, unable to keep eye contact as he continues to speak. "The Jana know much about things I never will, but I don't see the wisdom in casting away a gift— And it is a gift." "This we agree on," Usha says before downing the remainder of the libation. Sasa nods and looks to Runa who continues to stare down at the table. "When was your awakening? Not dreams or premonitions. It's usually unpleasant and intrusive—" "Two days ago," Usha says as she clasps her empty glass in both hands. Runa's mouth twitches with irritation. She wonders why her parents are being so welcoming yet guarded all at once. A peculiar tingling sensation trickles up her spine. Glancing between Usha and Sasa, Adanon sighs then closes his eyes. "I'm a parent myself. I understand the desire to advocate for your children," he says as he stops spinning the glass, "but I asked her."

CHAPTER 4

Usha looks to Sasa then back to Adanon who has placed his glass out of reach. "Kyr, Kyri," Adanon says folding his hands, the honorifics punctuated and lingering, "I want to harm your daughter much less than many in this world. A few moments are all I need." Usha shifts and glances sidelong to Runa with a sigh. Her eyes smolder at Sasa as she moves to go. "We will be close," she says as she sashays away from the table. Runa blanches as her father also stands and walks away, leaving her with the stranger. In well-practiced and intonated Esopt, Runa says, "I don't know what to say, Kyr." "Most start with their name," Adanon says with a small grin. Amber light from the fixture overhead casts short shadows across their faces as the ship rocks gently. "My name is Runa a'tah Shyena, but only so long as I call this ship home. Are you Mother's patron?" An abrupt, startling guffaw escapes Adanon, bringing his head close to the table. "Oh my, oh no." he says in amusement, "I am the Akroates, the prime seeker and subject of the Esoptrian Council. A Kasapna would consider me quite untouchable considering your culture's aversion to the gift." Runa cocks an eyebrow, finding several of the words unfamiliar. Adanon smiles and sips from the hereto untouched glass. "Ahem— I'm here on behalf of your mother's patron, Zidero. Your Esopt is excellent by the way." Runa relaxed her shoulders. After her conversation with Sasa earlier she has been worried about her pronunciation. "Were you sent to see what's wrong with me?" she asks hesitantly. "There is nothing wrong with you. Where your elders see the malign, we see potential. Our highest offices are held by men and women like me... and potentially you," he says with a twinkle in his eye as he holds out his hand from across the table, "Now, show me what you saw." Runa blinks at his outstretched hand and says, "Mom said—" Adanon sighs. "Contact is less acceptable when people abuse one's trust," he says glancing down to his hand, "As intricate as human communication is, it is flawed just like its creators. So please, take my hand and think on what happened." Swallowing against the lump in her throat, she clasps his hand and looks into his eyes. As she looks over his roguish features, despite his age, she finds him handsome. Adanon clears his throat, "Flattering, but focus on the incident, Kyri." Runa recoils then presses her eyes closed. She thinks of the things she saw on that day, the memories, the illness, the List's unpleasant father. Adanon pulls his hand away from hers and says, "Good. We'll make a Praxiat of you yet."

"What is that? You can see my thoughts?" Runa asks as she rubs her hand. Adanon smirks and pours another glass for himself. "This," he pantomimes the clasping of hands, "is passive. I receive only what you transmits. You have some experience with this, I think." Runa looks back to her hand, studying the lines of her flesh. Adanon begins spinning the glass as before, his forehead creasing as he says, "Before we go any further, you have a choice." Runa looks up from her hand, banishing her distracting thoughts. She knits her fingers then rests them on the table. "What's that?" she says as she leans in. She isn't sure of his intentions, but something about him insists on her trust. Just as she begins to puzzle over that notion, Adanon stops fidgeting with the glass. "I could lie and say your elders were mistaken; that you have no potential. I could teach you how to stifle your gift so you could return to the flotilla. But eventually, you'd slip up and be outcast all the same, never knowing what you could have achieved." He clears his throat. "Or you could come with me into the unknown." Runa stirs in her seat. He is offering her a way to stay with her people, but the draw of the unknown is too much for her curious mind. She stands, the chair scraping loudly. Then she strolls over to the porthole and glances out at the inky water. Fengari coyly lies somewhere below the horizon, not yet gracing the night with her luminous countenance. However, bright lights shrouded in fog lie off to the east. "Is that the harbor?" Runa says, breaking the silence. "Yes, it's a marvel. I wish I could see it again for the first time with the optimistic eyes of youth," Adanon says, his gaze distant, reverent. Runa paces across the breadth of the galley and stoops to glance out the other porthole. There is nothing to be seen to the west. Nothing but pervasive darkness. She considers how every meal she remembers had taken place in this room. How the wood of the bar top counter swells in the summer, smelling of sweet scenery she has never seen. She had wanted to do more, but she didn't know what that meant. This is her opportunity, at the cost of everything she knows. With difficulty, she sighs and says, "I think I would like to see the harbor." As she returns to the table, Adanon nods and says, "Very well."

"Why help me?" Runa says as she pulls the bottle of spirits close. She scrolls her fingers over the gilded script then looks past her brow at Adanon. "Praxiats have enough working against them within the civilized world. I cannot abide losing one to chance," he says. "Aye? Was there no chance in giving me a choice?" Runa says tilting her head. "A Pauker's gamble. Even humans can't resist something shiny," Adanon says as he leans back in the chair. Runa lets out a small chuckle. "I suppose that's true... Can you help me understand their distrust?'" she says. Mirth drains from Adanon's face as he says, "You mean your elders?" "Yes," Runa replies. "I can think of only one other Jana who left the flotilla to serve within my lifetime. But as I recall, their departure wasn't as... amicable. As for why, I suppose when your community depends on not sinking into the deep on the daily, any source of discord is to be excised expeditiously," Adanon says leaning in close and lowering his voice, "Besides, gleaning the thoughts of others is the least of our tricks." Runa leans in. "Why are you whispering?" she says with a curl to her lips. Adanon pushes his glass to the center of the table and says, "Take the drink. Our little secret." She looks at him, incredulous. After a moment she reaches for the glass and pulls it toward her, except the drink doesn't budge. The momentum pulls her toward the table. She blinks in confusion. The occurrence niggling her sense of what is and isn't possible. She tries to push the drink toward Adanon, but it's as if she is attempting to push the Shyena itself. Her eyes bounce from the glass to Adanon. From Adanon to her hand. Then she pushes the glass with her whole body, abandoning all caution. The table groans. With an exasperated sigh she relents and slumps into her chair. Then Adanon smiles, lifts the glass, and downs the contents with a shudder. "How? Magic?" Runa chirps as she glances under the table for some means of trickery. Adanon's face turns dark. "No such thing. For centuries that word and many like it were used to condemn us. Simply put, we borrowed an ancient word and idea to reframe our gifts as "Praxis." "Thus, the word "Praxiat," Runa interrupts, noticeably piqued. "Indeed... As for how, I think you've had enough world-shattering revelations today. Let's save it for another time," he says. "You can't do that!" Runa shouts, exasperated. A clambering heralds Usha and Sasa's entry to the room. Runa recoils in embarrassment as Adanon raises his glass to them with a grin. "Your daughter is delightfully curious," Adanon says as a toast, "Runa, gather your things, say your goodbyes. Delaying your parents would endanger them." Runa hops to her feet but pauses to give Adanon a quizzical look. "On account of the tide," Usha says with a smile. Adanon repeats the phrase with the same cadence as Runa hurries off to her room. A deep, frustrating guilt grows in her as she passes through the ship. Guilt for being excited to leave. Guilt for choosing herself over her family. "Why should I feel guilty," she wonders. The Janamudra were ready to be done with her.

As she passes into her cabin, the space seems smaller somehow. But everything does, this ship, the flotilla; all small against her imaginings of the world beyond. Her things sit where she left them, perched precariously on her cot, as if they never belonged. She opens the narrow closet which holds her finer clothes, most of them handed down from her mother. Running her hand along a lacy dress of seafoam and turquoise, she remembers. She had worn this for her Assay so long ago. "Delicate clothing for an indelicate affair," she thinks. Somehow the dress is undamaged after all these years. Likewise, the years haven't dulled the deep blue greens that remind her of happier times. Runa yanks down the dress and stuffs it into her pack. Then with a final glance about the cabin she sighs and wills herself to leave. The choice is made, in deed rather than word. She heaves the pack onto her back. Then with a final glance at Amil's bunk she whispers, "You will be fine without me," as she shuts the door.

Making her way back to the galley, she again notices she hasn't seen Amil since the incident the other day. It's unlike him to avoid her entirely. She ponders if she upset him as she passes into the galley to see her father capping a pen. Adanon stuffs a stack of paper into an envelope, then places it in his liner pocket. "Bureaucracy," he says in a jocular tone as he smiles at Runa. She nods and hitches the pack higher on her back. "Have you seen Amil?" she asks in Jana. Usha sits up straight then takes a deep gulp from her glass. Her parents are acting strangely. "He knows I'm leaving right?" Runa says. Both Sasa and Usha nod slowly. An acrid taste rises in her mouth as the seed of resentment takes root. She doesn't understand why they would let Amil act childish, avoidant. Perhaps they think it's easier to be rid of her quickly. Her posture changes and her expressive face goes still. "Let's not waste any more of these Jana's time," she says flatly to Adanon. "Please understand your brother is taking this worse than any of us," Sasa says, standing. A gruff sound escapes Adanon as he shuffles to his feet. Perhaps from the drink, perhaps from the motion of the sea, he steadies himself against the chair and says, "I will watch out for her. May your passage be safe." Usha accepts the sentiment with a delicate bow. Runa scoffs and marches to the door. Looking over her shoulder she says "It's a good thing this didn't happen to Amil. Your precious boy wouldn't make it on land." Usha is visibly shaken by her words, placing a hand to her mouth. "Watch your words," Sasa says with gravel in his voice. Runa huffs then strolls out onto the deck, breaking stride only to tosses her pack onto the waiting dinghy below. The commotion startles the flaxen haired woman. "Could you not?" she says, her gray eyes piercing Runa. Inside, Runa knows she is being petty and callous, but she can't seem to let her reason or compassion win in this moment. She climbs down into the smaller vessel and plops into a seat at the stern. It's as if all the emotion of the recent events has finally begun to settle on her. She crosses her arms and slumps into the seat with a sigh. Adanon climbs down into the boat and exchanges a few brief words for the woman. As he comes to rest aboard the boat he says, "This is Talin by the way. You may regret not saying farewell to your parents." Runa bristles as Usha and Sasa bid her farewell from the deck. Moments later their words are lost on the wind as they fade into the distance. Runa loses herself in the wake churning the dark water. She has never claimed the musical talent in the family. That is her mother's calling. Nevertheless, she remembers and sings a Jana shanty soft and sure:

Anchors aweigh Janamudra,
Janamudra fall away
our worries far astern today
one day we'll join the bones below

Brothers heave 'way and stow the load
Janamudra fall away
oh ne'er reason to fear that day
that day we join the bones below

Daughters mend here our battered hulls
Janamudra fall away
we gladly greet them on the day
the day they join our bones below

With a quivering lip, she ends the refrain. Then wicks away the tears at the corners of her eyes and chuckles derisively. The Shyena, where she spent most of her life has passed beyond her sight. Adanon and Talin exchange brief words over the sound of the motor and waves heedless of her discontent. Off the port quarter, Runa beholds Fengari rising to the northwest. Ethereal, pallid, and green as ever she was.

CHAPTER 5

The small vessel skips into the harbor, passing larger vessels in their haste. Runa shakes herself from her ruminations to marvel at the designs as they pass. Most are ships of war, titanic in scale of varying size and shape. Some considers some of the lines of the larger warships reminiscent of the profile of the Sabby back home. She puzzles over one ship lying low in the water. It's comprised of hard angles and flat surfaces, dark matte geometry amongst the proud armaments of the others. No bridge looms over the vessel. "Is that to avoid detection?" she asks, feeling a little better from the maritime distraction. Adanon shifts seats to move closer to her. "Glad to see you are done brooding. Yes," he says. "Scatters radio waves?" Runa posits. Adanon grunts in agreement. "The paint also absorbs electromagnetic radiation. Gets damned hot in the sun so the ship is semi-submersible." Runa gives a pensive hum then turns toward the boat's bow. The harbor ends as Talin pilots the craft toward a narrow channel between the thick concrete that forms the foundation of the city. Between the divisions of the deliberately planned city blocks, channels of water serve as means travel. As they pass into one of the channels, the waters behind and beside the craft churn an ethereal blue. Runa is no stranger to the effect. There were times that she needed to replace faulty electrochemical enzyme processors within the flotilla. Biolume is the standard among the flotilla and beyond. However, an entire city network implementing fluorescent algae for lighting, or aesthetics, is clearly designed to make an impression. The impression, much like the merchant tales of Esoptria, is boisterous and indulgent. In the flotilla, there were times that Runa needed to replace faulty electrochemical enzyme processors for lights, but the finer details of biochemistry have always put her to sleep. As she dips her hand in the brackish water, she appreciates the ephemeral spectacle with trancelike wonderment. A group of carousing young people shout and cackle on a nearby landing, stirring Runa from her daze. Talin steers the boat into an area that seems purpose built for docking small watercraft. Feeling the sudden urge to help, Runa hops to the dock and helps hitch the boat to the cleats. "She was worth every stone, Ad," Talin says with heavy sarcasm as everyone gathers their things and disembarks. Moments later, up a flight of stairs, they are on the ground level of the city. The closest structure is a marvel of steel and glass. Strands of vegetation hang down for the highest levels, presumably from a growing area atop the building. Off to the left, a bridge of glass connects the building to the roof of the next. The bulk of the immense housing construction overhangs a central core that supports the entirety of its bulk. Runa imagines the design is to avoid flooding in tidal swells, or should the seawall fail. Off to her left she has a better look at the shipyard and its massive cranes which loom over the wall that divides it from the city. Runa shifts her pack higher on her back, the uneasy stillness of the place settling over her like damp cloth. It reminds her of time spent on S'thara Anchorage. An unnerving, seemingly unnatural calm. She begins walking and the nausea dissipates. "Everything alright," Adanon asks, eyeing her quizzically. "My ears. I need to move, or I feel unwell," Runa says. "Then let's move, it's late and we all have places to be. Zidero will have to wait," Adanon says. Talin spreads a wolfish grin across her face and says, "He'll love that." Runa marks how Talin seems to dislike even the mention of Zidero. And so, they set to walking, past people and places peculiar. Boats that stand tall which function as floating diners. As Adanon leads, the structure of the buildings changes from the narrow and tall, to the flat and long. Each spans several city blocks, with more support around the vertices. As the group crosses a bridge, Runa looks back at the massive, illuminated sign that emblazons the face of the structure. "LyCorp," Runa says, reading aloud the letters in stark white. "Indeed," Adanon says. "Never heard of them," Runa says flatly. Adanon and Talin stop and look at her incredulously, then laugh. "You really don't know who you mother's patron is?" Adanon says with mirth in his voice. Runa shrugs, saying, "Some boot duster my mother entertains, I guess." Adanon clears his throat and continues to walk. "Sorry, the cultural divide still catches me off-guard," he says with a chuckle on his lips, "Zidero Lykios owns half this city, and the shipyard besides. For better or worse you'll get to know him soon." Runa looks back to the sign, imagining what such a man would looks like. Falling behind the group, Runa ponders why, or how Usha became involved with this Zidero. How she separates a part of herself for the wider world while maintaining a normal, sheltered Jana family. The carnal aspect of her mother's profession has never had a stigma among the Janamudra. Out there among the waves, the Kasapna are viewed as selfless, necessary. Runa catches up, locking stride with Adanon. "What do you think about them... us? The Kasapna. The Janamudra," she says, a tightness in her throat. "I've only had the privilege of knowing one Jana and that was long before you were born," Adanon says. "Aye, you said that earlier!" Runa says, snapping her fingers, "Who were they? Did they mention a ship? Oh, if it was that long ago it's probably changed names or families..." Talin groans causing Adanon to turn frown at her. A smile forms at the corners of her mouth and she says, "Kyr," with a slight bow and continues to walk. They all walk for a time chatting about small things here and there as they pass over the countless bridges and under the towering buildings. Runa mulls over the dynamic between these two. One moment Talin speaks freely and stands close to Adanon. In the next, she treats him with respect, almost reverence. They have clearly known each other for a long time, but propriety appears to override their familiarity. Runa watches Talin for a time. Under the glimmer of the city, her features are easier to see. Talin appears to be in her mid-thirties, with the first creases of age about the dimples of her cheeks and around her eyes. Her tawny hair hangs at neck length, just missing the high collar of her dark coat. She stands slightly taller than Runa, but the boots are a factor. Talin turns to see Runa staring at her, the lights from above revealing the freckles on her sand-colored skin. "Yes?" she says smiling only with her lips. "Are you a praxiat too?" Runa blurts. "Now is as good a time as any," Adanon says, glancing around. As he looks back, Talin glowers at him. "If anyone can bend the rules it's the Akroates," Adanon says thumb his own chest, "You see, Runa. You're a bit older than the powers-that-be would consider normal for assimilation. Too old to become a ward of the state at least. Most are fairly young. When were you taken in?" he says looking at Talin. "Five," Talin says, her features dark. She lowers her head and stares ahead, her face a placid mask. By Runa's estimation, Adanon has touched on something Talin would rather not remember. "Well then," Adanon says as he claps his hands, "It can't hurt to give you the big picture. There is a symmetry to the universe that is hinted at but is difficult to prove. For every bit of you, there is an opposing bit, but the masses and interactions betwixt are hazy maths of probability." "What?" Runa says. "The stuff that makes up everything," he says making a showy display with his fingers, "Most of it is missing on the other side, among its opposing, balancing twin. We, praxiats, just exploit this duality." "How do you do that?" Runa says, craning her neck. "Practice," Adanon says nodding, as if he said something profound. As they round a corner the view to the east and west opens creating a chasm through the city. They must have been traveling northeast as they went deeper into the city. To the east, through the towering manmade valley, sideways human likenesses peer back. One atop the other, the massive western-facing likenesses face the inky lagoon. The engravings decorate a large column which stands at the end of the channel which is part of a larger structure. The off-putting iconography sends an involuntary shudder through Runa. It reminds her of the Janamudra elders, not in the symbolism, but in the feeling it evokes. Adanon glances at her over his shoulder saying, "It's a bit much, I agree," with a comforting pat on her back. Then he strolls toward the structure with Talin in tow. Runa hesitates, looks back at the dark waters at the far end of the channel. That way lies despair and the pain of remembering. Ahead lies fear of the unknown, but the potential for something else. A something she doesn't understand, but she chose it. The nagging recentness of her departure clings to her. She shakes her head trying to dislodge the trepidation with force, but only thing that give her comfort is the relaxed confidence Adanon showed aboard the Shyena. If he is calm, she should be too. She glances past Adanon's broad frame toward the ominous slumbering visages, exhales emotion, then jogs to catch up. "What are they?" Runa asks, studying the thirteen placid faces stacked skyward. "They, are The Watchers of the Imminent Dark, as for the depiction. Could be sleeping, could be dead, who knows. Not much for religious symbolism myself," Adanon says with a shrug. Talin scoffs, but knowing scoff, as if there is some unseen humor in his words. "What is it?" Runa says. "I do love the curiosity," Adanon says, "but like our conversation earlier, this defies description. A temple. A mausoleum. A civic edifice. A locus of power. I understand your trepidation." "Aye, you do? I've never been here, much less seen anything like that," Runa quips as she motions to the building ahead. Talin cracks an unrestrained smile. "She has a point, Ad," she says, stopping in her stride. Adanon too stops, turning curiously to Talin who purses her lips in thought. "Listen, I can see you are clever; your being here is evidence of that," Talin says pointing to Runa's brow, "If you aren't careful they will take from you everything if you let them." Runa frowns, Talin's words hammer blows on the brittle steel of her nerves. "It was the same for you?" Runa says in a whisper between them. "I was a child," Talin says past her brow, "I can't say they will be as understanding given your... particulars." She looks Runa up and down. With a shudder, Runa glances to Adanon who stands with his back still to them. "Come off it,' he says without turning, "Don't let Talin's care of discontent rattle you."

Considering the circumstances, Runa has difficulty taking comfort in his words. Talin's gray eyes flash, seeming to take joy in Runa's discomfort. She doesn't know enough about the situation to stand up for herself, so Runa looks away and continues after Adanon. As they draw closer in silence, an unfamiliar scent to Runa carries on the wind. It is an unpleasant organic smell akin to the ammonia one would smell when working near algae production aboard the Sabby. Runa pinches her nose and trudges on. "Welcome to the marsh," Adanon says with flat affect as the courtyard-like area opens before the temple, revealing another angled pillar on the far end, similarly facing the west. They cross into the courtyard in front of the column of faces where the channel terminates in a ramp of gently rippling water. In the courtyard, a maze of spiraling moss grows in a path between the stones. Runa pauses to appreciate the attention required for such a display. The yawning maw of an entrance hangs open despite the large doors which stand nearly as wide as they are tall. A chittering from a high corner draws Runa's attention. Even in this place which gives her pause for its immensity, a careless creature nests in the trappings of human conceit. As she looks back the reflective interior of the temple, several people clad in dark hail Adanon. "There has been an incident in the south," says one of the figures. The thin-framed man with worry in his voice eyes Runa past his spectacles and raises a brow. The glassy sheen of the temple beyond begs for her attention, but Runa's gaze is drawn to the tension on Adanon's face. He turns to her and says, "Try not to be angry with me when you wake." "What?" she says as Adanon reaches out and places his hand beside her face. An assault of words assails her mind as she feels herself slipping.

"I am often desired but rarely remembered. I can be followed without ever taking a step. I am weal to some but woe to others. What am I?" the piercing voice in her mind echoes.

The fleeting moments of Runa's consciousness are tinged with nausea, confusion, and fear. The pain in Adanon's eyes is the last thing she sees before the dark.

CHAPTER 6

Adanon runs his fingers through his dark hair and sighs. The low lightning in the capacious temple beyond does little to obscure the infinite reflections of the interior off the mirrored floor. The rows of ossuaries baring the faces of revered men and women line the outermost area of the temple. The design ushers congregants into the wide middle aisle which terminates at a raised area obscured by long, sheer drapery. Beyond the orange drapery lies the mausoleum. The new construction, under which lies the atavistic monument, seems to devour its precursor with a metallic maw with gossamer teeth. "It's procedure, Kyr," the thin young man says pushing his glasses up his nose. Who then steps aside as the other acolytes tend to Runa. "I know procedure, Turios. She doesn't have worms or whatever they'll be testing for," Adanon says watching as the acolytes carry Runa away, "She's alone, confused and now she's going to be scrutinized in unpleasant ways, all for the sake of procedure." Talin scoffs and imposes herself between the two men, "We've all been through—" "What happened in the south? Another schism?" Adanon says interrupting her. Turios straightens his posture, the unflattering light from above casting harsh angles across his face while highlighting his ruddy teenage face. Adanon looks sternly at the young man, subduing his amusement at the fop of curly brown hair perched atop his head. "Kyr, no. A naval officer is briefing some members of the council. I don't have the details," Turios says, averting his gaze. Talin moves to speak, but Adanon makes a dismissive hand gesture. Her face goes from visibly flustered to blank in a moment. Adanon assumes, despite her usual calm and efficacious outward appearance, Talin is bothered by Runa. Is it jealousy? He cannot say, but he knows Talin well enough to know that it isn't personal, just petty. He looks to Turios and says, "Let's go then."

As Adanon climbs up one of the spiraling staircases that lies at the wings of the narthex where he found himself moments before, he is thankful that the spirits have worn off. Up and up the flights, into the glass upon glass of the council's showy temple top garden. Turios ushers Adanon and Talin in before stopping to wait within the tower. The air within is cool and drier than that and smelling less of the marshes. Beads of condensation run down the angled glass panels that meet above a ring of chairs. The chairs sit upon a raised dais surrounded by a fountain of trickling waters. On the dais an elderly woman with a coif of white hair towers over a man in military dress. Beyond the young man, another gentleman lounges in one of the many chairs looking disinterested. Talin waits at the edge of the surrounding fountain as Adanon crosses the smooth bridge. Beside the naval officer, Adanon drops to his knees before the two councilors, letting his forehead press against the cool floor. "I came as soon as I heard. A new prospective took some time to procure," Adanon says without looking up. "No worries, I am sure they were worth making us wait," the seated man says flatly, "The young man will just need to repeat the information once more." The elderly woman huffs. "I've heard enough," she says turning to the seated man, "we can continue this later, Darian." Before trotting down the stairs to leave, she eyes Adanon coolly with sunken eyes. Both Darian and the elderly women are on the Esoptrian Council, which serves as the final authority within The Federation. An institution which is at the heart of the oligarchy based on praxic merit across the thirteen prefectures. The understanding of how new councilors are chosen is a closely guarded secret. As the elderly woman leaves, Adanon stands, adjusts his coat, and glances to Darian with creased brow. Councilor Darian crosses his legs and waggles his hand at the officer as an unspoken command. The officer wipes the sweat from above his bushy brow. "Akroates," he says with a salute, "As I was telling the potentates- Contact was lost with the frigate Rushander three days ago. Her six-month patrol of Uxian waters was nearly up. Today, some of the locals found the ship adrift, without her crew." Adanon rubs his chin and glances at Darian, who looks bored. "What's more, the commissioned praxic cohort is missing," says the officer, lowering his head in reverence. "A somnial attack I'd wager. Your missing crew is at the bottom of the bay, Lieutenant," Adanon says. "Two hundred thirteen men, Kyr?" the officer says. "And five praxiats more than likely," Adanon adds, "Please ensure their relief is apprised of the situation. I'll speak with the replacement cohort personally." Darian sighs dramatically. "Ahem, thank you Lieutenant. You were very thorough and competent," he says tilting his chin to the ceiling as he sinks lower into the chair. With a salute to Adanon and a bow to Darian, the officer takes his leave. Out of the corner of Darian's eye, he watches the officer. His right eye tracking poorly and stopping before the periphery. It is a well-crafted glass eye, but the prosthesis has its limitations. The moment the naval officer passes beyond the chamber Daria lets out an exasperated sigh. "Why do you do that?" he says, waggling a finger at Adanon from his relaxed pose, "Speak to them as equals." Adanon takes slow and deliberate steps up to top of the dais. "Perhaps it's lost to your myriad years, but I remember what it was like being powerless," Adanon says as he glances down through the water and glass at the grand ossuary in the temple below. Darian chuckles and slides out of the chair. "They weren't powerless in the jungle. And much less now. Lest we forget," he says, tapping beside his glass eye with a hooked finger. Adanon grunts knowingly as he sits on the steps. "I'll be honest with you Adanon, the loss of a crew of shoal dredgers is tragic. I weep, truly," Darian says as he looms over Adanon, "but whomever harmed that cohort needs to be excised-made an example of." Adanon glances to Talin standing at attention nearby. "I'll keep a close watch on the situation, but I think the message was clear." "Then our reply will need to be just has clear. Some think the Dives' grip is too tight but given what Uxians can do with sticks and arrows, he may yet need to squeeze," Darian says through his teeth. Adanon raises a brow, still watching the motionless Talin. "At any rate, the council will discuss the best course of action, but I must admit. I'm tired, old friend," Darian says with a shrug. The honesty in his voice gives Adanon genuine pause. The council is a lifelong assignment. Death is to leave. To leave is death. Darian leans in and whispers, "If I left it all, would you join me in the old country?" Adanon's face twists as he looks at his once close friend, now made a figurehead of the State. The years and the burden of the council has changed the Darian he knew. He can't remember Darian ever wanting of returning to The Anvil. Even in the bleak terror of the trenches far from home, Darian sought to move forward, never reminiscing on their younger years. There are no fond memories for either of them in Stormanvil anymore, and the thought of the windswept domes sends a shiver down Adanon's spine. "No, my place is here," he says, pinching the bridge of his nose. A look of disappointment crosses Darian's face for a brief moment. Then he kisses his teeth and rocks onto his feet, saying, "Yes, of course. Duty and all that. A jape, my friend." He paces away from the stairs with a bounce in his step. His long sleeves sway in gilded strips about his knees as he approaches Tallin. She maintains her posture as he looks her over to an uncomfortable degree. "You took a pirate as your second?" Darian says in a haughty tone,

"A long way from home, brigand," This is not the first time Talin and Darian have met. It's a strange and demeaning game he seems to enjoy. "We take what we can get these days I suppose," he muses as he turns heel and returns to Adanon. Talin bites her lip out of his line of sight. "Talin has spent her whole life away from Orin, but that is true in any case. Our latest addition is from the flotilla, the Janamudra. Zidero is planning to sponsor her if she proves herself capable," Adanon says, watching Darian closely. In mentions past, Darian has always shown open disdain for the Janamudra, but not this time. A fleeting smile crosses his lips before he turns back to Adanon. "Curious..." he says as he returns to the steps beside Adanon, "One wonders what a man like Lykios intends for a Janny girl. But I'm sure it's nothing untoward." In the relative silence of the garden Darian cackles, causing Talin to startle. His laugher echoes off the glass ceiling giving it a thin, grating quality. "Oh, where has your sense of humor gone, Ad?" he chuckles as he elbows Adanon's side. "I donno. Something about the girl, or maybe it's me. Seeing these young praxiats makes me feel terribly old," Adanon says, fidgeting with a ring on his weathered hand. "It could be worse," Darian says with a chilling glance, "You could feel nothing!" he shouts with mirth. Again, his solitary laughter fills the garden. Adanon stands and smooths the back of his coat. "It has been a pleasure, Councilor," he says with a bow, "Next time there is a summons I will bring some of the data collected from the ruins of Rygell." Darian stands to see him off. "Yes of course. Nothing like the loss of thousands of Orin's sons to lubricate civic discourse," Darian says, winking at Talin. She accepts the jibe with a curt smile. Then Adanon turns to Darian and offers his hand, knowing the bidirectional threat it poses. Darian glances down at the extended hand, cocking his head but showing no emotion. He then moves in for a hug, taking Adanon off guard. The councilor embraces him loosely and whispers, "Brother, sometimes I wonder where you will be when the drums are on the horizon." Then, he pulls away with a smile and pats Adanon firmly on the shoulder. Adanon feigns a smile and gestures to Talin as he turns to leave.

Moments later, as they pass out into the stairway, Adanon swears under his breath. Turios is leaning against the wall looking bored, but quickly straightens as the duo see him. "Turios, make sure no one overhears us," Adanon says as he begins trotting down the long stairs. He slips into his habit of nervously clearing his throat. Halfway down he says, "It's as if he already knew about Zidero and Runa somehow. I need you to do what you do best," he says with an earnest look at Talin. With predatory quickness Talin draws a blade and turns on Turios. Before he can yelp or react, she pins Turios to the wall with her forearm and holds the blade against his inner thigh. "Today is the day we find what you're made of," Talin growls. "Loyalty to the council or an ideal?" Adanon says calmly to Turios, whose eyes dart between his betters. "Loyalty to you, Akroates," Turios grunts through the pressure on his clavicle. In this moment Talin assails his mind, probing for intent or deceit. Then after a prolonged moment, she turns to Adanon and nods. "Good," Adanon says as Talin releases the young man, "I knew you could be trusted. Oh, and your group will be taking on Runa when she passes. She's a good fit." "Kyr, how can you be so sure she will succeed?" Turios says with a tremor, still shaken by the sudden violence. Adanon smirks and says, "It's not a question of surety. I know she will because she must."

CHAPTER 7

An onerous darkness clings to Runa. There is nothing beyond her but the void until sound and sensation press through like the pinhole breaches in a hull. Her senses of beyond rise in fluttering waves, vociferous against the silence that was. The gentle hum of something without. The chill of bare skin. The pang of hunger. Runa sits upright with a gasp, remembering. She ponders on remembering. Much like the desire to rid oneself of desire is at its core, still desire. How does one remember to remember? With a difficulty her memories return in a trickle. She recalls Adanon's hazel eyes, falling back, then nothing. As she glances about, she takes in her surroundings. She finds herself in a room of muted colors, beige, brown, and white. While much larger than any accommodation at sea, this space lacks substance. To her right lies an unassuming door. A door with no handle or knob. The effect of the sedative that was used on her begins to wane, ushering in unpleasant thoughts. She wonders if she has done something wrong. A memory buoys to the surface as she shifts herself off the bed. Adanon. She remembers what he said before the darkness. "Try not to be angry," she mimics him saying with derision as she strolls to the door. With some lingering unsteadiness she crouches to examine the plate where a door handle should be. It is nearly flush with the door, having no fasteners, and the door itself is unreasonably solid. Upon examining the inner door frame which hides the hinges the realization settles over her: this door is meant to keep her in.

Runa looks about the room with a discerning gaze, noting again the intentional drabness. Inaccessible lighting, no fasteners, no glass. She rounds the edge of the bed and peeks into the dark room adjoining. White light blooms to life as she enters the area that contains a combined, minimalistic shower and latrine. On the outer wall there is a rudimentary mirror made of polished metal. Trying to calm herself as the sinking feeling rises within her, she runs her fingers around the edges of the mirror but finds no purchase with her fingertips. Then for the first time since leaving the flotilla she gazes upon her reflection. The clothes she wore have been changed into loose-fitting beige garments. There is a slight sense of intrusion that comes with the thought of someone undressing her and dressing her again. The colors of the clothes remind her of the traditional Janamudra burial linens. She tries not to dwell on that as she notices the bandage on her arm and begins to unravel the sticky fabric, knowing that her blood was likely taken. An inexplicable weight settles over her. Her heart palpitates as her mind recalls the past few days. She has left everything behind for this strange place and people who have seen fit to cage her. As she Runs her fingers through her curly titian hair, she searches for anything to ground herself, but the effects of the sedative and the suddenness of her situation frays her wits at the seams. With a whimper Runa turns away from her reflection and sinks to the floor. The cool tile is a shock against her bare legs. More shocking is the feeling of guilt that claws within her. Guilt for leaving and the fear of the unknown. "Mama," she blubbers into her hands as tears begin to fall uninhibited. She sits for a time as the weight of everything bears down on her, wanting to disappear. Between the heaving sobs Runa looks toward the shower. Then, in seeking some sense of normalcy, she drags herself into the shallow titled enclosure. Still clothed and sniffling, she turns on the water, then unflinching she bows her head as the cold streams over her and steadily grows warmer.

She sits there until the soothing warm water turns cold again. The motion-sensing light has long sense dimmed. She lost herself among the myriad droplets, but it was a welcome loss. Once the panic abates, she peels off her drenched clothing and climbs out of the shower. Heedless of the tangle of soaked hair about her shoulders, she strolls back to the room and flops on the bed. Then she folds herself into the soft, clean bedding as she wards off the intrusive thoughts which refuse to go. The thoughts, after a time yield to the solace of sleep. Her dreams are unremarkable, bleak. She wonders a land devoid of life and light with the whimsy that dreams often contain. She floats about pondering why she doesn't travel like this in the waking world. Then she comes to a rocky coastline, as ominous clouds form over the water, spiraling, writhing in their fervor. For every bit of mundanity of the dream before, the storm compensates with wrath, lashing Runa with wind and water. The cyclone that bows to embrace the sea fills her with dread as she tries to run. The howling wind and stinging rain envelop her, and she awakes again in a sweat.

Her first thoughts are unusual. Of things she hasn't thought of for some time. Her father's adherence to the Janamudra's faith. The sea... The Deepfather. His bride and sister Fengari, rent from the same fabric, so that all may prosper. Something about this fanciful tale stirs her memories. "Duality. On the other side," she says mimicking Adanon's cadence. She realizes that the boat she arrived on could have come directly to the strange temple by way of the channel. In a moment of clarity, she reasons that Adanon's wandering through the city must have been purposeful. He must have wanted her to see something. Reflecting on what was said and seen, she rocks herself gently while sat on the bed. She again pictures the faces of stone. "He had called them watchers," she says to herself, "How can they watch if their eyes are closed?" For a time, she weighs the implications in silence. Maybe they are watching for something that can only see without sight; or dead, as Adanon put it. Her thoughts flit back to her father the Jana belief that nothing awaits humanity in the end. Nothing but the dark. Rest is its own reward, Father would say. Which is a comfort to some, knowing that this life is their one chance to make a mark on existence. Runa sighs and tucks herself back under the blanket, feeling a chill. She begins to imagine herself dying or dead. She pictures herself bound in chains and resting at the bottom of the shallow sea. Wavering sunlight from above struggles to pierce the gloom, casting a ghastly sheen across her pale face. An imagining so vivid she can almost feel the bloat of decomposition pressing from within her. Or the wriggling and nipping of all manner of sea creatures at her former flesh. But dalliance with the macabre does little to calm her nerves. Then the thought of her brother, mother or father suffering such a fate shakes her deeply. As she pictures their contorted faces in the deep, she begins to weep silently into the pillow. For Runa, these helpless sensations are new. A tingling restlessness for want of rest. A mind that shows itself terrible and unwelcome things. She begs, the sky, the sun, Jana gods, and gods unknown. She bargains silently until sleep takes her again.

A loud, intentional slam tears Runa from her dreamless slumber. The door. She scrambles, fighting against the blanket that feels terribly heavy. Then the sight of the same door as it has been since she has been here. But something accompanies the vacuous silence. The scent of the sublime satisfaction of savory sustenance. Runa nearly stumbles over herself as she lurches for the steaming, covered plate on the side table. Lifting the thermal cover, she is greeted by a rapturous sight. A spread of a roasted beast served alongside a lumpy purple mound, all topped with a white cream. Runa doesn't know what it is, but it is the possibly the best meal she has ever seen. She tears into the food with abandon. Her mother is right, she thinks. Hunger is the best spice. This meal is much preferred to the compressed algae or smoked fish of the flotilla, she thinks. Something as simple as a warm meal has brought her back from the brink. Through her enjoyment of the piquant pop of the rooty mush, she reasons that her captors must want to keep her alive. Thus, the food and water. She pauses, a bone dangling precariously from her lips. The thought of poison crosses her mind. After a moment she chuffs audibly, then pulls the bone away with a snap. They are not trying to kill her, at least not yet she reasons. With the last morsels licked from the plate Runa begins to feel human again, at least for a moment. She lies back on the bed and stares up at the blank ceiling, thinking. She ponders if this is some sort of test. A test with no questions and a dubious solution. Even if testing her isn't the purpose of this room, she endeavors to escape in spite of her captors. If they should wish to see her fail, she will relish in success. For a moment she considers if Adanon had intentionally deceived her, but that isn't the impression she got of him. He seems earnest despite his obfuscations of what lay ahead. She reasons that she only knows two people in this strange new world. That being the case, she must place her faith in at least one of them. Considering the alternative, she chooses Adanon. Then once she has resolved to formulate an escape, she returns to the shower, washes herself under the hot water, then returns to the room renewed and resolute. Searching the small dresser, she finds several outfits identical to the one she awoke in. The thought that she may be under observation causes her to blush, and she dresses herself quickly.

Runa runs her hand along the outer wall, unable to shake the recurrent thoughts of home. It's inexplicable, her lingering on things old or forgotten when the present is pressing. It's as if she is forgetting something important but the details are out of reach. In slow, measured steps, she walks along the barrier as she hums in thought. She ponders her conversation with Adanon aboard the Shyena and the discussion on praxis. There is a tingle on her cheek. She touches her face with her other hand. In that moment she remembers. She remembers the words Adanon had forced into her mind before the dark. The fragile words of a riddle. "Often desired but rarely remembered. Followed without taking a step..." she murmurs to herself, struggling to recall the third clue. She plops herself onto the dresser and begins habitually kicking her legs off the side. "Weal or woe?" she mutters, struggling with the translation. Runa claps her hands and laughs. The riddle only works in Esopt, for the 'dreams,' when one sleeps and 'a dream,' such as aspirations, are the same word. "Dreams," Runa says with a smile and pictures the faces of stone. Runa hops down from the dresser and continues to pace around the room. With each step she pieces together anything she knows about dreams. There are a few Jana tales which involve dreams. One she recalls in particular with a dubious message.

It is a tale of a Janamudra fisherman of old. It isn't a happy tale, but myths rarely are. The fisherman would search for the fish in his dreams. As he slept the fish bade him to catch them, to free them from the frigid depths. To let them bask in the sun above, among the Deepfather's favored people. They convinced him that they wished to be caught. Each night before bed, the fisherman would recite a phrase before drifting off to sleep. "I fear no fetter when fetching Father's fish," he would say to himself to remember.

Runa says the phrase aloud in Esopt and chuckles as she struggles with the syntax. It sounds better in Jana, she thinks. "Maybe it's not the words," she says. The fisherman's fable ends when he is gobbled up by a pauk, the razor-beaked marine avian as long as five men tip to tail. The fish had deceived him, but Runa doesn't stop to ponder the allegory or its meaning. She sits on the edge of the bed after circling the room. Figuring she is already in the belly of a metaphorical beast; it couldn't hurt to try. So she lies on the bed thinking the Jana words, repeating the phrase until the words lose their meaning. As she slips into the somnial stream, Runa looks down on herself, and about the room. She has done it. The induced lucidity brings a jolt of excitement to her slumbering mind. A jolt which spirals her back to the waking world. With some choice Jana swearing, Runa slaps her hands into the mattress and stares up at the ceiling. This may be more difficult than she thought.

CHAPTER 8

Talin Argyra follows close behind Adanon through the opulent corridors of the Grand Cenobium. He had insisted on checking on the Janny girl after leaving Turios behind. Watching Runa slumber in the simple puzzle room had given Talin some twisted pleasure. "She doesn't know how good she has it," Talin says, fighting back the habitual urge to bite her lip. After all this time, some of the nervous vestiges of her childhood still remain. Adanon makes an indistinct grunt as they pass into the atrium where several young praxiats mingle in cliques. The murmur of youthful discussion falls away as he and Talin pass through the area until they leave through the tall arrowhead-shaped door. As they stroll along a footpath into the pitchy darkness of the swamp, they pass scampering unseen creatures accompanied by the droning screams of insects. Moments later they are standing before a secluded abode surrounded vegetation. Adanon places his hand on the handle, pausing for a moment, then enters. Standing just outside, Talin watches as Adanon moves about the entrance and activates the biolume. A soothing azure light washes throughout the home and Adanon turns to glance at Talin. "Come in," he says as he rummages through the cupboard and pulls out a large bottle of amber liquid, "you can drop the pretense." Talin waggles her eyebrows at him despite his attention being elsewhere. "Thought you'd never ask," she says in a sultry tone as she sashays in the door. Adanon uncorks the bottle and pours himself an immoderate glass before raising the bottle to Talin. She makes a hand gesture indicating she will take a small pour. Then she slips out of her woolen coat that marks her as a praxiat. Adanon crosses the room then sinks into a large leather chair, cradling the libation. Talin watches him with a sadness in her eyes, for she knows where he is heading for the evening. "What's on your mind, Kyr? The girl? Darian?" she says, walking to the far end of the living area, down the steps of the communal area, and up to the large window which face the pitchy dark of the swamp. The play of the light behind and the blackness beyond creates a warm reflection of the room against the glass. She looks at herself as she takes a sip of the bitter, smokey liquid. The drab sleeveless undershirt reveals her toned arms from years of service and training. Her eyes drift down to her feminine features and in that moment, she wishes she had worn something else. Glancing at Adanon in the reflection as he nurses the libation, she sighs. His gaze is distant, not on her, which she finds irritating. They have worked together in this subordinate relationship for nearly a decade. Never has Adanon shown any interest in her in a romantic way. In this moment she considers if he even cares that she is here. Talin turns away from the reflection and sits across from him on the low, cushioned couch, forcing him to see her. "Hmm? You said something?" Adanon says taking another swallow of his drink. "What's on your mind?" Talin says with a stretch and a yawn. "Darian," he says curtly before setting his glass on the ground beside the low chair. Adanon pinches the bridge of his nose and says, "He asked if I would go home with him. It was surreal. I didn't know how to answer him. Never has he... not even when—" he gestures to a picture frame resting face down on the counter top. Talin lifts the frame and studies the photograph within. It contains a fading image of Adanon's familiar face, but decades younger. He stands beside a woman while holding a young girl about his hip. Talin smiles at the thought of him being happy, despite the pain she knows comes for him later. "I'm sure they wouldn't want to see you two at odds, considering how close you once were," she muses as she places the frame back on the counter. Adanon furrows his brow at her from across the room. "You don't speak for them," he says with gravel in his voice. Talin glowers, an anxious sheen of sweat gathering above her lip. She knows not to bring up Adanon's late family, but the petty side of her wonders just how far she can push. It's not the reaction she wants, but it's something. And sometimes that is enough. His anger is passion, a passion preferable to the melancholy Adanon is prone to slip into. "You said he was also acting strange," Talin says in an attempt to deflect, "more duplicitous?" He scoffs and says, "That is an understatement," as he finishes the contents of his glass. She opens her mouth to speak but he interrupts her saying, "It doesn't change anything." She nods slowly. "Do you want me to look into it? I will be real quiet like. Nothing to tie you to it," she says finishing her glass with a grimace. Adanon chuckles. "Realistically, him mentioning it to me ties me to it, makes me party to his dereliction if I don't say something," he says with a sigh and waggles his glass at Talin, "No, I wouldn't ask you to do something I wouldn't do myself. It's just too risky to tail him without preparation- Saint's eyes, what if he were to catch you?" Talin pales as she fetches the bottle of liquor. "I would make sure I wasn't a liability," she says slowly, resting her hands on the glossy stone counter. "Come off it, I need to think first," Adanon grumbles. "You mean you need to drink!" Talin says raising her voice as she points an accusatory finger at him, "He told you that he intended to apostatize! Yet you won't give the order. Are you sure your judgment into clouded?" "Damn your eyes!" Adanon bellows, "Yes! Something is off, but we have to move carefully. Not hastily." "He was dismissive of the reports from Orin again. Why?," Talin says. "I don't know," Adanon says, pressing his empty glass to his forehead, "Even a blind fool can see that they are increasing, but they offer no solutions." "I know you don't want to hear this, Ad, but you are too close to the schism issue after... them," Talin says as she points at the picture on the counter, "I'm afraid it will break you." What she says is true. Any time the topic of the diaschisms is brought up, Adanon has a tinge of madness in his eyes. I wild, pained look, which the thought of causes Talin to shudder. She didn't know Adanon when he lost his wife and child, but she remembers the first schism. Who wouldn't, she thinks. Talin had been still a young acolyte at the time, but she remembers the news. How the displays in the cenobium had shown the dome crumbing to dust in the southlands. Two hundred thousand laid low under the home which became their tomb. As if the Anvilytes don't contend with enough of nature's indifference, they were the first to contend with a preternatural disaster as well. The men and women of Stormanvil are a hearty people, as sturdy and stubborn as the stones and domes of their homeland. But the schism had broken them the way empire never could "This is the second and last time I will ask you not to speak on them," Adanon says with venom in his voice. He swaggers over and wrenches the bottle from Talin's hand then swaggers back to the chair. As he pours himself another glass he chuckles and says, "Break me? Like the old book says, sometimes it takes a broken man to mend the world." "I don't think that's what they meant," Talin says skeptically. Adanon drinks deep from the glass. "An expert on theology now? Maybe Darian is right to mistrust an Oringian praxiat," Adanon says, hanging on the words as the drink takes effect. "You don't mean that. Adanon, I want what's best for us- you!" Talin says, pleading. "We can talk about it. Being there wasn't any easier for me when I lost my family, worse even. You can't imagine—" "It's my burden- You can barely remember your family. I had a whole lifetime with Diba before I met you." With those words, something flips within Talin; a mix of anger and senseless jealousy. "And some life it must have been, leaving her and your young child to play boy-soldier," Talin spits, her voice quivering. She knows that Adanon had no choice, but she loses the hurtful words regardless. After a silence that lingers, Adanon stands. He visibly fights back the tremors in his limbs. "Envoy Argyra, leave," he says, voice tight, measured. Talin thanks old and nameless gods that the effects of alcohol dull a praxiat's abilities. If Adanon had been sober, she doesn't know who would survive a mortal struggle between them. It's at this moment that she feels her pulse in her clenched fist about her blade, and she feels ashamed. She wants nothing more than to leave. Adanon has always driven her mad. "Akroates," she says with a slight bow as she makes her way to the door. Hot tears tease at the corners of her eyes as she gathers her coat then sees herself out. On the outside, among the croaks, chittering and chirps, she lets go. Deep gasps escape into the humid night as she fights for composure. She takes a final look back at the plain door then moves away, each step taking her away from the source of her passion and pain. But she knows it isn't grief. It's the deep, onerous affection she feels toward Adanon. On her walk back to the well kempt grounds surrounding the Grand Cenobium, she replays their conversation wishing to change the outcome. A junior praxiat hails her near the magrail station within walking distance of the cenobium but lost in her thoughts, she fails to return the pleasantry. On the dimly lit platform she awaits the next transport, dwelling on what to do about Adanon, Darian, everything. She tells herself she needs to sleep on the matter, not to be hasty, as Adanon had said. Perhaps tomorrow he will be more willing to hear her out. No, they need time apart. The deep resonant hum of the magrail's tracks alerts her to the approaching cars. As the transport arrives, she enters with a begrudging skip. Then with a sigh, she sinks into a seat at the rear of the empty car. In the brief moments before the car leaves, she relishes in the stillness. She ponders if his overt attention to new girl is a paternal side of Adanon that she's never seen. She is conflicted because she finds in endearing and irritating all at once. Talin closes her eyes as the rising whine heralds the coming departure. With a metallic clang, someone bounds between the closing doors, startling Talin. More than a startle. Something about the sensations and the stress of the evening takes her back to that day a lifetime ago.

She had curled herself into a ball as the dust fell around her in the street. Her mother had cried out. But no, it was more like a rattling gasp. As she had watched the crimson wet the sand around her mother, she looked up into her vacant eyes and wished to disappear. The projectile hadn't finished her father and brothers. "Where is your sister?" her father had said to her eldest brother as ricocheting rounds danced about the streets of Rygell. Her brother looked around the debris and dust for Talin's young body. Once, no twice, he had glanced over her in those prolonged moments following the concussion. She had not understood until much later that he couldn't see her. The metallic thump of the guns had drawn near as the crumbling stone wall gave way and pinned her father in a vicious thud. In hindsight, Talin ponders if her mother and father had been the fortunate ones. The pinging report and whine of the coilguns still find ways into Talin's mind. The trauma of having watched her brothers gunned down while she hid mere paces away. An awful sounds which cling to her still.

With a ringing in her ears, Talin is back in the car watching the man as he heads toward her. He approaches wordlessly, his face devoid of emotion. With feline grace and bated breath, Talin shifts to a nearby seat. Never taking her eyes off him as he slouches into the seat she had left. He neither says anything nor acknowledges her on the short jaunt back to the Esoptrian metropolis. Of course, this is because he doesn't know she is there. Choosing not to be seen is a skill Talin has mastered in the decades since that day clouded by death and dust.

CHAPTER 9

Over the course of several days, Runa awakes to the pleasant smells of prepared meals. Each seasoning is familiar to her palate, but the ingredients and preparation are often strange. One meal had been a soft egg served atop a crisp salad of white leaves. The runny yolk and coarse pepper served as an unusual seasoning. Back home, she had been no stranger to a seaweed salad, but this had been drier, less salty, and more terrestrial. The next, and her favorite, had been a flat disk of bread slathered with a tangy sauce and topped with delicate cheese and pungent herbs. She had giggled with each bite. This time there is no meal, and despite her many attempts to, she hasn't figured out how to escape. She has discovered how willing oneself to dream can be a reductive prospect. How long, she wonders, will her captors hold her, feed her, observe her. She is sure it's finite. Given what she has seen and heard, she is certain that the subdued empathy shown by Adanon is an outlier here. So, with the memories of her last conversation with her father, she sets her mind to a routine to combat the still lingering dread that overshadows all she does. Often in the steamy recesses of her waking showers, she muses on mourning, grief. Her memory goes back to when her father's mother had returned to the deep. Runa had been young, but the grief and sense of duty which had settled on her are still fresh today. Her Kasapna mother had never learned the finer details of maintenance and repair, so the duty had passed to her. Her paternal grandmother, her p'timah, had lost her sight before she lost her wits and Runa still recalls how her hushed voice had read to her before she never spoke again. A part of Runa resents the elders for not taking the elderly woman in. At sixty, older members of the flotilla are considered for such a position, but the needs of a ship often outweighed the needs of an individual. Therefore, she had overseen the Shyena until she could no longer, and often Runa wonders if she had been born earlier, if the elders would have let her rest. This had been years before the first and last time Runa had seen her father cry. In the light of the morning sun, as her p'timah sank into the depths, Runa had said to herself, "Rest easy, I will take care of Her." Now this memory of youthful resolve dredges up bitter regret, for she had lied. Trying to detangle her hair with her fingers, Runa sits on the end of the bed retreading familiar, resentful ground. Rather than anger toward her people, a bleak knot of self-loathing coils within her. Despite the thoughts of the contrary, Runa takes deeps, measured breaths as she pushes back on the intrusive thoughts of loss. She tells herself that thoughts come and go. That these thoughts don't define her. Then with a meager glimpse of hope, she endeavors to break free.

Sleep comes quickly as Runa feels her consciousness slipping into the dark. This time is different. When she recalls that she is sleeping, her mind doesn't reject her lucidity. A warm sensation courses through her as she looks around herself. It is the same room, but different. She imagines that she can feel the intent of each thing her gaze lands on. A tingling foreboding sensation sneaks up on her, as if she isn't meant to be here but she presses on. With loose, otherworldly motion Runa drifts to the door and wills that she should pass through it. First her hand, which is filled with a bitter chill as it passes through. Then with hesitation, she looks back to herself lying motionless on the bed. She struggles to understand the relationship between this state and the praxis she has seen and displayed, but there seems to be a connection. Once her excitement has passed, she crosses outside into the hallway beyond. Runa fights back the shock as the chill pierces her in places unmentionable. Then with a breathless gasp, she opens her eyes outside herself. This isn't a dream; she is sure of that. In a moment of elation, she feels herself drawn back, back to herself, her vessel. In a moment of panic, she glances down the ornate hallway festooned with drapes and rugs foreign to her. The tug of the self grows stronger the more she thinks about what she is seeing. Then she turns toward the door and grabs for the handle. Her hand passes cleanly through it. She can feel herself stirring. She's slipping, returning. In a desperate moment she places every drop of will and desperation into her hand , grabbing for the handle again. This time, it yields with click. Like vapor on the wind, she disperses. As if passing again through the blood and pain of that surreal moment of beginning, her eyes strain against the light.

Talin sits slumped in a decrepit rolling chair in front of several displays. She appears to be intently watching for something, but really, she is ruminating about her argument with Adanon. It has been two days since, but when she had seen him this morning, he placed her on this duty with few words and fewer smiles. The creak of Turios' chair pulls her back from her thoughts. She cuts her eyes at him, and he slumps in the chair. Talin has a keen distrust of Turios, despite having delved into the more intimate corners of his mind. He may be loyal to Adanon, but his familial ties could be troublesome by virtue of simply being a councilor's kin. "I would also rather be doing something else, Kyri," he says without meeting her eye. Talin sighs and leans against the simple desk, resting her chin in her hand. "This is work for neophytes," she says leaning back, "No offense." Turios crosses his leg as he sits back with a creak. "This is work for those assigned to it," he says objectively. Talin grimaces and turns her attention to the displays again. They sit there for a time, their faces lit by the soft blue hue emitted by the industrious biopixels. "What do you think he sees in her?" Turios says, breaking the silence. Talin looks at him curiously, hearing a sentiment of her own given voice by another. Losing some composure she says, "Adanon often sees the best in us. An easy way to be disappointed. People rarely fit into that idealized mold he puts them in." Turios lets out a subdued chuckle. "Speaking from personal experience?" he says with a thin-lipped smile. The clang against the desk as Talin stands betrays her frustration. With her back to him, she says through her teeth, "I need to stretch my legs," before leaving the room. Out in the hallway she curses under her breath as she plods away with heavy footfall. This level below the cenobium is seldom used any more. On occasion, it's used for assessment, or isolation of praxiats. This lower level once served as overflow accommodations for the young praxiats above, but the numbers of new talent have receded from that former decades old high. The only occupant for the past few days had been the Jana girl. Talin walks briskly down the hall, pausing to look at one of the nondescript doors. It looks like the others, but it is a cell. A cell designed to contain a praxiat. There are several reasons one could find oneself within that room, sedition, apostasy, dereliction, to name a few. But Talin shudders at the thought of one malfeasant act, illicit compulsion, the theft of will against another. She ponders for a moment how some of the apostates she hunted may have ended up in such a cell. The ones left alive at least, she thinks with a smirk. Then she turns and glances back down the hallway. A nervous shock shoots down her body upon seeing something unexpected. The fiery-haired sea witch's daughter stands several paces down the hall, staring back.

Runa watches Talin turn toward her with a protracted pause, as if confused- or amused. It's surreal seeing another person after isolation, she thinks. Talin assumes her predacious demeanor as she takes a step forward. "So, you managed to get out. That's good..." she says with some cheek, "... and bad. Certainly, no going back for you now." Runa tenses, unsure of what she should do. Talk or run seem like her only options. "Where is Adanon?" she says, leaning to glimpse the hallway beyond Talin. "I'm here at his behest. You can talk to me," Talin says with a glance to the open door, "You seem to have some skill at projection." Runa glances down at her dominant hand. "Is that what you call it?" she says, prickled flesh rising inexplicably on her bare arms. Talin hums in assent as she takes another cautious step. "What would you have done if I couldn't figure a way out of the room?" Runa asks, tilting her head. "You were under observation to see if you would manifest any other praxic abilities under duress, and you did. I'm sure Adanon will be pleased," Talin says, relaxing her tense posture somewhat, "Come with me and we'll wait for him to return." There is something persistently pestering Runa on the inside. A distrust of Talin that doesn't feel petty. She takes a longer look at the older woman. Behind her pleasant looks lies something manic, primal. Of the few things she understands about this place, how they had managed to sneak food into the room without alerting her gives her serious pause. "I think I'll wait for him here," Runa says coolly. Talin chuckles, saying, "You seem to think you have some agency here. Do you really think you had a choice on that merchant vessel you called home?" "What do you mean? He gave me a choice," Runa says as she tenses all over. "Maybe before your parents signed you away, but now, here, your service is compulsory." Runa feels nauseous. "They did it to protect me," she says, unsure. "Yes of course, and Fengari is made of Gaerdanian cheese. Now come with me, please," Talin says, reaching for Runa's arm. She jerks away, but Talin is quick and practiced. Runa stumbles back, then Talin is upon her. She clenches Runa's loose shirt and wrenches her sideways. Talin is deceptively strong under the showy jacket. Runa cries out as she flails against her. Talin's unnerving gray eyes narrow as she gazes into Runa. Then with a smirk, Talin lets her go. The pleasure Talin takes in such a chase is far from Runa's erratic thoughts. Not sparing a moment, she ducks away, bolting from her aggressor. She glances back for a moment, glimpsing only an empty hallway. Without warning, a blunt collision from her right bears her sidelong into the wall. She connects with plastered concrete with a thud then crumples to the floor. Dazed, she kicks at the unseen as it bends her, writhing, into submission. As she feels, not sees, the limber arm tense around her neck, Runa gasps, "I yield." "I asked nicely," Talin whispers in her ear as Runa's vision tunnels. "Kyri, she yields," a male voice says out of Runa's sight. With a tut, the knot of limbs releases from around Runa, leaving her a coughing, sputtering mass. "I just can't help myself," Talin says brushing off her coat. Turios hums in response as he offers a hand to Runa. Rising to a knee, Runa hisses as she touches the stream of blood running from her left brow. Then she fixes her gaze on Talin. The older woman smirks as she holds the rust-colored Jana girl in her gaze for a time, then turns heel. Runa accepts the hand offered in assistance from Turios, but never takes her eyes off the tawny haired tempest as she swaggers away.

C H A P T E R 10

Runa's thoughts are scattered as she follows Turios, who yammers for a long time about inconsequential things. After a subdued introduction Turios had begun rattling off facts about the building; several names and dates all of which are meaningless to Runa. Still holding a spare shirt from the room against her wound, she follows Turios into an elevator. "Turios, please," she says with a groan as he beings explain the of the lift. "Right, sorry," he chirps back, hanging his head. A short ride later they find themselves exiting onto a landing. The landing faces an atrium which slopes inward with each floor. Through darkened glass which forms the massive exterior wall of the structure, billowing white clouds drift across the artificially darkened sky. Farther beyond a peculiar sight draws Runa's eye. A structure which appears eager to topple. An inverted ziggurat that looms over a well kempt lawn dotted with periodic standing stones along a stone path with draws a line from this building and the ziggurat. "Come on," Turios says as he leads her toward one of the wings that serve as boarding for young praxiats. A short stroll later and he knocks on one of the inconspicuous doors once, twice, three times in a broken rhythm before a muffled voice responds from within. With a click and creek, the door opens revealing a young woman with skin as dark as a stormy sea. She smiles with her eyes at Turios, dimpling her pump cheeks under her prominent cheekbones. She stands a hand and a half taller than Runa, but her posture is warm and inviting, at least until she glimpses Runa. "Come in,' she says with a frown as she turns and makes her way into the spacious room. Compared to the room Runa found herself in not long ago, this space is rich in color and trappings. After a short entryway, the area opens up to the left and right with a dining area and kitchen, respectively. A communal area lies down carpeted stairs which surround it on all sides. The sunken square area is mottled with pillows and cushions perched precariously about. Runa is enamored with the unique décor. "What happened," the dark complected young woman says as she rummages through a kit on a small corner table. "Argyra," Turios says with indignation. She shakes her head as she pulls several tools out of the case then motions with her head for Runa to sit. Mirroring Runa, she pulls a chair in front of her then smiles as she takes a seat. "I am called Oma. Can you show me, please?" Runa pulls the bloody cloth away from her brow to show her. Oma kisses her teeth upon seeing the gash. "On such a pretty face too, but I can fix you up," she says pulling out a penlight and shining it in Runa's eyes, "What is your name?" Runa's attention wavers upon hearing a sound across the space. Another young woman sits sidelong to the commotion of the room, working on something. She has a similar dark complexion to Oma, but she is brawny. The muscles of her arms shine as she intently works on the task before her, heedless of Runa. Oma clears her throat, bringing Runa back to focus. "Hmm?" Runa says clearly distracted, "Oh, Runa a'tah Sh- just Runa." With a smile Oma leans into Runa's line of sight as the other woman continues diligently working. "That is Thand, my sister," she says with a sigh, "Thand isn't very personable." Runa hums then says, "And Turios is?" Oma lets out a genuine laugh as Turios squirms in the corner. "Humor is good, but you appear to be mildly concussed. But like I said, I can fix you up," she says, grabbing forceps from the table, "I know you are new to this, but I can shunt the pain from the stitches." Runa cocks her head considering Oma's words. "Through praxis?" she asks. Oma glances to Turios for a moment then back to Runa then nods. The shock of recent events has begun to fade for her, but Runa still has an anxious feeling. It's as if she is having trouble picking up on the intricacies of the conversation. She knows getting stitches will hurt, but her pride is more pained than her flesh. For a protracted moment she watches the bigger of the two sisters work from across the room. She thinks about her bother Amil, how eager he was to receive his first scars. While it is uncommon, for some Jana boys, the nervousness of cutting one's own flesh proves too much. Choosing to avoid the pain of scarification means shame and an existential pain far greater than a few cuts. Runa wasn't part of this rite of passage, being a shipmaiden, but she recalls talking with Amil about it at length. They had agreed that the shame of not belonging if the ritual is refused is unfortunate but necessary for the good of their people. She hasn't thought about this in years. Maybe she should reevaluate a great many things after leaving the flotilla, she thinks. "Leave the pain," Runa says with a tone of finality. Half a moment of doubt crosses Oma's brow, but after the moment passes, she gives a subdued smile and reaches for the stitching medium and needle.

The first plunge of the curved needle causes Runa's stomach to turn, but after Oma gets into her rhythm, resolve outweighs the pain. It is hard for her to focus on a particular point throughout the procedure. The pulling and tugging pain brings tears to her eyes. Wanting to remember this she closes her eyes until Oma finishes. "There, beautiful as the day you were born," Oma says as she presses the stem patch over the area. Across the room, the steady gritty sounds end. Thand holds up a blade then drags it laterally against her arm. Seemingly satisfied with the results, she nods and wipes the wisps of hair from the blade then slides to her feet. She plods over to Runa as she inspects Oma's handiwork in a small mirror. "Show me your teeth," Thand says bluntly. More confused than stunned, Runa obliges. Thand backhands Oma's shoulder harder than necessary. "Her teeth aren't green," she says flatly, "You owe me." Oma's face grows dark from embarrassment. An incongruent, nervous laugh escapes from her as she pinches the bridge of her nose. "I'm sorry. It's a song," she says as Than retreats to the other end of the room, "I told you she wasn't great with people. 'Jannie girl with the green teeth' is a folk song from Bujani D'we, our home." Runa stammers for a moment, but Turios butts into the conversation. "A pejorative and a stereotype all in the title. An efficient means of offense," he says shaking his head at Oma. Runa belts out a laugh, but it's cut short by the pain in her head. "Oh- don't make me laugh," she says with a groan as Oma and Turios join her in a chuckle. "Well then," Oma says with a clap of her hands, "Adanon has told us a little about you. I'm sure you have a lot of questions, so let's go for a stroll." She gets up and continues talking to no one in particular. She tells an anecdote about some of the items lying about the room, trinkets and the like. She pauses to glance at Runa periodically between her stories, to which Runa nods. "That was very brave or foolish," Turios says leaning in over Runa as he taps the corner of his eye, "I'm not sure which yet." Runa simply smiles as she stands and crosses the space to join Oma. "There was a temple with many faces, something about watchers, where is that? And what is this place?" Runa says, feeling more like herself. Thand has since retreated behind a closed door after her comment about teeth. "The temple is in the city proper. A short ride by magrail from here,' Turios says. Runa isn't sure what that is, but she nods knowingly to spare herself an explanation from Turios. "This is the Grand Cenobium. It serves to house and train praxiats until they have served out their commission," Oma says picking up a peculiar doll from a shelf. "And when is that?" Runa says. "Twenty-five. As we are assigned elsewhere in the federation, cohorts rotate in younger praxiats. Thus, how you came here to us," Turios says. "But I'm an outlier," Runa says. "Mmm, yes. Typically praxiats are assigned to a group at eighteen, but I think there are some special considerations in your case," Oma says as she fetches her boots. Thand opens the door, letting it bang against the stopper then huffs into the room. "Is it wise to discuss any of this with her?" she says stiffly. Turios saunters over, his entire demeanor shifting. "She is going to be in our cohort. It would behoove you to get used to it," he says, crossing his arms. Runa struggles to find a moment to interject on her own behalf. In a shout-whisper Thand says, "I don't think it's unreasonable to be wary, especially since she is tied to that heretic Zidero." Runa clears her throat and says, "I don't even know him, if that eases your mind." Thand chuffs. "It does not, and it's not simply a mistrust of you. Zidero is an outspoken opponent of the Church," she says to looking away from Runa, "We should all be concerned." Oma laces her boots tightly then stands. "Adanon assured us that it's fine. Besides, Zidero being a loud atheist doesn't inherently mean he is in opposition to the Church," she says. Runa has somehow found her way outside the ring of discussion since Oma walked over. "She's right," Turios says, "'Opponent' implies he actively resists the Church and the council, but he puts a lot of money into the foundling house." "Don't," Thand says, pointing her finger at Turios, "advocate for him." "Thandiwe, that's enough," Oma says, crossing her arms, "I'm going to trust that she belongs here. Do you think Adanon doesn't know what he's doing?" Thand knits her brow and says, "That, is completely different," before turning and returning to the side room. The argument draws to a close with the slamming of the door and Oma sighs deeply. "Let's take that walk," she says as she strolls to a closet and back again with a pair of shoes for Runa, "Probably not a perfect fit, but closer than Thand's." Runa admits that she wasn't paying attention to Thand's feet to the sound of subdued snickering.

Stretching her legs feels better than Runa had imagined, particularly so after her confinement. Oma leads the group down the tower making small talk. Turios is much less talkative now. Runa wonders if it's because of Oma. "How long have you known each other?" she says in a quiet moment. Oma smirks at the question. After some consideration she says, "We've all known each other from our foundling days. Turios loves talking about it." The color drains from Turios' face. He adjusts his glasses as he says, "What she means to say is, I still wake at the slightest sound because of the mischief the boys got into most nights. Fifty boys sleeping in one dormitory was an exercise in madness." Runa chuckles.. As they exit the elevator at the ground floor of the atrium, Oma leads out the cavernous east facing doors toward the inverted ziggurat Runa has seen before. "I take it that most praxiats are brought up in these 'foundling houses?'" "Most, yes. I'm sure Adanon told you that it's very unusual to have an awakening so late?" Oma says. Runa nods, saying, "The latest episode wasn't the first, I'm told." "She made up for lost time. She managed to project and manipulate the door..." Turios says as he glimpses at Runa, "An encouraging start, until Talin showed her ugly side." Oma claps her hands together as she glances off to the south where the well kempt grounds end at the tree line. "Speaking of," she says as she waves at the dark-haired figure in the distance.

CHAPTER 11

Adanon's head pounds as he shambles out onto the footpath. "May have gone a little too far with the drink," he thinks to himself as the afternoon sun assails his eyes. He raises a hand to fend off the headache inducing sheen. In the distance a group of young praxiats wave to him. He recognizes Omarosa, Turios and Runa. He feigns a smile and waves weakly to the young acolytes. He ponders how good they have it for a moment. But then again, that is the point. He could slip into the trap of distrusting or blaming the young for perceived wrongs in the world, but he has sought to spare them the hardships he had lived. Adanon runs his fingers through his unwashed hair and straightens his posture as he draws nearer. "Quite the trio," he says with a smile as he rubs the accumulation of dark stubble on his chin. Then his gaze lands on Runa. "What happened to you?" he says, setting jaw in anger. "Talin and I got into an argument," Runa says with a sigh and a gesture to her face, "Then, I got frightened and tried to run. I tripped and fell." "Unacceptable. I know Talin well enough to know that was no accident." Adanon says. Then he turns to Turios, "You were there too?" Turios nods. "And what is your assessment?" "Kyr, far be it from me to guess Talin's motives but she has been... agitated... these past few days," he says, looking at the ground, "Maybe I riled her up in discussion. I apologize." Adanon swears under his breath and says, "Oma, Turios, please give Runa a tour. Something requires my attention." Then he trots away before turning back and saying, "She managed a bit of praxis?" All three nod. "Well done," he says pointing to Runa before strolling away.

As Adanon crosses the verdant field toward the magrail station nearest the cenobium, he ponders his relationship with Talin. He recalls the first time he had seen her name on the transfer papers over a decade ago. At the time he had thought the woman must be either highly motivated or a bit mad to want to work with the Akroates directly after serving out her commission. Some praxiats choose that time to go out and start families or work closer to their homes after gaining some agency, but Talin chose the hard life of hunting down those she had more in common with than the rabble. In hindsight, perhaps Adanon should have seen the cracks. As he boards a magrail car, he feels the weight of his years more than he cares to admit to himself. The ride into Esoptria stands out no more than any other day. The whistle of the trees and hanging moss outside the window is a comfort in its familiarity. Even if everything fell to ruin, this place would remain to reclaim what Men had sought to control. In a shaded section of the track, Adanon's reflection peers back at him. Something catches his eye in the shade, a strand of gray hair standing out among his raven coiffure. He plucks the hair from his head, and despite the absurdity of it, he wraps the strand into a ball then places it in his pocket.

A short trip into the city later, Adanon exits the car. All about the platform young people chatter as they carry about their day. It's easy to hear the shifts in tone as one, then two people recognize him. He would like to think that it has never bothered him, but the reality is that it varies from day to day. The title of Akroates can be held in esteem or reviled depending on whom fills the role. Given what he had to lose to be driven to apostasy, Adanon isn't sure if any of the years since have been worth it. Since taking his rites he has never truly lived for himself. The worry that he could never count on being alone in any moment has faded with time, but the thought of a piece of himself resting in the hands of the council still makes him as ill as the day they took it from him. At the edge of the platform leading into the city, a young Gaerdanian girl hangs about her mother's legs, giggling. She smiles shyly at Adanon as her mother struggles to converse with another woman. With a smile and a finger-wiggling wave to the girl, Adanon pushes himself forward. Lifting his chin, he muses how sometimes, the smallest things save him from the dark.

The deep green door outside Talin's apartment looms over Adanon as he holds his hand up to knock. In the interim between his approach and the knock, he composes himself, not knowing which Talin will answer. He takes a deep breath, knocks, and waits for a reply. After a moment, Talin opens the door. She is dressed down in a white sleeveless undershirt with baggy pants. They don't exchange greetings as Adanon enters. The blinds are drawn on the west-facing windows, casting long parallel lines across Talin's lower half as she crosses the space. Adanon can't deny the grace of his subordinate, but his sense of propriety has always kept his more primal thoughts at bay. Talin is nearly the age his wife had been when she had passed in the schism. Over the years, Talin has grown more attached to him. Watching the muscles of her upper back shift as Talin reaches for a cabinet in the kitchen, he ponders if that is why they have been at odds recently. Retrieving two cups and a bottle of spirits, Talin moves to uncap the lid. "No, thank you," Adanon says, turning to peer through the blinds. He knows he should be firm, but delicacy may be more effective with Talin. It all depends on her mood. Talin wordlessly stops pouring the drink then walks over to him, hanging her head, unwilling to meet his eye. "I saw your handiwork on that girl," Adanon says, "Your behavior has been unacceptable recently, and it cannot continue." Talin looks up at him, eyes red, tired. "Kyr," she says with a nod. "Good," he says, stepping past her. Adanon has given it some thought but doesn't know how to address the wreather in the room. He has mulled over the scenario countless times since the news of the lost crew near Uxkukul. A seasoned cohort should have been able to handle most situations. If it had been a somnial attack, the natives must be harboring more praxiats than anticipated. It's a troubling matter, but Adanon has some hope that the colonial leaders will be able to control the situation. Even though his past few days have been a blur of drink and melancholy, Adanon has found time to read a more detailed report compiled by a praxic intermediary to the navy. "I have some news- about the other day," Adanon says after a protracted silence. Talin stiffens visibly, which Adanon notices. With a dismissive gesture he says, "You will not speak of our meeting with Darian. We watch how things play out." "As you say," Talin says as she walks back to the bottle she placed on the counter. She pours two glasses despite Adanon's prior declension. For a time, she stands with her back to Adanon as he looks about the modest apartment. It isn't much, Adanon knows. But considering the system in which praxiats are raised, it can mean a lot to have a space of one's own. He walks over to the high counter and props a leg on a stool. Talin turns to him and says, "Could you be convinced to reconsider?" Adanon shakes his head as he stares off at nothing. "No," Adanon says rapping his fingers on the counter top, "Here's the scenario. I meet with the council, placing my word against a Councilor's." His conflicting emotions hang plainly on his furrowed brow. The Akroates is beholden to the council's whims as much as any praxiat; if not more so. "Show them the memory," Talin chirps, unrestrained. "I'm not sure that would stand up to scrutiny. Darian can talk his way out of anything," Adanon says with a sigh, "Also, I'd rather keep them out of my mind if I can help it." Talin nods knowingly. Her eyes drift to the unattended libations. "I'm sorry for how I've been lately. I feel out of sorts. Maybe I need some time away," she says in a rare display of vulnerability. Adanon reaches his hand toward her then hesitates, falling short of contact. She doesn't notice, still fixating on the glasses to her left. "It's alright. Take a few days," Adanon says drawing his hand back and placing it in his pocket, "I will spend some time with our shady 'friend' and the girl. To be honest, Talin, it might go better without you." It's a blunt proclamation, but they both know it's true. Talin can be needlessly antagonistic at times, and considering her latest stunt, Adanon would rather avoid placing Runa and Talin in the same room. Talin turns to him and smiles slightly. "Thank you, Kyr," she says. Adanon smiles and nods to the unattended alcohol. "Save that for me. We'll share a drink after your leave." After a small farewell, he makes his way out. He hopes this time away will do her some good.

Talin bolts the door, hanging her head. She listens for the percussion of Adanon's firmly fleeting footsteps. One he has gone, she moves slowly, taking in the modest confines of her apartment. She had resolved to do this before he even came, but now his visit has strengthened her resolve. She moves to the closet and dresses herself in plain clothes. Plain so they won't distinguish her as a praxiat. Her eyes drift to the dark woolen coat hanging beside the entryway. Then she walks to her bedroom and begins to pen a letter. After much scribbling and groaning, she returns to the living room. The sun is setting off in the west. The light of the arc furnaces in the shipyard burn a deep orange, creating a second, artificial sunset. She had grown fond of the spectacle but even the familiar sight feels hollow in the face of her grave fantasies. She watches the evening haze from the marsh roll out over the harbor for a time before turning to the languishing glasses on the counter. She downs one glass and strolls over to gather her coat. She folds it neatly and places it on her bed. As she closes the bedroom door, she wonders how Adanon will react when he finds she has left. Then she returns to the counter, downs the second glass meant for another, and walks out into the bustle of Esoptria.

C H A P T E R 12

Runa sits alongside Oma on a drab bench near the magrail terminal. At first, she was fascinated by the technological marvel but over the last few hours, the overload of information from Turios and Oma has numbed her. Numb to the point of poor retention and weariness. "So, this Council holds power over the Church too. Why isn't Esoptria considered a theocracy?" Runa mutters. "That would be a question for Thand. I find myself falling more on the secular side of things—" Oma says in an earnest tone, "but don't tell my sister that please, she wouldn't understand." Runa nods, noting the trust such a statement seems to place in her. She considers whether Oma is particularly loose with personal anecdotes or if it is common for Esoptrians. Oma's demeanor since Turios turned in for the evening, and Runa has grown more curious about the interpersonal aspects of the cohort. Two sisters, dissimilar in many ways and a boy who doesn't notice social cues. Now Runa is set to join their group, but only after a nebulous initiation that is set to happen when she turns eighteen. Sitting on the bench she does the multiplication in her head. "Six thousand four-hundred eighty days," Runa mouths to herself. In addition to all the information she had been bombarded with, she must learn a new skill. A skill which until a few days ago would have read like a fanciful children's tale. All day she has felt as if she is forgetting something. Now in the solace of twilight she remembers. "Where are my things?" she says to Oma. "That's a question for Adanon," Oma says. As if summoned, a magrail car arrives and Adanon shuffles out onto the platform. Runa is a little too stunned to speak. "Good evening, ladies," he says with a grin. "How—" Runa says, "I was just asking about my things." Adanon rubs the scruff on his chin and nods. "Come with me," he says, "There is someone you need to meet." Runa turns to Oma, thinking how she is the first person to accept and be kind to her in some time. "Thank you, Oma," she says with a lighthearted smile. Oma grins and makes a gesture which means nothing to Runa. She assumes it's some way of expressing pleasure in doing something. Then she stands to go with Adanon.

A stroll in silence down a winding path past the cenobium and Runa finds herself in front of a house of sorts. Adanon welcomes her inside with a nod. Hesitating for a moment, Runa steps into the space. It is dimly lit and smells of dust inside. "I had to negotiate for you to keep this. I understand why you would pack something like that, but until your mental state was evaluated, it needed to be kept from you," Adanon says walking to a closet and presenting Runa's rucksack. She pinches her face, having no idea what he is talking about. Adanon returns a curious look. "May I?" he says reaching for the bag, to which Runa shrugs. Digging down into the bag, his face tenses as he searches for something. "I only packed clothing. Even left my books," she says, but is halted as he pulls out a long off-white object. It appears to be a sheathed blade. She knows it but it isn't hers; it is her brother's. Runa hesitantly walks over to the knife. "Amil must have snuck it into my pack," she says as Adanon rests the scrimshaw blade in her open palms. She looks over the familiar engraved handle and sheath. The image on one side is of a multitude of hands reaching up from beneath the waves. The other is a dynamic scene of a Janamudra man wrestling with a pauk beneath the waves. Given that the man has the razor-sharp beak held agape, Runa thinks the man isn't winning the contest. Runa lets a sniffle slip as she says, "This is a ceremonial blade. The one that cut each scar into my bother. It's a thing of great pride." Runa hangs her head. She recalls the tales of Jana men losing their blades to the deep. She has heard that some have dove into the black in search for their knife, never to resurface. For her, the message is clear. Losing Runa is tantamount to death for her Amil. "He wanted you to be safe," Adanon says. Runa lets out a half-sob, half-chuckle. Adanon, stunned with a slack-jawed gape, reaches a hesitant arm around her then pulls her into a weak embrace. As this young woman unravels before him, this moment of genuine empathy loosens memories within him. Long suppressed memories of the things he had been absent for. He recalls how Midora's look of disappointment in her younger years eventually faded into apathy. In a moment of clarity, Adanon sees himself being precisely where he is meant to be. Even though it can't make up for his past mistakes, he will step into this role he long ago forgot how to play. His insight tells him to find a solution for the sobbing child, but the wisdom of time reminds him to be still. This is enough. "It is an unusual and poignant thing to mourn the still living," Adanon says with a gentle pat on Runa's back. Then they hold there for a time until the moment passes. Eventually, Runa moves to the rucksack and shrugs it onto her back after depositing the knife.

Sometime later as they wait for the next magrail, Runa's mind returns to the unknowns of her situation. "Shouldn't I have gone to one of those foundling houses?" she says, staring out at the dark, croaking bog beyond the platform. "Yes, but like many things in life, favor turns heads and coffers alike," Adanon says. "I don't follow," Runa says as the brightly lit transport approaches the platform. Adanon grunts knowingly. "Even with government support, the foundling houses often rely on charitable contributions. I was asked to mediate," Adanon says, standing to board the car, "The solution I proposed was that none of them will house you due to your age. Ensuring Zidero's charity will be split among all parties and that you will be housed on neutral ground until induction." As they seat themselves on car, Runa says, "I'm glad your solution wasn't dividing me equally among all the houses." Adanon chortles. "That's remarkably similar to a parable from the old book," he says, still chuckling. "I think I'd like to read this old book," Runa says, looking at his reflection in the window across the cabin. He nods and says, "You'll need to learn Astoran in that case." Runa shrugs. "It's a language written in a runic syllabary from an empire that lasted one-thousand and one years. It's nothing like Esopt but the Church still writes exclusively in it," Adanon says. "Is it spoken?" Runa asks quizzically. Adanon nods. "Then I can learn it," Runa says crossing her arms and leaning back in her seat. Adanon throws his hands up in resignation. "I have no doubt," he says as they continue into the city. The weight of the day hangs on Runa's eyelids as she watches the gloomy swamp blur past.

A firm hand stirs Runa from her awkward, dreamless slumber. She blinks up at Adanon, struggling to remember where she is. The din of people coming and going from the magrail platform washes over her and she recalls. "This line circles the city then wraps around to the south before returning. I let you sleep awhile," Adanon says, as Runa groggily shifts to her feet. As they step off onto the platform, Runa breathes deep. The air smells different here, she notices as she exhales the vestiges of sleep into the humid night air. It smells of brackish tide and rain. She looks about the town she finds herself in. "Welcome to Cardis," Adanon says as they stroll away from the platform. Runa knows this place. She has seen the port several times, but not from land. The architecture of Cardis is like Esoptria but more distilled, simplified. The glass and hard angles of the stilted buildings is absent, replaced by stone and steel. The terraced gardens atop the city buildings are emulated here but, instead of canals every surface is paved with large reddish flagstones. They pass through a tunnel formed by overhanging trees into a plaza with scattered people moving here and there. At the center of the plaza is a fountain of trickling water topped with a stylized metallic figurehead of sorts. In passing, an elderly man kneels to kiss the wall around the fountain. Noticing the man, Adanon pulls up the collar of his coat and changes his pace, forcing Runa to walk to his right. He walks at an obvious angle to the old man, seemingly wanting to avoid the notice of the elderly man. Reverent mutterings unintelligible to Runa pour from the now supplicated man as Adanon continues. "What was that?" Runa says as she turns to glimpse the man lying on the warm stones. "Your first Astoran lesson," Adanon says with a grin. Then he turns down an alley and trots down a flight of stone steps, forcing Runa to skip to catch up. "Why was he acting like that?" she says, each step down the adding a bouncing rhythm to her words. "Well, where prefects and councilors enjoy the acclaim of the public, I do not," he says as they reach the end of the stairs and step out onto the open flagstone levee which overlooks the bay. "What about the metal sphere?" Runa says as her eyes take in the vast dark waters. There is something soothing to the familiarity of home. "It's a reductive and unsavory mode of representation. A smith may choose a hammer or anvil, a butcher a knife, but We are meant to be more than the ignoble tools of our service," Adanon says stopping to meet Runa's eye. She nods, somewhat following. "It's a weapon, a tool. But, just as a coilgun a solider doesn't make, so too is an aster to a praxiat," he says shaking an accusatory index finger. Runa stumbles over his syntax, but nods none-the-less. The tension in Adanon melts away. He seems satisfied with her response. Then he nods and continues to the west down the levee. Along the walk, Runa ponders how the sentiment is wholly foreign to where she came from. A shipmaiden maintains the ship. Her tools and craft are an extension of herself. She slows her pace, lost in thought. She looks inward, recalling how the loss of her home nearly broke her. How the grief still comes in waves. And how every little thing still reminds her how much she doesn't belong. But the thought that she is more than her skills or what others perceive her to be is liberating. In this moment she is glad to have met Adanon despite her detainment and treatment by Talin. Adanon slows and looks back at her, his head haloed by a biolume sign beyond. Smiling, Runa jogs to catch up.

CHAPTER **13**

Continuing their stroll along the sparsely populated street, Runa pauses to admire the bright signage. It appears to Runa to be some sort of general store or tavern with various trinkets in the window. Beyond the smokey glass window patrons gather around tables drinking and dining. She pulls away from the glass and reads the red lettering above. "Nambulite by the Sea," it reads with the leading and trailing letters curling into stylized waves. Adanon clears his throat, cutting her curiosity short. Blushing, she rejoins him. A bit farther away and down an inconspicuous dock, Runa finds herself following Adanon onto a ferry of moderate size. The pilot chats with Adanon for a time as Runa seats herself near the bow. As the boat putters its way out of the bay, the cloud cover dissipates, revealing the inky canvas of stars above. For Runa there is a peculiar comfort in feeling the rock of the waves again. She casts her mind back to the unremarkable nights looking up at the stars aboard the Shyena. She, Amil, and her father had often laid on the deck still warm with the radiant heat of the day and gazed up at the stars. Presently, on the deck of the nondescript ferry, Runa sinks onto her back, emulating the circumstance of those memories. The rocking of the small boat is a poor substitute for home but, in this moment, it suffices to soothe her anxiousness. Fengari still hangs below the horizon, giving a striking clarity to the contemplative sky. Runa recites the names of the stars recalling fondly watching little Amil wide-eyed and hanging on every word from their father. Then, after a time, she sits up noticing the hum of the motor has dissipated.

Ahead, an island stretches to the south, sheltering a narrow channel across from the cliffs of the mainland. The southern expanse rises to craggy peaks topped with a well-lit, sprawling estate. To Runa, it appears more suited for defense than habitation. Adanon shuffles to the bow and says to her, "Not a proper homecoming but I hope it's an improvement to a cage. I apologize for Talin, she has her own way of doing things and she took it too far." Runa turns to him. "Aye, it's alright. The experience was... edifying," she says, touching her brow. For the first time since the stitches, she ponders why she had refused to dull the pain. Had she sought to punish herself for the mistake of letting her guard down? "Adanon," she says as the island draws nearer, "thank you for the riddle, for the help I mean. Not sure I could have accomplished much without it." "It is granted. That can be our little secret. How did you find your trapse outside yourself?" he says with a grin. Runa shrugs and says, "Wish I understood more." "That's fair," Adanon says, "The duality that suffuses all finds its crux within us. Much of what you need to know comes from within, with time. Simply put, much of a praxiat's journey is personal, meaning, books and mentors can only take us so far." "Put simply," Runa says sardonically. Her last conversation with her father comes to mind. "I just have to find a thing and put my mind to it." "Sound advice. I presume you've found that something?" "I believe so," Runa says, eyes twinkling at the looming island, "What else can you tell me about this place?"

In the interim between then and the quay, Adanon relays a number of facts about the Lykios family. He tells her that much of their fortune stems from the transport and processing of magnetite, making him an integral part of the Janamudra flotilla's operations. After the war Zidero had brokered the use of existing Jana shipping lanes instead of maintaining a merchant fleet in the Federation. Both the parties have thrived off this arrangement. Then Adanon's exposition turns toward the more personal aspects of the family. Zidero has little family, save for a son in his mid-twenties. When Runa asks about the boy's mother, a touch of sadness creases the corners of Adanon's eyes. "Forgive me, that isn't my story to tell," he says as a man on the island calls out to the boat. Runa nods, not wanting to pry. "One more thing. Zidero can be- no, is rather eccentric, but he is far cleverer than he appears. Be mindful," Adanon says as he casts a line to the longshoreman.

After disembarking, Runa follows Adanon down the sizable quay which runs along the shallow channel on the eastern face of the narrow island. The permanent structure ends at a round landing which branches to Runa's right and straight ahead. The foremost path takes a gradual path up several wide stone staircases up to the estate. The stone construction is difficult for Runa to guess the age of, but some of the features are noticeably modern. A bloom of biolume runs along the steps, lighting the path with each step of their ascent. Adanon breathes a sigh of relief as they reach the final landing. To their left an overlook of the channel juts out over the precipitous fall. A courtyard of alternating red and gray stone stretches from the arch of the overlook to the large wooden doors in the distance. Columns topped with hanging vines usher Adanon and Runa through the space, past of gilded statues which occupy the fringes of the space. The stonework of the courtyard forms a singular impression for Runa, opulence.

As they approach, the heavy oaken doors unstick with a crackle, startling Runa. Beyond, a team of neatly dressed servants greet them with a bow. One of their number, a tall, stocky woman with a round face and dark eyes says, "Akoates, Kyr Lykios is finishing his dinner in the hall. Razmus has been... disagreeable." Adanon chuckles. "That's okay. Only a fool expects a warm welcome to a den of wolves," he says. The tall woman stands aside and welcomes Adanon in, pausing for a moment as she glimpses Runa. They press on into the depths of the estate unattended by the servants. Judging by Adanon's demeanor he knows this place well, Runa thinks. The hallways are much the same as the courtyard, beautiful and warmly festooned with crimson and gold. "I will say this now. If at any point you feel the need for me to butt into the conversation, let me know," Adanon says as they approach another set of large doors. Runa responds in understanding, but the creek of the large door drowns out her response. Upon seeing the cavernous room, Runa ponders how the word and the form of this room seem disparate. From the vaulted ceiling hang large fixtures of crystal and steel which scatter the light of a pale-white flame burning in a massive fireplace opposing the entrance. Various kinds of works of art lines the sides of the hall and an ornate table stretches half the length of the room. At the far end of the table a man sits watching Adanon's approach. He wipes his mouth and says, "I wish you had told me you were coming." Adanon walks around behind him and sits at the chair directly to his right. "I thought to spare your nerves. Undue stress ages us prematurely," Adanon says. The man glances at Runa then looks quickly away. "Is that your secret?" he says, pantomiming running his fingers over his receding hairline. Runa can't help but smile watching Adanon interact with this peculiar man. They seem to be nothing alike. He glances back at Runa. "Is she waiting for an invitation?" he says. Runa slips into the chair to his left as he watches her. "I'm sure you know who I am. You favor your mother very much," Zidero says, his gaze unwavering from Runa. There is a discerning look behind his heavy brow, and Runa is the first to glance away. A servant comes in through ha side door bearing a decanted bottle of spirits and several shimmering glasses. The Servant serves Zidero and Adanon libations then leaves quickly. "I do wish Razmus would come meet you. Maybe he will be in a better mood tomorrow... what is tomorrow?" Zidero says, but continues before Adanon offers a reply, "Yes Fenesday, he should be more agreeable tomorrow." Fenesday is the traditional mid-week day of rest. Traditionally the months had been broken into ten-day thirds. But one major contribution the Janamudra have given to the world is the eight-day week. A calendar based on Fengari, whose orbit takes thirty-one and seven-eighths days, just makes sense to Runa. She scoots her chair forward some and says, "Why is he more agreeable on a Fenesday?" "Ah," Zidero says as he takes a gulp from his glass, "Razmus fancies himself something of a racer, which is one of many reasons I've agreed to sponsor you. He has a team, but it was my suggestion that a Jana member of the team with lend some legitimacy and prestige to their number." "Aye? I don't know much about racing boats," Runa says. "Irrelevant. Sometimes the mere image of credibility is enough to massage the numbers," Zidero say, looking over his shoulder, presumably to have his glass filled, "Here is the expectation; you help my son with his hobby, I help you become a praxiat." Runa rests her hands on the table and says, "That simple?" The servant shuffles into the room and movies to top off the glasses of the men. Adanon places his hand over the narrow mouth of the tall glass, refusing more. A subtle look of frustration crosses Zidero's round face, but twists into a smile as he turns back to Runa. "It isn't lost on me that I may be the first outsider to the praxic mysteries you have encountered in Esoptria," he says. "Aye, that's true," Runa says, glancing away to Adanon who has begun rotating his glass like he had aboard the Shyena. "Some of us have to obey the rules as written by—" Zidero says before stopping abruptly to take a gulp of drink, "Oh, what was I saying... Yes, I want you to be comfortable. I hope that being here, near Cardis and the sea, will bring a sense of normalcy." Runa crosses her arms and says, "This is all very generous. All I have to do is live here, tinker with some boats and I'm set? What's the catch?" Zidero cracks a smug smile. "I don't think you grasp that the reason you were chosen is because of your heritage. My son has had a -prolonged- existential crisis that has grown more... disconcerting over the years without his mother." Runa sits up, seeming to understand. "Your wife was of the flotilla, Jana?" she chirps. Zidero nods slowly, casting his eyes down to the drink. Runa mulls over the unspoken understanding. She is meant to bring a sense of camaraderie to the young man. Runa fidgets with loose at the hem of her shorts. She can't bring herself to tell Zidero that she has begun to disavow the people who had cast her away. "Aye, I can do that," she says, drawing a subtle smile from Zidero, "but with one more condition." "Oh, shrewd and brash. Maybe you take more after your father," Zidero says with a wink.

Runa collects her thoughts for a moment but ultimately choses to guard herself against more pain. As she rocks back in the ornate chair she says, "If you see my mother again, I would rather not know." Adanon, whose face has been inscrutable the entire conversation, flashes a frown before pulling the cup to his lips. Zidero sits up, eyeing Runa as if now truly seeing her. "Resentment is a complicated and powerful emotion," Zidero says finishing the second glass, "I agree to this condition. I understand the sentiment well, so humor me as I relay an anecdote. Oh wait, care for a drink... no, too young. Ahem!" The servant scurries back into the hall from the side door. "Brew some shawhot ," Zidero says before the attendant retreats with a bow. Runa, despite her isolation, is familiar with the beverage, but she has only tasted it once. Among the flotilla it is a delicacy. Casting her memory back, she recalls one passage south on which her father had traded for some roasted beans from Uxkukul. She remembers the excitement in his eyes as he brewed and explained the beverage known in the native Uxian tongue as "xahuatl." Zidero clears his throat. "My father made me who I am, but not by virtue of his success, or lack thereof. Watching him squander our legacy taught me how to protect it," he says. Runa picks up his delight in talking about himself. She weaves her fingers together and says, "This was all before the agreements with the Jana?" Zidero mums in the affirmative as he turns his attention to the half-eaten plate of food. He pokes at piece of pheasant then looks back to Runa. "Mmm, precisely," he says, "Father was far too concerned with appearances. Anyone with a sad story would send him searching through his coffers. Until one day, he no longer had anything left to give." Runa kicks her legs as she listens intently. "I'm sure he was well liked for his generosity," she says. Zidero laughs and glances at Adanon. "Gratitude is fleeting, for we are fickle and foolish creatures," he says as the servant returns with the shawhot, "You see, charity invites manipulation. Reciprocity is the only way to ensure your means never run dry." "What happened to your father?" Runa asks. Zidero wipes his mouth with a cloth napkin. "Ah, he died with a bottle in one hand and debt in the other. I couldn't do anything about the 'friends' that bled him dry while he was still living. As soon as he was buried facing west, I moved to collect," Zidero says with a tinge of glee to his words. He then releases the napkin which he had wrung taut between his fists. Runa swallows and looks to Adanon, who is accepting the steaming bitter beverage from the servant. Once all present company has a mug of the brown liquid, Zidero raises his in a toast and says, "To family! May our friends never disappoint us quite as much," before taking a noisy slurp.

CHAPTER 14

Talin watches as the first dull blue glimmer of day creeps over the landscape beyond the windows of the magrail. She hasn't slept, choosing rather to pass the early hours in her thoughts. The arid savanna which stretches for hundreds of mille reminds her of pieces of her childhood, fragments really. Astoraph and Orin are half a world apart, but the dry, dusty air dredges up memories despite her attempts to keep them at bay. The sun creeps into the sky, casting long shadows through the tall grasses and wildflowers. It reminds her of chasing her siblings during some long forgotten festivity. She can recall red flowers, then the crimson memories ignite flashes of death. Taking in a shaking breath, Talin stands and exits the cabin to find a beverage. What kind she cannot say. Navigating the narrow hallway that runs beside the sleeper cabins, she spots an attendant. The young woman rummage through the cart as Talin approaches. She startles. "Oh my, you are very quiet," the attendant in blue says as she playfully touches Talin's arm. It's a strange thing, the guard that people lose when they don't know what you are. Talin smiles and says, "Can I have a cup of 'hot with cream?" The attendant nods and shifts to an alcove where the drink is brewing as Talin returns to her cabin without a word. There is a surreal mix of sadness and excitement fighting for dominance within her. Excitement to be doing what she knows must be done. Sadness in leaving her duty and Adanon behind. The irony of the situation is not lost on her. She has become the type of praxiat that she had often brough back into the fold. She believes that if she can find proof of Darian's misdeeds before she is found, the Council may be lenient. The attendant brings the energizing drink just how Talin had requested, then shakily hands her the cup and saucer. Adanon, a thought like an itch she cannot scratch. She wonders why he is so unwilling to act against Darian. As she sighs and returns to watching out the window, the scrubland falls away to lazy dunes. Talin knows she is close when the sand begins to gradually turn black, signaling the proximity to the former imperial city of Astoraph. What was once the great heart of empire has become a bolstering pillar of power production. Nearby, deep under the treacherous Fields of Vitrescence, is the only location in nature which the bacterium used for power cells can be found. Talin recalls the first time she saw the glassy fields aglow on a summer evening many years ago. The faint glow on the horizon had almost been inviting. That was until a hot spot on the vitrified landscape had erupted in an arc of lightning.

A half-hour later, Talin finds herself stepping off onto the dusty platform on the outskirts of Astoraph. Talin shades her eyes from the morning sun slipping between the black banners which dance between stately columns. She feels woefully ill prepared for this endeavor. As she passes out of the busy station the shouts of buskers and peddlers assail her ears. The particles in the air have already begun to sting her eyes. She sighs and thumbs the cylinder of lodes in her pocket, counting the reaming currency she has left after the trip. Broke and alive is better than lungs full of glass, she thinks as she makes her to the noisy merchant stalls. After an uncomfortable time haggling, Talin walks away from the market with goggles and filtration gaiter, which she had been assured is the best. She has her doubts, but it is better than nothing. Now properly equipped, she makes her way toward the heart of the city, past the endless many-tiered stucco buildings. It has been some time since she was last in Astoraph, but she has some idea how to navigate beyond the main avenues. She tucks into a narrow alley, fully cognizant of the danger. Danger for anyone foolish enough to confront her. In common dress Talin feels like a toxic creature that doesn't display its danger to witless predators. Something about the unfamiliar anonymity brings a smile to her face. As she passes several more blocks through narrow alleys and bustling streets, Talin finds herself in the central district, near the College of War. The absurd domed structure towers over everything else in the city. Aside from the obvious monument, aged railgun batteries hang precariously over the walls that divide the district from the rest. Pitting and corrosion mar the once lustrous metal surfaces. They are impressive despite their obvious signs of disrepair. They serve now as relics of a bygone era when might was measured by craters and casualties. Rather than entering the district, Talin turns before the gated entrance searching for markers from years past. Down another alley, she is confident she is on the right path. The person she seeks had been contacted only last night and has no praxic gift. The thought that he may have had a change of heart crosses her mind as she turns down another shaded alley. She is faced with a dead end. Pulling her dark goggles up onto her forehead, Talin dusts the surface of the wall. Under a layer of dust lies the ancient Astoran runes for "Sweet embrace." Talin smirks and steps closer to the wall, placing her weight as close as possible. Then the cantilevered stone beneath her feet tips forward, forming a short slide into the dark below. Though expected, she still lets out a stifled grunt as she hits the crawlspace below. Before her, a cloud of dust swirls through the dark, illuminated only by the slivers of sunlight streaming through the cracks above. Coughing, she crawls into the larger space beyond but freezes as a familiar sound fills her ears. It's deathly quiet in the dark save for the tell-tale whine of a coilgun primed to fire. "I never took you for one to shoot a person when they're down," Talin says, pulling down her gaiter and spitting. "You don't know me half as well as you think," a brassy voice rumbles through the gloom and dust, "but you know me well enough to shame me." The ringing from the weapon subsides. Talin stands, her eyes beginning to adjust to the dark. "How are you Ade?" she says taking a step forward into the dark, unsure of where to look. A mass shifts in the corner of the room. "I'm well. But you, you are still a flower too prickly to touch," Ade Jidun of the Bujani says as he activates a biolume torch which floods the room with a sickly green hue. For a moment, they stare at each other through the suspended viridescent particles. In this larger space Talin is able to stand upright but Ade hunches awkwardly to stand only a portion of his full height. A glinting bead of sweat runs down his dark face, then he smiles and steps toward Talin with arms outstretched. With a sigh, Talin accepts the hug. His wide hands rattle her as he pats her affectionately on the back. "Forgive me- for the- secrecy," Talin says, her voice skipping from the thumps on her back, "Things are- troubled back home." As they part Ade smirks, carving deep creases in the pocked scars on the left side of his face. "Troubled? With you in the mix?" he says sarcastically as he wicks moisture away from his forehead. Talin bristles but lets the remark slide. She needs him much more than he needs her, but there is no need for him to know that. There is about to be a negotiation, but Talin isn't playing by the rules. "I need to move north covertly, as a dredger," Talin says, running her hand along the coarse wooden crates that line the walls of this hidden space. "Then head north. It's that way," Ade says pointing a thumb over his shoulder. "No, I need your help and you will help me," Talin says. Ade blows out an unexpected laugh. "How is that? It seems to me that you are the one hiding from your own people. I'm sure the money is good for a runaway of your caliber," he says crossing his arms. "Probably, but is it worth more to you than the knowledge of what's become of your children?" Ade stiffens, his head hitting the ceiling. "You have no honor, Argyra," he growls. Talin sits on the edge of the crate and smiles. Then as she calmly inspects the nails of her hand, she says, "The ground is filled with the bones of honorable men. Do you accept my terms?" Ade stares at her past his heavy creased brow. "Damn you. I should have never—" he says, striking the crate with the side of his fist, "I want to see them too. Not just empty words." Talin smiles. "Deal," she says extending her hand, "that shouldn't be a problem if everything goes well in Gaerdan." Ade glances at her hand, visibly apprehensive. "No tricks?" he says after a pause. "I would never, besides the hug would have been enough if I had the mind to." Ade kisses his teeth, then clasps her outstretched hand. "Back home, a witch's bargain is struck in blood and bone. I think a handshake will have to do today," he says with a weight of sadness in his voice. Talin hums in agreement then moves to inspect the closest crate. Ade produces a crowbar then pries open the lid with minimal effort. Talin takes hold of the torch, changing the hue to a soft white as she peers under the lid. Within lie rows upon rows of tightly packed power cells. "You spoke of witches. Are there foundlings in Bujani dodging the system?" Talin says, as she inspects the power cells. "No, you've taken them all," Ade says, letting the lid drop. Talin catches the lid and looks sidelong at him, saying "Considering my current predicament, you don't have to lie," before letting down the lid gently. She ponders how unsafe it is to store cells within combustible crates but admits that this hovel is the last place she would look. "It's no lie. All we have left are herbalists and pretenders," Ade says as he walks away and returns with a small crate as wide as his shoulders. Talin accepts the box then rests it on the larger crate. Instead of nails, the box is held closed with a friction-fix wooden peg. She knocks the peg free and slides the grooved lid enough to see inside. She slides the lid closed upon seeing the contents. "How did you come by these?" she spits. Ade laughs with his belly. "Will you be walking your beautiful behind directly to the quartermaster to report me?" he says with a sardonic wink. Talin glowers for a moment, then open the case again. Inside lie several asters in perfect condition. Asters are foci so ubiquitous among praxiats that common folk have come to equate the weapon with authority. Talin runs her fingers over the iridescent metallic spirals. Then she pulls one free of the packing material and places it in her pocket without a second thought. "I'm still adjusting to life on the run," she says as she closes the box and strolls to another crate. An hour passes as both Talin and Ade sort through supplies in relative silence, exchanging nods and shakes of the head as they hold up items for consideration. They must pack light enough to blend in with a caravan but still make space for lifesaving or life-taking equipment. "May I ask you something?" Ade says as Talin sorts her remaining items, "Why Gaerdan?" "It's where runners always run to. The leniency of the Prefect almost invites them to try it." On the occasions Talin had worked cases in the north, the local authority had always failed to assist, but didn't interfere with the investigation. "You think someone intends to run?" Ade says. Talin smirks at him and says, "I do."

Stuffing the aster deep into an inside pocket of her pack, Talin turns to Ade and nods. In unison they shoulder their equipment and make their way to the far entrance. The daylight above is an uncomfortable reminder that Talin had removed her goggles in the storeroom. Letting Ade lead, Talin tries to shake off all thoughts of turning back. She knows she is too committed now. After much walking, on the other side of the northern gate, they hop aboard the magrail line heading north. This line ends before the geologically active mountains to the north, but they gladly take the reprieve from walking. At the end of the line, at a town called Greenview, Talin and Ade barter their way into a caravan crossing the mountain range into Gaerdan. Before the first step on the hard journey ahead Talin looks up at the looming mountains verdant with lichen and crowned by steam, imagining she can smell the scent of autumn on the wind.

C H A P T E R **15**

Runa gazes into the emerald eyes in the mirror. They are not her eyes; this isn't her face. It's a curious dream, one that churns the curiosity of her waking mind. Before she can cling to the memory, she wakes with a jolt. The dread of another unfamiliar bed cleaves to her before finally she recalls the night before. This is the room she had been shown after the late night in the hall of the Lykios estate. She recalls hearing the chatter of sea birds in the distance before sleep had taken her. This is to be her home for the next few months. She glances about the dimly lit, lavish room festooned with art and substance of little meaning to her. Dark wood paneling, crimson, and gold cover much of the surfaces. It's a stark contrast to the blues and grays of the flotilla. Be that as it may, she misses the sunsets on the sea but looks forward to exploring her newfound home. As she stretches, she makes a mental note to watch the sunset later if she can find the time

Her pack rests beside the entrance to the room, propped precariously against the wall. She doesn't recall placing it there. Making up for the lack of attention paid last evening, she rummages through the drawers and closets lining the room. There is a musty wooden odor to the beautiful clothing within the large wardrobe, but Runa doesn't find it off-putting. To her, it seems that there is personality infused in each garment this way. She not only flips through the dresses and furred coats, but she also runs her hands over them, smells them, and wonders whose they had been. With hesitation, she opens her pack then pulls out the ruffled turquoise dress. Frowning at the wrinkles in the lace, she places the dress aside then pulls out her brother's knife. As she glances about cautiously, she places the knife under the mattress with care. A knock at the door startles her. After a prolonged silence, the door creaks open, revealing a young girl with a porcelain complexion and wiry golden-red hair. "'scuse me Kyri, the quiet, I thought," she says closing the door. "It's alright. What's your name?" Runa says half-sitting on the edge of the bed and crossing her legs. Letting herself back into the room the little girl says, "Kaeln, Kyri. Forgive my Esopt, is bog water as he says." "Kaeln, can you do anything about these creases?" Runa says patting the dress. Kaeln nods apprehensively. "Is beautiful. Strong color for you," Kaeln says. "I prefer it to all the red," Runa says as she takes a closer look at the girl. To her, Kaeln appears to be only ten or eleven years old. Trying not to dwell on how a child came to be a servant in Zidero's home, she says. "Did you come to tell me about breakfast?" Kaeln turns a bright red. "Is half past the day, Kyri," she says shyly. Runa chuckles and shrugs. As she recalls some of the conversation from the prior evening, Runa snaps her fingers and says, "The boats," before moving past Kaeln in a hurry.

As she trots through the estate, Runa tugs through her hair with her fingers. Passing out the main entrance, all worries about her appearance fade as she hears the tell-tale slap of watercraft from the channel below. With fervor, she bounds down the long stairs that lead to the concrete quay below, taking moments in the flat sections to steal glances of the cerulean waters below. Then she sees them as they round the northern beach, the sleek boats skipping along the surface. One boat turns sharply toward the quay before running parallel to it, spraying the few bystanders with a wall of water. While Runa hasn't made it close enough to get splashed, she still tastes the kiss of briny mist on her lips as she descends. Approaching quickly, she hears Zidero cursing while several servants gather around him, patting him dry. "Glad you decided to join us," Zidero says, looking at Runa as he shades his eyes with a book, "but I think I've seen enough of Razmus' stunts for the day." He fixes a stray strand of his combed-over hair as he collects his things and heads into the nearby structure. From this quay, during the day the thin peninsula which marks the end of Cardis bay is barely visible on the northern horizon. Runa approaches the small gathering of people, all of whom Runa doesn't recognize. They don't appear to be staff of the Lykios estate. Despite her urge to watch the people, she takes an interest in the boats as they round the island again. As the pack of watercraft accelerate in the relative calm on the sheltered side of the island fountains of water crash down on the boats in the rear. Runa tries her best to estimate the speed of the craft as a narrow man with a puckered mouth turns to her and says, "Whatcha think?" She glances sidelong at him. "I think they probably struggle to maneuver at slower speeds," she says with an earnest look. A squat Esoptrian woman with a round face and greasy black hair scoffs. "Well, she's certainly sharp, noting a known flaw that's inherent in the design," she says, crossing her arms. Several bystanders chuckle at the remark. "Aye, judging by the defensiveness, I take it that you helped design it," Runa says, also crossing her arms, "I can see why Zidero asked me to consult. When you've done something a certain way for so long it's hard to see alternatives." The woman throws her hands up in irritation and walks away muttering. "Yithica is our self-proclaimed shipwright. She's very protective of our work," the man says rocking his peculiar face in the far direction of the quay, "The name's Bandon. I'm the fabricator fer Raz's ragtag team." Runa has trouble focusing on Bandon save for when the racers are on the other side of the island. In the scare glances she takes of him, she thinks he resembles a Shalladocian eel in the face. "How long do they usually go on like this?" she says, wrangling her hair which keeps catching on the southward wind. Bandon throws his hands up, saying, "Until they're content, or something breaks." As the pack of boats comes around again, they ease off the throttle and turn towards the island. The lead one, painted a warm orange hue putters over with care. Then in the last few boat lengths, the nose of the boat pitches down, accelerates under water, and pops out again like a cork. The boat bellyflops in the water uncomfortably close to the concrete, splashing several bystanders, including Yithica, again.

"I told 'em that's'n unlucky color, but he wouldn't hear it," Bandon says leaning in to whisper to Runa. She cocks her head, unsure what he means. She likes the color, as it's reminiscent of her mother's hair in sunlight. Farther down the quay the other ships slowly maneuver with assistance from those ashore. In the commotion Runa strolls down to examine the boat. The enclosed fusiform craft reminds her of a pauk, minus the bulbous head and the long beak. The cockpit of the orange craft opens revealing a young, broad-shouldered man. His brown, almond shaped eyes flit over, meeting Runa's as a perfect toothy grin spreads above his square chin. It is the look of recognition. The loose locks of hair that hang about his forehead suggest he is Esoptrian, but the tinge of wine among the curls and coppery tone of his skin betrays his Janamudra heritage. Runa recognizes him instantly as Razmus Lykios. He lifts himself out of the cockpit with handholds then shimmies himself onto the edge of the concrete as an attendant pushes over a wheelchair. In this moment it dawns on Runa, but she doesn't want to show her surprise. The Jana way of life doesn't mesh well with disabilities. She combs her mind thinking if she had known of anyone bound to a wheelchair within the flotilla and comes up blank. The implications sends chills down her spine. Razmus waves off assistance from two servants of the estate, insisting on lifting himself into the chair.

Doing so takes little time as he is exceptionally strapping above the waist. One would have to be, Runa reasons, to do so regularly without assistance. After sorting his legs out, he waves off the small crowd gathered around him, then he wheels himself toward Runa.

"Good wind, good waves, Sister," Razmus says in passable Jana before switching to Esopt, "Runa I presume?" Runa moves to hold out her hand in greeting, then reconsiders, pulling her hand away. "I don't mean to be rude, greetings have been trickier lately," she says. Razmus laughs and extends his hand, saying "I don't mind it. I doubt you'd probe my mind without asking me out to dinner first." Runa lets out a genuine chuckle as she accepts his hand. They exchange smiles and shake hands without incident. Runa takes an appreciative look at him. To her, he has genuine charm and striking good looks. Zidero isn't unattractive, but the thought does cross her mind that Razmus' mother must have had the brunt of the aesthetics in the couple. Her gaze drifts down to his legs. "Sorry, I—" she says looks toward the boats, "I have some ideas about your boat." "Already?" Razmus says. "Maybe. You use a thrust diverter for turning, braking?" she says resting her hand on her chin. Razmus nods. "I think maybe the angles are off. Judging by the poor response I'd say the reversed flow is creating chop near the intake grate." Razmus looks over his shoulder then back to Runa. "Not to be rude, but how is your Esopt so good? How often did "intake grate" come up in Rusty linguistics classes?" Runa frowns and says, "I don't like that word, it's a pejorative." Razmus' face loses color. "Sorry, I didn't know," he says waving his hands. Runa believes either he hadn't known, or he is an excellent liar. She crosses her arms and makes an indignant look. "It's alright, consider it your first lesson," she says with a grin as she uncrosses her arms, "As for the linguistics, we all have our strengths and weaknesses, Razmus." "True enough, but I am used to being underestimated," he admits as he wheels backward, "Now that we've gotten the social blunders out of the way, I prefer Raz." He then rolls toward the door Zidero had entered earlier and gestures for Runa to follow. The door automatically opens, revealing an enclosed glass and steel space large enough for several people to fit. Judging by the trail of light visible up the inclined tunnel, this is some manner of elevator. Yithica calls out to them as Raz rolls into the enclosure, but he waves off his friend dismissively. Runa joins him and says, "She looked upset." Raz hums and says, "She'll get over it," in a dark tone, "Dad's money has a way of smoothing my edges over regardless." "Is that why you think I'm here?" Runa says. Raz cocks a brow at her. "No, I have some idea why you're here, but the particulars are lost on me," he says as he touches the display. The elevator lurches to life, beginning the long climb up the island. "How's that?" Runa says, peering at him through the dim amber light. "At first, I thought it was weird, you being Janamudra. What with my mother and all, then I questioned Adanon's involvement," he says with a sigh, "But now you're here and it's not so strange." The yellow hue of the overhead lights casts long otherworldly shadows across both their faces. Raz rests cheek against his knuckles and says, "When I saw you watching from the shore, it reminded me of my mother. Which is weird, I know." Runa is taken aback by his openness. It's as if he had been waiting for someone to speak with candidly with, and now the hull of emotion is breached. "No, it's okay," Runa says. "It -is- weird though; I can't picture her face anymore, but when I saw you it all came back. You know, the emotions, the grief," he continues, morose. Runa can't help but empathize with him. As she rests her hand on his shoulder, she says, "Aye, I've been dealing with—" The frayed rope of despair snaps, freeing itself of its burden but Runa is the only one able to catch it. There is an intoxicating quality to being back in this space of conscious memory. In the rush of the electrochemical, she loses herself again, opening eyes which are not her own.

She is a child. A young boy nauseous with understanding. He hears the crying of the seabirds. Watches their flight as they flee the bloated body battered by the breaking waves. He looks up at the nearby structure which juts out daringly over the rocky shore. "She must have fallen," he tells his five-year-old self. Mother had promised to find a way to fix him. even when he had told her in his youthful optimism that there was nothing to fix. In those tender moments she had chucked and kissed his cheek with whispered replies of, "Of course, you're perfect my child." Quiet moments in which her silent tears had told more truths than her lips ever could. Then the surreal image of young Zidero knelt over his wife's corpse wrenches Runa back.

She gasps, floundering in the unknowing of when and where she is. The subtle clacking of the elevator has a familiarity on which she finds focus, equilibrium. Then, looking up from a slumped position, she sees Raz looking down at her with concern pressed into his features. "Are you alright?" he says as the elevator clunks to a stop and daylight pours through the opening doors.

CHAPTER 16

After a day of onerous errands, Adanon finds himself returning on the path to Zidero's island home. While one day didn't seem sufficient to acclimate Runa to her new surroundings, it will have to do. Though the day had been taxing, he does find it odd that Talin hadn't at least contacted him despite her intention to take time for herself. As the evening fog follows the sun over the town of Cardis, Adanon arrives by magrail lost in his ruminations. Upon arriving at the Lykios estate, he proceeds directly where he had been told to find Runa. Playing at his already frayed nerves, a servant girl relays unsolicited information as he makes his way through. He thanks the girl then enters the room without knocking. Inside, Runa is reclined on the bed, crunching on ice chips meant for her head. "What happened?" Adanon says, crossing the room. "I'm fine," Runa says, crunching more ice, "but Raz insisted I rest. So here I am, resting." Placing his hands on his hips, Adanon glowers, silently scolding the young woman with his eyes. Runa pushes the bag of ice away, yielding to his gaze. "We were just talking, then I had another vision," she says as she sits up on the bed. Adanon relaxes somewhat then says, "Care to share?" "Not really," Runa says as she throws off the large comforter, "it's a little unsettling." Adanon nods as he slides over a chair and takes a seat. "The vision was unsettling, or the way it made you feel?" "Both. Is—" Runa says as she waggles her hand, "is the euphoria normal?" Adanon is keenly aware of the intoxicating effect that meddling with the mind can have on a praxiat. "It's expected," he says, "The trouble comes when we chase that feeling by meddling beyond observation." Runa sits up straight, watching Adanon closely. "Beyond in what way?" she says as she rests her chin on her clasped knuckles. Adanon looks back at the door, then turns back, clearing his throat. "It's one thing to live someone else's memory. A completely different thing to change them, remove them," he says leaning in to whisper, "It's malfeasant and the kind of thing I'm tasked with stopping." Runa swallows against the lump in her throat then says, "I haven't had any control over—" Adanon holds up his hand, saying, "I know that, and you have nothing to be afraid of. Malfeasance is practiced. It takes immense patience and familiarity to break someone's mind. And I don't say this lightly: It is evil." Runa shudders. Adanon didn't want to be so direct with her, but fear is often enough to stimy youthful curiosity. "I understand. If we're all products of our experiences, meddling with memories fundamentally changes who a person is," Runa says. It's a statement wiser than her years, which gives Adanon pause. It's a hard truth for many to hear, that mankind is more than the nature written in their bones. That some mysteries cannot be reasoned with, same as the symmetries of the universe yearning to break. What better way to emulate the absurdity of the cosmos than to be human? Adanon chuckles past a grin and leans back in the chair, sighing with resignation. "Do you ever question if you're doing the right thing?" Runa says. Adanon steeples his fingers, pressing them to his chin. Another complicated statement "You don't have to believe in yourself to believe in what you're doing. That keeps me going," he says with a grin of self-satisfaction, but Runa has turned to the windows. It was good advice even if Runa seems to have moved on. "Is it nearly sunset?" she says. Adanon nods and says, "Probably past, you'll have to scamper." Runa flings herself off the bed and bounds out the door without hesitation, leaving Adanon mildly dismayed at the display of youthful enthusiasm. Moments later, past the library, the greenhouse, and the servant's quarters Adanon finds himself facing the western facing overlook. Voluminous purple clouds hide the sun, leaving a thick ribbon of clear, vibrant sky on the horizon. As he walks down the walkway which hangs out over the crashing waves, Adanon watches Runa more than the sun dipping below the clouds. Catching on an upsurging eastern wind her copper hair frolics, salient in the dying light. It's a moment Adanon doesn't wish to ruin with words. So, he watches her in the prolonged minutes until the sun touches the horizon. Then Runa turns and says, "What is the significance? One of Raz's crew said orange was an unlucky color." Adanon places his hands on the railing next to her and peers over the edge. "It's just superstitious nonsense," he says with a stern look, but Runa doesn't look away, "The sun sets over the shallow sea, wherein your people, known for their titian hair also reside. Even Esoptrian funerary garb is traditionally orange." "By that logic, they associate Jana people with death?" Runa says. Adanon lets out an affirming grunt. The warmth from the sun fades from Adanon's face as the sun sinks lower. While it is true that orange is symbolic of the end, it also suggests a beginning, the promise of rebirth. For the sun always returns in time. Runa continues to watch the spectacle for a time, then says, "I don't blame them." There is a weight to her words that Adanon cannot contest. As it isn't his place to tell her how she feels about her own people. They stand there in silence for the remainder of the sunset then leave as the biolume activates on the walkway.

On the path back through the estate, Adanon says, "Tomorrow you'll meet with Oma and Thand, early. Here is the simplest way to get to the cenobium." He hands her a slip of paper. Runa reads the instructions several times then places the paper in her pocket. "I want to be honest with you. Four months doesn't give you a lot of time to learn a great many things," Adanon says as they stop in front of Runa's room. The nineteenth day of the Month of Doors, is four months and three days away, placing it in the new year. There is a part of Adanon that wants to tell her that she will be fine, but there is no guarantee. Most praxiats have much of their young lives to prepare. "Adanon, what happens to the praxiats who fail this test?" Runa says, crossing her arms. Adanon looks away. "Orange?" Runa mutters, holding up a clump of her hair. Adanon nods slowly as he says, "Orange." Runa lets out a blubbering sigh as she leans against the wall. Rubbing the scruff on his chin, Adanon says, "You'll do fine." It's not a convincing lie. However, if he didn't think she had the capability she never would have left the Shyena alive. He still hasn't found the courage to tell her that two killers met her on her last day among the Janamudra. With a hesitant nod, Runa tucks into her room, leaving Adanon alone in the hallway.

On his way out of the estate, Adanon takes a course toward the lower floor. He seeks out Raz's room. A servant stands precariously outside the door. A raised male voice can be heard through the floral plastered walls as he approaches. "How... ...be stupid," the muffled, broken voice shouts. Upon seeing Adanon the servant knocks loudly on the door. More less-audible words reverberate, but Adanon can't make them out. With a smirk Adanon says, "I can come back," but thudding footsteps approach the door as he turns to leave. Swinging the door open, a red-faced Zidero storms out into the hallway. "Akroates," he says before shouldering past Adanon, "Forgive me, I need rest before my trip. I don't have time to humor you or that boy," then he turns and thuds away. The tall female servant raises her chin to Adanon. "I'm going in now," he says, heedless of her standing partially in the doorway. A flash of irritation crosses her brow, but she stands aside. Within the room, Raz sits at a chaotically organized desk covered in tools, looking glasses, and various bits of wood. On the wall are rows upon rows of model ships, each constructed by Raz in his free time. The collection is a familiar sight to Adanon, albeit larger than the last time he had been here. "I thought you were—" Raz says as he turns away from the model, "Adanon. Sorry." Adanon smiles at the young man then turns to admire the craftsmanship of the models on the wall. In the past Adanon has occasionally spent time with Raz through either pity, or a need to mentor. Zidero refuses to speak of his late wife, often shutting down at the slightest anecdote. While Adanon had never known her as a wife and mother, he knew her as a praxiat and warrior. She had been a member of his and Darian's cohort. Of course, Adanon never tells Raz those stories. Often, he finds himself repeating the same stories. Stories which mingle with happy memories of his own family. Raz has never stopped Adanon from repeating the same mundane tales, which is a kindness or unspoken understanding between them. Adanon clears his throat and says, "Did I ever tell you—" "No stories please," Raz says, interrupting. Humming in response, Adanon moves to admire another model. "Maybe a different kind of story?" he says, as he slowly makes his way down the wall. "I think not," Raz says as he takes off the magnifying visor and hangs it on the workbench, "I think we could all use a break from our past, right Akroates?" Adanon looks at the young man, understanding the sentiment but disliking the implication. Then he turns and makes for the door. As he sees himself out, he says, "Maybe another time?" Without looking back, Raz says, "Maybe."

After leaving the Lykios estate, Adanon finds the town of Cardis dark and deserted. To the northwest only a scattering of light from Fengari is visible through the thick blanket fog which clings to the bay. Despite the liminal quality of this time and place, he prefers this to the gawking, the whispering, and the staring of the masses. On the most direct route to the magrail station, he passes through the same square he had passed through with Runa days before. The fountain she had remarked on is lit with an amber glow. Under these conditions, the cascading water resembles whimsical flames. Everything in the square is as it should be, save for the child sitting restlessly on the rim of the fountain. Even though the child appears to be only nine or ten to Adanon, he approaches with care. As the young boy notices him, he looks down to a letter then back to Adanon several times before hopping down. Adanon stops to address the child, but before he can form the words the young boy says, "He told me to tell you not to bother me. I don't know anything," each word punctuated with a rhythmic bounce in time with his footfalls. Then the child forces a paper-wrapped box into his hands and runs off into the fog without hesitation. Judging by the cryptic and off-putting nature of the delivery, Adanon assumes Darian is behind this.

Adanon inspects the rectangular box, which is as long as his forearm, then glances around the empty square. There is no one and no sound save for the whisper from the babbling fountain. As he props his leg up on the fountain, he begins to unwrap the drab paper. Curiosity has gotten the better of him, and his mind imagines all manner of things secret within. The reality is more harrowing than any of his imaginings. He continues to unwrap, leading to a hand scrawled slip of paper. He turns over the note and reads the words, "Be Free," before wiping a bead of sweat from his brow. His trembling hands unwrap the rest as he sees something he had never thought to behold. The cardboard box falls away revealing a cylinder of glass encasing a lattice of translucent white crystal. The object glows slightly under what little of Fengari's light pierces the fog. It's not the crystal that unsettles him, it's what it encases; the pieces of him long removed. The shards of bone are only dark smudges through the crystalline growth, but it is unmistakable. This is what keeps the Akroates under the thumb of the council. This is the check that balances his permission to live. This is something the Akroates should never possess. But now, he does. Again, he glances around and curses under his breath. Adanon must steady himself against the fountain, taking several breaths before tucking the reliquary into an inside pocket. Then by shifting the balance through his will, the remnants of the packaging curl, blacken, and turn to vapor as he walks away.

CHAPTER 17

Runa awakens in her room after a fitful night of sleep. The revelation that she might not have much longer to live has weighed heavy on her mind all night. Despite this, she endeavors to rise early to keep from languishing. With a stretch and yawn, she makes her way groggily toward the dining hall. A thought crosses her mind as she strolls through drafty outer hallways. Her having little time left has always been the case. That knowing unequivocally has changed nothing. This only strengthens her resolve to succeed. Kaeln scampers past bearing breakfast to the hall ahead. Still yawning, Runa sits at the near end of the long table within the hall, then asks Kaeln for a cup of 'hot. The servant girl doesn't ask how she takes the bitter beverage before running out of the hall. Runa sits for a time simply picking at the contents of her plate, pondering the times before. They seem very distant now in this terrestrial home filled with excess. But aside from a sense of normalcy and her family, she misses her things. And not just anything things, her books are sorely missed. She is certain she could recite most of them from memory, by the sensations are not the same. As Kaeln stumbles back in with a steaming pot of shawhot and a bowel of fresh fruit, Runa recalls the library within the Lykios estate and makes a mental note to visit later today. Zidero storms through the hall arguing with his retinue. This barely registers with her sleep deprived brain. Even when he picks a link of sausage off her plate, she shrugs and takes a sip from her mug, disaffected. The 'hot is scalded, in desperate need of sweetness to combat the bitterness. Just as Runa finds herself nodding off before the jitters from the caffeine, the sight of Raz coming into the hall stirs her to attention. In a self-conscious moment she checks her appearance in the distorted reflection of a silver bowl, then not-so-discretely fusses with her hair. When her fingers catch in a tangle, she gives up and smiles just as Raz settles into the space next to her. "Good morning," he says, eyeing the prodigious offering of fruit. As she brushes her hair aside and behind her ear, Runa says, "Fresh fruit is a rarity in the flotilla, often reserved for expectant shipmothers." Raz grabs a lumpy purple fruit from the bowl and takes a bite. "Mhmm," he mums, followed by a slurp. It appears that he knows this little bit of Jana trivia. With a crooked grin, Runa leans in and grabs a bulbous red fruit which barely fits in her hand. She inspects the fruit, its smooth, waxy skin conjuring memories of the shimmering red schools of ruby finches near S'thara. As she moves to take a bite, Raz grabs her wrist. "Not that one," he says, taking the crimson fruit from her hand, "Dad loves these. On account of my mother, I do not." Runa can't tell if he is playing a joke. "Aye? Well, I'd still like to try it," she says, beckoning with her empty hand. Raz leans back and tosses the fruit to her. "Suit yourself, but I tried to spare you the trips to the toilet," he says with a sigh. By his tone Runa can tell he isn't joking. Raz watches her for a moment, then leans in intently and setting the fruit aside. "My turn to teach you something," Raz says as he takes another bite of the purple fruit and waggling it at her, "The Navy loves this fruit. Karpomo are extremely high in ascorbic acid, so it keeps scurvy at bay. But you don't know about scurvy, do you?" Runa shakes her head. She finds his self-assurance distracting. Raz spins the fruit on a wobbling path to the other side of the table, then says, "Mom taught me that Jana descendant folks have the gene to synthesize the vitamin which most humans lack. So, eat it if you want but your stomach is gonna have a bad time." Runa had never given it much thought. She had known that certain adaptations made the Janamudra lifestyle easier, but never had never known everyone else had such a deficiency. Draining the remainder of her mug, Runa exhales dramatically. "Guess I should thank you then. But—" she holds up the empty cup of shawhot, "this won't be kind to my stomach either." She stands and sees herself out after letting Raz know that she doesn't want to be late to her first real day of training.

After the ever-available ferry ride to the mainland, Runa finds herself walking back through the streets of Cardis. However, this time the town is bustling under the fast-retreating fog under the morning sun. She peers into the curious store with the red sign, but it appears closed. Then she passes back through the square enroute to the magrail station. Just as her mind replays the mnemonic she had made for the transit back to the cenobium, she is overwhelmed with a putrid smell. Acrid and offensive to her nose, the scent comes and goes before she has time to react. With a glance around, she stops to make sense of the phenomenon, but reasons it must have been her imagination as she notices no one else similarly stricken. She looks again to the nearby fountain then continues on her way.

An hour and several platform changes later, Runa steps off the magrail car and the Grand Cenobium. Looking bored, Turios is leaned against the wall waiting. Runa yawns and waves to him as she walks over, but he doesn't offer the warmest greeting. He simple welcomes her back and begins walking away at a brisk pace. So brisk that it forces Runa to almost jog keep up with him. A cool morning breeze whips across the verdant grounds as they follow the path to the cenobium. Turios slows and looks at Runa as they reach the entrance. "You look different," he says before turning and leading into the building. Runa isn't sure what he means by that but shrugs. "Well, last time Talin had rearranged my face somewhat," she quips. Turios arches his thick brows and takes another look at her. "That's not it," he says flatly then trots down a ramp which runs under the atrium. It is the beginning of a series switch-back ramps that lead into another underground area. To Runa it appears to be some sort of fitness hall, complete with a running track and additional rooms around the perimeter. It is one of these rooms which Turios heads directly toward. Through the transparent wall, Runa can see Thand and Oma talking. Oma waves to her, Thand does not. As they enter the room, Turios flips a switch, and the glass wall turns opaque. Thand crosses her arms then says, "Glad you could take time away from suckling the wolf's teat. Let's see how sturdy they make Jannies these days." Then with a pompous, toothy grin she holds up her scar-covered hands in a defensive posture. Runa looks from Turios to Oma, then back to Thand. Oma says, "They expect you to be able to defend yourself." Runa frowns. She knows nothing about fighting. Jana men are expected to be proficient with a blade, but she had been expected to be proficient with a spanner. As she watches Thand's eager eyes, she laments not watching Amil spar more.

Runa sinks into a similar stance to Thand's then shuffles forward. Just as she works up the courage to swing at the much larger woman, Thand speaks. "If you manage to hit me, I won't humiliate you," she says, throwing Runa off. It's a goad, but the nervous energy from the 'hot or the smug condescension throws off Runa's reason. With an advancing jab, she aims for Thand's face. But Thand easily, brushes her strike aside and taps her softly on the cheek. Taking a step back, Runa says, "I don't— What does this have to do with being a praxiat?" Incredulous, Thand looks to her sister, who nods apprehensively. Before Runa can speak another word, Thand lunges forward causing her to flinch. She cradles her head instinctively, but no impact connects. Instead, her legs are swept out from under her. She topples her back under the strength of her opponent. Runa's mind races as she struggles against her assailant. There is a familiarity to this hopelessness. It dredges up memories of her recent humiliation from Talin.

Next her mind jumps to Adanon and fear of disappointing him. Inexplicably, her mind returns to the small moments spent with Raz this morning. She pictures his perfect smile as she feels Thand's arm press around her neck. Just before giving up, she thinks of her brother Amil. How ashamed he would be of her utter inability to fight back.

The tension around her abates, allowing Runa to roll away. Gasping and beside herself with frustration, she looks to Oma and Turios, but neither offers any encouragement. Thand sits cross-legged, waiting. When Runa has regained some composure, Thand says, "Talin roughing you up left an impression. You don't want to disappoint Adanon, which is adorable. Strangely, you had some licentious thoughts about Zidero's son somewhere in there. Oh, and something about your rusty brother, seemed like shame." Runa sits there, aghast. It is like the times she has intruded on other's thoughts, but purposeful. Thand hadn't lost consciousness, nor control of herself as Runa was careless with her thoughts. The lesson was short but effective in demonstrating how little she understood about praxis. "Can you show me how to control that?" she says to Thand. With a grin, Thand says, "I will teach how to not let that happen a third time," while patting the rubbery floor. Oma interjects, "What she means is, Turios and I can help you with the more nebulous aspects of praxis. She will help with the physical." Runa looks to Turios. Before she can ask the question, he says, "They fancy me a bit of a dreamer. So, my dubious tutelage with cover projection. Runa cracks a sarcastic smile and says, "So, you're saying your best work is performed on your back?" Turios turns a deep red as Oma erupts in laugher. Thand purses her lips, fighting off a smile teasing at the corners of her mouth. Turios turns and excuses himself from the room to the waning laugher. After the moment passes Runa says, "He's a delicate sea moss, isn't he?" Thand clears her throat as she stands. "Shy, not delicate. Now focus," she says taking a step toward Runa. What follows is a practice in Runa learning how to hit the ground in the least painful way. Oma demonstrates form against her sister but leaves the lessons to be learned by Runa's flesh. Eventually Turios returns, looking dower and avoiding eye contact with Runa in the brief moments between physicality.

Hours later Runa hobbles down the docks of Cardis looking for the ferry home. She knows she had planned to visit the library but her mind provides myriad reasons to rest instead. She opts to take the inclined elevator instead of the stairs once faces with the choice upon the island. Something about the place feels different. It is sense of calm which has settled over the entire estate. No servants shuffle about. Zidero isn't arguing with someone about something. It is quiet and it puts Runa in a better mood. At the last minute, she passes her room and heads toward the small library. The heavy door of dark wood has a stubborn seal which takes considerable strength to overcome. Inside the environment differs drastically from the rest of the estate. It is dry and cool to the point that Runa worries that her breath and sweat will throw off the delicate balance of this place. It is a bit of a marvel to her. Books would never last long in the conditions at sea. Which makes this place a bit of a marvel to her. As she scans the shelves, she pulls out several books and rests them at the table which runs down the center of the library. Once she has grabbed a book for each subject she finds interesting, she sits and opens a pristine tome about military history, then promptly falls asleep.

ACCRETION

CHAPTER 18

Adanon sits in the dark within his secluded home in the swamp. The shades are drawn but slivers of twilight slip past, etching sepia bands across the carpeted floor. His face is illuminated from the pallid glow from the reliquary that sits before him. In habitual fashion, he rotates his waning glass of spirits as he gazes into the cylinder. A chill passes through him as he imagines he can feel the ache just below his ribs where these pieces of himself had once resided. Darian has given him a dangerous and frustrating "gift." Frustrating because he has been given a choice, a choice he should never have been given. Dangerous because the suspicions of the council will be firmly fixed on Adanon unless he handles the situation well. As he takes another gulp of the stinging libation, he ponders if the council even know that the reliquary is missing. They certainly will with time. In that eventuality, Adanon would like to be rid of it. Perhaps he should return it. He has been considering it more as the day has grown long and his sobriety thin. It would certainly be an ingratiating gesture to return this to the Council, but the questions that follow will not be pleasant. Adanon shakes his head and sighs. If he had intended to return the object, why had he obfuscated Darian's involvement?

Taking another drink, Adanon thinks back on the disagreement with Talin. She had been right; he is too slow to find fault with Darian. Perhaps due to their closeness as youths, or that he is the last nostalgic link to a world that no longer exists. Despite how much Darian has changed over the years, Adanon still considers him like a brother. For at one time they had effectively been brothers. Adanon's ruminations lead him down a melancholy and destructive line of thinking. When drinking heavily, his memories of his mother are incessant. She had never been a virtuous woman, but she had taken Darian in after his mother abandoned him. Adanon tops off his glass with an unsteady hand. They barely had the food for the two of them, but she still took him in. Of course, there would have been more food had she not spent her money goldcap. Recalling the joy in his mother's eyes when he first had his awakening brings a lump into Adanon's throat. He knows now that it wasn't joy for his sake. Every citizen within the federation knows of the government stipend paid to parents of young praxiats. In addition to this, there a program that rewards those who report parents who fail to alert the state. Regardless, that joy in her eyes only grew when Darian also displayed the gift. She would be set, she had thought. Two less mouths to feed and a sizable income. But Adanon remembers how that joy had turned malicious as the assessors told her that she was to receive nothing for Darian. He wasn't truly her child. Adanon lets out a stifled, wistful laugh at the thought. Then he ponders if she is still alive. Only four decades have passed, but old age rarely claims the impoverished or addicted. With a sniffle, he recalls what had pained him the most in those days. Every night as the three of them had huddled together for warmth, Mother's shivering would always stop once the goldcap had taken effect. Those were the easy nights. Adanon knows now that her shivers had not been from the cold.

Adanon grunts to fend off the rising tightness in his throat. Just as he considers placing the reliquary in a safe place then passing out, a knock comes from the door. He had not planned for this. In his drunken state, he being to worry that somehow the council knows he has the reliquary. No, he doesn't even know if they know it is missing. In frustration, he finishes the glass of spirits then prepares to put on a show. He may not know who is at the door, but deception is second nature to him. As the knocking repeats, Adanon pushes the bottle off the counter where it explodes upon the tiled floor. With feigned drunken curses he makes his way across the room and stuffs the accursed reliquary in a false-bottomed vase which accommodates a stringy sapling. He then drops a towel on the spill as a third knock comes. "I'm coming, damn your bones!" he shouts as he thuds over to the door. Upon opening the door, he is greeted with the sight of a tall Gaerdanian man with light wispy hair. He has skin so pale it appears blueish, or corpselike in the shaded entryway of Adanon's abode. He is a shoalie courier of the council. A commoner with sunken, glassy eyes. There is only one reason he would be here. "You have been summoned, Akroates," the pale man drones. Adanon throws the door wide, exaggerating his slurred speech. "Of course! Only- let me clean the mess. You really caught me at a poor time," he says as he shuffles back to the spill, "It's such a waste. Thirty-four-year vintage." The pale man enters, his movements floaty, but almost mechanical. "Let me help," he says as he stoops beside Adanon and taking the rag. His movements to sop up the liquid are purposeful, but imprecise, like that of a young child. Adanon knows what this is, but he will play the fool. For he is being watched by the man, but the man is not under his own control. A malfeasant possession by another praxiat guides his actions. As Adanon walks away and retrieves a broom, the man fixes him in his unblinking gaze, holding his head at a peculiar angle. They must know, Adanon thinks. It takes every bit of willpower for him to remain calm. He knows that whoever is controlling this man has limited perception. For this is one of the forbidden techniques that brought Adanon to be the Akroates. He likens it to dreaming. All the senses are dulled or muddled. His suspicious are confirmed when he returns to see the man continuing to wipe the floor with the now bloody and sodden rag. It appears he has cut himself on the glass but fails to notice the injury. While it was just a suspicion at first, this confirms his initial impression. Adanon thanks the man for his help then they make their way out of the house.

As they approach the platform that leads back to the city, the pale man hisses in a labored breath. Whomever had been controlling the man must have ceded control of the vessel. Adanon doesn't like any of this. "Do you know what the summons pertains to?" he says, with concern in his voice. The pale man only looks at Adanon for a time then looks away, offering no response. As they draw closer to the city, Adanon can feel his heart racing in his chest, partially from the unknown, partially from the drink. The central hub of the city is near the temple, leaving little time for Adanon to formulate a plan. Adanon chuckles with a glance at the pale man. He assumes it is no coincidence that the summons had come as he had been drinking. Despite the overarching melancholy, he can find the humor in the situation. It also proves a sentiment of Talin's true; he is self-detrimental. A trickle of nervous sweat runs down his spine as the car comes to a stop in the station. A few days ago, he would have never foreseen his current predicament. But he has always been a survivor, more so than Talin even. As they approach the Temple of the Watchers, Adanon straightens his posture and runs his fingers through his hair. The pale man prostrates himself at the entrance of the mirrored hall, leaving Adanon to approach alone.

The sun has long since set, leaving the only light in the temple filtering into the main space through the shear orange fabric which separates the new from the old. Adanon can see them from the entrance, the cowled councilors waiting near the ancient mausoleum. As he approaches, he notes that their number is wrong. There should be thirteen councilors. A sense of dread settles over Adanon as he reaches the end of the corridor and supplicates himself. "Akroates," a chorus of voices says, sending shivers down his sweat drenched back. "Potentates," he says, fogging the reflective floor with his breath. "Do you know," the councilors say in unison, "the whereabouts of envoy Argyra?" Of all the things Adanon had prepared for mentally enroute to the temple, inquiring after Talin had never crossed his mind. "Potentates, she requested some time away from her duties, which I granted," Adanon says, unsticking his forehead from the floor. Scoffing filters through the dividing fabric. "Was she always fond of the begrimed vistas of Astoraph?" one of the Councilors says. Adanon struggles to make sense of the question, "How do you mean?" "Someone matching her description was seen in the east." Adanon's feeling of dread had been apropos of the situation.

After a silence, a female Councilor says, "Something important has gone missing." A chill runs through Adanon. They are speaking about the reliquary, he knows it. In a desperate moment he ponders if he is sober enough to defend himself. No, not against several Councilors, he reasons. Even a praxic genius the likes of Agrios would fall under these circumstances. Throwing out the idea of conflict, Adanon leans into deception. "What has gone missing, Potentates?" he says calmly. He thinks he seemed genuine. After another prolonged silence, the council says, "Our dear friend Darian has slipped his reigns." The words send Adanon's mind into spiral. Over the course of a few days everything has begun to crumble. Had Darian intended that Adanon take his joke about apostacy seriously? As his mind jumps through the chain of events, he struggles to keep his composure. Talin's flight pains him more than Darian. Hoping beyond hope that her actions are sound, Adanon chuckles into the floor. "Potentates," he says as he raises his head and rises to a knee, "I am your listener, but I have failed to hear the truth from Darian's lips. Allow me to bring him back to stand judgement." It is a ploy. If the council knows that his reliquary is missing, they will never let him leave this place. How can he hope to outsmart the collective wisdom of the ageless? While Adanon has been faithless for as long as he can remember, he does what men do when the outlook is hopeless; he prays. Prayer offered to the unknowable that he had glimpsed on his long-obscured days of bliss. Bliss reflected in the eyes of his daughter. Despite his mental flailing, the weight of the silence foreshadows the council's reply. His sins have caught up with him and he will be replaced. "Very well," the council says, "If anyone can bring him back into the fold, it's the Akroates." Adanon struggles to contain the tremors in his limbs. As he stands, he builds the courage to address them without fear of reprisal. "I will leave expeditiously. I have a feeling he fled to Stormanvil," Adanon says, lifting his chin, "Please see to Talin as you see fit." "So be it, we will be watching you closely," they say. They won't. They can't without the reliquary. He has the upper hand thanks to the man he is tasked with hunting. "As for Argyra, a cenobium was razed by insurrectionists in western Gaerdan. She has less allies there than she may think," one Councilor says. Adanon is familiar with the cenobium, having spent time in Gaerdan as a young praxiat. The cold driving wind of Stormanvil is no preparation for the frozen mirelands of Gaerdan. The memory of tramping through the frigid bogs sends shivers down his spine. "If I have your leave, Potentates, I'd like to be hasty. Darian is several steps ahead," he says. It's no lie, Darian has forced Adanon to seek him out. His delivery of the reliquary had been calculated. The huddle of twelve separates. "Then go Akroates, but do not return emptyhanded," a husky feminine voice says. With that Adanon bows and turns away. He must be quick. As he exits the temple, his mind turns to his newest recruit. But he reasons that there are bigger things at stake. Runa wouldn't understand yet anyway.

CHAPTER 19

On the boulder field which merges into a deciduous forest north of the mountains, Talin finds herself watching the sun draw lower through the bare branches of the bone white trees. In another month's time this area will be locked in frost, closing off their passage to all but the most brazen. She doesn't mind the cold so much. What she does mind is the attentions of the other members of that caravan. The guide, a man not native to Gaerdan but who claims make the trek often, lets out a shrill whistle signaling the end of the day's travel. Talin is glad to be done for the day. Watching the shadows grow long over the fallen blanket of leaves, she figures there is only an hour or two of light left to make camp. Ade tromps up next to Talin who has since sat on a boulder half as tall as her. Wordlessly, he begins to unpack the tent as Talin watches the others unload and tie off their beasts of burden to the barren trees. One of the louder men proclaims how he finally gets to use his hammock. As Talin picks up a piece of dead wood, she ponders if this is the place for such a sleeping arrangement. Over the past month she has tried to remain distant with these people. The less they know the better. But she and Ade had crafted a believable tale to avoid suspicion. They have posed as a married couple seeking refuge in Gaerdan. The specifics have been left to the imagination, which has frustratingly piqued the curiosity of the more perceptive members of the troupe, the children. One in particular annoys Talin, a little boy around ten who always seems to be watching her. She had felt terrible on one of the early days in the trek when she had asked if "he had something he wanted to say," only to be informed that he was in fact mute. He is the youngest member of the caravan, the next being his teenage brother. As Talin sits lost in her thoughts, thoroughly exhausted with travel, the boy comes running past, chasing his older brother. It's a slice of life that Talin has long forgotten how to relate with.

The shadows defuse as cold and bitter clouds move down over the peaks of the mountains to the south. Talin picks at the piece if wood with her knife as Ade finishes setting up the tent. He does a good job, she thinks, at acting the part. Naturally, he is working off the experience with his own wife and family. Talin has already uprooted the man and borrowed him for an indeterminant time. Fabricating their history together has been easier than discussing their very real baggage, so they have left it alone. Perhaps that is what she finds so irritating, not the circumstances, but her ease at adopting this false life. Had she been so ashamed of what she had been that she was eager to change? The young boy circles the encampment again, but trips over Talin's foot. Her knife slips, nicking her flinger slightly. Her look of anger is harsher than she intends as the boy scrambles to his feet and signs an apology. At least, Talin assumes it's an apology, she doesn't know the language, but it is a distinctive gesture. His father calls out to him red-faced as the boy slinks away. With a frustrated grunt, Ade sures up the last stake to the tent and calls out to Talin, saying, "Darling, would you care to help?" She would not, Talin thinks, but sighs and joins him at the tent. "The grapes need watering," Ade says with a thin smile. He means the beasts that have been their means of conveyance throughout the journey. The terrnoceros is an indigenous species to the forests of Gaerdan. The affectionate nickname stems from the grape-like keratinous protrusions that grow in clusters from the middle of their shaggy faces to above their brow. The 'horns' do resemble bunches of grapes standing in defiance of gravity. With a sigh, Talin makes her way to fetch water for the animals, but not before wrapping herself in a furred cloak.

Stomping through the brush, Talin makes her way to a nearby stream, of which there are several. The streams of snowmelt make their meandering way down the mountains, eventually converting in the mirelands and lakes west of the capitol of Hleifden. Talin has never been out this far in the untamed wilderness of this land. Most of her time was spent in the towns and cities. She dredges up a memory of asking Adanon why runaways wouldn't brave the wilds over seeking asylum in civilization. At the time she hadn't thought the answer of, "Try it and see how that goes," was appropriate. Today, the reality of the hardship is palpable. After nearly tripping over a dozen small stones, she makes it to the stream. There are a few lone trees among the boulders, though the density of the woodland begins rather abruptly to Talin's left. The setting sun and low hanging clouds give her an uneasy feeling as she peers off as far as she can see into the trees. She can't shake feeling that she is being watched. After bagging the water, she makes her way back to the encampment. As Talin returns to the caravan, she does her routine count of the group. It has become habitual through the journey. She, Ade, the boy, his parents and older brother, the shifty barber and his much younger wife, the guide. Nine travelers accounted for and settling around the fire. Talin calls out to the guide, named Youm, as she offers water to the first foul smelling terrnoceros. Reluctantly, Youm shuffles over to her. "Yes, Kyri?" he says with an imposed deep voice. Talin thinks he fancies her and doesn't hide it well. "Is this place dangerous?" she says, looking out into the darkening forest. Youm loses some of the color in his beaded face. "Yes and no Kyri. No worries..." he pauses seeing the concern on Talin's face, "I have made this trip many times." Talin studies the man's eyes as he smiles. Then he breaks her gaze to pat the terrno's shaggy flank. Talin wants desperately to rely on her gift. It would be so simple to see if Youm is lying, but she has gone without using praxis thus far and would like to continue to do so. "If—" Youm says, stilling looking at the pack animal, "if you get frightened, you may join me in my hammock." She looks at him, incredulous, then scoffs as she strolls to the next animal. "Don't worry kyri," Youm says, as he pats the terrno hard enough to make a sound, "they will alert us of any danger," before moving to sure up his nearby hammock. One by one, as the dark creeps in and the cold seeps into their backs, the travelers retire to their tents. Talin joins Ade after taking a final glance into the endless rows of trees. "I don't like this place. Keep your weapon close," she says to Ade as she fishes her blade from her boot. "I always do my blushing bride," Ade replies with a smirk as he turns off the lantern.

The shrill resonant hooting of the terrnos jolts Talin awake. All she can see through the dark is Ade's eyes looking back at her. He reaches for the biolume lantern, but Talin stops him. Ripping noises ring out over the terrified bleating of the animals. "We have to do something," Ade whispers as he thumbs off the safety on the coilgun. Talin desperately wants to grab for the aster secreted in her pack, but reconsiders as she remembers where she is. A bout of muffled pleading in the distance spurs her into action. Talin rolls over and slashes open the tent as Ade barrels over her and out into the unknown. With nothing but her knife, Talin's eyes dart around the camp. The fire has died, leaving the area so dark that even the smoldering embers seem bright in comparison. A light dusting of snow falls through the gloom and the only sound that can be heard is the whine of Ade's weapon. Another blast of screams from one of the animals heralds its flight as it tramples from out of the trees, bounding and thrashing. It lands squarely on one of the tents in its gallop then tumbles into the fire kicking up a lot of embers.

It's then that she sees them. The reflective orbs within the branches. "My God," Ade says seeing the gashes on the felled but still breathing terrno. Its entrails hang exposed, it's fetters and flesh torn to ribbons. Without hesitation, he shoots the ailing creature, ending its suffering. Talin whips around looking for the rest of the party. Youm is missing. "He said he knew this place," Talin mutters before growling in frustration. Then she scrambles forward to the nearest, untrampled tent, cutting through to check on its occupants. Inside is the weeping mother of the two boys. A plinking shot rings out. Ade must have seen something. "Where is your husband? And your boys?" Talin says hurriedly. The woman stammers, "They- they went to- pee." She breaks down into sobs. "Stay here," Talin says, then curses as she pops back out of the tent. It's too dark. There is a bloodcurdling cry from the forest, sounding like something between a howl and human scream. Then the scraping of branches and bark carries through the night air. Talin needs the aster. "How many?" she shouts as she slides back to her tent. "A dozen or more!" Ade responds as he loses another volley at shades among the trees. In a panic Talin digs deep into her pack looking for the aster. She's about to throw out the past month of work. Anyone who sees her use this will know she is a praxiat. There is a scraping sound from the small wagon used for carrying the heavier items. One of the beasts clambers over the top of the wooden vehicle in a blur of shadow. It lunges for Ade as he turns toward the sound. He fires only once before it is upon him. As the razor-like maw snaps at his face they tumble away from the light. Ade is able place his feet against the animal and launch it back toward the wagon but he doesn't escape unscathed. He lets out a groan past clenched teeth as dark slick stripes bloom across the back of his beige shirt. The woman within the tent panics at the commotion, stumbling off into the field. Talin has found the aster. She emerges from the tent to see the woman fleeing into the night. The animal that Ade had launched picks itself up, holding a fore limb clutched to its chest, visibly injured. Talin abandons all caution and activates the lantern, flooding the campsite with crimson light. It flickers, the power cell struggling in the cold. Then heedless of who will see, Talin focuses her will into the aster. It activates with a thin metallic clank. Still holdings the focus in her clutched hand, she wills the metallic sharks barreling toward the animal in a cascade of pain. Through the arcing motion, she draws as much mass and energy into each razor-sharp slivers as she can muster. Before the impact, Talin grins and aligns each edge with malice. Then the torrent of hardened alloy collides with the unsuspecting creature in a chorus of death, each note driving through flesh and bone while bearing the animal down in a metallic cacophony.

The last sound from the beast is the rattle of death that escapes as the pieces of the aster squelch free from its corpse. Just behind the viscera Talin sees an unexpected sight, the mute boy is looking out from under the wagon, wide-eyed and trembling. "Stay there," Talin says as she recalls the pieces of the aster into a cluster around her. Ade takes a hissing breath as he fires off several more shots into the darkness. It appears he has found his mark, as a tumbling mass falls from a tree several paces into the woods. Talin rushes forward, whipping the cloud of metal in a crescent toward the trees. Several chittering yelps resembling human laugher echo through the night air. "Reloading!" Ade shouts as his weapon falls silent. Talin wishes desperately to see what she is facing. She had heard stories about treehounds in the past but has never seen the animals. Gaerdanians speak of them in hushed, reverent tones, as if they are the embodiment of this savage and timeless land. A commotion erupts within the trees, branches rattling, snapping, scrapping. Shapes shift, darting through the tangle of limbs. Talin has made a mistake. She had gotten too close to the tree line. Turning to the tree a few paces away, she summons back the fragments of the aster. But it's too late. A pale shape washed a vivid red by the lantern's crimson light clings to the trunk of the tree. She sees the gaunt figure and unblinking dark orbs set within the vulpine face. All she can to is stumble backwards as she fumbles for her blade. It's lunges for her, claws outstretched. Two reports ring out as the mass of the animal slams into Talin, bearing her to the ground under its substantial weight. Pain shoots through whole her body. What a way to go, she thinks. Her chest burns like fire, but she isn't dying. She takes a gasping breath. The wing had been knocked out of her by the creature which presently lies atop her, leaking dark ichor. "Help! Ade!" she cries out. After a moment, Ade lifts the creature off her by the scruff of its neck with one arm then sets it aside. Talin thanks him wordlessly as she picks up the focus for the aster she had dropped in the scuffle. Then in a moment of manic rage, she recalls the aster and flings it back into the trees with a primal yell. She hits nothing but air and branches, but the wanton fury feels good. The chittering laughter resounds deeper in the forest, seeming to signal a retreat. But the only sound Talin can hear is her labored breathing punctuated by her pulse pounding in her ears.

Ade rests his hand on Talin's shoulder, causing her to flinch. She turns to him, as the dusting of snow continues to fall. They have lost the cover they sought to keep in one desperate struggle. Any witnesses to Talin using the aster will cause problems. As her heartrate slows and her composure returns, Talin turns back to the wagon. Ade calls out her name, but she tramps directly through the now blood slick camp and peers under the vehicle. The boy blinks back at her, ever silent. He has pressed himself under the shelter of the wheel and rear axle. Talin thinks back to the events before the attack. Then she frowns as she mimics the sign for an apology before grabbing the child by his lapel and dragging him out into the silence.

CHAPTER 20

Runa zeroes out the regulator on her welder before flipping up her helmet shield to inspect the still glowing bead. She is lying on her back under a section of Raz's boat that has become something of a project for her. Since holding her hands over her face for any amount of time is agony, she is glad to be done with the weld. Bruises and soreness from the lessons with Thand have found a way to inconvenience her every day. Walking upstairs, bending, even sleeping have all become chores to the muscle soreness that never seems to abate. Simply put, the past month has been an exercise in exhaustion. On the days she doesn't get wrung out by the sisters, she reads and works with Raz and his team. She has taken a liking to him, that is, when he isn't brooding in his room. She has seen in his room once but has never been inside. He seems very protective of the space. It's a stark contrast to her room, which had the décor changed out in a day as Runa had been at the cenobium. No doubt Kaeln had relayed Runa's remarks on the garish trappings, which spurred the change. After a week Zidero had returned angrier than before he left. His temperament is hard to read, leading him to blow up at the slightest inconvenience. Runa slides out from under the suspended watercraft and takes off her helmet. She sits there on the roller board ruminating. One instance that showed her who Zidero really is under the pomp, was when a servant had forgotten to order more of his favorite fruit. He had ranted and yelled about how much he liked it because it reminds him of his late wife. Which is a fabrication if Raz is to be believed. After Zidero had reduced the woman to a sobbing mess, he had apologized by giving her a gross sum of money to go purchase things for her family. It had been at that moment that Runa had understood how and why the staff are so inclined to work here. Despite the abuse she has observed, he has never been cruel or unkind to Runa, and she has lost some sleep pondering why. Several times she has wondered if the lascivious implications by Talin had been true, but never has she caught him in an inappropriate stare. Just the thought of it, considering that he has been with her mother, makes her ill.

Slipping out of her coveralls, Runa shudders as the chill of the shop sets in. Without the heavy garment, her sleeveless shirt and shorts offer no warmth on this seasonally cold day by the sea. She exits the shop then turns to the mountain of stairs up to the estate. She purses her lips at the sigh. She'd rather not scale those due to the ache in her legs, so she shuffles to the elevator. In the interim between praxic lessons and being a shipwright, Runa has read voraciously. She hasn't made progress with languages or finding any manuals about praxis, but she has consumed several volumes on history. While she hadn't sought out accounts about her people from an outside perspective, she had come across mentions dating back to the praxic knights of the Astoran Empire. She hadn't considered how long the Janamudra have called the sea home. Another area in that had caught her attention was the more modern development of naval weaponry. She has yet to bring it up to Raz and his crew, but she has several ideas about implementing wartime torpedo technology into the boat. However, she hasn't figured out how to broach that topic without sounding mad. Sighing at the thought of Raz being melancholic, Runa steps off the lift into the stuffy halls of the estate. Everyone else may tolerate his bouts of sadness, but she doesn't want to sit idle when he could use some consolation. A thought occurs to her as she strolls through the warm, dry air in the lower level. Staying busy has helped her cope with the overwhelming shifts recently. Maybe that is what Raz needs, something to focus on other than his own thoughts.

As Runa approaches Raz's room she lets down her hair then fluffs it as best she can. It has become unmanageable as of late, but she considers the attempt soothing enough for her anxiety. She knocks loudly. After a moment, Raz cracks open the door with a glare. His brow softens somewhat upon seeing Runa. "Hi," she says peering through the crack at the warmly lit interior. "Good morning," Raz says, making no attempt to welcome her in. "Aye, close enough," Runa says with a shrug. It is nearly dinner time. He still hasn't invited her in, but she is determined. "What are you hiding in there?" she asks, leaning against the door frame. "Not hiding, it's just private. It's not a secret or anything, but my dad calls it kids' stuff," Raz says quickly. "I've got a secret I can trade. If you show me yours; I'll show you mine," Runa says matter-of-factly, resting her hand on her hip. Raz sputters. She blinks at him through the crack, oblivious of the implication.

"Let's not say that," Raz says as he relents and opens the door, "A secret for a secret sounds like an equitable agreement to me." Runa hops into the room without hesitation and glances around. Her rust-colored eyes glitter at the sight of the wall of model ships. "Ooh!" she exclaims as she rushes over to the display, "You made all of these?" She walks the length of the wall, stooping to admire each shelf from the bottom to the top. Raz simply watches her, his mouth a thin line. "This is amazing. Seriously you- the Sabby!" Runa chirps, recognizing the ship even though the model is a mockup of its wartime configuration. Raz lets out a chuckle, saying, "I thought you'd think it was childish. You're the only other person that's had anything nice to say about them." There is a genuine air of gratitude to his words. Finishing her perusing, she makes her wat to the desk. There is an unfinished model, or what used to be one. It is a destroyed old sailing vessel. Its wooden decks, rigging and sails lie strewn about in tatters as if thrown across the room. She doesn't need praxis to piece together what had occurred. She looks at Raz, with sadness in her eyes. He sighs as he looks away, saying, "He's always been like that. Vindictive, cruel... overbearing" "You don't have to make excuses for him," Runa says. "I'm not. I said he's always been that way, but I can almost remember a time before. When he wasn't." Runa thinks back on the memories she had trespassed into on that day in the elevator. Raz clears his throat. "He's still my dad and I love him despite how hard he makes that sometimes," he says as he turns and pushes himself to the door, "Let's get out of here. I heard there's another petty secret around."

As they traverse the halls Runa thinks about her family. She hasn't thought about them in some time, not since focusing on her training. A pang of guilt rises within her. It isn't the sharp ache of first losing them. It's the annoying pain of wondering if things could have gone differently. To get her mind into a different space, Runa says, "So who was it?" Raz looks at her perplexed. "The other person you said showed an interest your model ships." She continues holding up a finger enthusiastically. They arrive at Runa's room then she opens the door. Raz follows her in, saying "Adanon." Runa nods but drops the discussion there. She hasn't seen him for several weeks. Whenever she had questioned Oma about his absence, she's been suspiciously dismissive. "I have doubts that your secret is anywhere near as embarrassing as mine," Raz says with an exaggerated sullen look. Runa glances at him over her shoulder as she rummages under her mattress. Then with a flourish, she flips the scrimshaw blade end-over-end and offers the handle to him. With a candid reverence he takes the blade, as if he already understands its significance. Leaning forward, he inspects the engraving and says, "I was right. This is keen. Not embarrassing at all." Runa slides over a chair then straddles it, saying, "Can I confide in you?" Raz gives her a curious look before nodding slowly. "In addition to helping with the boat stuff, Zidero asked me to tutor you in Jana culture, which is something I'm increasingly apathetic toward," she says, resting her chin on the back of the chair, "If I'm honest, it has been easy to let go of." Raz chuckles. "Of course it is. That's what they do," he says offering the blade back to her. She waves off the gesture, questioning his meaning with her bemusement. Raz opens the blade, revealing the long, fixed blade of etched metal. "The institution," he says, breaking the silence but pausing to consider his words, "To them, you're just like this engraving. It was only a bone before someone thought to change it. The process takes away to create something new. To them, you are unfinished, so they chip away." It's a rough analogy, but she follows his reasoning. She can't say she has experienced any explicit push to expunge her of her heritage. It was her choice. "Aye? Except I've had these reservations about the Jana since before leaving the flotilla. Also, I think Adanon would have expressed that if—" Raz's expression cuts her short. "I think you know what I'm talking about," he says narrowing his eyes. "I understand point they are trying to make, but I don't think you can draw a comparison between a material and a person. For every bit I may be losing, I'm gaining something else," she says vehemently, "Right? I'm not a block of wood or stone to be shaped." "Let's just agree to disagree," Raz says, handing the blade back to her with finality. "Aye. Let's," she responds, taking the blade with a despondent look. She knows he meant no offense, but sometimes, paradoxically, when she wants to get along with him, she finds herself arguing. She hasn't always been so combative, and it annoys her. Sighing, she moves to leave the room but not before saying, "I think a change of scenery is in order. I have some ideas about your boat, Kyr." She mimics the bow which the servants often use with Zidero. He smiles as he accepts the gesture with mock reciprocation.

A short time later in the library, Runa scampers about, pulling books from the shelf and placing them on the table in front of Raz. Skirting the table, searching for another volume she says, "I know there are regulations about the gross weight of the boat but is there anything that says the craft must remain above water?" The question noticeably catches Raz off-guard. Most of the boats are capable of diving below the waves to a degree, but to do is to sacrifice speed. Raz shrugs, saying, "As long as the craft crosses the finish line on the surface, I think it's fine." "Good," Runa says slamming down the last book and grinning. Before him is a fold-out diagram of a torpedo. "Here," she says pointing at cylinder on the diagram, "can agree that the density of water is greater than air?" "Wouldn't debate it but I'm not the praxiat," Raz says with a crooked grin. "We will have to add more weight. A rocket motor and cylinders of compressed air- Oh! And mounting, all heavy. But if you could travel faster under the water than you can above, would you?" "How fast?" Raz says, interest piqued. Runa scratches her head and says, "Maybe two hundred knots, give or take. It will take some calibration—" "Bog off," Raz says with an incredulous laugh. She looks at him, crestfallen. "You're right. I thought it was worth a mention," she says closing the book. With a discerning look, he stops the book from closing and says, "Show me how it would work."

CHAPTER 21

The following morning, well before the sunrise, Runa drags her tired body out of bed. Shambling through her morning routine, she pauses briefly to check her reflection in the mirror. The gash for Talin's throttling has long since healed, but the faint scar still forms a slight crease whenever she furrows her brow. Her attention then turns to her hair. It has grown overlong, the long-faded ends split unruly to the point that she is considering cutting it herself. She mutters to herself in frustration then bundles the mass of hair into a bun as best she can. After layering on clothing, she sets out into the frigid morning air.

The commute goes as usual, with industrial workers piling into the car alongside Runa, only to disembark in Esoptria. The longer route that doesn't require a changeover is preferable some mornings. By the end of the trek, she finds herself alone as she approaches the cenobium. The transit Adanon had insisted on saves only twenty minutes of travel. Some mornings she'd rather spend the extra time preparing, mentally. This particular morning her mind has been dwelling on something Raz had said. No one has forced her to change who she is, even if a select few have been antagonistic. She ponders if that had been his point. That many gradual cuts are less noticeable than one great blow. She sighs. It's still an annoying analogy. Annoying in is aptness, she thinks, but flawed under any logical scrutiny. Still lost in the autonomous motion of the early morning stroll to the practice room, Runa has a delayed reaction to someone calling out her name. It's Oma. The two young women exchange pleasantries for the rest of the walk. Upon entering the room, Thand places her hand on her hips and says, "It's graduation day for you, Kelp Queen." Runa rolls her eyes at the new insult as she crosses the room. Turios backs away from Thand as she puffs up her chest. Runa has a good idea about her nature at this point. She doesn't dislike Thand the way she seems to dislike her. They are simply too dissimilar. Thand respects results but has ardent faith in the intangible, a notable contradiction. This was a point of frustration for Runa until she gave it serious thought. One evening after a particularly grueling day of training, Runa had arrived at the thought that everyone, even she, has a facet of life they are willing to overlook to remain comfortable. But today Runa doesn't have time to muse on her biases. So, she approaches the much larger woman and sinks into a low, defensive posture.

Thand shifts forward, letting out leisurely, probing strikes with her scar covered hands. Throughout their sparing, Runa has grown to be close friends with Thand's fists and feet. The scars on her hands betray some traumatic event Runa hasn't dared ask about. In a lax moment, one of those very same hands strikes hard against her ribs. Their eyes meet. The jab had been a warning. Despite the size of her arms, her legs are Thand's weapon of choice. She had been adamant that utilization of one's legs is more important than one's arms in most situations. Presently, Thand says, "I'll concede that you've learned something," as she takes a large step forward, "but you still fall for the classics." She reaches past Runa and grabs her hair, pulling her into her substantial bulk. Before Runa can mount a defense, she finds her neck trapped in a triangle of muscle. It's a headlock, again. The difference is this time she is ready. With her outside arm, she reaches between Thand's legs. With her other arm, she reaches behind the woman's broad back, clutching her shoulder. Then with all her strength, Runa lifts, bearing Thand up, then over, toward the ground; right where she wants to be. Now with the leverage of her core and back she overpowers the grapple. Runa can feel through their contact, Thand is wavering. It's another small victory. She seizes the opening with purpose, pinning Thand's free arm with her leg as she climbs atop her. Sometime in the scuffle, her hair has broken free, hanging about her in mad, blazing curls. She crashes against Thand's mental defenses like the raging sea. Each blow building with the beating of her heart. Then she sees herself through Thand's eyes; untamed, crowned in a halo of flame against the backdrop of the ceiling lights.

She's trapped, pinned under a burning wooden truss. This is the day Thand had bargained never to be powerless again, for her sister. If only she could press the burning timbers from atop herself, she could get Oma out of the inferno. Her chest compresses under the weight with each exhale. Wriggling her arms up against the crackling timbers, she presses with every bit of strength her young body can muster. The flames sizzle the flesh of her fingertips. "Salvation comes to the worthy," she thinks to herself as the beam begins to move.

Runa snaps back to the sensation of hands pulling her away. "She yielded," Oma says calmly from over Runa's shoulder. She hadn't lost consciousness this time, but she had lost her composure. Runa flexes her hands, still feeling the pain from Thand's memory. Silence hangs over the room, broken by the shifting of Thand to her feet. Shame crosses her face and body as she glances at Runa. Then turning without a word, she exits the training room.

Oma rests a hand on Runa's shoulder and says, "You did nothing wrong." A warm sensation passes through her body from the point of contact. It is a curious thing, as if the emotion is filtered through Runa's own perception. And while it is a shifting synesthetic experience, the intent is communicated clearly. It's pride. Runa understands now that the scope of what praxis can do is wider than she had ever known. "You still have a long way to go, Runa, but now you can see that praxis isn't just a gimmick," Turios says with a nod. "Turios means he feels a lot safer with you being able to defend yourself," Oma says as she offers her hand to help Runa up. After she stands, the group makes for the door. Letting Turios walk ahead, Oma stops Runa then says, "I don't know what you experienced, but it's best to keep it to yourself. Any old fool with eyes could tell Thand was upset." Runa nods. "I've learned more from everyone, more than they know," she says, patting Oma on the shoulder. She is alluding to the trauma she has experienced through Thand, Raz, and even List. There is a disquieting shame that lingers in the back of her mind. Shame at feeling so distraught over losing her place among the flotilla. She could have lost so much more, and still has much to lose. But she is unwilling to let that happen. Unsure how to communicate the feelings, Runa thinks of a bittersweet memory. It's a memory she doesn't even know is real. The memory of her grandmother rocking slowly as Runa read a children's book aloud. It's a mix of pride, hope, and longing, that she wills to share with Oma. With a shudder, the lingering static in her fingertips fizzles silently as she pulls away. The corners of Oma's cheerful mouth tighten for a moment before returning to a smile.

Catching up with Turios, the two young women make faces at him. Runa elbows him in a manner reminiscent of greeting her brother. She stifles the emotional memory with a cough, then rests her arm on Turios' shoulder. "I say, where are we going, Kyr?" she says, mimicking his proper Esoptrian accent. His thin, forced smile is Runa's reward for invading his personal space. She has grown to enjoy teasing him alongside Oma. Thand, on the other hand, has little patience for any display of affection. Shrugging off her arm, Turios says, "The quartermaster." His foreboding tone is echoed on Oma's face. Runa sounds out the title in a whisper, oblivious to its meaning. "Sound like a military position," she says, straightening her relaxed posture. No time for basking in a victory, it seems. Turios grins awkwardly, saying, "More like paramilitary, but it's a bit of a tongue-in-cheek name for an establishment, not a person." "Yeah, it doesn't make sense," Oma adds. After a long elevator ride to nearly the top of the tower, Runa follows the others into a space of drab grays and whites. Compared to the sterile surroundings, the three young praxiats are a splash of color. Close to the entrance of the elevator is a reception area where a single bald man sits watching the group approach. "Whatcha want?" he says, scrunching his hooked nose at Turios. "I need to requisition an aster," Turios says, looking down at the man. "Whenzya date of deployment?" the bald man says. Clearing his throat, Turios leans on the desk. "To be determined." The bald man picks up a book from the desk then returns to reading. "Fresh out," he says without looking up. Not wanting to deal with another obstacle, much less an avoidable one, Runa steps up to the desk. "Listen, I really need whatever this thing is, I think," she says. "Ya 'ear that Jov, she really needs it," he says to the empty wall behind him, then he looks at Runa out of the corner of his eye. There is a look of recognition in his eye. He sets down the book. "I've gotta note 'ere that says give the sad lookin' Jannie girl whatever she needs," he says, holding up a piece of paper and flicking it. "Really?" Turios and Runa say in unison. "No," he replies as he picks up the book again with a self-satisfied grin. The white wall behind him makes a sound like perpetually cracking glass as a line forms in jerking motions. The line traces a door frame, then a woman steps out as if she hadn't just stepped out of a wall that had no portal moments before. Runa watches the pale woman with frizzy black hair flop beside the bald man. She pushes her large circular glasses higher on her square face then glances at Runa. "Isn't that the one?" she says, kicking at the bald man's chair. "Hmm? Oh," he says, looking under the desk. The woman shoos him, reaching under the desk as well. A moment of clattering passes before she reemerges. "This was supposed to be delivered to Cardis. Surprised it ever left Stormanvil," she says flopping a heavy envelope on the desk. It is torn open and stained, but the address is still legible. "You this Runil? Note here says to deliver to the Janamudra girl in training," the bespectacled woman says, tapping the crumpled parcel. Runa corrects her mispronouncing her name. "Close enough," she says, slapping the bald man on the arm, "Another satisfied customer." Runa examines the parcel, pulling out the paper within. It's from Adanon. "How long has this been here?" she says, incredulous. "Few weeks'er three," the man says. Oma butts into the conversation, "We still need an aster." The dark-haired woman yawns and says, "You- know the procedure. Need some of that red collateral." Turios rolls up his sleeve in frustration, as does Oma, while Runa scans the lengthy handwritten letter.

ACCRETION

CHAPTER 22

Talin watches the shallow breathing of the young mother of the mute boy as they rock in the back of the covered wagon. The boy sits across the wagon from her, bundled against the cold. His mother's head rests in Talin's lap. A few times she has glimpsed the woman's fevered and pitiful dreams. They are the only members of the caravan left. Only gore of Youm had been found among the ribbons of his hammock. Not nearly enough to bury. The terrno that blundered through the camp had trampled the old man and his young wife. "At least it had been a quick death," Talin thinks. After a grim, one-sided discussion with the mute boy, Talin had searched for his brother and father, but they were never found. Ade had found the mother, catatonic, among the boulders. The working theory is that she tripped in her flight and hit her head against a stone. The poor woman hasn't woken since. Despite Ade's insistence, Talin dares not attempt using praxis to heal her. Mending is a gift she sorely lacks and has never claimed to possess. "Boy, are you hungry?" Talin says. He doesn't respond. Ade claims to remember his name as Eklin, but he responds to almost anything Talin calls him. Often, she wonders if that is out of fear. And he should be afraid. She had been moments away from sending him along with the rest of recently departed. Scoffing at the thought, Talin rests the mother's head back on a soft sleeping bag. She still isn't sure why she had spared him. At the time the panic and fear had clouded her judgement just enough to allow Ade to stay her hand. Perhaps it's because he is mute. "I said, are you hungry?" Talin repeats. He just shakes his head as he stares out the back of the wagon. It has been a tense three days. Each night the chatter of the treehounds can be heard during the night watch. Often, in those long hours of delicate silence, she wonders if it could only be her imagination. Regardless, she keeps the aster close. She intends to keep it until they get closer to Hleifden. Talin reaches over her shoulder, parting the canvas to speak with Ade. He glances at her with a cool expression. It niggles her. Out of earshot of the boy Talin had implored that they abandon the woman. She clearly has severe head trauma, and Talin counts it as an anomaly that she has survived this long. But Ade had insisted, again invoking her conscience, just like the boy. "No seizures?" he says. Talin shakes her head. Ade nods then says in a hushed voice, "I hope she can hold out another day. We've just passed another standing stone." Neither of them knows the exact distance but judging by the speed of the only surviving terrno, the stones are approximately three mille apart. Which is disconcerting, as the mirelands should have begun by now, but then again, neither of them is certain. Talin rests her head against the wagon and grins at the absurdity. She has never wanted to see a crowd as badly as she does now. Her only company for the past few days has been a mute, a catatonic, and Ade, who has been uncharacteristically quiet. There is an irony to the loneliness that is not lost on her.

That evening they bed down in a coppice clearing, the first sign of recent habitation they have seen north of the mountains. The area is overgrown with short bushes covered in vibrant red leaves. At first, the sight had been unnerving, but being away from the trees offers a degree of comfort not afforded to them in some time. Talin takes the first watch, letting Ade rest after a long day. As flurries of snow begin to fall, she takes out that same scrap of wood from before and sets to whittling. She had no purpose to the carving before, but now she has roughed in the shape of the terrible creatures that had preyed upon them. She thinks back on the shape of the animal, the one that was felled but not reduced to a formless mound. The tree hounds have long curved claws on the end of their three middle digits, with the two outside digits having more mobility. That coupled with their long, tufted tails makes them well adapted to life in the trees. Talin shudders at the memory of the gaunt animal. They must have been starving. Talin notches deep into the wood, attempting to shape the animal's tufted ears. On the counter-cut, she slips, knocking what would have been the ear off. She sighs deeply and tosses the carving into the distance with a whisper of an impact against the shrubbery. In the inky void beyond she glimpses a light. A flickering blueish-white flame off in the distance. She blinks and it appears to move. She shudders before bundling herself more in the woolen blanket. She knows what this is. It has many names; a fool's flame, a wisp of will, a witch's lantern, but Talin knows what they truly are, vestiges. The dead aren't conscious or malign, but remnants such as these have unwittingly led mortals to join them in the deep. With nothing to occupy her time, the watch is taxing on her mental state. Just as she considers following the whimsical light into the dark forest, Ade stirs to take his watch.

Talin doesn't mention the light, she knows Ade is a superstitious man. Maybe not as superstitious as Gaerdanians, but before the annexation Bujani had been filled with both powerful and pretender shaman of ancient wisdom. Some of whom had stumbled upon convergent tenets of praxis, but now they are a husk of their former glory. No one is left to continue their traditions but those who knew nothing of the truth. All relegated to crude alchemy and impuissant blood magic. Talin knows Ade will not follow the light even if he sees it, and they will never discuss it. Ade climbs out of the wagon, hissing against the icy needles in the air as Talin rolls over the bench while trying not to let too much heat escape. Ade breaks the silence, repeating his sentiment about the woman doing well. Talin offers nothing but a grunt as she bundles up next to the infrared heater at the center of the space.

In the morning, everyone shares rations. They discuss how long it has been that the woman has gone without water, but they don't want to make the situation worse. Talin tends to the woman, then turns her on her side to place small bits of ice in her mouth. This had been Eklin's idea communicated by pantomime. And while Talin feels the woman's death is a forgone conclusion, she helps keep her clean and dry. There are other ways to save the woman, but that is a line Talin has never crossed. With that thought and for the first time since she left, she sorely misses Adanon. She clasps her hand over her mouth and lets out a painful gasp. Both Ade and Eklin look at her curiously. "I'm fine," she says, blinking away tears. It will not be adversity that breaks Talin, it will be her attachment to him. "I was just thinking that Ad would know what to do," she admits in a rare moment of candor. Ade nods knowingly. "We do what we can until we can't. Let the sky sort out the rest," he says in a whisper as he shake's Talin's shoulder reassuringly. She feigns a smile then shovels down the last of the rehydrated slop in her bowl.

Shortly after leaving the crimson clearing the terrain begins to turn. What had been a dry whisper of a road gives way to the wet depression of one. The paving stones lie scattered and cracked on this stretch, through the perpetual cycle of freezing and thawing. It is a welcome sign that they are making progress, even if the terrain is much less accommodating. There are several times throughout the day where the wheels spin in the deep grooves in the mud which have filled and frozen over. They have entered the mirelands. The relentless dusting of snow abates as the sun shows its face for the first time in days. Then the dark comes as Talin and Ade sit at the front of the wagon watching the fleeting purple sky. It will be a long dark, as Fengari has passed beyond the horizon. Ade stirs Talin from her admiring of the darkening sky by saying, "I will drive on through the night. It's her only chance." Talin furrows her brow but shrinks back into the bench without protest. She knows he is right. There has been no food or water for the woman in three days. Talin rubs the reddened tip of her nose. "Should I send her on her way? I'd want it for myself." Ade looks at her, cross. Talin nods ahead, cutting her response short. A new lightshow has begun to the north. Ribbon like arcs of ethereal emerald light undulate across the horizon. It is the polar lights. "The sky burns," Ade says, gazing at the spectacle, "A good omen." It is beautiful, but Talin has seen the phenomenon before. Never the less, she spends a long time watching the lights as the trees grow sparse and the ground more frozen. Ade insists she gets some rest after an indeterminate amount of time, stirring her from her trancelike state. She mutters in agreement, then tucks back into the wagon. Eklin rushes across the space, startling her. She has nearly drawn her blade by the time he pushes a scrap of fabric toward her chest. On the scrap of canvas is a message in crude Esopt with poor spelling. "Please don't hurt my mommy," Talin reads the message aloud, then looks at the young boy's tear-soaked face. She squirms with irritation. "She ran away. I saved you," Talin says thumping her chest. She hears the insecurity and anger in her own voice, but she can't help herself. Eklin stumbles back, landing in the opposite corner. "Stay over there. I'm upset with you... and I don't know how to handle it." Ade asks if everything is alright through the canvas, which Talin dismisses. "Eklin, you know if your mother makes it, she probably won't be the same. She may need help doing everything." The boy scratches on the other side of the canvas. "Then it will be my turn to take care of her," Talin reads, interpreting past his poor spelling. "You don't know what you're saying," she says with a sigh, "It would be a great burden on you. Do you know what a burden is?" More scratching. "Like when you protected me," reads the note. Talin shakes her head. "No- I spared you, there's a difference. I'm not your mother and—" Talin says, feeling shame as the words leave her mouth, "the only person I can protect is myself." Eklin sinks deeper into the corner and turns away. The sound of him slowly scratching another note fills the wagon. He tosses it at Talin and turns his back to her, replacing the steady scribbles with low sniffling. She waits until the boy falls asleep then slips the note from his hand. "I think you'd make a good mommy," it reads. The sentiment grips her. What follows for her is a bout of self-loathing and self-reflection. She ponders what Adanon is doing in the spaces in between. Then Ade's voice breaks her out of the repetitive rumination. "Hey," he says, banging on the wooden bench. Talin pops up and sticks her head out of the tent. "I told you it was a good omen," Ade says. Ahead, past the gently sloping landscape, the trees fall away to a great sheet of ice. The dancing aurora above reflects slightly off the surface of the grand lake. Talin nearly overlooks what Ade had been alluding to. To the northeast, slowly strobing red orbs of light dot the icy surface. The pattern ripples to the edge of the lake, beckoning eastward.

CHAPTER 23

Adanon stands on the wind worn stones of the upper fortress town of Stenandra. The rest of the town rests firmly down the mille and a half tall cliff face. While this upper portion had once been an Avilite fortress, the area has since been relegated to tourist attraction. The plateau, the majority of which was formed through eons of tectonic upheaval and erosion, forms the prime territory of the prefecture known as Stormanvil. Adanon has spent the better part of two weeks investigating leads in a low town. Despite his position, many of the Esoptrians that occupy low town had met him with a fair amount of skepticism. Despite the mingling of Avilites and Esoptrians at this transitory town, there is still a physical, social, and ideological division between those above and those below. Adanon frowns as he watches a sailcar approach from the southeast. His wife Diba had been from Stenandra's low town. Things hadn't been so tense back when he met her bartending in a seedy cliff-end bar. Perhaps he had just been young and smitten, unable to see the issues past the sheen of her raven hair. Adanon sighs and looks back at the aggressively sloped buildings of the austere fortress. This had been the site of the last stand against the long reach of empire. Now it is a gift shop. While the grievances are old, and the aggrieved full of pride, Stormanvil couldn't survive without being part of the Federation these days. The few resources on the plateau make that a certainty. Even fewer tradesfolk come from the anvil, save for brewers, masons, and slime gardeners. Any that make a name for themselves leave. Adanon doesn't blame them: this place is where dreams die, having never taken flight.

His time in high town had been just as vexing, but for different reasons. Either out of a sense of wanting to be helpful or to ingratiate themselves with Adanon, many of the locals had claimed to see Darian. This had led to several more days of false leads. Presently, the sailcar arrives at the crumbling wall Adanon is perched upon. Then a young Anvilite man with a wisp of a chin beard exits the cockpit of the vehicle. His eyes grow wide with recognition, his rapid speech betrays his nervousness. "She pulls a little to the right, Kyr," he shouts, his longish hair whipping in the wind. Adanon tips him enough lote to heat a home for several months. He accepts the stack graciously, grinning uncontrollably. Adanon hitches his leg into the vehicle. "My- my sister looks up to you. Wants to be like you and councilor Darian someday," the young man says. Adanon stops, placing his hand on the open door as the locked sail vibrates in the breeze. "How old is she?" he says, glancing at the man. The man puffs up proudly and says, "Eight, Kyr." Adjusting his collar, Adanon turns and heaves himself into the car. "She still has time then," he says, before pulling the door closed. But he earnestly hopes the boy's sister grows to find better role models.

On the zig-zag path eastward, memories long repressed vie for Adanon's attention. This is the same path he had taken all those years ago after the news of the dome collapsing. The anguish he had felt on this lonely road is still palpable twenty years on. The danger of pushing the sailcar to its limits that day hadn't even been a consideration. What had he expected to do? As countless tonnes of stone had lain atop tens of thousands of people, not to mention the reality shattering effects of the diaschism. He had known the reality of the situation, but was compelled to try in testament to mankind's defiance of a cold and unfeeling universe. With a pinch to the meaty part of his leg, he stifles the painful ruminations. "Think of the good things," he says to himself as the diffuse morning light chases away the gray monotone landscape. This works for a time. He reminisces on his days as a young praxiat, pondering his youthful, optimistic desires to change the world. But reality is the cruel adversary of expectation. Adanon had no luck in getting Darian to visit home after they were free to come and go as they pleased. The closest Darian would ever get was the bottom side of Stenandra. None of his cohort had passed up the opportunity to carouse in Stormanvil's shadow. Partly to gloat, and partly to soothe his insecurity, every weekend Adanon had taken the magrail to Stenandra to debase himself in the shade of his youth. It was on one of those weekends that he had stumbled into the odious bar where Diba worked.

On the horizon, a massive collection of domes emerges from the haze of the morning air. Long, cultivated rows of native amethyst maples stretch to the south as far as the eye can see, in seemingly endless waves of fluttering purple. The dew which clings to the sheltered swathes of the low-lying maple trees is the only moisture the plants may ever see. The unique geology of the plateau means the surface of Stormanvil never sees its eponymous weather. Instead, the humid air from the jungles of Uxkukul travels up and over the territory, sending cool air tumbling off the northern precipices into the warm marshlands and fertile prairies of Esoptria. The effects of this eternal dance are great and thunderous deluges as regular as clockwork. He recalls watching them from near the edge, the great walls of clouds roiling and climbing ever upward. The surreal beauty in the power which Man can observe but never truly capture. Things which must simply be experienced, as the imperfect tools of prose and poetry faulter in the face of forces beyond human faculty. Presently, the sun glints off the nearest dome, drawing Adanon back. He parks the sailcar near the arch-shaped entrance. Entering here will instantly mark Adanon as an outsider, as residents use the network of tunnels bored through the rock to move between the domes. Only four domes remain of the original five marvels, each of which houses over twenty-thousand inhabitants. These titanic structures have accomplished what the countless lives lost to wars of conquest never could; subduing Anvilites in cages of their own devising. Adanon chuckles at the thought as the heavy gate folds open at the seams. This is a reunion he will not enjoy.

A reverberating howl shakes the narrow entryway as the winds beyond tug on the stagnant air. As soon as Adanon steps into the tunnel the chattering doors close with a clunk behind him. A squeal and a crackle come from a speaker somewhere unseen, which welcomes him formally as the Akroates. Then he is alone. A series of biolume fixtures light his way deeper into the structure, activating in response to his pace. The first sign of another human is a wheezing cough echoing down the tunnel. Slime-lung most likely, he thinks. A horrible way to die. The oxygen generating radiosynthetic plankton used in respiratory applications are generally safe, but the main commodity from the domes is not. Cultivating the slime mold used in memresistors is hazardous on the best of days. The powers that be must consider the technological rewards greater than the human risks. Unfortunately for the people of the domes, their homes make an ideal environment for slime circuit production. This coupled with the slime's affinity for the native maples makes Stormanvil for a perfect storm of misfortune. The person who had coughed slips out of sight into the murmuring corridors of dome one. Perhaps it is folly, Adanon muses, to pursue Darian among these old haunts. But, as he repeats what the council had said like a mantra, he presses on. For if anyone will succeed, will be him.

Adanon makes his way through the corridors, keenly aware of the hushed whispers of his name from the midst the shambling masses. He will start in the only place he can remember; the beginning. So, he makes his way down to the settler district. Named for the dust that fails to get filtered out, making its way to the dregs of the domes and those who have lost care for living. Like the dead particles of skin and dirt, people too settle out here among the bleak, colorless corridors. This is where Adanon and his mother had lived. Not that he considers it really living. He supposes he should be thankful that fate swept its feet through this pitiful place, kicking him up, never to settle again. He laughs to himself. He had still settled, just a little higher. Adanon makes his way past a steadily dripping pipe running along the ceiling of the passage. Then, past the sound of trickling water, voices carry through the hall. This place hasn't changed. An intersection of passages lies ahead in a cobbling of stalls, a market of sorts. Adanon stops to glance about, pausing on the sullen faces and shoddy wares. Much of the things that hold no real value in the outside world find a second life down here. A scrap of cloth or an endcap for a pipe could bring a settler warmth or collect recycled water. He stands out drastically. He is cleanly dressed, if not cleanly shaven. Too caught up in his thoughts, he has made a grave mistake. A hoarse, young voice behind him says, "Gimme ya jacket, real slow like." Something hard presses into Adanon's side. He sighs. He won't get out of this without mussing up coat. A slender man from just out of Adanon's line of sight storms over. A thud and a whimper are all he hears. "Ya haf any idea who this ism, boy?!" Adanon turns to the man, unrecognizing, despite his familiarity. He looks to be Adanon's age, but he has a youthful roundness to his face. The felled young man scurries away as the man feigns a kick at his backside. "Adanon, I know you won't remember me, but I never forget a face," the man says, offering his hand, "Fabir." Adanon narrows his eyes at the man as he takes his hand. Resisting the urge, he doesn't glean any thoughts. "Saint's eyes, man. Fab and Ad of the Lodestone Boys, reunited," Fabir says grinning a gap-toothed smile. "Of course," Adanon says patting the man firmly on the arm. Only fragments of his childhood memories remain. "Forgive me, I don't remember much from those days," he says. Fabir waves a hand dismissively, saying, "S'allright, ya got more important things to think about. As for me, my community comes first. Ole Fab is the proprietor of this and many other humble hovels." Adanon lets out a decompressing chuckle. "It's quite a coincidence that I ran into you, Fabir," he says. "Ya don't know the half of it," Fabir quips, as he rests his arm around Adanon's shoulder.

The two men walk together for a time chatting about the past. Their laughter cuts in stark contrast to the pall of this place. Before long, they ascend several floors the dome. "You seem to have done well for yourself, Fab," Adanon says, noting the top-level signage, "I have some hard questions I need to ask." Fabir walks ahead some, approaching a door in the corridor. Looking away, he says, "That can wait." Furrowing his brow Adanon says, "I assure you it cannot." Fabir stops, wearing a serious look for the first time since they met. "Wantcha to understand, I never thought I'd see ya again. Did what I thought was right. Kept my promise to Darian," he says, sweat beading on his forehead beneath his thin, graying hair. Adanon puffs up, stepping close. The threatening aura seeping out of him presses Fabir back against the wall. Speaking slowly, Adanon says, "I've suddenly lost my mood for nostalgia. Speak plainly." The shorter man shakily reaches for his pocket and says, "Easier to show ya," has he draws out a jangling set of keys. "Smart," Adanon says taking a step back, "Now, when was Darian here? A week, maybe two?" The door creaks open, letting out the sounds of squabbling children mixed with the general din a household. Fabir slumps his shoulders. "I reckon I don't know, Ad. Use your tricks to see I'm not lyin'," he says walking in, "best guess is twenty-somethin' years ago." Some of the tension drains from Adanon's shoulders. "I don't understand," he says following Fabir into the abode. A dozen children across a gamut of ages play and cavort around the communal area of the living room. Some are as young as two, while others are teenagers. A middle-aged woman hops up upon seeing Fabir. She looks tired, bedraggled. One of the older children grabs a younger one as they tumble into the Esoptrian style stepped common room. "Papa!" another child cries out as she comes crashing into Fabir's legs. It's all a little overwhelming for Adanon. "Are we having a guest for lunch?" the woman says. Fabir nods, then turns to Adanon, saying, "This is my wife Ebra... Ebra, this here is Adanon. He's come to see Yeeyee." Ebra presses her hand to her mouth then hurries to the kitchen. Adanon grabs Fabir's shoulder and says, "Who? What game are you playing?" Fabir shoos the children who have gathered, wide-eyed and prying. "Peace, brother, peace. Easier to show ya, I swear it on my family," Fabir says. Adanon takes a deep breath then releases the man's shirt. Then he follows as Fabir leads on. In a room far from the entrance, Fabir stops and casts his eyes to Adanon, then down and away. Not knowing what could be on the other side of the door Adanon's hackles are raised as enters with a creak.

Inside, a warm light imitating the golden rays of the sun saturates the wallpapered walls as a radio plays long dated music. Adanon doesn't register the light, or the music, he is fixated on the figure sat motionless in the corner. It's an elderly woman, gray of hair, staring blankly across the room. Great, dark bags hang under her eyes and a blanket draped across her legs keep the chill to bay. Adanon waves his hand in front of her from the middle of the room. "Should I know her?" he says turning to Fabir. "Goldcap and time haven't been kind to Yeeyee. Take ya 'nother look," Fabir says, smiling at the old woman. Adanon approaches her then drops down to his knee to meet her eye. Her distant eyes are a deep hazel, dulled by toil and time. The recognition settles over Adanon like a chill. The woman Fabir calls Yeeyee, an affectionate Anvilite word for a matron, is Adanon's mother.

CHAPTER 24

Holding the segmented chromium disk in the palm of her outstretched hand, Runa forces her will into the object to solicit any sort of response. She growls and pushes her hair out of her face, breaking her concentration. Oma takes the aster from her hand with a tut. "Think that's enough for today," she says pocketing the device. This version of the aster is devoid of all the aspects that make the real thing a danger to its wielder and others. "That's alright, you can't be a prodigy at everything," Turios says, snapping his fingers, "you've done well with projection besides." Runa visibly bristles at the remark. "Aye? Two months, Turios. You'll miss me if I don't pass this test. You could at least tell me what it entails," Runa says, tucking her hair into a bun as the others gather their effects from within the training room. Turios blushes. "No, we really can't. The test is tailored to the individual," he says. Runa rolls her eyes. Turios and Thand lead out with Oma and Runa falling to the rear. Oma leans in and whispers, "He would, as would we all." Runa arches a brow. With a nudge, Oma smiles and says, "Miss you, as you said." Making a puttering sound with her lips, Runa trots to get closer to the other two before saying, "There is a place I've wanted to look at but haven't had the time. What with this training and being a wrench wench in my free time? Could you humor me?" She ends with an exaggerated pleading gesture. Oma and Turios mutter in agreement. Thand walks on, only turning her head to listen. She has been quieter than usual ever since what Runa calls 'the incident.' She isn't foolish enough to consider her silence as shyness or fear. She knows it for what it is, Thand learning from her mistakes. It isn't friendship, or anything close to it, but considering their beginnings, Runa will take it.

After an uneventful transit, the four make it to the docks of Cardis. On the magrail, Runa had regaled the others of the finer details of the upcoming race and modifications to the boat, but only Turios had seemed to take a genuine interest in the conversation. Thand had sat nearby watching the world pass outside the window. Periodically, Oma had interjected with questions that revealed her lack of experience with the subject. Nevertheless, Runa gladly answered the questions, becoming more animated and enthused the longer they spoke. In these rare moments she can feel herself slowly becoming part of the team. They arrive at the red sign outside the establishment called Nambulite by the Sea. "Isn't it cozy?" Runa says, shading her eyes as she peers through the tinted glass. Inside a stocky man scuttles about speaking with patrons. "It's something," Thand says as she opens the door for the group, holding the door as they shuffle in. Inside the smell of cider and smoke take Runa's stomach in their clutches. Her appetite has been insatiable since taking up the training. Even on days she does the quiet work of the mind, she still finds time to exercise out of necessity. She had been so active in the flotilla, and the nutrition very calibrated. At times she imagines herself getting fat just by looking at the savory and bready foods served at the Lykios estate.

As the group stands about no one acknowledges them. Thand calls out to the apparent owner, but he continues on heedless of her. Then he walks past but Thand steps in front of him. He simply steps aside and continues around the broad young woman. "This is strange," Runa says, "why's he ignoring us?" "I donno," Oma says, "Let's go." A tangle of dark frizzy hair and pale skin pokes around a far-off booth. From the grating voice, Runa knows who it is before she fully sees her. "Runa!" Yithica shouts across the tavern. She had warmed significantly to Runa from working together on the boat. Bandon also pokes his head out of the booth. Yithica plods over and pats Runa on the shoulder. "We were about to leave," Runa says nodding to the barkeep, "he was ignoring us." "Pish- the old man is just following the Uxian way. A patron has to introduce you," Yithica says before screeching, "Hey, Pa!" The barkeep comes over smiling and wiping his hands on a towel. His complexion is like a cup of 'hot with a splash of cream. His face is worn and creased, but the lines are full of mirth. He bows to Yithica, then looks at Runa expectantly. "This is Runa, she stays at Zid's. I've told you about her. Smart as a whip and says the craziest things," she says, her neck and upper chest blushing. Runa improvises, imitating the bow. "Welcome," the man says, before turning to Thand. Runa follows. She must now introduce Thand. "Aye, um- This is Thand," Runa says, "She is strong and proud, but I wouldn't change her. She's taught me a lot." Thand's mouth twitches, as the man welcomes her. Thand returns the bow, then the man looks to Oma. Thand looks at Runa wide eyed. Social encounters are not her strong suit. With a shrug Runa urges her on with her hands. "Yes, this is Omarosa, my sister. She is too kind, like our father. But we're family," Thand says tensely. Again, he bows in greeting before turning to Turios. Oma stammers for a moment, looking at Turios. "This is Turios. His personality is too thorny for most, but his smile is worth the hassle," Oma says, knitting her fingers behind her back.

After the peculiar introductions, the group joins Yithica and Bandon at the wrap-around booth in the far corner of the establishment. It's a tight fit but there is enough room for everyone, including Thand. Runa finds herself farthest from the exit to the booth, and despite reservations, she simply goes along with the experience. This entails letting Yithica and Oma, the two most socially inclined individuals talk until the drinks arrive. "Runa," Yithica says, stirring Runa from her passivity, "I didn't know you had such wonderful friends. You're really such a social glimmerfly." It dawns on Runa. All of the praxiats are in common dress, appearing just like any other citizen in Esoptria. She had made a concerted effort to avoid talking about the particulars of her agreement with Zidero. Looking about she realizes everyone is looking to her. "Aye, Yith, all of my friends are praxiats, members of my cohort," she says matter-of-factly. Yithica grows paler than Runa thought possible with her already fair skin. "Erm, right, I—" she scoots back in her seat, not so discreetly glancing under the table. Runa had known that there was a social divide between commoners and praxiats, but she has never seen the mingling of the two until now. As the silence becomes palpable, Yithica throws up her arms and calls out to Pa, "A round of drinks for our new friends," she says. "I'm too young to—" Runa begins, being cut short by Turios, "Law says there is special consideration for religious ceremony, Thand?" Sitting on the outside of the group, Thand looks about, dazed by the mention of her name. "Right, um," she counts off the days on her fingers then says, "It's Saint Minim's feast day. Bow your heads." Everyone complies, except Runa, who is both amused and a little confused. "Bless this which we are about to imbibe, in memory and anticipation of your return. Ahm," she says as the others join her in an apathetic chorus. Afterward, Turios claps his hands together and says, "There, now it's a religious function. Drink up." Pa arrives, skillfully carrying six flagons on mystery liquid. A sinking feeling settles over Runa. As Oma passes the wooden vessel to Runa, she leans in and whispers, "Don't be surprised if praxis is difficult when you drink that." Runa takes the oversized mug, smelling the contents as bubbles tickle her nose.

Despite Runa's momentary misgivings, the social lubricity of the drinks has the entire group talking freely after a short time. With a giggle,

Runa says, "You call him Pa, is he like your father?" Yithica, whose face has turned ruddy with drink, gives a half-smile. "It's a term of endearment. Pa was displaced by the war, but that's all he'll say 'bout it," she says before taking a deep drink. Turios perks up, saying, "He doesn't wear the half-mask, maybe he doesn't see himself as Uxian despite the greeting tradition." "Maybe," Yithica admits with a shrug. "Well enough. Best to be rid of things that don't serve us," Thand says, noticeably more talkative. The heady beverage causes Runa's cheeks and forehead to flush. "Is that what you and Oma did when you left home, just left it behind?" she asks. Turios shrinks back from between Oma and Thand, leaving Runa looking at the two sisters. "No, leaving that behind was a practice in discipline, at the end of a cane," Oma says. Runa swallows hard. Raz had been correct about how young praxiats are treated. "Aye, I talked to Raz about this. The longer I stay here the more I hate the Janamudra. Maybe it's self-loathing," Runa admits. Oma firmly squeezes Runa's shoulder as she says, "Then let it go. To us, you are another praxiat, closer than our real families." Maybe it's the drink or the setting, but seeing everyone nodding to the sentiment moves Runa, giving her the courage to do something she has only fantasized about in passing. "Zdramas!" Yithica shouts, lifting her drink in a toast along with the others. Despite all her misgivings and tribulations, Runa would not trade this moment for home even if she could. For once, she feels like she truly belongs. Then with tears in her eyes, she raises her mug to the toast, echoing the others in the Esoptrian exclamation.

Later swaggering off the quay on Lykios isle, Runa makes her way directly to Raz's room. After a long time banging on the door, he answers with a disgruntled look. Looking her up and down he says, "Have you been drink—" Runa presses a finger to his lips. "Come with me," she says as she walks away. Entering her room she shuts the door, leaving Raz outside listening to the commotion inside through the door. When she opens the door again, she is wearing the gaudy dress from her Assay. It still fits her somewhat, but the sleeveless turquoise top is much tighter in the bust than it had been in her ceremonial rites years ago. The skirt of seafoam lace falls about her knees in waves. Raz is taken aback by the change in wardrobe. Runa taps the scrimshaw knife from her brother against her hand, then walks barefoot past Raz. She heads toward the west end of the estate, passing the library, garden, and ultimately arriving at the jutting overlook of the sea. Without hesitation, she stomps up the metal grating as a brisk northern wind catches her dress. She had made it in time. The setting sun lights the stratus clouds aflame in a myriad pallet of oranges and shadow.

Runa simply stops and admires the sight for a moment as Raz looks on from the end of structure. Then, unsheathing the blade, she cuts free the band struggling to bundle her hair and begins cutting. Each handful she saws away is a wordless prayer that she lets catch on the wind. As the light slowly fails, she cuts away the last long strands, her arms burning from the unexpected physicality. But her body isn't the only thing exhausted, her mind longs for the satisfaction of letting go. So, she takes one last look at her brother's blade then hurls it into the sea. She watches it tumble end-over-end, feeling a semblance of release. It hits the waves without a sound. "Such a monumental but trivial thing to cleave to," she thinks to herself. Imagining the blade sinking into the brine, then exhales a breath held overlong. Together, Runa and Raz return to the interior. Then she bids him good night with a prolonged gaze then shuts the door. When she is sure he is gone, she slumps to the foot of the door and quietly lets out a sob.

CHAPTER 25

"Talin," Ade whispers, drawing her out of her slumber, "You'll be late." Talin's eyes pop open. The bakery opens promptly every morning. She had not wanted to mingle with the locals in Hleifden at first, but over many weeks the benefits of the ruse outweighed Talin's desire to be alone. It had seemed purposeful, the suggestions from Ade. So much so that she had to concede that he knew more about blending in with common folks than she, which still perturbs her. Ade can't exercise the plans. He is far too imposing of a figure and far too foreign to avoid suspicion. That is how Talin had come to work in a bakery near the shuffle district. So named for its impermanence. In the winter, the banks of the lake freeze solid, allowing the poorer communities to expand onto the ice with sled houses. Talin swears as she shuffles about their temporary home above the ice. "Where is Eklin?" she asks as she ties her heavy fur lined boots. Ade fetches Talin's coat, holding it up for her to slide into as he says, "To see his mother." "Already?" Talin exclaims, stuffing her arm into one of the puffy sleeves. "It's late morning," Ade says gently. Talin looks to the door absentmindedly. No morning light would be visible there even if the sun was up. But of course, it won't rise for another hour, then it will linger for six hours before again retreating below the horizon. Talin hates it here, not because of the people or the environment, but because of the general malaise of the place. While working in the bakery last week, a woman had offhandedly remarked that her brother's wife had walked off into a storm never to be seen again. It was then that Talin had truly understood that even the locals are suffering in this forsaken landscape at the end of the world. For Talin, understanding and caring are mutually exclusive. Despite showing no interest in being friendly with the other women in the bakery, they have made a concerted effort to include her. Perhaps they take her withdrawn personality for meekness. How wrong they are, she thinks with a smirk, then exits the room. The sled house is cramped, the next room separated only by a thin hallway. Every few paces, a ceramic grate blows warm air up from the maze of ductwork below. Despite her general distain for this place, Talin must admit that the Gaerdanians know what they are doing. The comfort within makes stepping out into the dark and cold a daunting prospect, but Talin pulls up her hood and steps outside without hesitation. The sledhouses route any biting winds under and over the structure, which is fantastic on the inside, however, as Talin steps down to the surface level of the lake a gust catches under her coat, turning her warm sweat to a dreadful chill.

The walk along the compacted path of snow bricks is routine, if not tedious. While Talin is nonplussed about having to work a menial job, the repetition of measuring, kneading, and bundling the assortment of bread has given her something to lose herself in. She almost enjoys the banality of it. As on other days, a line of shuffle residents trickle into the city proper to work their menial jobs. The opposite direction, others make their way farther onto the lake to fish. Over and between the tops of the repetitious buildings, a single structure looms. Perhaps it is better to say two halves of one structure. Much like the Grand Cenobium, the prefecture building is comprised of two sharply angled sides rising like jet black wedges, except there is a void between the two. The two skyward daggers are connected by a bridge halfway up. Talin shudders, recalling how she had looked down from that vantage years ago. How small the rest of the city had seemed under the gaze of its overlords. She imagines the Prefect looking down on her now, appearing as spec of snow against the white backdrop of the city of Hleifden. A familiar bundled shape waves to Talin as she approaches the bakery. Someone else seems to be late. Both women exchange muffled greetings, but Talin isn't sure who it is under the scarf and hood.

After settling in and removing her layers of clothing, Talin nods to the other women and sets to work. She moves to the back of the kitchen and washes her hands. Lusa, the head baker shouts, "Welcome Thala, Ulva. It's about time." Thala is the alias Talin had chosen. It's close enough to her name to illicit a response but different enough to make her comfortable amid these strangers. The shift goes by quickly. There is always something to do. Fetching this, washing that, it's very mechanical, but Talin doesn't forget to do what she set out to do; listen. Esopt and Gaerdanian are sister languages, having shared loanwords and tonalities over the centuries. Most of the women are from Gaerdan and speak in the harsh tongue, but when addressing Thala, they practice Esopt. It's all part of the ruse. A few have even expressed an interest in Thala teaching them to speak like an

Esoptrian. At the time she couldn't tell it they were being condescending.

As the ten-hour shift comes to an end, Talin is washing up. She can feel the women gathering behind her. Like gravel, the stocky Lusa says, "Thala. We know about you." Talin's heart leaps. She eyes a long blade under the sudsy dishwater. It isn't ideal, but a chef's knife could dispatch these women handily, if not cleanly. Despite her herself and her heart suddenly racing, she can't assume their intent. Talin turns, placing her hands behind her and hanging her head. "Look at me," Lusa says, "you've nothing to be ashamed of. Fleeing Esoptria took courage. You're not Gaerdanian but you have spirit." "What Lusa means is, there's a gathering tonight. We'd like you to come. Likeminded individuals only," the tall, homely woman Heid says. Talin unclenches her hands and looks up at the women. Finally something she is good at. She thinks of the mistreatment in the foundling houses. Then the feigned tears come as she says, "They took my family from me, treated me like a slave—" she lets out a sob. There is a truth to her words that adds affect, making the act all the more believable. "See, old Lusa has an eye for these things," Lusa says, pounding a fist on her chest, "you are among friends, Thala." Talin goes in for a hug from the wide-faced woman, catching her off guard. Lusa reciprocates the gesture to a chorus of heartfelt sentiments.

Talin and the others close the bakery then congregate outside the building. She glances back in the direction of the lake, thinking that she should tell Ade and Eklin that she will be late and not to wait up. This is an opportunity she can't squander, for trust is a hard-won currency. As Lusa gets her attention with a pat, Talin turns away from the lake and follows the women toward the prefecture tower. After some considerable walking, they tuck into a narrow passage. If Talin had been distracted she would have missed it. She follows them closely. The biolume lantern Lusa carries pulses slowly from the cold as they walk to the end of the space. It is cold and cramped waiting for whoever is speaking to Lusa ahead. Then the queue shuffles forward, each woman stopping to remove their hoods for the individual at a door. When Talin's turn comes, she does the same for the tall man who peers at her through a dark mask. Only his emotionless, pale gray eyes are visible. He looks toward the open door, then back to Talin. Before she can react, his cold fingers are climbing up her leg, then the other. "Tsk, she is with us," Lusa says, having doubled back to the door. Still his frigid hands probe for a weapon which isn't there. As his hand reaches under her jacket and touches Talin's midriff, her patience runs out. She bats away his hands and steps into the door. He offers no protest as she retreats alongside Lusa. "Forgive him, all newcomers get the same treatment," Lusa says, as they make their way down lightless stairs. At the landing and around a bend a large room opens. It is an abandoned root cellar, but many times the size of any Talin has seen. One thing is certain, it isn't used for storing roots.

The permafrost floor has melted, turning the mud and aggregate to a crunchy slurry beneath Talin's feet. Alongside the other women, she and Lusa crunch to a stop. All around is a murmuring mass of people chatting and facing the far wall, waiting expectantly. It isn't long before Talin's questions are answered. The lights atop a raised platform dim, then a figure clad in long vestments slowly faces the crowd. Talin recoils at his inhuman face. No, not his face. It's a mask made of a treehound skull, hollowed out, allowing the wearer to peer through the sockets of the dispatched beast. For a time, the figure simply looks over the crowd. Then he speaks, raising his hands, "I am proud. Proud of you, and all you have done. Proud of our pack, and what we have yet to do." He pauses, letting the crowd shower him in adulation. Even Lusa lets out a cry, startling Talin. While Talin's Gaerdanian is weak, she manages to follow much of the rhetoric. "They sit in their towers, monuments to their hubris, dolling out judgement on the rest of humanity. As if we—" he thumps his chest, "are less human than they. But I tell you my friends, they are the ones who have lost their humanity. I would pity them if had any pity left to give." Talin leans in close to Lusa and whispers, "Who is he?" Lusa replies, "Just a man." As the crowd settles back into silence, he continues, "Praxiats, they say, are more than us. But we know what they really are. Baby stealers! Fungus sippers! Mind rapers!" The crowd cheers with each exclamation. "Today is a glorious day brothers and sisters. Soon we will take back what is ours, here and abroad. Things are in motion that will break them as they have broken us. Are you with me?" More whoops sound from the crowd. The speaker looks around, slowly panning from one end to the other. "So many new faces. It warms this old hound's heart," a chorus of laughter comes from the crowd. Talin isn't laughing. With each passing minute she has become more paranoid. Why had Lusa invited her specifically? Do they know? She glances at the older woman, who nods and smiles. "I've heard all of your stories, you know my heart if not my face. As I always say, I am not important, YOU are. Together we are mighty, as a pack we thrive." Something about the way the man speaks tickles Talin's memory, but she can't place it. The prospect of knowing who this man is only heightens her fear. Her pulse throbs in her ears. "Are there any new pups that would like to share their story?" the speaker says. Lusa jumps, heaving her considerable girth off the ground, and waves her hands. "Ooh! We have a pup!" she cries out. "Be silent," Talin hisses. "You there! What is your friend's name? Bring her forward. No need to be shy," the speaker says. Talin's head spins. She looks to the door. It's closed, a multitude of attendants between her and escape. "Lusa I really don't want to," Talin says. The crowd pushes her forward. Before she knows it, Talin is near the stage, only a few paces from the speaker. "Even the brigands of Orin find a way to our cause. Let us welcome our wayward sister!" he shouts, and the crowd imitates the chittering yelps of treehounds, "Your name little pup?" Talin is trapped. She chose to come here. It's time to see how good she truly is at deceit. "Thala, Kyr. I don't speak the tongue well," she says. "Oh, that's okay, sister. I am nothing if not accommodating," the speaker says in perfect Esopt. The voice is even more familiar now but still muffled by the mask. Talin can almost make out his eyes through the boney voids that surround them. The crowd, which had risen to a fever pitch, grows silent, expectant. "Join me, regale me, weave me the tale that brought you so far from home," he says, offering his hand. With trepidation she takes it, then he helps her to the stage. Talin resists the urge to use praxis. She could so easily see who this man really is if she took the risk. It's subtle, but as she pulls her hand away, she feels it, the tingling and lingering touch of a praxiat teasing the corners of her mind. She freezes. She can see his eyes. One eye of flesh, the other a void. With a chuff, he says, "But it would just be a lie, wouldn't it, Talin?" "Darian," she gasps as she steps back, heel hanging off the stage. "This man isn't who—" he pushes her hard, sending her wheeling into the crowd. Among the yipping and the shuffle of feet Talin hears him say, "Seize her," before the crowd swallows her.

CHAPTER 26

The creased paper doubles over in Runa's hand as she rereads the neatly scrawled script. She lies on her bed, bouncing her legs absentmindedly mouthing the familiar words. They are relatively innocuous lines from Adanon, but one sticks with her. "You can never let your opposition define you, or they've already won." Runa sighs. His absence has been longer than his presence in her life. Still, the absence is palpable. Thand, Turios, and Oma are excellent teachers and comrades, but there is a frankness to Adanon's tutelage that is lacking in her peers. Runa lays down the letter and looks at the dress still hanging on the back of the door. She groans then rolls off the bed before stiffly crossing the room. Opening the door she says, "Kaeln, I asked you to get rid of—" Outside Zidero looms with a thin smirk. "Am I interrupting?" he says, limply gesturing. Runa backs away from the entrance saying, "No, I just asked Kaeln to do something. I think she forgot." "Far be it from me to guess the motivations of a child, but maybe she doesn't want to?" he says as he steps into the room uninvited, "Kaeln is not forgetful." Clasping his hands in front of him, he paces about the room, looking in corners and paying no mind to Runa. "This was my mother's room long ago. Funny, the women bound to this room hold such a spell over Lykios men," he says, finally looking at Runa, "Some things never change- Hmm, trying to remember why I came- oh yes. I know how much you've helped my son..." he trails off, pausing at the sight of the Janamudra dress. "Aye, those were the terms," Runa says, placing her hands on her hips. "Yes, I know, but that's not what I meant," he says, running his finger over the surface of a side table, then inspecting the dust, "He fancies you, so I want you to be mindful, whether you succeed or fail as a praxiat, the outcome is the same; you are going to leave. I have no control over that, but I do have control over this house. Tread carefully." Runa is dumbstruck. She and Raz have had less contact since the day she cast away her brother's knife. "Kyr, I..." she stammers. "Don't placate me with your mother's tongue. I am so tired of every word from Razmus revolving around you and your charms. Speaking of your mother, she's just as annoying. Last time we met she could only tell me how you are, what you are doing, when all I care about is bending her over. Obnoxious." Runa face burns with rage. With her voice quivering, she says, "I asked you not to bring that up. I can't control how your son perceives me. If you want me to avoid Raz, I can, but do not insult me or my mother." Zidero turns around, glaring at her. Having watched him interact with the staff, Runa knows she has made a mistake. The one thing that seems to bring Zidero Lykios true joy is controlling others. "How ungrateful you've become. I took time out of my busy day to give you some guidance," he says shaking his head. Runa lets out a sardonic chuckle and turns away. She puts on a jacket and collects her shoes heedless of the vindictive man. "Look at me, you think you would have become a praxiat on your own merits?" he says leaning over her as she finishes putting on her shoes, "Every day you've lived off the Shyena is a gift from me to your whore of a mother." In the commotion Kaeln has arrived at the door, watching everything unfold. Runa looks up at her, solemn but unbroken. Then she stands and walks out of the room, leaving Zidero ranting behind her.

The ferry ride to the mainland is strangely comforting. Despite the argument being a pall on the morning, Runa refuses to let it break her stride as she makes her way through Cardis. For today is the eve of the winter solstice. This is the time of year that the Jana move far to the south for the warmer climes of the southern hemisphere. They too have a celebration for the end of the year called the festival of coruscating lights, but today, Runa is focused on landbound tradition. Some prefectures burn a sacred log, while others place gifts inside shoes. Still others skate on frozen lakes with their families or simply exchange gifts to ward off melancholy. But Esoptrians celebrate the holiday in a fashion of their own; with a race. It isn't the final race of the season, but the top competitors of the Aneletide day race will move on to the prime circuit. After all the testing and modification to the boat, Runa has eagerly awaited the day. She strolls into the Grand Cenobium with her head held high then proceeds to Oma and Thand's room. After a moment Oma answers the door, squealing with joy at seeing Runa. Her usually short, tufted hair is sectioned off and braided, merging into a singular plume at the back. It's a striking hairstyle and it suits her, Runa thinks. They greet with a hug. Through the contact, Oma conveys a sense of joy, while Runa unintentionally expresses disappointment. "What's wrong?" her friend says, welcoming Runa inside. "Just someone showing their true colors. I'm trying to carry on as usual," Runa says, waving to Thand, who sits on a chair with her hair teased out. "Not a word," she mouths to Runa as her sister commits to braiding her hair again. "I don't want to interrupt. I can go practice with the aster," Runa says, thumbing over her shoulder. "Come," Thand says, stomping her foot in the space in front of her, before wincing as her hair is pulled tight. After a moment of hesitation, Runa sits in front of her. With a tut, Thand releases Runa's high ponytail. "I still can't believe you butchered your hair so," she says as she combs out Runa's hair, "Jana do know about scissors, yes?" All Runa can do is laugh. She can't explain her desire to break the chains which bound her to the anchor of her heritage. Again, Thand hisses in pain. "Be kind, tender-head," Oma says, full of mirth. With a hesitant grunt, Thand says, "As you say," sectioning off Runa's hair before setting to braiding. There is a comfort in the intimate ritual. For Runa it dredges up memories of her mother. Wanting to avoid thinking about passing into a near year without her family she says, "How did you celebrate Aneletide in Bujani?" In an uncharacteristically long-winded recounting, Thand describes the local traditions of her former countrymen. Even though she is generally humorless, she does acknowledge the humor in burying brooms by their handles to ward off malevolent spirits. Runa asks if it works, followed by laughter.

As the last braid is locked in place, Thand squeezes Runa's shoulders firmly. With youthful enthusiasm Runa hops over to a decorative mirror. Starting from the center, five thick braids interwoven with her hair trickle into a neat bun. Runa tries to subdue her emotion, but something about the day or the company makes her eyes misty. "Thank you!" she says, bounding back to Thand then hugging her. The musclebound woman grunts. "Well done, Sis—" Oma says warmly, "but I'm not done with you." Thand winces as her sister begins braiding in the next set of extensions. Most of her head is covered in perfect little braided knots which are twisted into mounts at regular intervals. Since Runa has known the sisters, Thand has never done anything with her hair other than keep it short. Something about seeing the sisters caring for each other this way makes her smile. In the spirit of conciliation, she invites the sisters to the race, offhandedly mentioning her superior vantage from the maintenance barge. As they accept the invitation, Oma offers to let Runa spend the night. Despite Thand quoting procedure she relents when her sister reminds her of the holiday. The quiet comfort of the living room is warm and inviting, but Runa still struggles to sleep. When she does sleep, she dreams of darkness. An all-consuming void, broken only by two eyes shimmering like glass. As the clattering of dry bones accompanies the unblinking eyes, Runa wishes only that the dream would end.

In the morning, the three young women shamble about, preparing for the day. Oma insists on helping Runa apply makeup before they leave for the race. A little eyeliner and malachite eyeshadow make her feel a little less out of place when she sees both sisters don their very official praxic coats. As she pulls on her plain gray jacket from the day before, they set off to fetch Turios. Disheveled and glasses askew, he answers the door with a trickle of drool still around his mouth. It doesn't take him long to get ready. It never does, same as Amil. The brief thought of her brother tugs at the wound of throwing the knife away, but Runa has learned to push those feeling down. Turios too looks very professional in his praxiat garb. Runa supposes that is the point of the uniform. Dredgers treat the coat with a confounding deference. Oma nudges Runa out of her daydreams, then they set off for the lagoon.

Arriving before the fog has lifted, Runa has to argue with a taxi pilot to take the group to the barge. Normally, she, Raz and the others would arrive together before dawn. The pilot needs little more convincing after Thand steps forward and whispers something in his ear. No sooner do they arrive at the barge before the waterway is closed to all boat traffic. While the lagoon is shallower than the sea, it is still thirty paces deep in most sections, which makes onsite emergency crews a priority, especially in the cold. At yearend temperatures, racers can be expected to become hypothermic from only fifteen minutes in the water. Runa had expressed discomfort over the racing conditions to Raz, especially considering his disability. He had been nonplused but had assured her that he would be fine. By the time Runa and company make it to the portion for Raz's team, the boat is already in the water. Yithica and Bandon greet everyone warmly. Though, the former is clearly nervous, biting her nails with each radio transmission from Raz.

As the fog burns off, a perfectly clear winter sky opens up over Esoptria. "Can I talk?" Runa asks as the boats begin to line up. Yithica passes off the headset without hesitation. Taking a deep breath Runa says. "Raz? Hey, I'm here." "Hey, change frequencies, one-one-five," he responds mechanically. Runa adjusts the radio, then tucks into a nook created between equipment, saying, "Hey, we are all here. Everyone came to watch." Raz crackles through with a chuckle, "Not everyone. Kaeln told me about my dad. Seems he has something more important to do." "Aye, it doesn't matter. Focus on the race," Runa says, cupping her hand over the microphone. After a bout of unbroken static Raz crackles through in Jana, saying, "Good wind, good waves," before going radio silent.

Not long after, a bright white flare streaming into the sky signals the start of the race. The growling pack of boats pulls away from the starting line in a wave of foam and fury. At one end of the barge is the starting line, which gives Runa and the others an excellent view of the straight-away which borders the marshy peninsula. The course then turns along the shipyards of Esoptria, the most crowded section. Then following the lagoon, the track skirts the sea wall before arcing back past the barge. One lap around takes roughly fifteen minutes at speed, possibly longer if the conditions are choppy, but today the lagoon is a calming aquamarine under a cloudless sky. Taking time for herself to just enjoy the moment, Runa walks away from the others at the front of the barge, making her way to the rear. She plops down, hanging her legs off the side of the barge as the racers skip past the seawall. Then, as they turn toward her and the barge, she closes her eyes, imagining how it feels to be on the razor edge of disaster at any given moment. The first boats, one of which is sunset orange, rush past, sprinkling cool sea mist over her face. An unhindered shudder reminds Runa that soon, she too will know how it feels to risk everything to soar.

CHAPTER 27

It has been pleasant, Adanon thinks, spending the past few weeks with Fabir and his family. While he continues to search for Darian throughout the domes, he still returns to their warm and welcoming abode. Even more than the agreeable atmosphere he enjoys sitting with his mother in the evening. Each night Adanon recounts the events that she had missed. Not out of spite or absolution, but to put to words what he never could. Despite his many hours beside her not once has she spoken or reacted to his presence. Adanon knows her mind is too far gone, which is a burden. Today he intends to leave, but there is something he must first do. Something which has been in his power, but his pride wouldn't yet allow.

After recounting an adventure that he and Darian had shared in Gaerdan, Adanon closes the storybook of his mind and lets out a sigh. As ever, his mother stares off at the wall, serene and unmoving. Strolling over to her, he places a hand to her cheek. A tingling pulse ushers Adanon's sight beyond sight into the fractured recesses of her mind. He isn't searching. He's simply trying to connect with her. Every sharp feeling of heartache, every fleeting moment of joy, every mild contentment in-between, he distills them into a stream of thoughts, sharing them all with her. But none of this is what he truly wants to show her. He still can't forgive her. Forgiveness is complicated. Nevertheless, he encapsulates every bittersweet feeling of unconditional love for those closest to him then lets it slip from his fingertips. As Adanon opens his eyes and focuses on the room again, he feels the moisture on his hand. Warm tears fall from his mother's glassy, unmoving eyes onto his hand. He nods knowingly then says, "I have to go now, Mom," as he walks away. A hand brushes his weakly. He stops. For the first time her eyes fall upon him, beckoning him back. Her hands tremble as they places his hands on her face again. Her eyes implore him to look again. So, he does.

Memories bubble to the surface of her mind. Memories of this same room, flickering through the years. Darian, had sat here just as Adanon has. His young face smiles at her as her mind had slowly fades. Flickering images of him aging out of youth. Then abruptly the space is empty, until Adanon watches himself enter back into his mother's live after forty years.

Darian had visited her when even Adanon wouldn't. This is the Darian that he remembers. The man who sits on the Council is so very unlike his recollection, bitter and ruthless. "What happened to us, my friend?" Adanon thinks to himself.

He wordlessly bids her farewell, his own hands trembling. Then he passes through Fabir's spacious home. He smiles at the multitude of children playing, imagining how things would be different if he had grown up under these conditions. It may have made no difference, but who can say? Gathering his coat he heads for the door, before wishing Fabir and Ebra well. Then, sparing no time, Adanon proceeds to the connecting tunnel to dome two. Several people speak to him as he passes but he spares no time for pleasantries. He is determined to make this last stop before returning to Esoptria emptyhanded. Ascending to the base level of dome two, he exits the seldom used surface portal into the typical driving wind. His destination lies to the east, a monolith of equally gargantuan proportions to the domes. Turning slowly, the cylinder of stone which marks the spot of what had been dome three. Adanon shields his eyes against the oppressive sunlight scattering through the layer of haze over everything. A haze which evokes the emotions Adanon is, and has been internalizing. Mourning long forestalled and reflection which has been sorely avoided by Adanon for far too long. He walks the distance to the monument, the wind buffeting him sidelong, threatening to topple him. But he persists. Upon reaching the base, he thankfully tucks into the wind shelter in the base of the structure. Craning his neck to take in the full height of the structure, a grimace crosses his face. The names of the lost are engraved on the surface of the solid stone. A low humming reverberates around and through the monument. It will play in tribute until the day its bearings grind to dust. While the slow notes reverberate in his chest, Adanon is overcome with shame. "I'm sorry it took me so long," he whispers into the driving wind.

The eternal dirge is known to most Anvilites. Of Stone and Storms, hums from the baffles and channels built into the cylinder. It's a lullaby and folk song, the words often misremembered. Adanon chuckles. The lyrics proclaim a savior to be born on the winds of the Anvil, the imagery mirroring how this land births mighty tempests. Adanon can't deny his fanciful thoughts as a child. Thoughts that maybe he would be the one. "Which do you think will last longer?" a voice calls out over the droning. Adanon turns toward the unfamiliar voice. Leaning against the inner wall of the monument stands a fair skinned man with golden, braided hair in the Gaerdanian fashion. His appearance doesn't give Adanon pause, but the black praxiat jacket does.

"Sorry, what was that?" Adanon calls out to the young man. With a sigh, the Gaerdanian pushes off the wall then repeats himself. "I said, which do you think will last longer? The stones or the stories?" He nods to the moaning monument. "I'd say the stone would last longer, but I don't think remembering is the point," Adanon says. "How is that? You're saying a monument to the fallen isn't about remembering?" says the young man. "I think it's about guilt. A kind of prayer for absolution etched eternally, in the hopes that any of this means anything," Adanon says, casting his eyes away. The young man clicks his teeth. "I've trod fields and mounds knowing what proud cities below lie. We remember when even the stones are forgotten," the man cuts a smug grin across his face as he meets Adanon's eye, "If I dug up a stone, would it tell me what sort of man shaped it or why he chose to be a mason?" What had been a chance and unusual conversation has turned toward the unexpected. Adanon narrows his gaze and the blue-eyed man and says, "We haven't met, have we?" The man spreads an unnerving smile and says, "We still haven't, not in flesh and bone." At those words, Adanon's face grows grim. Understanding washes over him. Placing his hands in his pockets, he says, "Let him go." The young man lets out a peculiar giggle. "Have you always been so dour? Darian said you were like this even in your youth..." the young man says waving his hand dramatically, "I don't think I'll let him go just yet... This sweet little colonial is the first northerner I've gotten to try on." Adanon isn't mistaken, the man is possessed, and the possessor is goading him. Only a praxiat of the highest skill and disregard for decency could break someone's will like this, much less puppet one like fleshy marionettes. Adanon takes another step toward the man, saying "What's his name?" "Oh, wouldn't you like to know, errand boy," the man says, placing his hands on his hips. His tone is relaxed, but his body is tense. That is the second sign that Adanon should be weary. "He's still fighting. Wants to cry out, to say his name. Oh my! He wants you to end his suffering. Really Holfnir? You'd rather die than serve your Queen?" Adanon takes another step forward. "Holfnir? If you can hear me, keep trying. I can help," he says, holding out a hand to the young man trapped inside his own body. Holfnir twitches as he stands to his full height, then his face contorts. "Oh, please Kyr, save me from the scary little girl," he says mockingly. Seizing the initiative, Adanon lunges toward the man. But too slow. A single shot rings out over the wind. Then Adanon's body hits the ground as the echoes within the monument resound. "I like this one, good reflexes," Holfnir says to himself, clasping his face in ecstasy. As he removes the coilgun, he inspects the magazine while standing over the motionless black mound that had been Adanon. After a moment he narrows his eyes at the elder praxiat's crumpled form and says, "Get up Adanon, honestly."

Adanon breaks into sputtering, ragged breaths. Coughing, he lifts his head from the polished basalt with a groan. A burning, throbbing pain courses through his chest. He had only just reinforced his jacket before the shot. The dense fabric had caught the projectile, but only just. As he picks himself up, he plucks the deformed projectile from his coat then flicks it at Holfnir's feet. "What if I didn't stop that?" Adanon says, still sputtering. "Now that would have been an interesting and unforetold circumstance," Holfnir says. Adanon dusts off his coat as he collects himself. "Did you come all this way just to gloat? Or is there a purpose to your dubious visit?" he says, still aching. "Come home Adanon. Home to the jungles what made you," Holfnir says.

"What did you say?" Adanon says, raising his voice. Holfnir mocks his seriousness by throwing up his hands. Stony faced, Adanon stares down the young man. With a sigh Holfnir says, "I'm sure my retinue are awaiting my return. Do you think he will miss me when I'm gone?" Adanon turns red. "Just go! Before I make you," he shouts. "Ah, finally dropped the sanctimonious pretense, have we? You'd do this too if you could get away with it, Ak-ro-a-tes," Holfnir says, waggling the coilgun at him. Adanon scoffs, saying, "Be gone. You're nothing but an artifact, a parasite." Holfnir clicks his tongue and says, "I have more to do with your predicament than you know. Come home. Bringe the girl." Then he levels the coilgun at Adanon's face. With a crooked smile, his eyes roll back, and he buckles at the knee. Adanon rushes forward, barely catching Holfnir before he crumples to the dark stone. All around the two men the wind buffets in a ceaseless cacophony. The council seem to enjoy toying with the Akroates, but even they pale in comparison to the whims of the Prophet Queen of Ux. He curses, then places a hand on Holfnir's face, ensuring that the man is still alive. He is, but his unconscious mind is chaotic. She had overpowered this man's will for weeks or months without end, a truly dismal existence. To be an observer within your own body is a uniquely cruel torture. Adanon is unsure, but Holfnir must have been aboard the vessel that lost its crew and praxic cohort. Except the cohort wasn't lost, but rather they were overpowered and enslaved. But how, Adanon wonders as Holfnir slowly comes to. The young man's eyes swim around the hazy blue-gray sky for a time before turning to Adanon. As if the words are too heavy to speak, Holfnir stammers incoherently as Adanon cradles his head. In a whisper Adanon says, "I know," as sounds of agony escape the broken Gaerdanian man.

CHAPTER 28

"Today is the day," Runa says to herself in the small hours on the morning of her birthday. It is less a statement, than it is an invocation to steady her nerves. Raz had done well at the Aneletide race, placing high enough to quality for the prime circuit. However, the thrill of the race had only lasted a few hours in the face of her own trials. As she readies herself for the day, she recalls the terrible things Zidero had said to her and how small she had felt. Her ability to walk away had been an edifying bit of growth. Luckily, he has been gone for much of the last month, even for the celebration of Raz's qualification. If anything, it speaks to his character more than his cutting words, that he hadn't been there for him. Before leaving the estate, Runa stops by the western overlook. Why, she doesn't know. It has become a bit of an exercise in clearing her mind, to stare down at the white-capped breakers. The thought of the knife below hardly bothers her anymore. "What are we throwing over today?" Raz says from behind her as he approaches. He catches her off guard. Their friendship is in a precarious place. "Nothing," she admits, gazing down at the gloomy sea. "Ah, casting away the intangible now?" Raz says. "That is kind of my thing now," she replies, feigning a haughty stance. Raz presses an appraising finger to his mouth, humoring her. "Yep, that's really sells it. Conjuring fire would really give it that extra something," he says. Runa places her hands on her hips and nods. "I'll see what I can do," she says, looking down her nose at him. The warmth of their friendship keeps the oppressive overcast discontentment of the morning at bay. They speak at the same time, "I—" "Listen—" "Go ahead," Raz says. Runa clears her throat. "I just wanted to tell you not to worry," she says with a shrug. "I'm not worried," he says, "No that's not true. I will worry, but not about your safety. I know you think the change is a good thing, and it can be, it's just—" Runa bends at the waist and hugs Raz. Then she whispers, "Have some faith in me," before strolling away.

Runa's solemn trip to the mainland is short lived. Turios, Thand, and Oma are all waiting for her in Cardis. Their somber faces match the mood of the day. Everything along the path, from the muted clothing of strangers to the worn stones beneath their feet, are tinged with gray. Runa doesn't know why she finds comfort in the prosaic atmosphere of the day. Perhaps it is the absence of vibrancy which makes the details seem more vivid. Or the ceaseless sameness reminds her of home on the endless sea. Outside the magrail station, a chain of dark-clan praxiats stand in rows, shoulder-to-shoulder all the way the entrance to the temple. It's painfully apparent that they are waiting for her. She has received no instructions on how to proceed or what she should expect. Perhaps that's the point, giving the praxiat agency for the first time.

As she steps off the magrail, Turios says, "We'll see you on the other side." The sisters nod, then Runa begins the long walk under the watch of countless eyes. She had convinced herself that she wasn't going to be nervous. But the reality of the situation is proving more trying than she had anticipated. Somewhere beyond the file of praxiats, the drone of liturgical Astoran and the odor of burning censers carries through the air. Runa follows the path around the temple and into the open front doors. As she passes the slanted pillar of faces, the coarse hands of fear claw for purchase within her. The smokey perfumed scent outside was only a prelude to the oppressive smoke wafting from within the structure. The interior of the temple that she remembers as dark and clear is now smokey and bright. A layer of white haze clings to the vaulted ceiling above as she enters. The space is empty, save for the white flame braziers and sarcophagi stretching toward the raised and obscured mausoleum. Beyond the orange drapes, twelve hooded figures await Runa as she approaches the rear of the temple. For a moment she looks between each of them. As she thinks to speak, the heavy stone door of the sharp-angled mausoleum opens. On her periphery the pressure differential draws the drapes toward the dark void of the unknown. Then she passes the enigmatic figures for the ancient stone door.

Stepping in, the door closes behind her. Inside, the air is warm and dry, free of the sickly saccharine perfume. It isn't hot but compared to the winter day and the interior of the temple, it warms Runa's face. Without a second thought, she removes her coat and sets off into the dark. After a moment, her eyes adjust to the darkness. The only sound within the mausoleum is her steady breathing. Some distance ahead a dim light lies just out of sight down a sloped corridor cut through the rough-hewn stone.

Making her way down, Runa notes the peculiar effect on sounds within this place. It's as if the sound doesn't propagate. She stops halfway down the slope, then purposefully scuffs her foot against the stone, confirming that there is no echo. Any sound she manages to make has a thin and irritating quality the likes of which she has never experienced. Even her inclination to speak into the darkness is stifled. Confounded, she presses deeper into the tomb. At the bottom of the slope she sees the source of the light. On either side of a passage divided by a wide pillar, are walls of perfectly smooth black stone penetrated by a spectral glow. The light blooms brighter as she approaches. The engravings are not in Astoran or Esoptrian, or any script Runa recognizes. It must be older. The letters are restrained, composed of broken lines and loops with space between each. This is an opportunity to do something Runa has excelled at. She approaches the script and opens her mind, imagining whoever cut these words into the stone. The line between her and the unbroken past is tenuous. When she pushes, to delve for understanding, the wall pushes back. Sound isn't the only thing that faulters in this place. What would normally be a resonant and warm feeling, comes in flashes devoid of context, mechanical in quality. The time this had been carved is either so long ago that it is unfathomable, or the remnants have somehow been expunged. So little remains. It's akin to a fleeting transmission, stretched thin and delayed by time. Her own curiosity makes it hard for her to let go of what these words must sound like or what enigmatic people created it. The moment she lets her conscious, curious mind slip and falls into the rhythm of the modulation; the intent becomes clear.

"In those early days, when God's tears bore men unto the world, we learned of the dark. A shadow so deep and inextricable that it fractured the foundations of our understanding. To know the ineffable was a burdensome gift so we sought the illumination of all. We failed. This hallowed ground is dedicated to those who have yet to come. May you not make the same mistakes."

The words ricochet through Runa's mind as she finishes running her hand along the carved stone. Then the ghostly light rises within the wall, revealing images of catastrophe inlaid. Depictions of a nameless people in victorious poses, radiant and proud. Then calamity, with men, women, and children crying out, faces twisted in agony. Finally, the carving depicts a desolate landscape, the bones of the fallen covered by the sands of time. The light makes a final swell, blinding in the cracks of the letters of the relief. The light reveals that the stone which appeared like jet, is in fact a deep and unnerving crimson. Then the light fades, leaving Runa again in darkness.

If she hadn't been nervous enough, a sense of foreboding washes over her as a red light rises in the next room. This time as Runa exits, instead of a corridor, a steep staircase of the same worn stone leads deeper into the next room. Within, the light shifts to a neutral white. A long slab of stone cuts through the middle of the room. The absence of sound here is even more pronounced. The imperceptible noises of her moving joints and pumping blood are uniquely loud in the silence. At the near end of the dark stone slab is a geometric platter of pearlescent metal. Resting at its center is a single dried mushroom. Curiously, the light catches on the fungal body as she lifts it to inspect it. It shimmers like goldleaf in the drag of the air, flaking off thin, gilded pieces which catch on imperceptible eddies and drift away. Runa looks back over her shoulder cautiously; nothing but the aberrant silence stares back. She is ignorant of the uses of this mushroom, but she has heard of it. 'Goldcap' is an apt name based on its appearance. She considers what to do next. After a tense moment, she pops the mushroom in her mouth.

Chewing the fibrous stem proves a challenge as she makes her way to the other room. Not only is the texture terrible it also tastes of bile and smoke. She crouches to peer down the steps. The next room appears the same as this one. As she stands the nausea hits her, followed closely by a chill in her extremities. Trying not to panic, she plods down the stairs, but her limbs swing haphazardly. She chuckles silently at her brazenness as she reaches the next room and presses toward the long slab. At the near end rests a cube. At the far end, an even larger cube. Runa shudders and exhales, her breath condenses in the frigid air. Another step then Runa's perception splinters, fracturing into a million facets. Every surface of the room shimmers, reflecting an otherworldly light. It's a familiar sensation but under unfamiliar circumstances. She is projecting. A muttering comes from behind her as she begins to reason out what is so familiar. It is an all too familiar voice but thinner, labored. Runa turns toward the voice. She has seen herself from outside her body before, but never has it been as jarring as this. She is looking at herself, slumped to her knees. Her heavy-lidded eyes and incoherent murmuring give her pause. Then she moves toward herself. As she reaches toward herself, her body's hooded eyes grow wide, rising to meet her incorporeal gaze. An unseen force rises in tandem with a crescendo of disembodied voices, rebuffing Runa's advance. The message is clear, she isn't in control here.

Then something wholly unexpected happens. She watches her body stand. It approaches her. And as she stares, so too do her glassy corporeal eyes. It reaches out and, impossibly, seizes her by the wrists. She lets out a voiceless cry. The strength of the grasp is unbreakable. Her body subdues her, looming over her menacingly. "Why are you here?" her body vocalizes in Jana, as the vice grip grows ever tighter. Runa winces. Through praxis, she impresses that she has a right to be here. Her body cocks its head strangely, then leans in and breathes deep. Barely perceptible spectral tendrils enter her body's nose, followed by erratic eye movements. "Too soon for him. Too late for her, but just in time," her body stammers along with the chorus of voices, "Speak not of this. Go." The ghoulishness of her features and the voices disperse, then her body topples through Runa.

Unfettered by the constraints of a body, Runa drifts over to the small box, attempting to ignore the fact that her body is still muttering on the floor. Upon closer inspection, her heart sinks. This palm-sized box appears to be made from the same material as the aster. She never made much progress in controlling the device. As she rests her hand near the device, it returns the same minute praxic feedback as an aster, which confirms her presumption. Runa focuses her will into the device trying to trigger the mechanism, but after a few moments she drifts away to examine the other cube. While it is made of the same material, it doesn't give her the same feedback. Knowing that, she figures that the other must open the larger one. The bitter feeling of defeat settles over her. Reflecting on the past half-year, she shakes off the self-doubt. She may not be able to solve it the way they want, so she will solve it her way. Bracing against the coming discomfort, Runa reaches her hand through the metallic cube, sending cold needle-like pain through any part of her that intersects the material. Through the cold burning, she feels around the base of the cube for any sort of latch or mechanism. It is disorienting, overcoming the pain while attempting to feel details unseen. Working her way around the outside of the box she finds what she is looking for. A circular plate on the inside of the cube, seemingly holding the box closed. She withdraws her hand for a moment to think. Knowing something about how the master works, some sort of motion must free the lock. Now comes the hard part. She reaches back into the unseen and attempts to grip the circle plate. She has practiced projection with Turios, but she has only had middling success moving objects. However, lifting a feather isn't exactly noteworthy. Her most successful manipulation had been the door to the observation room all those months ago. She focuses on that moment of desperation. Her life is more on the line now than it had been then. Feeling the metal press into her would-be flesh, Runa forces her will into her fingertips then rotates. The box clicks. Quickly, she clasps the side of the box and heaves. The one side of the cube falls silently to the slab. She lurches backwards at the sight within the cube, a human skull. Golden orbs sit in its empty eye sockets. If she had her body, she would shudder. There is an enthralling nature to the gilded skull. Less so for her finding it. More so for the perplexing nature of the thing. "Who is this person?" she wonders as she reaches a spectral hand toward it. As she feels the tingling surge from the contact, she gets surges of emotion. It is hard for her to place. It is resolution, joy, fulfillment. No, she thinks, it's rapture. Runa pulls away from the macabre relic. It's in this moment that she understands what is expected of her.

Runa returns to her body, then lingers there, catching her breath. "Looks like it's just you and me Kyr Bones," she says, her warm breath clinging to the cool stones. Deliverance is near, she can feel it. Throughout her lessons there had never been any communion with human remains. Runa nods. Maybe that is the point of the test, to see how flexible praxis can be. Still, something feels wrong, and it's not the lingering effects of the goldcap. Her vision and equilibrium seem slow to recover, and delicate shapes dance on her periphery. It's as if a cog in her mind had been missing teeth, and this experience has bridged the gap. Nevertheless, praxis now feels less like an obstacle for her to master, than an ally to enlist on her journey. She smiles as she rights herself, walks to the slab, then tenderly picks up the skull. It's incomplete, the lower jaw missing, and Runa can only guess at the significance of the off-putting substitutes for eyes. Her delving is gentle at first, like the handling of dear friend. There is nothing inside this cranium but a void, no memories to glean, no lifetime to share. She nods knowingly. She hadn't expected there to be anything. Tales of haunted ships filled with the vengeful dead had once kept her up at night. She wonders if there is something in our nature that makes us cleave to the departed in such a way. Perhaps ghosts just make for good stories, she thinks with a shrug. Then she remembers the wall. Perhaps mortal remains could hold similar echoes as the carvings. Having nothing left to try, she closes her eyes and attempts a similar approach.

The rise and fall of the waves are gentle at first, gradually becoming more pronounced through each crest and trough of thought. As Runa is reminded of home, the waves fall away, sending her senses reeling into a foreign time and place.

It's sunset, she surmises by the light. No, it's something else. From the perspective of this person, she is lying on her back, facing the sky. And what a sky it is. Fengari hangs over her, blocking out the sun, casting a great shadow over the land. An eclipse. The person through whose eyes she is seeing turns to the side, taking one last look at the silent crowd gathered around. This was the source of the joyous pride Runa had felt while inspecting the box. As she turns back to the sight of the eclipse overhead, strange words pass her lips. In an archaic dialect of Astoran she says, "Though I am a wanderer, wonder still remains." Then a flash of steel arcs through the edge of her vision. The bite of the swing of the executioner's blade across her neck cuts clean and true, rending the sinew and flesh. Whoever's remembrance this is not afraid. But the pain and viscera are real for Runa. She wants to scream, but she is trapped as a spectator to butchery. The sword rises, glinting like silver in moonlight then falls again, crushing bone. A hot spurt of blood splashes across her face and chest as Deliverance rises a third and final time. Her vision tunnels to black, the final words she spoke repeating like hammer blows in her mind.

Snapping back to the present, Runa clutches at her neck. The phantom has left hot needles in her flesh and tears in her eyes. Wasting no time, she returns the skull to the slab then staggers away. When her head stops spinning, she makes her way back through the rooms, unable to shake the experience. As she reaches the entrance again, the stone door opens. Outside the mausoleum a congregation of praxiats is gathered in the temple proper. The twelve cryptic individuals look to Runa expectantly. She supposes there is only one thing that she should say. "Wonder still remains," she says in lilting Astoran. The congregants echo the words with a thunderclap of voices. The farthest figure approaches her with a coat as dark as midnight, the inside a sheen like the surface of the sea. Runa is overwhelmed with being the locus of attention, but her attention changes as a face in the front of the crowd draws her attention. Donning the coat which fits her perfectly, Adanon returns her gaze from the front.

PART 2

CHAPTER 29

As the temple begins to clear, Adanon approaches Runa and her while they stand about chatting. Though she had seen him amongst the crowd, Runa bounds over and hugs him aggressively. Through praxis, she imparts a feeling of joy and relief. Adanon returns the sentiment with a smile and a pat on her head. "I'm sorry I was gone so long. We have a lot to talk about," he says, looking over her friends. Holfnir shadows Adanon but stays far enough away as to be less conspicuous. Runa pulls away from the sidelong hug, then peers around Adanon, taking notice of Holfnir. She waves to him, but his attention seems to be on Adanon. Slowly noticing Runa's eyes on him, Holfnir turns away while making a clicking sound with his mouth. "He's been through some things," Adanon whispers to Runa. "Aye..." Runa says as Holfnir continues the tic, "did you just arrive? Did you visit Raz?" Adanon shakes his head, saying, "Not yet, how is the better little Lykios?" "He is fine, I think," Runa says with some hesitation. Adanon really has been gone for too long. But, if he is to be any help to Talin, Runa or more recently, Holfnir, he must first help himself. The upcoming predicament has been all that has occupied his mind since leaving the barens of the Anvil. The predicament of misleading the council a second time will require tack and cunning that Adanon fears he lacks. As he appraises the young praxiats with a smile, a hoarse but sultry feminine voice from behind him calls out, "Akroates, how fortunate that you returned from your assignment today. For all our sakes, I hope it was fruitful." "Duty calls," Adanon mouths to the young praxiats before turning away. "Councilor Aoifia," he says with a deep bow, "I'd be remiss if I didn't congratulate our newest praxiat. She is to join your great nephew's cohort, after all." She glances briefly at Turios. "Indeed?" she says, her thin lips curling, "Always the dutiful leader, Akroates... Join us in our haven. Now." Adanon bows as the procession on councilors make toward the wings of the temple.

Aoifia takes up the rear of the train, walking just in front of Adanon. "You know Akroates, I make an attempt to remember the face of every praxiat that passes or fails their assay. But your shadow, I don't remember him." Adanon looks back as they begin the lengthy stair ascent. He nods to the young man, prompting him to speak. With a slight stammer, Holfnir says, "F-forgive me Potentate, I have a forgettable face." "What I think Holfnir is trying to say is, that for a woman of your years, it's only natural for you to forget a few faces," Adanon says. Aoifia lets out a rusty hinge of a laugh. "Ah humor, often the accompaniment of truth. It is soon time for at least one of us to move on. This is why I hope you have good news Akroates," she says. Clearing his throat, Adanon says, "I certainly have news, Kyri. The rest is subjective." As they enter the garden above, Holfnir is asked to wait at the entrance. It's the same as the last time Adanon had been here. The same water trickles slowly through the fountain. The view of the mausoleum below is unchanged. Why then does it feel so different? Has learning that Darian knew that their mother was alive and cared for her really changed anything? The last councilor sits in a ring at the center of the space. Adanon clasps his hands behind his back and says, "I have found no trace of Darian in Stormanvil. I believe he may be seeking asylum among our enemies. I'm prepared to head abroad—" "This is outrageous," Councilor Phacian says, "we warned you about returning emptyhanded." The elderly man turns to Aiofia on his left. "I told you we should have pulled his reliquary to keep an eye on him," he continues. Aoifia makes a dismissive hand gesture to the man, keenly watching Adanon. "Unfortunately, Potentate, you would have had no such luck," Adanon says with flat affect. Phacian struggles to his feet and shouts, "You are subservient to us! We give the orders and do as we please." "No, you are bumbling through this life just like the rest of us, and Darian has played you for fools," Adanon says. The Council erupts in jeers. "Let him speak. He returned despite failing his mission, that takes bravery or foolishness," Aoifia says. Several of the councilors grumble in agreement. Aoifia stands and speaks over the others, "We are not your enemy Adanon. I know that we seem to be at times, but you were chosen by this council. Now, if you please." If earlier comments had been walking on a thin ice, Adanon is about to jump in with leaden shoes. He chokes down his fear and says mournfully, "I've thought for so long how to go about this. And despite my love of pontificating, I think my actions have always spoken louder. What I mean to say, Potentates, is- you wouldn't have found my reliquary if you thought to look." He reaches slowly into his liner pocket and produces the accursed cylinder of his excised pieces. There is an audible gasp from members the council. He then walks the few paces to the dais and sets it on the polished granite. Aoifia rests her face against her splayed hand, smirking as the council deliberates noisily. She watches Adanon keenly, saying nothing. Councilor Vergia shouts, "Do away with this son of a rock scraper! We must choose another Akroates." As uncertain as his future is, Adanon still believes he has made the right choice.

After a long time, the council comes to order. Aoifia is the first to address Adanon directly, "It's no wonder this council has become so impotent, given our inability to listen. Tell us how you came to possess this, Akroates." They have taken the bait. Adanon prostrates himself before the dais and speaks loudly, "Potentates, my shadow, as you called him, Holfnir, was one of the members of the cohort that went missing off the coast of Uxkukul. He was held captive by the Prophet Queen until which time she sent him home with the reliquary." All of it is a fabrication, but Adanon desperately needs them to believe. "And how did that schismatic beast come to possess it?" Aoifia hisses. "I can only speculate. Darian must have sent it as a gift of good faith," Adanon admits. Pacian groans and says, "You can't possibly know that," slamming his fist into his armrest. "I said it was speculation, Potentate. Perhaps another among you removed it from the vault?" Adanon says, rising to his feet. His words are a poisonous barb of suspicion. The men and women of the council share glances. Rubbing her temples, Aoifia says, "It was Darian. Thank you for returning it, Akroates. It's bought some favor with me at the very least." "Yes, yes, very courageous. Unfortunately, that isn't the only thing with which Darian absconded. We cannot perform our rites as it currently stands and the next convergence is soon," Councilor Vergia says. "Potentate, has there been word from your prefecture?" Adanon says, teasing a scab of discontent. Vergia slumps in her chair. Vergia is a younger councilor, not yet middle aged, but time or stress haven't been kind to her. "Things are bad everywhere. Even in our collective memories things were never this dire, not even in the war," Aoifia says. "Speak not of the war," Vergia mutters. Over the years Adanon has been able to piece together Vergia's aversion to the topic. Her previous iteration was killed in the war. No doubt those memories are fresher, more poignant than those in her past lives. "What do you make of the stirrings in the north, Akroates? Didn't your second run off to those frozen wastes?" Pacian says. "Unfortunately," Adanon says, shifting uneasily. He continues, "To your point, I would request assignment to the north. Talin isn't a lost cause, just... troubled," "I think not Akroates. Is difficult as you are, you still didn't choose dereliction over your duty. Should she return, she will be subject to our laws the same as any other apostate," Aoifia says with bile.

Councilor Jures from the distant archipelago of Qualam clears his throat. Adanon finds he is often the most observant and subtle of the Council. He says, "Put it to vote. Akroates, after making us wait for months, I'm sure you can spare a moment for deliberation." They do not dismiss him. This seems to be a power play, to deliberate over his fate with no considering of his presence. Several of the councilors bring up the peculiarity of Adanon's reliquary ending up in Uxkukul. Only Vergia votes to send him to Gaerdan. The others quash her insistence by iterating that navigating the growing pall of Gaerdanian xenophobia may pose an impossible task for even the most skilled outsiders. As he listens on, Adanon intones a whispered plea for forgiveness to Talin. He will have to try something different at a different time. Exposing the reliquary and lying about its acquisition had the opposite effect to what he had intended.

As the chamber grows silent, Adanon queues into the silence and focuses back on the council. "Akroates," they say in unison. From the congregation, Aoifia stands and moves to the edge of the dais. "We have decided to send you to Ux. We would very much like to know how their aberrant monarch came upon this," she picks up the reliquary, "Perhaps she's had a change of heart about us. Don't you think?" Since the war much of the territory of Uxkukul has been annexed by Esoptria. The conditions of the treaty had been considered unfair even by those who penned it. The jungles and mountains of Ux are rich with natural resources which the Federation is unwilling to cede to anyone. All that remains of the Uxian resistance is a city tucked far away in the jungle, headed by a monarch younger than anyone that fought for it. Legend says that the leader who sold Uxian freedom killed herself with the same pen with which she signed the treaty. Adanon doesn't know if it's true, but Darian would. He had been there. For one reason or another, the Eighth Star had taken an interest in him. Adanon sighs to himself. All of that had been a lifetime ago and a world away. "Orin has been posturing more and more near our southernmost colonies. Seek out this puppet ruler, sus out her intent. Should anything interfere with our affairs, destroy her like the malfeasant creature she is. You are dismissed," Aoifia says. "Speak and I listen," Adanon says in Astoran as he turns away. He casts his mind back to Holfnir's possession by the separatist queen. Somehow, she had known this would be the outcome. "Perhaps her odious title has merit," he thinks to himself as he makes his way out of the temple.

CHAPTER 30

In the oppressive darkness of her dreams, Runa watches a pair of serpentine eyes staring through the shadows. Fear and sweat cling to her as the eyes press closer. The grip of sleep loosens, as a feminine voice from the formless dark says, "You think yourself a slave to the past, but the path to salvation is woven at your heel like unbroken tapestry." A rumble of thunder jolts Runa awakes in the predawn hours. She struggles to remember where she is for a moment. Then the ubiquitous stillness within the Grand Cenobium ushers in remembering. It is the second Sunday in the Month of Storms, and she is glad to no longer be dreaming. Her dreams have been fitful ever since her first taste of goldcap at the ceremony. As she sits in the dark, she pushes away the sweat-soaked sheets and shudders. The dreams are incessant and strange, feeling more like forgetting than absentmindedness. Nearly every day a twinge of regret follows her through her morning routine and she doesn't know why. She nods, thinking that she should ask Adanon, then slides out of bed. She shuffles out into the common area, glancing at Turios' closed door. He's still asleep. He has been an accommodating roommate, mindful of messes and going out of his way to cook meals for the two, or four of them. It had taken some getting used to. Despite her first impression, he is so very unlike her brother Amil, At times, when she lets her guard down, Turios feels like he belongs in her life. Scavenging for something to eat in the pantry, Runa wonders if he feels the same way about her. There had been moments when she had caught him staring. She smiles, knowing that if she ever brought it up to Oma or Thand, it would be more ammunition for their ceaseless teasing of him. Still rummaging through the pantry, her mind turns to Raz. She intends to see him today. Then, she sighs, remembering her departure from the Lykios estate. Raz had taken it well enough, but she misses the small, knowing glances. His father still remains abroad, leaving Raz there alone save for servants or when she visits. Even before Zidero showed his true colors, she had pondered what he had expected two young people to do under the circumstances. How could he get mad at them growing close? She sighs again then pushes the hardly touched xahuatl away. Perhaps Zidero is the kind of man that orchestrates his own outrage. Even though she still considers him small for how he treats those he is closest to, she imagines regret is his greatest bedfellow. It would be easy for her to vilify his narcissistic tendencies, but surely narcissists suffer like the rest of us. She is stirred from her ruminations by Turios leaving his room.

Sometime later, Runa is strolling along the brick pavers of Cardis in her praxic coat. The change in people's perception of her hasn't been subtle. Where she had once been a Jana girl simply going about her menial day, she is now a figure of elevated repute. It's the kind of attention Adanon abhors, even though she sees an excessive amount of it with him. Even when his name isn't known, his title is, and she has come to have some idea why. Adanon did something grave in his past to earn the title of Akroates. While no one in her cohort has been forthcoming with the particulars, it must have been malfeasance, Runa is sure of it. Approaching the ferries, she is taken aback by the sight of Raz waiting. She had said she would spend time on the island. It seems something has changed. Morning sunlight breaks through the fleeting storm clouds as Raz waves to her.

They exchange a lingering hug and a knowing gaze. "I know I've said it before, but the dark doesn't suit you. You should add some color," Raz says. Runa simply scoffs. "But think of the regulations," she says with an imperious tone. Raz gives her a half-hearted smirk, then begins to move away. "Let's go to Pa's place to talk," he says. Runa raises a brow. She hadn't known that Raz was familiar with the tavern. She shrugs. Of course he knows of the tavern, he seems to know everyone despite being somewhat of a shut-in. With time, Runa has come to understand Thand's misgivings toward the Lykios family. Through his father they seem to have their hands in everything. As they make their way into the tavern, Runa says, "Ad asked after you. Have you heard from him?" Raz knits his fingers as she sits across from him. Without meeting her gaze he says, "He still playing parent to other people's children?" Though she had just sat, Runa scoots back primed to stand again. "Where is this coming from? Why are you in such a foul mood today?" she says in distress. Raz looks around the mostly empty tavern. He throws his arms up in surrender. "I don't know. Maybe some of the things my dad said are starting to get to me," he admits. Runa rocks back in her chair. "Raz, your dad is a strange man," Runa says flatly, "He facilitated us living under the same roof, then got upset when we grew close. Does that make sense?" Raz waves down Pa who is hunched precariously over an antique radio atop the bar. The volume is so low no one besides Pa can hear the broadcast. As he makes his way over, his face isn't the leathery image of joy that he usually is. Raz gives him an exaggerated smile then says, "I'd like a cup of 'hot, the Anvilite way- and make it a double. And whatever Runa is having." Pa looks at Runa. "Water," Runa says flatly, before Pa bows and shuffles away. "Water. Really?" Raz says, rolling his eyes, "Worried you'll have trouble reading minds or something if you relax a little?" Runa leans forward. Raz is acting very out of character, almost like his father, she thinks. For half a second, she considers saying so. "It's not 'or something.' It's the balance that holds the universe together so don't be so condescending," she says. Raz makes a dismissive gesture, saying, "Spoken like a true zealot." Even before he can regret his words, he leans in and says, "Alright, fine. I admit things have been weird. Zidero has been ever since you showed up. Always going somewhere. Today marks three months that he's been gone." "Aye, that's a long time. And now I'm gone too," Runa says, casting her eyes down to the rough wooden table, "I think I get it, not being accustomed to a void in the family," she says, offering her hand to him. "Adanon and I spoke about this sometime after I came to Esoptria. He likened it to grief." Raz scoffs and crosses his arms. "Why do you cling to him the way you do? You really don't owe him anything. How many times did you read that letter? Like a pet awaiting its master's return," he says, clearly frustrated. "Raz, stop," Runa says clenching her teeth. "I just... It feels like everyone leaves, and the way things are going abroad, I'm just worried." Runa's demeanor shifts. She sees that he is coming from a place of fear, not malice. Her mind turns to her first glimpses into his past. His mother's suicide. It's a bad look, but better than his father's. A group of regulars enter the tavern and begin chatting with Pa.

Drawing her attention away from the newcomers, Runa slides into the chair beside Raz. As she places her hand on Raz's, she says, "There's no easy way to say this, but your mother. Do you think Zidero knows why?" Raz lets out a sardonic chuckle and presses his hand to his face. Refusing to meet Runa's eye, he takes a long time to form his words. While Runa could form a deeper understanding through praxis, she knows well enough not to let her curiosity overstep her decency. "She," Raz says, hanging on words, "was tireless in her pursuits. Always working in her laboratory, but still took time to make me feel seen. Hiring servants to play with me was my father's way after she was gone. That's to say, no, she left no note for her suicide." He chuckles. "When did you make off with those memories?" Runa recoils. "I stumbled into it. I would never purposefully—" Pa arrives with their drinks. Raz grabs the steaming concoction and downs it over several prolonged heartbeats. Runa's disapproving look says more than her words. "Now that you've come up for air, what is this really about?" she says. "I'm worried about what you'll say," Raz says, his face flushing, "After this next race, I'm giving up racing. I want to be far from this place and the sea. I've enlisted in the pilot training division." Runa knits her fingers, watching him past her knuckles. The advent of heavier than air flight had sprung from the wind-swept barrens of Stormanvil some years before the war. Its adoption for warfare had been haphazard and swift, but due to the ubiquity of the magrail network, its spread post war has been slow. On top of the inherent risk of air travel, the consequences of crashing and rupturing a power cell large enough to maintain flight are often catastrophic. "I don't want to ask the obvious, but is such a thing advisable? Have you told Zidero?" Runa says. "Another!" Raz shouts to Pa from across the tavern, "Of all people, I thought you'd understand wanting to succeed when others think you'll fail." Runa smiles wryly. "Aye, I find that endearing about you. But recognizing our limitations isn't failure," she says. Raz scoffs, saying, "What limitations do you have exactly? Every time I get into that boat I imagine myself sinking beneath the waves, unable to swim. But all of that—" his voice breaks. Never has he brought up such a fear, even in the small moments of vulnerability they have shared. Runa struggles to find her words. The young man who had seemed so confident had always been afraid. For a time all Runa had known was fear. Her fear of loss. Loss of belonging, loss of identity, loss of purpose had been her struggle until she found new purpose. She now sees that Raz has been suffering the same. But how can she explain that such fear is paralytic? That sheltering oneself or another from strife is damaging and at the very least, reductive. It's the same fear that guides Zidero's overbearing reactions. And it's a balancing act that Runa hasn't, nor thinks she will ever master. For a time, they simply sit without regarding each other. Then Runa says, "I'm sure you'll make a fine pilot. Just tell those military folks who's the best mechanic you know." Raz looks away, a sheen in his eye. "Pa!," he shouts looking to the bar, but the elderly man is still listening to the radio. Without turning, Pa makes a beckoning motion in their direction. "He seems to have it backwards today," Raz says, but Pa says nothing, only turns up the volume. The voice on the radio is reading a report which is at first indecipherable to Runa. Numbers of riots in Gaerdan, damage to the magrail lines to the north. But what catches Runa's ear is the mention of the Janamudra. This time of year the flotilla heads back to the northern hemisphere through the Straits of Mulsyn. The commentator continues, mentioning a blockade. An Oringian blockade near the inlet of the shallow sea. Runa clasps her hand over her mouth as the report continues, mentioning Janamudra ships being attacked and sunk. "They are defenseless," she whispers as the reporter begins estimating the souls lost to the sea.

CHAPTER 31

"Wake up," a masculine voice says, cutting through the dark void that is Talin's perception. Her limbs are heavy. As she shifts them slightly, the clink of chains pierces the rift of unhearing. Even her eyelids struggle against their weight. A hoarse croak escapes her throat as she attempts to speak. "Where- am- I?" she rattles, her eyes straining against the light. "I'm very busy Talin, if you would hurry up, I'd really appreciate it," the male voice says. Then the cold hits her. Not just cold, also wet. Frigid water soaks her face and clothes, sending her reeling into lucidity. As she sputters and gasps, Talin focuses on the two figures in the hoary room before her. One is Darian. The other appears to be a man of similar build but wearing the frightening treehound skull mask. Talin feels awful, sedated. Aside from the water sapping her warmth, nausea and confusion pervade her mind and body. She lulls her head toward her bound hands. That's when she notices the intravenous line near the crook of her arm. She is being sedated in a way that keeps her bound to her corporeal form and incapable of praxis. "A precaution," Darian says, taking a step closer. "Do the dredgers really not know who you are?" Talin slurs. Darian snaps his fingers, then the man in the mask throws more icy water on her. "People see only what they want to see. I presented myself as a savior for the downtrodden, so I became one," Darian says with a flourish, "but I am asking the questions. How did you know I was in Gaerdan when even Adanon didn't?" Talin lets out a chuckle. "You can't even fathom it, can you? Failure. I see failure around every corner. Plus, it was a lucky guess," she says, ending by smacking her dry lips. "Lucky? I wouldn't be so sure," Darian says coolly, "Hurt her." The man in the mask steps to Talin, lifting her head by her hair then smacking her weakly. Talin lets out a half-laugh, half-gasp. He barely hit her at all. "Your goon lacks your courage to hurt defenseless women," Talin says wryly. Darian walks slowly up to her, placing a knee between hers. Then he takes her arm with the intravenous line and presses hard. He rolls and pinches the catheter imbedded in her flesh until her face twists in pain, but she holds his gaze. "You should hear what I have to say before hurling insults. You are very dull-witted at times, has Adanon told you that?" he says. Talin looks to the other man, who looks away. "Sorry, I thought this was torture, not foreplay," she says, rolling her head and eyes around the room. Darian backs away and the masked man whispers to him. Gesticulating wildly as he says, "My associate reminds me not to waste good resources. I am trying to make a better world, can't you see that? The petty squabbling, the breakdowns in communication, the tribal mentality of 'us' versus 'them.' If everyone was given an equal footing, we could achieve so much more." "Is that what you told them, the dredgers?" she says. Darian scoffs. "You saw how they are. Animals. I tell them a convenient lie because they can't even conceive of our understanding." Talin coughs with laughter. "Artificially instilling praxis is in people is impossible. It's been tried before," she giggles. Darian storms back to her, pushing the chair she is chained too onto its side. "It is not!" he shouts, watching Talin squirm helplessly against her restraints, "I have made great strides. If you only knew what I sacrificed for my work—" he trails off, gaze distant. "What do you want from me?" Talin asks, exasperated. "Nothing. Sparing you would be a kindness to a friend. He seems to have some misplaced affection for you." Talin chuckles, rolling her head on the cool stone floor. How wrong he is. The affection is one-sided. She looks toward the other man. Perhaps she can take advantage of his apparent indecision. "What are my choices? Agree to help you with your grand plan or die?" she says as she slowly begins shifting the manacle up her arm. "Oh no, your help is not needed, Kyri. The plan is well underway, I just think Adanon would miss you terribly. Although, he is no stranger to loss at this point," Darian says with a sardonic chuckle. He makes Talin ill. But for the first time she recognizes why. His ruthlessness, the singular focus, the abuse of power, she sees all of it in herself. What a strange place to learn a harsh truth. Letting out a resigned sigh, she says, "Can I have some time to think it over?" Darian cuts a crooked smile, clearly pleased with the situation. "Thirty minutes. We're missing the revelry elsewhere. Check her drip and let's go," he says. The masked man checks the glass hung from the stand, then moves to upright the chair. But Darian snaps his fingers. "No. Let her spend time with the stones she may yet be buried under," he says, turning away and heading toward the door.

The moment she is alone in the room Talin feverishly forces the manacle higher on her arm. Then, flexing her arm, pressing the sweating iron bangle into the crook of her arm just above the catheter. She grits her teeth against the discomfort, but after a few moments the tingle in her arm lets her know that she was successful. She isn't sure if thirty minutes will be enough time, but she must try. As the time ticks by, she scoffs at the thought of accepting what Darian is offering. Perhaps she has changed. The old Talin would have jumped at the chance to save herself. For her, this last act of defiance will be worth the heavy price. She only regrets giving up on Adanon because he was right. Catching Darian in a game of his designing had been something she was woefully unprepared for. She comforts herself with the thought that she couldn't have guessed that he had been hiding among dredgers. A few months ago, the thought of the councilor leading an anti-praxiat movement would have been insanity. But, hadn't she thought to hide among the commoners as well? Either he is not as clever as he seems or there is more to his plan. Talin is inclined to believe the latter. She looks down at her arm which has turned an unnerving shade of purple and smiles. None of it will matter soon.

After what seems to be the shortest half hour of her life, the door to her cell comes open again. Talin relaxes. She has many regrets. Chief among which is dragging Ade along on this foolish quest. The masked man strolls over. As he stoops to upright her chair, Talin readies to pounce. She has regained some focus despite the sedative still lingering in her system. Watching the man through feigned heavy lids, she notices that there is something familiar about him. The metallic chair scrapes onto its feet and her along with it. This is the moment. Talin grabs the him. Then, with words that cut like a knife, she commands, "Free me." From across the room, Darian bellows, "Back away!" But it is too late. Talin has ripped through the man's mind like an armor piercing projectile. Curiously, much of his mind is fractured, obfuscated. Vast areas are dark. This must be Darian's doing. Despite the scarring throughout his mind, his will crumbles like ashen paper. She does know this man. "Lykios," Talin whispers, as the masked man steps places himself between Darian and Talin. It is pointless. Darian taps the man on the chest, sending him buckling to the stone floor. He spares not a moment for the man. His ire is aimed at Talin. Before she can react, Darian kicks her in the chest, sending her skidding back to the stones. The glass bottle of fluid shatters somewhere out of Talin's sight. "That- was a mistake," he says, leaning over her as she labors to breathe.

"I swear to you, in this life or the next, I will be there when you fall," Talin sputters. Darian smiles, saying, "Join the queue." She spits at him. Unfazed, he simply leans over her and speaks in a hushed tone, "You know, I am somewhat of a collector. It's a great injustice that so few have seen my collection." Talin shudders as Darian steadily removes his dark leather gloves. Then he delicately caresses Talin's face with the back of his hand. She recoils. "Now, I think this only fair after you hurt my friend Zidero," he says, feigning concern for the incapacitated man. "You've have harmed him more than I," she says, wincing again to his touch. "I doubt you'd understand. You bumble through life forming no attachments with anyone," Darian says with a shrug, "Now, let me show you my first." With slow, deliberate movements, he takes Talin by the hand. The force of his will crashes into Talin. Primal, swift, and without remorse in its efficacy, her mind yields to his.

Sound, it's muffled. Talin looks up, the light of the sun etching ephemeral shapes on the surface of the water. She fights against her bindings, holding her last gasps of life-giving air in her screaming lungs. It is agony. Darian is forcing her to live the last moments of this unfortunate soul. Each protracted spasm of pain is hers to experience. The primal struggle between mind and body, the war to inhale the brine is one she will lose. Hope against hope that she might yet take one precious breath. As sinew strains against steel, her vision tunnels into oblivion.

Talin surfaces from the imposed memory, gasping. "Not to your liking? Perhaps you'd prefer the final moments of a despondent geriatric, whose final thoughts are chaos and fear? All alone. All alone," Darian says, fixing stray hairs clinging to Talin's face. As she turns toward him, hot rage trickles down her face. She's at his mercy, of which he has none. Staying her quivering lip, she glowers at him in silence. He tuts, continuing to caress her hair. "You know, I poked around a bit," he says, pressing a finger hard against her forehead, "I'd like to know where your large Bujani friend went. I'd really like to meet him. But the boy..." Talin bucks against her restraints. "Oh, the mother passed. A mercy, that. Eklin though... He's very enamored with praxis, thanks to you I think," Darian says, false sweetness in his voice. Attempting to feign ignorance or uncaring, Talin's face relaxes as she stares up at the featureless ceiling. "You think you hide your madness well, but you don't," she says. Zidero, coming to his senses, lets out a muffled groan. Darian looks to him, then back to Talin with a smile. Then he leans in and whispers, "The boy will make a fine subject for my experiments." Sparing not a moment, Talin whips her head sideways, connecting with a crunch and sending Darian reeling backward "Just can't help yourself can you, Darian!" she cackles. "Darian," Zidero says as he pulls off the mask and scoots to his side. A guard from the door peeks into the room. "Kyr, everything alright?" he says as Darian stymies the crimson flood from his nose. "The old mouser still has claws," Zidero says to the guard. "Right," he responds, then clears his throat, "I have news, from the spires." In a nasally tone, Darian says, "This had better be good, interrupting my work." Zidero helps Darian to his feet as the guard says, "Kyr, we've taken the day. The prefect has surrendered." Talin's laughter peters into silence as the three men congregate near the door. Patting the guard on the shoulder Darian says, "That is good news." Talin can see Zidero's profile from her vantage. His face is placid, but he seems to hang on Darian's every word. Snapping his fingers, Darian turns to the guard and says, "This prisoner is a pox on everything she touches. She deserves everything that comes next." It's subtle, but Zidero winces at Darian's words.

CHAPTER 32

The rising sun pierces the morning fog over the shipyards on the western banks of Esoptria. Runa stands together on the docks with the members of her cohort looking up at the superstructure of a warship, the Nurval. The invigorating spring light glints off the armor of the ship, the class of which replaced the Sabitum and its sister ships years ago. The protective plates overlap the fore and aft sections of the bridge and other points of convergence like the layered pauldrons of ages past. It seems to Runa that each segment is held fast to the structure anywhere the engineers thought might need protecting. The Nurval is smaller than the Saby by fifty paces, but twice as fast, and the bioreactor is powerful enough to handily sustain a modest city. It's an imposing sight, and it gives Runa chills. It hasn't settled in that she and the others are to be stationed aboard this behemoth vessel. Turios nudges her gently. "You'll have to change your name," he says, alluding to Janamudra naming conventions. Runa's eyes jump from one detail of the ship to another, disregarding his comment. Oma kisses her teeth. "Doesn't have the right chime," she says, brushing off her shoulder, rejecting the suggestion by proxy. Runa nods in approval. Under the cover of her coat, she fidgets with the aster secreted in her pocket. Running her hand over its surface, she wonders about the armored plating on the warship having a similar geometry. She had requisitioned the aster upon receiving their orders to accompany the battlegroup heading for the southern colonies in Uxkukul. Runa wishes they hadn't been so rough when they took her blood for retainer, but given her last interaction with the 'quartermaster,' she isn't surprised. From behind her, a familiar voice calls out, "Ho there, breaking curfew miscreants?"

Adanon saunters up, feigning a salute to the large posters stuck to the face of the warehouse running along the wharf. The posters read, "Purchase Energy Bonds! Ration Heat for Victory." Runa had grown blind to the propaganda plastered around the city over the last few weeks. Each poster is a reminder of how dependent Esoptria had become on the Janamudra. The military had scrambled to pick up the shipping of raw materials from various territories, but the loss of diplomacy with Gaerdan has struck another dire blow. Zidero's disappearance, Gaerdan's repudiation, and Orin's blockade, all at the same time. All of it seems purposeful in its disruption. Runa makes a sour face at the thought of what is happening far to the south, before turning to wave to Adanon. He appears to have been drinking. "I thought curfew didn't apply to praxiats," Runa says. "Ostensibly," Adanon replies, knitting his fingers, "Many peculiarities these days." He pauses to look over the snip, nodding his head. Then he says, "I've heard Razmus wants to fly. They'll have need of pilots soon." Runa perks up, unsure how Adanon had heard. Turios scoffs, crossing his arms as he says, "Was being a racer not enough for him?" Runa gives a noncommittal shrug. "He has a gift for operating machines. He may do well," she says earnestly. Turios rolls his eyes. Before he can say anything, Thand muscles into the conversation, visibly flustered. "On the day of judgement woe betide he who squandered His gifts," she says, cutting her eyes at Turios. "Ahm, and well put," Adanon interjects, clapping his hands. Turios clears his throat and says, "Kyr, have you come to see us off?" "See you off?" Adanon says with exaggerated incredulity, "My boy, I'm coming with you." Turios' jaw hangs slack as Adanon slides to the gangplank and begins boarding the vessel. "Oh, help him with that," he says, turning back and pointing to Holfnir who approaches with arms full of luggage. Before slipping out of sight, Adanon beckons to Runa with a curled finger. She hops to join him on the deck of the Nurval.

"How are you feeling?" he says, glancing up at the sky. Fengari cuts an arc high through the afternoon sky. "Kyr, it's... strange going back to sea," Runa blurts out. With a hum, Adanon turns to her and says, "Couldn't have picked a better day if you tried. Should be quite the spectacle." She knits her brow at him. "I don't follow," she says, turning to see Thand assisting Holfnir with the baggage. "It's good you are getting out. With your nose to the books you can't see the sky," Adanon says, pointing to the sun and Fengari with separate hands, then pulling them together. For a moment Runa puzzles over his meaning before she hums and nods. She had forgotten that there was to be an eclipse, the penumbra of which will be visible for much of the continent. For the briefest of moments, the vision of the execution within the mausoleum flashes to the front of her mind. The memory of which is interrupted by a nudge from Adanon. "Go check your quarters. The commander of this vessel is an old and sour man. Doesn't hide his distrust of us, but—" He presses a thumb to his chest. "You expect trouble?" Runa says, glancing back up at Fengari and shading her eyes against the glare of the morning sun hung over the city. Adanon chuckles, saying, "Not many old salts like him left in the navy, I just don't like him. It's nothing I can't handle." Runa clears her throat, saying, "Kyr, I thought maybe you'd be heading north." Adanon squints at her, seeming to sus out her intent. "No, they chose their path. There's much bitter fighting still to be had in Gaerdan, but my place is elsewhere." Runa nods, inferring that by 'they' he means 'Talin.' "I'm going to look at these quarters. They can't be worse than the Shyena," she says. Before Adanon can quell her youthful optimism, she is around the corner catching up with the others.

Runa trots down the series of stairs until she catches up with Turios below deck. The line of praxiats comes to a halt before an open bulkhead. Holfnir, at the head of the pack glances back, stammers for a moment, then steps into the long corridor through the belly of the ship. Every chatty sailor standing about the passage falls silent before tucking into their quarters. The hall falling silent gives Runa the impression of how this voyage will go. As she steps through the portal, she breathes deep, taking in the familiar scent of forced air, bodies, and steel. "Just like home," she remarks to Turios, who looks at her nervously. "I wouldn't be so sure," he says, averting his eyes from the leering sailors within their quarters. As the group passes each compartment large enough for over thirty sailors, Runa peers in each room, disregarding the countless gazes. At one hatch, a sailor calls out to her, but Turios turns and pulls Runa along, saying, "Sorry, she's just curious." As she is dragged away, Runa says, "Some many people for so few showers." Turios shushes her. "The Janny girl is right!" a sailor calls back to a chorus or rowdy laughter. "Come on," Turios whispers as they reach the end. A hatch leads to another Corridor with stairs heading topside on either side. Turios groans. "You mean to tell me we could have come here from the deck?" he says to Holfnir, who stares at him blankly. "S-s'pose so," the tall Gaerdanian admits. Runa lets out a chuckle, pushing past Turios in his embarrassment. "I like this one. He irks Turios without even trying." All the young women let out a whoop of amusement. Turios fumes at the entrance, before deflating and following the rest. This space is cramped, and ahead the typically straight corridor of the ship diverges in a wide arc to port and starboard. It appears that the hatch across from where they entered leads into a circular room at the center of the ship. Runa's curiosity is interrupted but Holfnir, "Three per room. Ladies," he points to the port side quarters, "M-m-me and mopey," he continues pointing across the hall. Inside the quarters are wide, comfortably padded berths stacked three high. Each room contains a couch, two lavatories, and copious amounts of storage space by way of lockers. The cohort's effects are waiting within, having been delivered by porters. Holfnir sets the luggage he was carrying in front of the hatch leading into the circular room. As soon as Runa begins rummaging through her pack, the biolume shifts red and a voice reverberates throughout the ship mustering all the personnel to the deck.

Back above, hundreds of sailors stand at attention facing the bow of the ship, where the commander and officers have gathered. Turios urges that the praxiats should join Adanon as they slink toward the front. Even during her formal initiation, Runa hadn't felt this out of place. Joining Adanon just below the lip of the forecastle, all the praxiats turn toward the multitude of crewmen. "I'm glad you could join us," the commander says dryly, but only loud enough for those nearby to hear. "We have an important mission," her shouts in a commanding voice, "This battle group is to relieve a stress brought on by powers outside our control." Runa can't help but feel as if the comment is directed squarely at her. "Let's do our best work, to remind them and ourselves that no one person, no one creed, no one people bind this union together. We all have a job to do," he pauses to pull something from his pocket. He fiddles with the cigar for a moment, then lights it. "I earnestly hope it is enough. Let's get to work." He steps down, nodding to his executive officer, then strolls over to Adanon. His stark white uniform is blinding in the morning sun. From the officer, a series of orders are given to the crew as the commander takes a long drag from his cigar. "Akroates. I saw the last-minute changes to my crew roster. I don't enjoy suffering praxic oversight of my command. I'll be frank, I hope your presence will keep them in line, I wouldn't want to suffer the paperwork should something happen to them," he says, flicking the ashes of the cigar in Runa's direction. Adanon slicks back his dark hair, and smiles at the commander. "I promise you, Commander. If anything happens to them, you won't have to worry about the burden of command," he says charmingly. The grizzled older man chuffs, his pockmarked, leathery skin twitching slightly as he assesses Adanon for a time. Then he takes a long drag of his cigar and walks away.

Shortly after, the mooring lines are retrieved as busy sailors and officers trot about the deck. Then to a chorus of horns, bells and voices, the slaps of the churning props herald their departure. It's surreal for Runa, watching all these people going about their duties. Partially because she is on the other side. Watching the determined faces of the sailors, she feels almost powerless. In short time the Nurval, accompanied by four other ships, makes for the sea wall. Runa's vision drifts up to the two celestial bodies which will soon converge. Her mind wanders, thinking about how those men and women on the face of Fengari must feel. Surely nothing she has experienced is as daunting as leaving the world behind for the verdant forests of the unknown. It has been some time since she has mused over the grander things which leave her with a feeling of powerlessness. But her mind is cast back to her last conversation with her father. Adanon says something as he watches the eminent eclipse, but a prolonged blast from the horn drowns out his words. The Nurval and the other ships ride high in the water as they near the lowered flood walls. Runa looks at each of the other members of her cohort, taking in their faces. Oma and Thand are both the picture of delight. They are undoubtable sisters when they smile. Turios is stony faced, looking between the sky and Adanon in equal measure. In the moment she understands her feelings for them all. Unlike Raz, whose fear of loss drives him to push people away, she chooses to embrace her circumstances. If these people are to be her family, she will protect them as if they truly are.

Out upon the open sea, the viridian goddess converges with the sun, casting everything in shadow. All around Runa the world reflects the ephemeral beauty of the sky, stretching forever like sapphire in twilight. Adanon was right, this is a fine day to return home. Sniffling, she wonders what her family is doing at this very moment. Then, as quickly as it began, the eclipse ends.

CHAPTER 33

Talin's eyes strain at the patches of biolume passing overhead. The nausea from the sedative hits her all at once as she retches over the side of the gurney. It's a dry retch. She hasn't eaten anything in so long. There is no way to tell how long for sure. He limbs are like stone, but she manages to hold her eyes open long enough to glimpse Zidero walking beside her. "Welcome back," he says, "I'm sorry for how things turned out, but you left Darian no choice." Talin rasps, searching for her voice. "Give her some water," Zidero commands someone nearby. No water comes. "She's still human. Give her water, or are you no better than your overlords?" After a moment, cool life-giving liquid meets Talin's lips. Weakly, she says, "You're wrong." Zidero leans in to whisper, "How's that?" "He had a choice. We all have a choice. Being rid of me is the easy way out," she croaks. Zidero shakes his head vehemently, saying, "No, we don't all have a choice. Let's keep moving." Talin is reminded of the state of Zidero's mind. The nebulous areas of darkness that pock every corner. It can't be easy living like that. Zidero isn't being contrarian; he's speaking the truth. He has no choice but to obey Darian. "Zidero, I can help you. Free you from his influence, with time." Talin says. Zidero lets out a sigh. "You seem to be confused. What gave you the impression that I don't want to be here?" he says with a chuckle. How could Talin foresee that he had chosen such a pained existence? Under what circumstances would a man choose to lose his free will? Talin struggles to reach her hand toward Zidero. He bats her flaccid hand away. "For what it's worth, I'm—" he clears his throat, "Forgive me, I feel the urge to confess in the old ways. Would you grant me intercession, though I don't deserve it?" Zidero says to Talin as much as he does to the person pushing the gurney. It's an outdated practice of passing burden onto the soon to be departed. "Be quick," a man says outside of Talin's view. Zidero helps her sit upright. "You think I don't know you, but Adanon has spoken loosely about you on occasion. Despite my philandering I have only ever loved my late wife," he says, trailing off. "Wanting me to put in a word for you?" Talin says. "No, I want you to know for next time, that we often become strong for our partners, thinking strength is what is required. But moments of weakness, of kindness are all that matter when there are no more memories left to be made." "Why are you telling me this?" Talin groans. "It's my way of apologizing. I don't wish things were different- I wish we were different. I hope next time we will be," Zidero says, his voice cracking. Talin, regaining a bit of her lucidity, smiles at the floor. She looks to him past her brow and says, "That's not how this works." "I know," he whispers, "I'm just voicing my regret. I know how the world sees me. I did everything in my power, but it wasn't enough to stop her. Now I carry that burden and the hatred of my son..." he says, voice tight with emotion. Talin leans forward and softly says with a grin, "I don't care." Zidero pulls back, hatred flashing in his eyes. He calls out to the attendants that have walked away. Before he turns, he says, "I hope it's agony. Die as you lived, Talin Argyra." As Talin slumps back to the gurney, she says, "That's more like it." Then, Zidero strolls away.

The minutes pass like hours as Talin is rolled through the complex. She wonders how they'll do it, If only she could contact Adanon. Suddenly the gurney stops, then a rosy faced young woman with raven hair leans over her. She touches Talin's face with her cold fingers. A feeling of disgust washes over Talin, but it comes from without. The young woman is a praxiat. A poor fool following Darian into madness. "You must have done something terrible. Try anything and we'll take our time with you," she says sweetly as the man from earlier moves alongside Talin, then heaves her onto his shoulder. "The door," he grunts, as Talin's head swims. The lithe young woman opens the heavy door to a small chamber, then the man drops Talin inside with little care. Whatever sedative she was given does little to dull the impact of the metallic floor. Then the door closes with a clank.

Talin pulls herself up against the wall of the tiny space, looking out of the metallic mesh and glass window in the heavy door. She lets out a weak chuckle. So, this is how she ends. Everything up until now has been a dirge for the despair that is her life. A lament for the woman she might have been. Outside the cell the woman grins wickedly as she taps slowly on the glass. Beside her the man fiddles with a control beside the door. Then the hum of the magnetron starts. A sound which chills Talin to her core. It's subtle, the penetrating heat from the invisible rays striking her exposed flesh. Talin whimpers. This is torture of the cruelest kind; to cook her slowly from the outside. She had thought she would be calm in the face of death, but being pelted with microwaves breaks any illusions she had of bravery. The rest is instinct. She tucks into a ball covering her eyes and ears as her skin begins to warm. Then the hum stops. Talin peers up at the woman, still tapping incessantly on the glass. She mouths something Talin can't hear, then the assault begins again. Each second that passes is agony, before a momentary reprieve. Talin fights back the tears. She had been cruel in the past, but she told herself it was a justifiable product of her upbringing. Of how the other foundling children had bullied her for being from Orin. What little kindness she had been shown was obligatory of the instructors, but disingenuous. She retreats into those memories as her cells begin to die. The blistering heat on her flesh is like those yearly years under the uncaring sun.

In a moment of respite, Talin struggles to her feet. She presses he palms of her hands against the glass and stares at the raven-haired woman, who stops tapping. She assumes a posture similar to Talin, mocking her. But Talin doesn't look away. She knows it's foolish. Her eyes will sizzle and burst if unprotected, but she doesn't care. One last act of defiance before the end. The woman says something to the man operating the machine, then the hum begins again. Talin presses her forehead to the glass, unblinking through the pain. The woman simply smiles back. A concussive blast outside the chamber causes Talin to jump. The glass is splattered in crimson. The young woman's face falls limp as she slides and topples against the door. Talin looks on, confused by what's transpiring. A dark mass barrels into the man from outside Talin's view, bearing him to the ground. Either the shock or the drugs distort her understanding of the situation. "Am I dying," she wonders. Unable to keep her eyes open any longer, Talin crumples back to the floor. Then, mercifully, the machine falls silent. Every surface of her aches as hot, stinging sweat trickles into her eyes. For every reason and for none in particular, tears pool at the corners of her eyes as the door to the chamber opens. A familiar gravelly voice stirs her to her senses. "Are you well?" Ade says, voice heavy with concern. She looks over her shoulder at him, incredulous. "Not well," she rasps, "but not gone." Ade offers his hand to her, and she rises to her feet. "Your eyes have never been more beautiful," he jokes. Talin looks down as the blood smeared floor, the young woman's body crumpled behind the door. "Don't count that one among your prayers, Ade. You did the right thing," she says, making a hand gesture indicating the woman was a praxiat. "Can you move, fast?" Ade asks. Talin grunts a non-answer as a groaning sound comes from behind Ade. "I'd like to think I'm better than them," Talin says nodding at the man. Ade hums, checking his coil gun diligently. The eyes of the man who had tortured her grow wide with fear as Talin approaches him with slow, measured steps. "But sometimes on our journey, we stumble," she continues as hold the man's fearful gaze. She places her hand on the man's quivering face. For what comes next, Ade frowns but says nothing. He only turns his back and strolls farther down the corridor. With dulcet words, Talin compels the man, "You'll get in the chamber for me, won't you?" He nods, powerless to resist, and crawls the several paces into the machine. Without emotion or hesitation Talin latches the door. Then before turning away, she sets the machine to run for an hour. The man's muffled cries stir no remorse in her as she crouches to rummage through the dead girl's pockets. The strands of her blood slick hair undulate in the sanguine pool as Talin disturbs her corpse. Talin is no stranger to blood, but she can't bring herself to look at the girl's lusterless eyes. She pauses to close the girl's narrow, upturned eyes. The girl must have been no older than the Jana girl, Runa. Rummaging once more, Talin gasps, finding what she is looking for. Then she hobbles over to Ade holding the absconded aster.

In the face of recent events, Talin struggles to focus. The burst of adrenaline from the pain has long since passed, leaving her hands shaking and her gait unsteady. Ade looks at her out of the corner of his eye and says, "Not to be imprudent, but shall I carry ya?" Talin walks on. Her mind is hazy, hanging on distant and unimportant things. For some reason she keeps thinking of the time in the forest after the tree hound attack. "We have to find Darian, put an end to this," she says. Ade stops. "Discretion. You can barely walk. An opportunity will present itself, just as it for did me." "What did you say? "I waited for Darian to leave before even attempting to come here. "An opportunity will present itself; they always do. If you are over eager you will miss the signs." Talin sighs. He may have a point, but everything in her wants revenge. Ade nods ahead, saying, "We must hurry. Besides, we have a deal. I will see my children after all of this." Talin chuffs. "That wasn't part of the deal," she says. Ade walks on, disaffected. "I will pray for both of us. Killing a child also wasn't part of the deal." Talin nods, unable to argue the point, so she trudges on beside him.

CHAPTER 34

Before sunrise aboard the Nurval Runa climbs down from the top bunk with a thump. She doesn't want to wake the others. Besides, more hot water for her shower if she's the first in. She relishes in the steamy washroom until the others rise. It had been an interesting day at sea. She is sorely unaccustomed to leisure time. Before long, a knock comes at the privacy glass. Thand waits outside, arms crossed. She's not as imposing as Runa had once thought. She would even consider her demeanor toward her friendly, considering the alternative. Runa shuffles past Thand to the mirror, pausing to look herself over. Runa has always been thin, but over the past few months of persistent exercise some definition has begun to show in her shoulders and arms. Thand watches her for a time before saying, "You've put on weight." Runa sighs. Thand has a way of picking at anyone's insecurities. Before Runa can respond, Thand says, "It's good weight. Do you know what today is?" Runa ponders for a moment. "Typhsday," she says with a shrug. Thand cuts an awkward smile and says, "That's right. It's leg day," clapping Runa on the shoulder a little too hard. Then she steps into the shower and shuts the door.

As Runa slips into her clothes, Oma pulls a pillow over her face and groans, "I wish you two weren't such busybodies." Just to irritate her, Runa begins whistling as she retrieves a comb, then plops onto the couch. Over time she has become more proficient at braiding her own hair but it's never as neat as when the sisters do it. As Oma gives up and rolls out of her cot, Runa braids her hair into a wide plait down her neck, whistling all the while. After some time, a knock comes at the door accompanied by Adanon's voice. Runa hikes on her praxiat jacket then answers the door. Adanon looks her over then says, "Lose the jacket. Let's go." All three of the young women share a glance before shedding their dark coats and following Adanon. They don't have to follow him far, for they stop at the circular room a few paces away where the hatch hangs open. Inside, Turios and Holfnir are leaning over a console speaking in hushed tones. Turios gives a slight nod to the others but doesn't pull his attention away from Holfnir's instruction. Adanon shuts the hatch and secures it with a crunch. He beckons to Runa, pulling her aside for a moment. "How are you with this?" he says, flashing an aster from his pocket. Runa gives a timid shrug. It's a point of embarrassment for her. Adanon pulls away from her, toward the center of the dome-shaped room. "Turios, you stay there. Thandi on comms. Omarosa, you're here," he says knocking on a large metal half-cylinder resting lengthwise but offset from the center of the room. In line with the cylinder, placing the space betwixt at the very middle of the room, is a table of similar proportions. Runa strolls up to the table and hikes a leg up on it. "Me, I assume," she says, rapping her fingers on the glass surface. Adanon gives her an affirming grin before moving to help Oma open the chamber with a pneumatic hiss. "Things have changed a lot sing my day, but Holfnir is here to help with the particulars," he says, helping ease Oma down into the glowing chamber, "Runa, here. I know in the excitement your position might be the most trying." He tosses a small sachet to her. Her catch lets a fine puff of golden dust suspend in the air. It's powdered goldcap. Runa considers protesting, having flashes of her experience in the mausoleum. Once Oma is entombed in the metallic sarcophagus, Adanon makes his way alongside Runa. "Can you hear us, Oma?" he says, offering a canteen of water to Runa. Oma's voice crackles a confirmation over an unseen speaker. Speaking to Thand, but looking intently at Runa, Adanon says, "Request the bridge make ready for drills." "Kyr," Thand responds, placing her hand on the headset, undersized relative to her proportions. Runa sets the sachet of goldcap on the table and pushes the canteen back toward Adanon. "Don't need it," she says as she lays back. Adanon hums in response. "In a less controlled environment, you may change your mind. Remember, while you're out there let this room ground you. Your mind is the stanchion of consciousness; likewise, this room to the ship," Adanon says as he toggles a switch on the side of the table. Closing her eyes, Runa begins to slip into that meditative state as the table hums to life. Even with her eyes closed, the light coming from behind her is bright enough to color her vision a fleshy red. Taking in measured, purposeful breaths Runa steps outside herself as she has done so often before.

She drifts up through the bulkheads, each one a wash of ice against her incorporeality, until the rays of the sun fill her with warmth. It isn't just warmth, it's a synesthetic dance washing over her senses, conflated in the light of the sun. She is far above the Nurval now, watching as it drifts off to the south. She spins about herself, keeping her eyes on the horizon which is blue upon blue. A voice, Adanon's, says in her mind, "What do you see?" All she need do is think a response. "Everything for mille," she replies. "Good. Come close, you'll want to see this." Her curiosity piqued, Runa closes the distance to the Nurval within the blink of an eye. It is something to behold from her vantage, like glittering fortress of steel borne on the waves. "They are releasing the safeties," Adanon says, a twinge of glee in his voice. Then a multitude of clanking and hissing sounds from the Nurval. At first Runa thinks there has been a malfunction, as the armored plates sag in place after the cacophony. She understands now why the shapes had been so familiar. In synchrony the plates drift away from the hull in fluid motion, seeming to orbit about the ship. It doesn't simply resemble an aster. Runa watches in awe as a ring of sixteen forms a ring about the ship, holding in place at measured intervals. She intuits their purpose. The ring is meant to act as a compass of sorts, but not for observers from the ship, but for Runa. As she thinks to pose a question, a commotion from the stern and bow interrupts her. From within their encasement just below the deck two hulking railguns emerge into the pristine sunlight. They twitch to life, then swing hard to starboard, stopping perpendicular to the path of the ship without any perceptible sway. The cloud of metal around the Nurval clusters on the starboard side, compacting in a wide arc between the muzzles of the weapons. It's a shield. Then the guns roar, belching fury and flame toward the horizon. The entire ship lurches sideways, snapping Runa back to her body in an instant. Adanon stops her from sliding to the table's edge. "Thus, the goldcap," he says with a haughty grin. Runa lets out a nervous chuckle. "Forty-seven thousand Lotte down the drain for that," Turios mutters. That's nearly twice the median pay for a household in Esoptria per shot. Over the next hour several drills are performed, from docking the armor to navigating by the instructions from Runa.

Runa's stomach growls loud enough for all to hear as she returns to her body. "I second that," Adanon says, "chow time." Holfnir chooses to stay behind as everyone else heads for the mess deck. It's peculiar, despite not wearing their praxic jackets, everyone still stands out in their plain clothes amid the throngs of uniformed sailors. Just outside the mess, a melody resonates through the bulkhead as Adanon opens the door for the young praxiats. Upon entering, the music and chorus of sailors falls silent. Toward the center of the room a man holding a curious instrument catches Runa's eye. She knows of them, though she has never seen one in person. It's an iliophone, which is comprised of a biolume display and a crank for tempo control. The man starts the white noise hiss inherent to the instrument before placing his fingers at points on the screen, peaking the frequencies of the static into harmonic tones. Runa falls in line at the food counter just behind Turios. She leans in and says, "You know a lot about this ship?" He gives a noncommittal shrug. "From you, that means yes. I'd like to see the reactor. Can you show me?" Turios sighs as some lumpy green slop is ladled onto his tray. "Sure," he mutters. The music from the sailors reaches a crescendo then comes to an end. After a murmuring silence and the time it takes for the praxiats to take a seat, another melody begins. It begins slow, with sailors beating a chugging rhythm on the tables of the mess hall. Adanon smirks at Runa and says, "You'll like this one."

From the shores of ole Esoptria
to fair Bujani downs
In days of yore, the story of
the man who'd bear the crown
Agrios cut the world in twain
or so the masters say
but not before he 'gan the pain
we suffer still today

Oh, they say we're wrong and their boots make them right
But what do they know of a poor dredger's plight?

Where would they be without you'n'me
who toil and scurry and fuss
for without our ingenuity
their world would fall to dust

Though sting of whip came to end
they claim to save us all
still they take our children,
pride begets the fall

Oh, I say that they're lucky not chosen by rite
But what do they know of a poor dredger's fight?

The crowd erupts in a raucous chorus. "Well, what do you think?" Adanon says, nudging Runa. The song is clearly a scathing take on the fundament of Esoptria and praxiats as a whole. Nevertheless, Adanon seems to have enjoyed the performance. Runa clears her throat. "Well, they are no Kasapna, but there was a certain charm to their performance," she says before scooping the nondescript contents of her tray into her mouth. Thand shakes a spoon in Runa's direction from across the table. "Maybe you can show them how it's done," she says. "My mother was the musician. Best I can do is whistle in tune." Oma rests an arm around Runa's shoulder. "Trust me, we know you can whistle," she says, jostling her friend side-to-side.

CHAPTER 35

Talin sits hunched in the back of cabin of the all-terrain vehicle. At first it had been to keep the power cells warm within the insulated cabin. Now it's to comfort herself away from the judgmental gaze of Ade. She knows he means well, but she can't shake the feeling that they are fleeing when they should be doing something. "Ade, they have Eklin. Darian gloated about it. Saint's eyes—" Talin cuts herself off, "Listen, Zidero is involved in this. We have to get out of Gaerdan." "On that we agree," Ade says, "but I we can't make a trip back through the mountains." Even though it is spring and the melt on the mirelands has begun, they have no supplies. "I get it," Talin says reluctantly as she slumps into the corner, "do you think we are being followed?" Ade rubs the stubble on his head. "I think given the chaos in the city, we are not a priority," he says. Talin pokes at a patch of blistered skin on her forearm and says, "So it's true." She is referencing the coup that deposed the prefect. Things had been tense for a long time in Gaerdan, but the authorities were still loyal to the council and the federation. Now nothing is certain. "How are you feeling?" Ade says, looking back at her. Talin stares off at nothing for a time. She ponders the vital information she must deliver to Esoptria through a hostile territory. The sound of an exhale from over her shoulder startles her out of her ruminations. There is nothing behind her but a bulkhead. The vehicle rocks from side to side on the suspension, and Talin laughs. "I think I need some sleep, real sleep," she says. Ade nods then says, "Rest. We are passing back the way we came, then I'll head for the coast once we are farther south. I'll wake you if there's trouble." Sparing not a moment, Talin slides to the floor and pulls a blanket over herself.

Around five minutes pass before sleep begins to take Talin, but just as she feels herself letting go of consciousness, a voice calls out her name. She lets out a yelp and pulls herself upright. "God on High, you startled me," Ade mutters, looking over his shoulder. Talin pulls herself up into the fore cabin then says, "Stop, stop, stop." Ade looks at her incredulously. The sun has set. The last vestiges of light slip beyond the budding trees as Talin pans the landscape outside. "Kyri, I really think we should—" Talin shushes him. A voice as thin as Oringian silk whispers her name again. "Did you hear that?" Ade makes a concerned face. "You said an opportunity would present itself. Pull off to the right here," Talin says feverishly, "Did we pass this way all those months ago?" "It was near here, looks different in spring. Look, mounding rouge weed," Ade says pointing off the left. Talin climbs over the passenger seat and opens the door. Ade brings the vehicle to a stop just as Talin slides out the door. From outside the cabin distant pops from the northeast, in the direction of Hleifden can still be heard. This can't be a coincidence, Talin tells herself. Ade pulls the vehicle into the tree line, then rests his head on the wheel for a moment before joining Talin. Fengari is nowhere to be seen in the dusk sky, promising an exceedingly dark night. Talin hasn't tread far from where she left the vehicle. She just stands there looking at her feet as Ade approaches. As he moves to speak, she holds a finger to her mouth. "Can you hear them?" she says, shuffling her feet. Ade's confusion only mounts as Talin stoops to pick something from the overgrown foliage. It has been an entire season in the elements, but when she stands upright, she is holding the wood carving she had cast away on that winter evening. "This is witches work, Kyri. Let's go back to the out wheel," Ade says, nervousness tinging his words. The older generations in Bujani are superstitious, but Ade is right to fear this place. Not a sound can be heard save for the sound of their breathing. A smile cuts across Talin's face as the sound of breathing from others unseen joins them. First one, subtle in its mimicry, then two more. "You're right to fear the unknown, Ade," Talin says nodding into the forest, "but I'm the only one at risk here."

The briefest orb of light drifts between trees in the forest, waggling on wings of whimsy. Ade unbuttons the leather loop of his under-arm holster and thumbs off the safety. Talin takes a step toward ephemeral light, motioning for Ade to stop. Again, the light weaves between the trees deeper, illuminating the underbrush and trees with blue-green light. Without hesitation Talin walks in the direction of the light as it vanishes again above a patch of knee-high spline cabbage. Trotting in her ill-fitting boots, the squelching sound of the mireland accompanies her steps. Ade closes the distance between them, a soft prayer lingering on his lips as he brushes against Talin. She hardly registers his presence, as another whisp of light appears several paces away. Then she is off again, chasing the unknown through the dark. The humor isn't lost on her. Whatever is trying to get her attention had tried to do so before. At the time she had been too cautious and proud to let it pique her curiosity. She can't be too harsh on herself. Perhaps she just had to be this close to the grave to hear them beckoning. The deeper she draws into the dark the more she can hear the voices tugging at the corner of her mind. Then, her foot hits something hard as a wisp flickers just a few paces away. The spectral flames light the cracked and crumbling sections of pavement. It appears to be a path leading deeper into the forest, but completely obscured from the view of the road. Years of thaw and freezing have split the manmade structure into a nearly unrecognizable, alien landscape. As Talin steps out on the crumbling walkway, she glances off to her left. As if they had never been, the murmuring voices stop in an instant. Ade clomps out into the clearing breathing heavily. By the time he finds Talin in the darkness, she is heading in the direction of the shadow at the end of the lane. "I hope we can find the way back through this accursed forest," Ade says in a whisper. Talin glances sidelong at him and says, "The veil is thin here. I'll understand if you want to wait in the out wheel." Ade groans and pulls out a glim to light the path.

After following the broken road for several minutes, the area opens somewhat. Instead of trees in the clearing, small mounding rouge weed have reclaimed where the trees have not. As they step into the clearing, the glim lighting their way dims and dies. Just visible through the gloom is the chaotic outline of a toppled building. Beams and slabs of stone jut at odd angles from the marshy courtyard. Talin exhales, her breath condensing in the unnaturally cold air. She and Ade watch as the cloud of warm moisture paradoxically drops and pools on the ground. "Talin, please," Ade says, alarmed. Disregarding him, Talin presses forward, sure this is what she is meant to see. "What's happening? What was this place?" Ade says. Circling the structure Talin surmises this was once a cenobium based on the layout of the courtyard and what little structure still remains. There are several dotted across Gaerdan, but she finds it peculiar that she doesn't know this place. Regardless of its current state, something terrible must have happened here to wear the veil so thin. "It was a cenobium. I need to get inside," she says. As they round the far end of the structure they stumble across a basement entrance marred with the telltale signs of fire. By some stroke of luck, Fengari begins to show her face over the trees, giving them a minute amount of light. Ade mutters another prayer and wrenches open the brittle door. Talin slinks down the steps which end in dark, foreboding water. Ade tests the depth with a broken piece of the door. "Quarter pace and melt water. It's freezing," he says. Talin nods. "We'll have to be quick then," she says as she splashes into the ankle-deep water. Nothing can be seen in the darkness save for the nearby ripples. Talin motions for the glim, which Ade relinquishes gladly. Despite her efforts to get the light working, Talin gives up As Ade splashes into the water and lights a small lighter. "Will have to do," Talin admits as they press on.

Ade hadn't been exaggerating, the water is freezing. As if they didn't have enough to contend with, now frostbite is a concern. They move deeper into the basement, Ade holding the lighter out to inspect objects, desks, the walls, some equipment clearly covered in a layer of soot. There had been a fire, but surely Talin would have heard about a cenobium burning. In the far corner the weight of the building above has buckled the ceiling precariously. They give the area a wide berth, breaking the silence with their splashing footfall. Machinery is strewn about carts and desks. Talin runs a hand along one of the warped contraptions. "Does this look like medical equipment?" she whispers, to which Ade grunts in agreement. As she follows just behind Ade, she says, "I don't know why—" Ade stops dead in his tracks. Peering around him, she sees why. A mist undulates at chest level near a hallway that connects to the rest of the basement. Before Talin can react, the mist disperses as if reacting to their presence. No longer whispering, Ade recites another prayer as Talin maneuvers past him to where the mist had been. "This way," she says, passing out of the light of the single flame. The passage slopes down. It isn't a hallway, it's a staircase. The cracked door frame of the next room can be seen just above the waterline. "No," Ade says, but Talin removes the light jacket and takes several nerve-steeling breaths. Then she plunges into the frigid water. Being unable to see, she feels around the space beyond the door. It appears that a slab of the ceiling has collapsed against the door, partially or entirely blocking the passage, she can't tell. Talin resurfaces, trying to calm the involuntary shivering. "I don't think you'd fit anyway, Ade. Give me the cell for this," she says tabbing where his coilgun is under his arm. Ade hesitates, but nods seeing the determination in her eyes. Then, taking the power cell from the weapon and unsheathing his blade, he hands them to her. "If there's no way through, you'll know pretty quick," she says, tearing a sleeve off her discarded jacket. She dunks the fabric in the water, ensuring it is sufficiently wet, then wraps it around the cell. Then, pressing the cell against the wall and brandishing Ade's ceremonial blade, she pauses. Ade says, "You'll only have a few minutes of light." Talin punctures the top of the cell, filling the space with a blinding blue-white flash. Once exposed to atmosphere the matrix within the cell will burn until only magnetic slag remains. For how long, Talin can only guess as the technology isn't meant to be used this way. She dives back into the water holding the cyan flare. Even submerged in water the jet of fury persists, giving ample light as she pulls herself down under the slab of broken concrete. She wiggles through the space, kicking up particulate into the icy water.

Surfacing on the other side, Talin sees the collapsed parts of the structure. What she had been under gives her pause. The brunt of the collapsed building rests as a mountain of stones and broken bent steel near the opening she had passed through. It's a wonder that the whole structure hasn't collapsed. Talin carefully treads away from the chaotic mound knowing her time is short. She takes another breath, diving into the murky unknown. The burning power cell helps, but the water is cloudy with debris. She passes more rusted machinery, then as she surfaces again, she sees something that gives her pause. Steel cages, stacked to the ceiling all along both walls. They are bolted into the ceiling and look terribly sturdy. She ponders if they are the reason this entire room hasn't been crushed. Back into the water and she makes her way along the bottom scanning for anything that can clue her in to what happened here. Then she feels it. All the air is forced out of her lungs in an excitement as she feels familiar shapes, bones. It isn't a small pile either. She rummages through until she finds a skull and her suspicions are confirmed, these were people. She has what she needs. Through praxis she can see the lingering vestiges of this person. By experiencing their last moments she can hopefully understand what happened here. The radiant flame in her hand sputters once, striking her with primal fear of dying alone in the dark. She swims in a panic back the way she came, still clutching the skull and makeshift flare. Once near the piled rubble, she dives under the surface scrabbling to pull herself through the narrow opening near the floor. Her light flickers again. In her haste she pushes the skull ahead, needing her hand for purchase on the jagged debris. As she pulls herself through the crush, her pantleg catches on something. Had these unfortunate souls sought to bring her here to join them in their grave? Talin drops the flare ahead and yanks at her pants trying to free herself, but her last gasp of air is running out. The light flickers once more then dies, leaving her in the inky black. Everything is cold. Maybe it would be easier just to stop fighting. She had been nothing but a burden for so long. So scared that seeing others suffer brough her a modicum of peace. She has changed though. She acknowledges the wrongs, is that not enough? No, surviving isn't enough if the cost is her humanity. Talin lets out her last breath and kicks off her ill-fitting boots, wriggling against the wet fabric of her pants. Whatever has snagged her pants scrapes at her flesh as she yanks free of her would be tomb. With her lungs screaming for air, she kicks for the surface.

After a lingering moment of glorious breath, she finds the skull and joins Ade. She strips off the wet clothing as her knees begin to give out. She feels hot. She knows what is happening but can't help herself. "You are far braver than I, Kyri," Ade says, as he wraps his large jacket around her. Then he stoops to scoop her into his arms, then makes for the exit. Through the uncontrollable shaking, Talin never takes her eye off the skull she had risked her life for. Even when her senses somewhat return, she can't seem to do what she has done countless times before. Where there are always remnants of a person's last moments, she finds none. Somehow, whatever happened to this person has removed any vestiges of their consciousness. That should be impossible. "Thank you, Ade," Talin whispers as they make their way through the forest. "You would do the same," he says, giving her an affirming squeeze. She smiles but isn't so sure that she would. After a silence, Ade says, "Did you learn anything?" Talin drops the skull unceremoniously. "Say an extra prayer for those in that tomb. The dead have never been so quiet. It's as if their souls were stripped away before they died."

CHAPTER 36

    Runa dreams of her family. They sit around the table aboard the Shyena discussing the events of the day when she notices an unsettling detail. Though they are looking at each other, they have no eyes. Taut canvases of flesh cover the spaces that would be their eyes. Nevertheless, they turn to each other as they speak, seeming not to notice their impairment. Someone calls out her name, making her turn. In the time it takes for her to turn back to her family, their faces are gone. The same featureless flesh covers their faces. Runa cries out as she rises to her feet. She wills herself to wake up. But wake she does not. A voice calls her name again. She turns, no longer aboard the Shyena. She is surrounded by a void of glittering darkness. A slender figure steps out of the darkness. It is a young woman with straight, black hair which hangs down past her hips. Her skin is darker than Runa's, like a cup of xahuatl with a kiss of cream, but patches of her flesh are white. Her face is fixed in a smile, but her discerning gaze is unsettling. The nameless woman holds out her hand to Runa and says, "I look forward to meeting you again," then a scream draws Runa awake.

    A man's voice cries out aboard the Nurval. Runa can hear his words clearly through the bulkheads. "She's here! She's here! Saints save me!" the man screams. "What in the world?" Oma says climbing out of her cot. She and Runa make for the hatch to their quarters in time to see Adanon entering the opposite room. He must have been sleeping in the praxic nerve center which they have come to call The Stanchion. The curious young women follow him into the open hatch to see Holfnir flailing on the bottom berth. His eyes are wide, highly dilated, and erratic in their motion. Adanon pushes Turios aside and firmly grabs Holfnir by his nightshirt. "Calm! Be calm," he half-shouts. In his thrashing Holfnir strikes Adanon in the face. Without hesitation Adanon clasps the manic praxiat by the face. The biolume fixture in the quarters flickers out as pressure surges within the room. Then Holfnir falls still with Adanon crouched precariously over him. "Rest easy now," he whispers, as he stands. It is only then that Runa notices his relative state of undress. His bare back in a mass of lean muscle, pocked with curious scars. Runa catches herself staring at the two mirrored hypertrophic scars at his midback, just below his ribs. He turns to see Runa and Oma watching from the hatch. "Is he?" Oma says, still looking at Holfnir. Adanon furrows his brow at the implication. Then Holfnir draws in a blubbering snore, cutting through the tension in the room. All the young praxiats let out a sigh of relief. Adanon motions with his head for all to exit. After the hatch is closed, he says, "I don't want to see any of you compel someone like that. Do you hear me?" "Yes, Kyr," the young praxiats says in unison. "Good, now I need a cup of 'hot," he says turning to go. Runa interjects, "Kyr, do you have a moment to talk?"

Sometime after their morning routines, Adanon pulls Runa way to the deck of the ship. "What did you want to talk about?" he says as they slowly make their way astern. Runa walks along beside him watching the seabirds frolicking to the east. "I just have some concerns. My dreams these past few weeks have been strange and Holfnir's episode this morning... But If I'm being honest, what I really want to say is: I feel like I'm failing." They reach the aftmost deck. Adanon peers over the railing trying to catch a glimpse of the toroidal propellers amidst the churn. "Show me," he says, still looking over the edge. Runa reluctantly pulls out the aster and knits her brow. Despite her intense focus the aster simply falls apart in her hand, scattering several pieces on the deck. Adanon shrugs, places his hand over the aster and recalls the pieces gently to Runa's hand. With a smile he says, "I don't think you have anything to worry about." Runa bristles somewhat, quickly placing the aster back in her coat. "How can you say that? The others are much better at it. You see how easy Oma makes it look," she says, gesturing to a nearby armor plate. Adanon leans back against the railing. "Potential is tricky. Think of it as material for a boat." he says, gesturing as he speaks, " So, you shouldn't concern yourself with skiffs when you're building a frigate." Runa leans on the railing as she looks sidelong at Adanon. Then she smiles. At times he knows just what to say. A blast from the horn from the Sophir, their missile cruiser escort, causes them to turn toward the bow of the Nurval. "Land," Adanon says cheerfully. Runa shudders as the Nurval returns a blast that reverberates in her chest. She can't shake the feeling that she is crossing an unseen threshold as they draw closer to Uxkukul.

The praxiats gather in the stanchion as they have done every morning. "Holfnir, I want you to stay aboard the Nurval," Adanon says, rubbing his hands behind his back. Holfnir lets out a deep sigh of relief. "Speak and I listen," he says. Adanon nods then continues, "The rest of you, leave your coats, pack light, and keep your heads down- Turios, how is your Uxian?" Turios adjusts his glasses. "I think it's passable," he replies in Uxian. "Leaves something to be desired," Adanon replies, placing a hand over his mouth as he speaks "See, tonality is different with your mouth covered. Uxian has a unique post-labial fricative on account of the masks." He demonstrates the sounds several times, repeating where Turios had been mistaken. Runa is fascinated by the peculiar popping and hissing sounds unlike any other languages she has heard. "That settles who's doing the talking. Let's get moving, we are nearing the delta," Adanon says. Sometime later, after packing and sorting through clothing, Runa saunters up to the deck with her pack in tow. The open sea has given way to brilliant turquoise waters teaming with life. Off to the east, small islands of dense jungle spill onto white sand beaches. It's a drastic change from the swamps of Esoptria. Even though she had been this way on the yearly migration in the Flotilla, staying far out to sea had always been a priority. The color of the water reminds her of Apudar Anchorage, and for the recurrent homesick feeling rears its head again. In the spare moments since they left Esoptria, she has thought about them more and more. She knows that her parents did the best that they could given the circumstances. But that doesn't blunt her malignant anger toward the elders. She brushes aside her thoughts of family as the costal jungles come into focus. After a time the untamed wilds cede to the formulaic lines of human agriculture. Endless rows of rubber trees flicker against the misty backdrop of the breathing jungle and it is unlike anything Runa has ever seen. She can make out the figures moving from tree to tree, presumably harvesting the rubbery sap. The fields end abruptly in haphazard rusted shacks on the outskirts of a settlement. Oma joins Runa just as the buildings of the port town emerge from behind the hovel town that forms a crude wall. Most of it is unremarkable, a sore Esoptrian thumbprint on a beleaguered foreign land. What is remarkable and cause for Runa's concern are the numerous Esoptrian warships moored along the port. She glances down at the water. Without her noticing the water has gone from clear to silt-laden brown. "Why does this place feel so familiar?"

she says to Oma as she adjusts her pack straps. Placing her arm around her friend, she says, "I can't say. But if Adanon's stories are true, it should put many things in perspective." The sound of thunderous chain clatter from the anchor being dropped stirs the friends from their brief conversation.

Gathering at the rear of the ship the praxiats watch as the amphibious vehicle known as an out wheel approaches from the shore. "That would be your ride," the Commander says, shuffling up behind them, "Can't say I'll miss any of you." Adanon laughs, watching the transport bob on the waves instead of meeting the man's eye. "If things come to blows, you'd prefer we were here. Plus, Holfnir will keep you company while we're gone." Commander Lamphros produces the spare end of a burnt cigar then lights it. Runa glances around, unsure of what to do as the two men openly antagonize each other. The large floating vehicle butts up against the port quarter of the Nurval as crewmen secure the lines and ladder. Taking the initiative, Thand is the first to head down to the metallic monstrosity. "Ah, yes the even more eccentric eccentric. Can't promise the crew will be kind in your absence," Lamphros says, tilting back his head and exhaling smoke. "You might not be able to, but I keep my promises," Adanon says, resting his hand on Runa's shoulder before she moves to disembark. She looks back to Adanon and Lamphros before entering the top hatch. She knows Adanon can handle himself. His safety isn't her concern. Lamphros lets out a derisive chuckle then says, "No, no promises in the navy, only oaths. How can you expect discipline from these children when you are so lax?" He takes a long puff from his cigar, "Then again, I think perhaps you're where you belong. To my mind you're a child that never grew up." "I'm flattered you think of me, Commander, but I don't think of you at all," Adanon says as he climbs down the ladder to the roof of the out wheel. Lamphros scowls and flicks what's left of his cigar at him. Though he is balancing on the bobbing vehicle, Adanon catches the burning cigar. With a grin, he clenches his hand around the embers. A moment later he opens his hand to show a plume of black smoke. Then he wipes the soot on the drab gray hatch cover and closes it behind him.

CHAPTER 37

The acolytes within the out wheel sit in silence, save for the occasional gasp from Oma. The rocking of the transport is having some adverse effects on her. "Press here," Runa says, taking Oma's wrist and pressing firmly into her flesh a handsbreadth up. Though unintentional, she sees a memory that Oma uses to calm herself. It's of a homestead somewhere in Bujani. All around, the punchy scent of pepper sorghum warming under the summer sun fills her senses. Spliced with the calming scents are memories of her playing among the frolicking alabaster grains atop the current of green. Oma exchanges a glance with Runa. "It's a nice memory," Runa admits in a whisper to her friend. Without warning the out wheel hits the sandy shore with a jolt, shocking even Adanon. "These seats need more cushion if the rest of the ride is like this," he says to the pilot. The gruff looking man glances back but offers no response. He looks to be twenty years Adanon's junior but is already showing gray about his temples and chin in his well kempt beard. Turios shifts in his seat, leaning in toward Adanon. "Kyr, we haven't been briefed," he says, almost apologetic. "Right, slipped my mind with the morning's activities. We are to be guests at the Medon's estate, then tomorrow, we'll set off into jungle to reach the grave of stars, the Gibbous City, where I'll meet with the queen to discuss trifles," Adanon says, rubbing his beard. "Trifles?" "Medon?" Turios and Runa says at the same time. Adanon turns to Runa. "Medon is the man's name, but it has become synonymous with his title. The territory around New Astoraph isn't an Esoptrian prefecture, so Uxians have no representation on the council. Medon has been the interim governor of Ux for decades in place of a Prefect." "Until what time?" Turios says. Adanon throws up his hands and shrugs. "I can't see anything," Runa says, standing up and opening the hatch. She then pulls herself up onto the roof. She braces against the railing but avoids touching the metal with her bare flesh, as the equatorial sun has heated it to an unbearable temperature. To Runa's right the wall of sheet metal shacks blocks her view of the city proper. All that can be seen are the few tall Esoptrian style buildings and railgun batteries facing in every direction. "Does the Medon not live in the city?" Runa says, sticking her face near the hatch. As she rotates to the other side of the road, she catches sight of the women and children working in the cultivates grove. Some of the young women cutting at the bark of the young trees have swaddled babies on their backs. "The Medon lives in compound on the banks of the river. We are heading there now," The driver shouts. Thand also climbs onto the roof, giving an approving nod to Runa, but only frowns. "It's their way of life," Thand says, "It's not ideal, but neither is a Kasapna having to spend a few days aboard the Belly Ship after visiting a patron." Runa cocks a brow at her, wondering how Thand knows about the Belly Ship. "Aye," she says, lost in thought about this strange place she finds herself. Even as they women and children are toiling in the field; they have masks over their mouths obscuring their features. "I know we talked about it at Pa's place but it's my first time seeing it. They are striking," Runa says. Striking is hyperbole, or kindness. The masks themselves are plain in design but their execution is what Runa finds remarkable. "It must be important to them to work in this heat like that," Thand remarks, turning to look ahead of the out wheel. In the distance the red clay road, which is pitted and cracked like reptilian skin, slithers past and away from the plantations toward the fog laden jungle.

The crenelations of the compound, the driver's word, had been visible from over the horizon a few mille away. Runa wipes the sweat from her brow. She wouldn't call it a 'compound.' To her mind it is a storybook castle, complete with battlements, portcullis, and drawbridge. The stone of the construction is coarse and unsettlingly dark. As they draw nearer Runa tucks back into the cabin. It is shockingly cool inside. "You have to see this," she says, pulling Oma by the arm. "I really wouldn't—" the driver says as everyone climbs atop the moving transport. Even Adanon pokes his head out. The clay road ends in a bridge made of the same pitted, black stone. Runa makes an uneasy face at Oma, not trying to hide her feelings about this place. From their vantage atop the vehicle the banks of a river can be seen feeding the moat. Runa would think the land on the other side is an island if she didn't know better. They come to a stop on the bridge, seeming to wait for the drawbridge to be lowered. The heat is unbearable now that they have come to a stop, so Runa climbs down the few rungs of a ladder on the side then hops to the ground. Despite seeing people moving about through the crenelations above, the bridge doesn't lower. The driver of the vehicle begins blasting an ear-piercing horn. After several minutes of the acolytes standing in the shade of the machine the bridge drops. With a number of choice words, the driver pulls the out wheel into the courtyard with Runa and company in tow.

The driver storms out, shouting for the guard in charge. A young man, a boy really, comes down to face the blustery man. Before even saying anything, he strikes the Uxian boy across the face, breaking the clay mask and bearing him to the ground. "Don't ever make me or guests wait like that again," he shouts at the cowering child. The boy gathers the pieces of the mask and covers his mouth before skittering away from the gazes of everyone. "He was probably just being cautious," Runa whispers to Oma, "We are an odd-looking group." The others nod with varying degrees of agreement. Runa looks to Adanon who has made his way over after the confrontation. He says nothing, only resting his hands on his waist as the driver joins him. Runa doesn't know what she expected him to do, but his doing nothing is more unnerving. The driver introduces himself formerly as Mithragen, the overseer of the Medon's estate. The man is very proud of this place, telling small details as the group travels from the courtyard to the hall proper. Every stone used to construct this place had been shipped from Esoptria. Falling behind, Runa runs her hand along the rough masonry, opening herself just enough to feel. She recoils, sensing what she had already known: this place is a palace of despair.

"Runa," Adanon says, stirring her from praxic ruminations. "Aye," she says, not sure what he said. "Forgive me saying so, you all look worse for wear. The servants will help you clean up for the party," Mithragen says, glancing sideways at the acolytes. Up until this point he has only spoken to Adanon. Runa finds him truly irksome, even more so than the Commander of the Nurval. The graying Esoptrian snaps his fingers then a dozen servants slink from around corners. With three to each acolyte they are ushered away through the unfamiliar halls. Roughly and in silently the attending women undress Runa. One draws a bath in the stately room as another appears to be taking her measurements. It is almost degrading, but the women's lack of banter blunts the awkwardness. Runa imagines if they were whispering in their native tongue she would be much more out of sorts. A perturbed shout, from Thand can be heard from a nearby room. The thought of her enduring the same invasive routine brings a smile to Runa's face. After nearly an hour of forceful scrubbing, plucking of hair, and applying of salves, she is left alone in only a towel. Checking the door on the other side of the room, she sees that this is some sort of receiving room to a larger bathhouse. She strolls out into the Esoptrian style bath to see Thand and Oma kicking their feet on the edge of the steaming pool. "That was certainly something," Oma admits as she slips into the water. They spend quite some time lounging there in the water until their fingers and toes wrinkle. All the while they chat about offhand observations about the place. But Runa's mind is elsewhere. Sharing that memory with Oma makes her think of all the other times she has glimpsed raw moments of emotion from others. Oma's mindfulness, to shift her thoughts toward something pleasant has inspired Runa. She thinks perhaps she needs such a memory for herself. The sisters notice her uncharacteristic silence. "What's the matter?" Oma says. Runa gives a noncommittal shrug then says, "Thinking about memories. I've gotten past my anger but now thoughts of home are tinged with far of the unknown. Is my family safe? Were they among the ships sunk in the blockade?" Oma scoots closer. "We're no strangers to tragedy, Runa, as I know you've seen. If I can think of home without thinking of fire, you can think of home without thinking of loss," she says, with a nod of approval from Thand. Runa hears her and begins to respond but is interrupted by Turios angerly barging into the bath. "Leave me be!" he says, shutting the door behind him. Runa reactively sinks to her chin in the water. They may have been roommates, but this is different. Oma darkens, either out of embarrassment or anger but says nothing. Turios strolls over wearing an unusual suit of satiny black, trimmed in silver and embroidered with colorful stars of magenta, gold, and sky blue. "Not a word. It was the only clothing in my room. I assumed they wanted me to wear it," he says. Then he seems to notice the women's state of undress and turns a deep red. "I didn't see anything," he blurts as he turns away, "There is probably similar dress for you in your rooms." Without waiting for a response, he speedily makes an exit.

An hour later and much more invasion of privacy later, Runa is done up to an excessive degree. She looks herself over in the full-length mirror in her room. Her hair was braided halfway back in an up-do and teased into a mane of loose curls. Her eyes are covered in a deep shadow of malachite makeup. And she is squeezed into a dress of the same fashion as Turios. Except, it has detached puffs of black lace which pretend to be sleeves and cinches tightly around her belly before flaring into a long bell-shaped skirt. Runa tests the security of the strapless top and makes her way out of the room.

As she exits, she spots Adanon. When he notices her, his face contorts in confusion before walking over. "Take it off," he says, gesturing at the dress. "Why? It's beautiful," Runa snaps back. Adanon pulls her aside and says softly, "Because it's a traditional Uxian dress. Where did you find it?" "It was left for us," Runa says as she fidgets with the folds of the skirt. Adanon pinches the bridge of his nose and sighs. "It's Uxian. This gala is for Esoptrian dignitaries. This," he flicks the puff of fabric around her arm, "is an insult. Implying we are servants. And if I know anything about the Medon, it's intentional." Runa looks at him incredulously. He means well but seems to have forgotten that she knows much about being underestimated. "I'll wear it anyway," she says with a smile. Adanon leans against the wall, tapping a finger against his mouth for a moment. Then he straightens and walks past her. "Never change," he says with a smirk that she cannot see.

Later, when the sun has grown low and the guests have begun to arrive, Runa and the others find themselves standing against the wall in a grand hall. Servants scurry here and there within the grand room festooned in wine colored drapery. It is the picture of opulence, and it reminds Runa of her time at the Lykios estate Throughout the area are showcases of artwork and relics from times and places she has never seen. Near where they settled, she finds herself fixated on a glittering tree-like sculpture. She reads aloud the caption placarded to the display, "Memories of Shwari. Natural glass sculpture procured from the Fields of Vitrescence. Lent by Zidero Lykios." How something so delicate had been transported these thousands of mille is a point of wonderment for her. "Looks like Adanon was right, look at that," Turios say, nodding to the gathering crowd of people wearing white. The men and the women are draped in similar loose folds of pale linen which fall about their ankles. It's a traditional Esoptrian festive garb often paired with wine festivals. The intent is for the clothing to be ruined throughout the revelry. "Turios," Runa says, "An insult is only as effective as your reaction to it. This was a jape and nothing more." Thand grumbles in agreement. She is clearly uncomfortable in the dress. Her broad shoulders and back make for an almost comical. "Your hair looks nice," Runa says to Thand, coaxing a smile from her. "And they didn't mutilate my scalp," she says in a clear jab at her sister. Both have their hair done up in locs with beads of matching colors to the dress which hang at the neck and part down the middle. Just as they are beginning to settle into the festivities the crowd falls silent as a train of individuals parades in. Runa's curiosity gets the better of her as she pushes toward the alley formed through the center of the room. Reluctantly, the other praxiats follow. Runa need not push her way through. Curious and awkward looks from revelers precede making way for the oddly dressed acolytes. She can see Mithragen walking near another man wearing an ill-fitting suit of cream. Heading the procession is a large animal held on a leash by the suited man. At the shoulder it stands a pace and a half high, has stark white fur with a gray undercoat that shows through as it approaches. The creature is noticeably overfed, its belly hanging halfway to the ground. Runa turns to Turios with a quizzical look. "Treehound," he whispers, as the rotund man greets guests halfway down the procession. Runa reasons that this must be the Medon. "It looks unwell," she says to the others. Turios knits his brow, "Leave it be, Runa. It's not worth agitating this man." Thand lets out a grunt of irritation and elbows him. "Woe betide he who has the power to defend God's creation but chooses not to," she says through her teeth. Medon and his entourage are drawing nearer. "Leave it be, I'm begging you, Runa," Turios says just as the treehound comes up sniffing some of the guests a few paces away. "It's not about that. You can tell a lot about someone by how they treat animals. I'll only respond in kind," Runa whispers. "That's what I'm worried about," Turios says, before slinking back behind Thand. The Medon jerks at the leash of the beast causing it to lie on the floor a few paces from Runa. The red-faced, corpulent man tips his nose up at the praxiats as he takes a few steps toward them. "Ah, my most distinguished guests," he says, looking down at Runa. She returns a slight bow. "It's interesting to me. I see you here, without your coats and your masters. You take them away, and what are you?" Medon says with a smile. Without hesitation Runa replies, "An envoy, a praxiat, and a daughter of the wind and waves. The clothes don't make the person, Kyr, but thank you for lending us these dresses." Medon hands off the leash of the animal to Mithragen and shoes him away. "I know how little acolytes have to call their own. They were a gift, not lent," he says. "Aye, unlike many of your treasures here. I'll be sure to return it in the same spirit it was given," Runa says with a wry smile. Medon lets out a dry and humorless chortle. Regardless, many of the guests join him. "I see what they say is true, you can take the Janny out of the brine but you can't take the brine out of the Janny," he retorts. Runa places her hands on her hips and snickers. "It must be true. You're the only tenth person to make that joke since I came to Esoptria," she says. The Medon turns a violent shade of purple. Just then, Adanon appears from behind him, placing an arm around Runa. "Sorry I'm late. Last minute alterations," he says, running his hand along a suit that matches the other praxiats. Medon's demeanor changes completely. He almost appears to smile genuinely. "Akroates," he says with a flourish, "Enjoy the festivities." Adanon bows courteously. As the Medon plods away he says, "Quite the mouth on that one," to no one in particular.

"What did I miss?" Adanon whispers to Runa. Oma pops up, saying, "Oh, Runa exchanging insults with the fat man." Adanon blanches, glancing at Runa with concern. "Oh no, Runa held her own," Oma adds. "Aye, I learned a few things around Zidero," Runa says with a shrug, "What is that?" She points to a troupe of cloaked people entering the stage which runs along the opposing wall. A swell of music fills the chamber as the biolume dims, casting the area in darkness. Oma bounces giddily. "Scar dancers," she half-whispers clapping her hands in excitement. The barely visible figures on the stage turn their backs to the crowd, then as the music transitions to a soft and pensive piece they drop their cloaks to the stage. To the rhythm of the music, they begin to move, first with subtle gestures, then with more intensity as the music builds. It's not their dancing that affects Runa so. With each step, biolume pulses under their skin in a luminous spectacle. In synchrony, the shifting colors trace mysterious patterns along their bodies. Runa is transfixed by the otherworldly display. Too soon the show comes to an end with a round of applause. Then the lights rise and servants weave in and out of the crowd with libations. It's only then that Runa notices Adanon has slipped off somewhere. An Uxian busser walks by with a platter of overfilled wine glasses. Runa grabs two and turns to Oma, saying, "When in Ux."

The festivities drag on into the night. Runa's favorite event besides the scar dancers is a traditional drinking and gambling game from Esoptria. It revolves around an octagonal table with an oversized goblet affixed at the center of the table. Within the goblet is a hollow tube which acts as a siphon. Each player takes turns tossing wine into the bowl until the point that it reaches the top of the post. Whoever makes the toss that sends the contents splattering about the feet of the players wins. It's a ludicrous and wasteful game, but Runa finds herself enjoying the competitive and addictive nature of it. It is nearing midnight when Runa looks down at the wager pot filled with various odds and ends that she finds herself without anything else to bet. All the Lote are clumped together in a mass before Turios. He pushes up his glasses on his face flushed from drink. "You're done. You have nothing to wager," he says. Ebikos is a curious game with a social contract that accepts anything the players find of value. Throughout the evening

Runa has watched patrons wager anything from a ring around their finger to a deed to villa. "What about a kiss from a Kasapna's daughter?" she says, glancing at the croupier. She is sure this toss with trip the table. The croupier looks to Turios and the middle-aged woman still in the pot. The woman bows out, but Turios accepts with a smug grin. Then Runa lobs the contents of her cup into the bowl. For a few moments, the contents slosh about, licking the side of the central post. Holding her breath, Runa looks at Turios' cheeky expression. But the splatter of wine about her feet heralds her victory.

CHAPTER 38

Runa's hands ache. It's so very familiar, this place. She looks down in the basin, the water streaked with scarlet. The crimson won't come off as she scrubs as the dark ichor staining the edges of her nails. Then, as she gazes in the mirror above the sink, she sees a face that is not her own. It's the young man with eyes of emerald green. His face is placid, unfeeling. A stark accompaniment with the mechanical, repetitive motions of washing. But a voice from the nearby door draws her attention. It's Adanon. Not the Adanon she knows. He's so very young and full of concern. He grabs ahold of her and shouts something she doesn't comprehend.

Runa comes to her senses. Turios is standing where Adanon had been in the dream. "Are you alright? I heard the water running from my room," he says. Runa looks to her shaking hands. "I don't know. Was I sleepwalking?" she says, turning off the faucet. "Seems like it. It's pretty common for some folks in unfamiliar places." Runa sits on the edge of the ornate bathtub. "Aye... it wasn't a dream though. It was like a memory," she says still looking at her hands. Turios leans against the door frame and says, "I think you should talk to Adanon about it." "Aye," she replies as he turns to go. After a few moments Runa drags herself through the room, looking toward the tattered dress in the corner. The fringe of the skirt is torn and stained. She cracks a sly smile. She hadn't been lying about how it would be returned. They are to set off into the jungle today. Parts of her wish she had considered that more last night as she dresses in beige and green trekking clothes with black boots.

Runa drops her pack in the courtyard that terminates in terraces which kiss the banks of the mighty river. The Seprinos, so named by Esoptrians for its yellow hued waters, is the largest river in the world. It carries as much fresh water to the shallow sea as the next six largest rivers combined. This isn't what the natives of this land called the river. 'Yatlrin,' the Uxian word for water, hadn't been categorical enough for this land's colonizers.

Runa marvels at the surging current in the yellow-pink light of the stratified sunrise as the others gather on the highest terrace. "We have to cross that?" Turios says, already beading with sweat. Adanon pats him on the shoulder, but as he begins to speak Mithragen strolls up. "Afraid of getting wet, boy?" he says, tipping his brimmed leather hat. There is a collective groan. "Are you our guide?" Runa says, incredulous. The smug man snaps and whistles, a native Uxian boy shambles over, shoulders arched in discomfort. The boy is wearing little but hempen trousers, soft rubber shoes and his Uxian mask. "Nah, you need an introduction at the Gibbous City. I'm coming along to make sure this one doesn't run off," Mithragen says, pushing the boy. "And what's his name?" Adanon asks. Mithragen thinks for a moment before saying, "Oti." Adanon sighs, knowing that isn't the boy's name, but the Uxian word for a ceramic pot. After some time inspecting their supplies, the unlikely crew set off through a gate and along the south shore of the river.

An easy five mille of walking later, a pylon bridge spanning the Seprinos comes into view. It appears to Runa to be a magrail bridge but the tracks are incomplete on this bank. Turios remarks how there have been setbacks in the construction of the system. Given the state of corrosion on the access staircase, Runa would think that this has been here for decades. As they reach the top and begin crossing the perfect squares of rare-earth magnets, Oti protests. Adanon is the last to ascend the stairs, pausing for a moment to regain his breath. Oti grows more insistent prompting Runa to ask, "What is he saying?" Mithragen produces a leather crop from his belt then strikes the child. "Just superstitious nonsense- Oti, they are praxiats," he gestures to the group with the crop, "there is nothing to fear in that jungle." Oti's eyes jump between the praxiats as he mutters something in Uxian. Mithragen chuckles as he turns. "That's right, 'The eyes of the jungle see well the hands of the gods.' Now move." The boy moves but periodically looks back to meet Runa's gaze. The pace of traversal slows considerably beyond the northern bank. In places the Jungle has reclaimed the tracks but there are pockets of small saplings which offer little resistance to Mithragen's armlength clearing blade. After several hours, as the sun grows dim beyond the imposing canopy, everyone unpacks for a long night in the steamy, bug-infested jungle.

The group sets up simple lean-tos just off the tracks with the last bit of light. "Oti, go get firewood," Mithragen commands the boy. Runa hops up from the moss covered stone on which she had been resting, saying, "I'll help." The short medium complected boy treks out into the jungle heedless of Runa in his wake. Runa soon find that there isn't much dry wood but the child has bundle under his arm before she has two or three rotted sticks. Before moving back toward the makeshift encampment, Runa drops into a squat, meeting Oti's eye. She covers her mouth and says, "Why do you choose to stay? To help them?" The boy looks at her curiously. In broken Esopt, he intones, "Why do you?" as he pinches a bit of the skin of her forearm. His intent is clear. Runa is unlike Esoptrian this boy has ever seen, but she is still an acolyte, a servant to the council. Runa nods slowly. "I don't like how they treat you all the same," she says. Oti simply pushes past her in the direction of the camp.

After a bit of banter around the meager fire, Runa tucks into her sleeping bag and slips into a deep dreamless slumber. The following morning, she is awakened by droplets of rain hitting her face. They set off again after a breakfast of sundries and roasted xahuatl. Despite herself, Runa is in good spirits. Everyone is particularly chatty on account of the caffeine. Turios regales everyone with tales from Ux during the war but is sensitive to the fact that Oti is near. Many of the stories revolve around bravery and sacrifice of Esoptrian forces throughout the conflict. Several times Runa catches him looking back at Adanon, who has been quiet. "And so, the somnial division proved itself a vital part of the war effort. Can you imagine the psychological impact on an army being unable to sleep for weeks on end? Pure chaos," Turios ends a particularly harrowing tale. Adanon lets out a chuckle. The terrain has become more uneven, and the magrail tracks ended several mille back. In the late afternoon it begins to rain, bringing their travel to an end for the day as they seek shelter. Despite being unable to start a fire, Mithragen sets up an infrared heater for everyone to congregate around in the crook of a massive tree with thorny bark. Runa marvels at the tree in silence. Not even ten men could encircle the tree with their arms. In reddish glow of the heater, she turns to Oma. "Give us a story," she says with a pat on her leg. Oma shakes her head, saying, "I think it's your turn." Runa slumps back against the trunk of the tree. Adanon pulls out a canteen and takes a grimacing swig, making clear that it isn't water. "What about an allegory?" Runa says. Mithragen groans and rolls over, appearing to sleep. "Aye, an allegory of the man and the grain of sand. There was a man who returned to his ship and his family after a salvage on the bottom. He washed away the salt and the sand, but still a grain remained on the sole of his foot. Now the man carried about his day, piloting his ship along. Later, when he least expected it, winds caught the sand, driving it up and finding its way into the shipfather's eye. It was painful and blinding, leading the ship off course." "Wait, what's the point? Sand hurts if it gets in your eyes?" Turios says. "It's not about sand, Turios," Oma says, "It's about the power of the seemingly insignificant." Thand chimes in, saying, "Same applies to praxis. Adanon hasn't told a story yet." Everyone looks to their elder mentor. "Nope. Get some sleep, I'll take first watch," he says before taking another swig from his libation. Runa looks at him with concern before tucking into her sleeping back. She knows he had been here in the war but the particulars are nebulous. His disappearance during the gala and his diminished communication have been a point of concern for her. It can't be easy being here after so much time. As she drifts off to sleep the stories Turios had told rattle at the fore of her mind until the dark takes her.

Runa wakes surrounded by the darkness of the jungle. The drone of insects fills her ears as the pallid crescents of Fengari's light filter through the high canopy above. She sits up, looking about the camp. Noticing that Mithragen and Oti's sleeping bags lie empty, she rummages for her handheld glim. Carefully, she covers the lens and clicks on the red hued light. She is unsure whose watch it is, but no one appears awake. Cursing under her breath, she nudges Oma who sits up with a groan. Pressing a finger to her lips, she leans toward her friend. Not wanting to wake the others, she communicates the situation to Oma through praxis. Together they step away from the camp until sure the din of the midnight jungle will muffle their movements. "Do you think they went to relieve themselves? I've got to go myself," Oma admits. "Aye, maybe. But, no one is on watch, so let's not go far," Runa says as she sweeps the glim beam across the undergrowth. The young praxiats trudge a ways into the brush before separating to take care of the call of nature. Past the perfectly still veil of broad-leafed ferns Runa sees a light. It's a clean, white orb of luminescence which flickers as she shifts her vantage. She stands to see if she can spot the source of the light, but it remains masked behind foliage. "Psst, I see something," she whispers. "What?" Oma replies. "A light, might be Oti and the boot duster." They convene beside a felled and rotten tree. "Should we wake the others?" Runa says. "I'll get Turios," Oma says sitting on the ground and leaning against the stump. Runa turns back toward the light. A chill runs down her neck as she waits in the eerie silence. It is at this moment that she realizes just how quiet it has become. Not an insect is chittering. No leaves are rustling. It's akin to the silence of the mausoleum in which Runa had proven herself. A few moments later, Turios whispers, "Where are you?" as he tramps into the jungle. Runa waggles the glim in his direction. "This had better be good. I was having such a dream," he says. Oma makes a gagging sound as she stands to join them. "One of those types of dreams, huh," Runa says, punching Turios lightly in the arm. It's dark but they all know he is blushing. "Anyhow, what could that be," she says pointing. Turios shrugs then pushes a fern aside. Cautiously they make their way toward the curious light. "It's too quiet," Runa says, but the others offer no response as they press on. "Runa," a familiar voice says from ahead. She must be imagining things. It sounds like her brother Amil. Despite her knowing at the back of her mind that something is amiss, she moves forward as if compelled to see what lies beyond. The group quickens their pace until coming to the edge of a clearing of loose sand. Above, Fengari hangs high and full, casting enough light to make out the edges of the space. At the opposite end of the oblong clearing is a deposit of smooth river boulders, but that's not what draws Runa's eye. A figure stands obscuring the source of light. "Runa," the voice says again. "Amil?" she says incredulously. No, it isn't Amil, but the voice isn't coming from the male figure standing with his back turned to the trio. Runa looks to the other two on either side of her. They seem equally transfixed by the glimmering light. Something is wrong, she tells herself, seeing the blank expressions of the others. As she steps to the side to nudge Oma, she sees clearly the source of intrigue. At the center of the clearing is a cluster of luminous crystal jutting from the sand at a slight angle away. It stands nearly as tall as Runa with a milky coloration but the light does appear to come from within the structure. It is beautiful, she thinks. Then her mind slips back to the trancelike state. All she wants is to get closer to the spire of crystal. Sparks like the embers of a roaring blaze crackle withing the crystal as the pillar shifts. It rises, the boulders in the distance tumble over each other without so much as a sound. No, not stone. Runa watches in disbelief as the coils heave the crystal skyward on a black mass. Whatever hold it had on her is broken, but with no time to react, she watches as the dark form with crystal in tow fall to her left, crushing the man beside her. She yelps and stumbles sideways bearing herself and Oma to the ground as the mass swings over both of them, then back until connecting with Turios. Only then does Runa comprehend what she is seeing. The gargantuan serpent recoils, holding its head high in the moonlight. The crystal, which has diminished in brightness, is part of the creature. Its unblinking eyes fix on Runa. She kicks Oma, "Oma! Move!" she screams as the creature opens wide its jaw, exposing rows of horrible teeth which flex outward. She scrambles for purchase on the sunken pit of sand as a horrific vocalization emanates from the serpent, like a dozen branches snapping in synchrony.

Runa looks up at the titanic predator as she struggles to her feet. Oma too has regained her footing. Neither dare take their eyes off the monster. In her pocket, Runa searches for her aster. She curses under her breath. It must have fallen out in her sleeping bag, not that she could put it to much use. "Oma, get to the camp," she says sternly. Without a word Oma sprints for the tree line. The snake lunging its great maw in chase. It crashes into the yearling trees, snapping them effortlessly as it tumbles into the thicket. Runa can't tell if Oma had made it as the snake's mass obstructs her view. She takes the opportunity to dash toward the Turios sprawled near the sandy pit. "Tee, wake up," she says, shaking him. He lets out a groan. Runa glances sidelong at her assailant. It has yet to double back on itself. Rummaging through Turios' pockets, she mutters, "Please." A faint spark of hope flares within as she feels the cold touch of steel. Another glance toward the serpent; it's turning. The dim crystalline mass on its head flickers again like flame as it slowly arcs toward its tail. Runa rises to her feet, brandishing the aster. Focusing her will into the object she feels the reverberations from the world beyond worlds. Doubt courses through her mind as she commands the aster to move. What could she hope to do? This creature must be over 30 paces long. The pieces lift away from the focus, then fall to the ground. Runa lets out an agonized grunt of frustration and throws aside the focus. She needs a weapon she knows. Laboring to breath, her heart throbs within her chest. As the snake coils under itself, the last bit of tail passes Runa and Turios. Then it rears up again, preparing to strike as Runa looks on hopelessly. It is a surreal moment, as if her mind can't process that the end is near. She reaches out, her vision filled not with the present danger, nor the moments of her short life, but of that day she had cast her past away. She sees the scrimshaw blade tumbling end-over-end into the sea. She feels the frigid waves crashing over her as it sinks beneath the breakwater. Emotion subsumes her. How could she have cast such a thing away? The serpent leans toward Runa, as if perplexed by her stillness, its forked tongue flits from its mouth. Runa watches as the blade handle wears smooth by the driving waves. Watches as the sheath comes away and the metal rusts to nothing in the face of unyielding time. "No," she says, reaching for the blade. Her flesh burns. In this moment, her mind touches the realm of consciousness from which all things are wrought; the fundament which collapses probability into certainty. Then she closes her hand around the Janamudra blade.

With a rumbling shudder which ionizes the air, Runa pulls. The blade comes away in a spray of seawater which wets her face. Looking up at the snake, then down at her brother's blade, she is beside herself. It's impossible, and yet, the knife is here. The snake lets out another chest-rattling vocalization, then lunges. In a defensive crouch, Runa yanks away the sheath. The jaws large enough to devour her whole close in. She dodges to the side and drives the blade into the citrine, serpentine eye as momentum carries it past. Then the coarse body strikes her. The impact drives the air from her lungs and sends her sprawling to the sand. The immense reptile writhes, whipping its tail through the jungle, creating a cacophony of noise. The next thing Runa sees is the star-streaked sky above, Fengari illuminating the canopy in a sea glass hue. She takes in a jagged breath as she rolls to her side. The serpent is coming about, its blinded eye dripping dark jelly. An unbearable pressure presses down on Runa, as if gravity has doubled. The snake also senses it, its head swivels past her, and over its body. A shrill call emanates from it as the crystal on its head grows blindingly bright, like the sun in the midnight jungle. Then it ruptures, sending the shards skyward as the beast lets out a reverberating screech. With prejudice, the crystalline daggers dive home with a squelch, as a flashing pinwheel of light carves a crescent shaped hole through the back of the creature and sprays gore atop the bone-colored sand. Runa can only watch as Adanon step-hops through what had been the creature's spine. He glances at her and Turios, then walks to the head of the serpent. The tail twitches at the other end of the clearing as Adanon crouches next to the dying animal. Runa staggers over, overhearing Adanon speaking softly to the animal as it takes its last belabored breaths. And the jungle falls still.

CHAPTER 39

In the morning, Runa stares off into the greenery as the jungle awakens. She hadn't slept well after the encounter with the Wreather. That's what Adanon had called it. She had been led to believe that only humans know how to tap into the power of praxis, but the animal had clearly been able to disorient them all. She doesn't know if it's testament of the creature's wisdom or their weakness. Judging by Adanon's reverence and silence, she thinks it's the former. Nevertheless, she is shaken up by the affair. She picks at a bit of crust stuck to the handle of the Jana blade as the others collect their things. Oti is missing and Mithragen is dead. The Wreather had dispatched him handily. He had been a bit of a pain and cruel to the Uxians, but he didn't deserve to die here. Runa sighs. "Nice knife," Turios says, hobbling over, "Where'd you get that?" His leg had taken the worst of the impact. Lucky for them, Oma is a skilled medic and a praxiat. Runa looks up at him. "Always had it," she says flatly. It's a lie, but he accepts her answer and goes about his business. Shortly after, they set off.

As they depart the encampment, they pass near the Wreather and Mithragen's final resting place. Adanon had taken the time to dig him a shallow grave and placed him on his side facing West, in the Esoptrian tradition. Thand had said words. It is startling how fast the jungle has reclaimed the putrefying flesh. The profusion of feeding insects reminds Runa of life's perpetual capriciousness. Shuddering, she looks away. For a time they cut their way through the jungle, the only sound the woosh and hacking of the aster under Adanon's control. Runa speaks up, "Are you upset with us?" "No," he responds tersely. After a moment of silence, he turns and says, "I'm upset that I had to kill that magnificent animal. If we set camp up farther away, or if the Wreather had eaten elsewhere, it could have gone on for centuries. I can't blame the creature for wanting to survive." The young praxiats nod. "What about Oti?" Oma says. Adanon chuckles sardonically. "That wasn't his name. He's long gone, which makes getting an audience where we are going precarious at best," Adanon says. "Then what's the plan?" Runa chirps. Adanon turns back to slashing through the jungle, saying, "Let's get there first." It's a grueling day of travel where the pace slows to one or two mille per hour. Crossing countless gullies they travel northeastward. Where morale had been high the first two days, now the smallest perturbation frays everyone's nerves. When they don't reach their destination by the end of the third day, they make camp near gnarled old tree under which a stream trickles meanderingly westward. Bedding down and gathering around the pot of odorous beans, everyone sits in quiet contemplation.

"It is my turn to tell a story," Oma says, looking at her sister. Thand looks at her sternly, but doesn't object. "This was back before we were foundlings. I think some context is important. In Bujani, fire is sacred. It cleanses things, places, people. We would often see the neighboring families burning their fields, but the really auspicious occasions were home burnings. A few things constitute such a burn, a matriarch passing on meant that the house too must be cleansed." Oma pauses, gauging the look on Thand's face. "Another occasion for a fire cleansing was when children meet an untimely end or ill omens. That is how we arrive at the story proper. Mother had suspected that Thand had the gift from an early age, but since we were so close in age, she wanted to wait until I was older to see if I too was so gifted. Bringing both of us to the authorities together would, in her mind, guarantee we wouldn't be separated. I was young and didn't understand the ritual significance of burning the house. I remember thinking it was a punishment for being different. Mother had insisted on keeping the tradition, and my Father kept telling me that I had done nothing wrong..." Oma trails off. Thand clears her throat then says, "It is a hard thing to ask a child- to just accept that their home is going to be destroyed because that's what everyone else has always done. After living away for so long, it seems backwards to add the grief of loss to an already tragic situation. But, I think I've come to understand that the tradition is about remembrance and rebirth." Runa is a little beside herself with this opening up from the sisters. She recalls the memory from her tussle with Thand, but hadn't worked up the courage to ask about the event which had left her hands and mind traumatized. Runa's stomach turns as she relives the feeling of flames against flesh. She hugs her knees to her chest as she listens to Oma continue. "Father told me to stay with Thand. I was young and impetuous. I remember running off as our parents went to burn down the only home I had ever known. It seems foolish now, hiding in a barn only a dozen paces from an inferno. I'm sorry Thandiwe. If I had known—" she catches on her words. "It's alright Sister. We can't undo the past. If you hadn't run away, we might never have gone to the foundling house together," Thand says looking at Runa, "You see, Oma's first praxic act was to shunt the pain from my hands." Turios holds up a finger and moves to speak, but Adanon, who is reclined beside him, clears his throat loudly. Runa nods. She thinks she understands the point of the story. She also knows what Turios was going to say. Surely it was something about 'how some things are just coincidence, or a statistic.' She would like for there to be meaning to their encounter with the Wreather. Perhaps she just can't see it yet. After bedding down, she drifts off to sleep clutching the Jana blade close to her chest.

The morning comes uneventfully. It's unusual for Runa to sleep past the others in her cohort, but she awakens to the sounds of the others shifting around the campsite. Four days in the jungle has been four too many, she thinks to herself as she rolls out of her sleeping bag. The terrain has become more and more difficult with each day. It's not the endless vegetation or the incessant insects. It's the gradually increasing slope and precarious pitfalls littering their sojourn. As they pass a particularly harrowing hollow under a tree, Turios begins to talk about the network of tunnels dug by Uxians during the war. Everyone protests so he relents to the sounds of the jungle. Just when Runa is feeling delirious from the drudgery, Oma lets out a cry. It startles everyone, ever Adanon who is leading. "Look!" she says, pointing ahead through the trees. It is dusk, but the sight of the clearing ahead is unmistakable. Everyone rushes ahead, stumbling out into the open air. It's a jovial scene, the young praxiats laughing amongst themselves as they take in the mountainous view. It is a familiar yet foreign sight. Beyond meadows of low-lying fruit trees stands a lonely mountain. From that mountain protrudes a structure of stone seemingly carved from the living rock in a single piece. Runa marvels at the construction, for under the hundreds of paces high stone overhang lies a human settlement; the city of Stars This is Gibbous city which they had sought. Thand mutters a low, thankful devotion as Adanon strolls past. "We haven't made it quite yet," he says as he continues toward the orchard that surrounds the city.

Adanon looks back at the hesitant youths. He supposes it can't be helped. Making passage through the wilderness is its own challenge, encounters with the wildlife notwithstanding. He endeavors to maintain the appearance of calm, for he knows too well the effect of poor leadership on the young and impressionable. He steadies his eyes against the failing sun to his left. This is Teft'tun-Metzglan in the native tongue, the place of Sun, moon, and stone. Adanon has never been within the city, but he knows its people well. Darian had made sure of that. As he crosses the verdant fields, Adanon reminisces on the man that his friend had once been. Darian had never let him dehumanize the enemy no matter what they faced. Things certainly would have been simpler is he had. This place overturns memories better left to lie. Adanon glances back at the trailing acolytes. He sighs to himself, thinking it better they hadn't seen the state of him on their night day in Ux. And he is glad none of them have asked where he had gone during the festivities. The kiss of the bottle is less than kind these days. Particularly so for processing the guilt of letting Talin go. She had deceived him but he hadn't be surprised, only caught unaware. On that evening in Esoptria had been too copacetic. Talin's brashness had always been something he liked about her. Adanon lets out another sigh as they reach the outskirts of the settlement just before the sun has set. There is no wall or gate to bar their passing: They simply walk in. Around them the people carry about their business unaware or unconcerned by these outsiders. Adanon leads on as the praxiats chatter to themselves. It isn't for ignorance of the situation that he presses on. He is only preparing mentally for that which is about come. They pass through snaking streets of traditional clay roofed homes. Here and there they pass stalls of clay wares, Uxian half-masks of differing materials, and fruit and vegetables. It continues this way until they reach the clear demarcation of the city which falls in the shadow of the stone structure above. Golden twilight casts no shadows here. A stout man with a silvery mask steps out in front of Adanon as he presses forward.

Runa swallows against the lump in her throat. The man in front of Adanon is not as tall, but very wide. His hair is shorn down to the skin save for the wide, dark band above his nape which is pulled up and affixed to the top of his head. Curious hairstyles aside, the weapon slung over his shoulder and his glower give her pause. Adanon addresses the man in Uxian, holding the purlicue of his right hand just under his nose in a makeshift mask. The man who Runa assumes is a guard narrows his eyes at Adanon. "I don't know you," the masked man says in stilted Esoptrian. Runa looks about, the nearby stall-tenders have tucked into buildings and the streets is suddenly barren. The tension is palpable on the humid air. "I was summoned to audience with the Queen," Adanon adds. Again, the man repeats his prior sentiment but slower. Adanon nods, glancing sideways at Runa and the others as he takes a step toward the nearby stall. Something in his eyes says not to be hasty. Fine glazed pots, masks, and delicate ceramics are stacked in abundance on the shelves of the wooden stall, same as many others they have passed. Adanon extends his arm then shoves the ceramic contents of an entire shelf to the pavers below, filling the street with a terrible clatter. The guardsmen unshoulders his folded coilgun, priming it for action, but doesn't point the barrel at anyone. Again, Adanon sweeps more laborious treasures onto the ground. Runa clutches at the Jana blade in her pocket, sure the others are equally on guard. Adanon bends and unlaces his boots, tossing each one to the side along with his socks. Is this some Uxian custom Runa is unaware of? Then, to her dismay, Adanon steps on the broken shards of the shattered finery. Oma lets out a gasp as the first brittle pieces crunch against the stone. Without hesitation Adanon takes several steps, then turns and walks back across before looking to the guardsman with a blank expression. After a protracted silence, the guard lowers the muzzle of the weapon and says, "I do know you."

CHAPTER 40

The guardsman removes his half-mask, revealing the magnetic attachment points at the lobes of his ears and upper lip. They are not simply magnets, they are Lote embedded in his flesh, leaving the denominations visible. Runa cocks an eyebrow at this. Surely this is some sort of display of status. The gesture of removing his mask is shocking after never seeing an Uxian without one, except Pa. Adanon gets out a low grunt, picking a particularly heinous sliver that had found its way into the sole of his foot. Oma slinks up to him. "Do you want me to look at that?" she whispers. Adanon declines with a gesture before pulling his socks and boots back on. Then he stands, saying, "I'll pay for the damages of course." The guardsman smirks, showing no teeth. "No need, it's potter's work. You know our ways. You in the war, old man?" "Something like that," Adanon admits. "Akroates Adanon Chlorosa," he extends a hand to the guard, "your Queen is expecting me." The guard looks down at his hand, then to the other praxiats. "You may call me Potzl. You are praxis," the guard says, deigning to shake Adanon's hand. Some hesitations appear to be universal. Runa assumes that Adanon must be used to this by now, for he shows no displeasure at Potzl's refusal. "We are all praxis, as you say," Adanon says gesturing to the others. The stout Potzl reattaches his mask and nods, turning toward the far end of the city.

Runa has several questions, but the grandeur of the half dome draws her attention away from her silent stroll among the shadow city. The houses are made more modestly than those they first passed. In place of clay roofs, some have none, exposing their upper levels to open air. Others have a combination of open roofs and moss-covered thatch. Runa had overheard someone calling this the city of stars. She doesn't understand why, for the first stars of night are hidden behind the canopy of stone. At the rear, where the megastructure intersects the ground, a newer less surehanded construction of small stone marks an entrance which continues into the rock face. A retinue of similarly kitted guards greet Potzl and talk for a time as Adanon rests against the wall of layered sheets of rough stone. A guard leaves and returns with a shambling, elderly person draped in folds of dusty gray linen. Their face is gnarled like a knot of petrified wood, but their eyes. Their eyes are keen orbs of hazel amidst a face of jowls and grooves. The ancient crone hands something to Potzl, then points to Runa before shuffling back into the cave from which they came. Potzl approaches Adanon and hands him a missive of yellowing paper. "She has no words for you, Esoptrian..." he says, placing his hands on his hips, "but she has for her." Runa meets his gaze. "Me?" she says. He slumps down heedless of the jagged stones gnawing at his back. "Go. Be wary, for every bit of cunning she is twice as cruel," he says, placing the paper on the ground beside him. Potzl stands tall then announces in a percussive voice, "The Ninth Star. The Queen of all. The herald of the end, who was begotten in shadow, who was born without blood, and whose words make the world tremble, summons you to speak..." He raises a brow at Runa. She chirps her name, which he then repeats emphatically.

The passageway is narrow and gradually getting lower until the point that Runa has to duck. Potzl had escorted her to the entrance after she had doffed her pack but he had followed no further. She can't help but wonder at the hunched old retainer making taking the same path. At the point which the last sliver of light vanishes, Runa reaches an opening. She places a hand on the vertical rock face behind her in complete darkness. She isn't alone. A slight wheezing breath at her shoulder startles her. The old crone rasps in Esopt, "You come as you are or not at all," their eyes, iridescent orbs in the dark. They shimmer like the night eyes of the Wreather, then they are gone. There is a flash of brilliant white light which flares bright enough for Runa to take in the scope of the cavern, but only for a moment. The light dies down, leaving the afterimage emblazoned across her vision. The brazier that had risen in a blinding swell calms to a warm sanguine glow. "You know, it's meant to resemble a womb," a childlike voice echoes around Runa. The feminine voice giggles. It is only then that Runa notices the language she had been addressed. How seldom she had spoken or thought in Jana since those early days in Esoptria. She wets her lips and moves to speak but is cut short, "It is only a mountain of course. Theatrics of those long gone to rest and returned again." Runa approaches the crackling fire, shading her vision against the light. Just beyond the illumination rests a figure on a mass, a throne. She slides out of her throne wreathed in shadow just close enough to make out her features. "I know you," Runa mutters. This is the young woman from her dreams. The voice, the eyes, the figure of a young woman with long raven hair. "Aye, we have known each other before and we will know each other again. But, Tell me, how was it? Bending the rules to their breaking point," she hisses through a half-mask unlike any other Runa has seen. It is a fearsome amalgam of bone and teeth perched precariously on the young woman's face. "I don't follow," Runa admits. The queen removes her mask, letting out a side-splitting laugh. "You are as funny as you ever were- The knife my guards absentmindedly left on your person," she says taking a gliding a step closer. Runa tenses. In the commotion the weapon had slipped her mind. However, the queen doesn't seem threatened.

"It's not that you have it," the queen says, "It's that it should be mired among silt and stone, shouldn't it?" "You can't know that," Runa mutters, crossing her arms. "I can and do, as does Adanon." Runa looks away from the queen, choosing the gaze into the smoldering brazier. "You do know Adanon then. Why not speak with him?" she says. "Your Akroates, his reputation moves before him like a wave. And like a wave which passes under me, I remain unmoved. I told him what he needed to hear, much as he does to others." "He is a good man. I wouldn't be alive if not for him," Runa says. The queen sighs and says, "And many of my people would still live if he had never. He is lost and unwilling to see what is plainly before him. So, no, not a bad man. His masters are bad men and women. He knows this yet does nothing." Runa grits her teeth. This young woman seems to know more about Adanon than she, and it annoys her. Not wanting to deviate from the topic, she says, "You mean the Council—" "May I see the blade?" the queen interrupts. Runa hesitates. It is a curious, almost devious tact. From conversing in Jana, to the kind sentiments about Adanon. All of it seems planned, curated. "Why are you so interested in the knife?" Runa says in a combative tone. In a flash of rage, the queen spits, "It's not the knife!" The flames flare, revealing more of the chamber. For the briefest moment the smooth stone ceiling, the osseous throne, and the plane of glittering dark beyond are visible. It feels as if she is being pressed from within. Her very bones chatter within her as the light dies back to its former luminosity. "May I see the knife? I'm not... accustomed to asking," the queen says in a slow but saccharine tone.

Runa runs her fingertips over the engraved handle of the blade she has secreted about her waist and says, "I've spent a lot of time among the boot dusters, but despite myself I can't escape my father's penchant for bartering." She's meeting the queen's feigned sweetness with a façade of shrewd indifference. "One thing for another," she ends, holding out her brother's blade. The queen looks her over, as if seeing her for the first time. Her lips curl deviously as she says, "Very well. Name your price." Runa struggles to mask her excitement. "A name and a tale. That's my price," she says holding out the sheathed blade. They exchange a nod amid the crackling gloom. As the knife changes hands, the queen says, "I go not by name but by number. Naahui is what I am called by those that know me best. Naahui... Nine. Nine for the lives I have lived. And nine for the lives I will live. As for a story..." she scoffs, "Stories are a filter by which we make reality palatable. I have a story, but you must live it." Something in her words grips Runa with fear. Naahui seizes the knife. At the same moment she seizes Runa by the hair and presses into her mind with a force of will unparalleled by any before. She sieges the walls of Runa's mind, and although she resists, her senses crumble to the subsummation.

It is dusk. Somewhere in the rainforest leaves rustle. Doubtless, life carrying on heedless of human existential agony. She knows what she must do. Her ardor to do so is fleeting, so she stays her trembling hands around the blade. Yet, they are not her hands. Again this is a moment from someone else's life. It's filled with dread and despair. Saints save her. She turns over the blade once more, quieting her nerves as she points it toward herself, her face. Nothing could have prepared Runa for the pain and fear as the hateful point draws close. The point is true. Hot tears well in her eyes as it slips behind, under, and through the flesh of her face. Her hands tremble as tears and blood blur her vision. Then nothing but the bestial moans of agony as the warm, warm liquid slicks her cheek.

Runa collapses to the floor as Nahui releases her. She retches in to the dark from the aftershock of pain. "Why?" she stammers. Naahui is unmoving, seemingly more interested in the knife. "I wonder if the great serpent thought the same as you drove this home," she says flatly, testing the weight. Runa struggles to her feet, rage flaring in her belly. Through gritted teeth, she says, "Why show me such a terrible memory?" "You see, we all must give up a piece of ourselves to become who we are meant to be," Naahui says, drawing the blade free of its sheath, "How is it that it isn't rusted or marred after all that time? Testament of its craftsmanship or something else entirely?" Of course, the thought had occurred to Runa, but she hadn't dwelled on it. "I plucked the knife from thin air thousands of mille from where I left it. Is it more, or less probable that it doesn't have rust?" Runa says, still picturing the ghastly point entering her eye. Naahui chuckles dryly. It's a terrible sound which Runa should never like to hear again. "You are going to help me. I want that bloated anemone which gloats over my land and people. I want to drink his blood and watch as the light leaves his eyes forever." Runa recoils. "Medon?" she says. "The beast has many names here. Less so the one he chooses. Yes, The Medon," Naahui says with a sardonic flourish. Runa wipes the sweat from her brow and says, "I am no friend to him, but I can't harm the man." Again, Naahui laughs. "I'm not asking you to harm him. I'm asking that if given the choice, how would you do it?" she says with venom on her lips. How had they come to this conversation? How is it that Runa is considering sedition with a woman she has just met. Runa speaks slowly, choosing her words with care, "I don't know- I was only in his castle for a night." "Would it ease your mind to know that he is the reason you are here? He has many dealings, the least of which is secrets. I doubt he thinks I would tell you this... Nearly a year ago a certain ship with a fresh-faced crew and a cohort of praxiats was making trouble for Medon's less scrupulous endeavors. Imagine my surprise when I received their float plans out of nowhere." "I hadn't heard of this," Runa says. "That's very like Adanon. It's the reason you are here, well, one of many. Suffice it to say, the sailors and praxiats Medon thinks are bones in the ocean are alive and well. A bargaining chip for a most singular occasion. Now, answer my question." Runa tips up her chin. "You are bargaining all wrong. Neither party means much to me," she says. Naahui hands the Jana blade back to her. "I knew you would say that. But I have the upper hand and always will. The dreams, are they getting worse? The green-eyed lad in the mirror," she says. Pulling out a small pouch and dangling it by the drawstrings, Naahui grins. "I have the answers to the questions your subconscious asks itself." Can Runa trust that this is true? She heard this woman was something of a prophet. Even if that is an exaggeration, she clearly has the upper hand. Hanging her head, Runa says, "The crew goes free and I receive what you claim are answers?" She feels ill. The flames flare, casting enough light to see Naahui perch herself back on the throne. Then she crosses her legs and smiles. "The handler of his grounds is... recently deceased. There is an opportunity to work someone into his circle, but he seems to only trust Esoptrians. I can't say I'm any good at this. All I remember from the party is dancing and strange animals," Runa says. "Strange animals?" Naahui says, resting her chin in her palm. "There was some sort of hound. Freakishly overfed. Another woman had a bird in her hat..." Naahui's demeanor changes suddenly. "Thank you, Runa. The captives will be freed at first light and—" she tosses the small pouch, "Don't partake of that until you are certain you are ready. Truth is a blade with no handle." Runa catches the bag. "I never told you my name," she says. The old crone shuffles into the light. "And you'll never have to- See they are well taken care of, Xixhup," Naahui says, waving her hand dismissively.

CHAPTER 41

The rest of the evening is a whirlwind of people and places. From porters to showers, all of it is backdrop to the tempest of Runa's mind. She wonders if she had done the right thing. It had seemed like such a small price, a dodgy answer to an even dodgier question. She can't help but feel like she made mistake. As she had recounted the events from the cave, Adanon had seemed unmoved by the revelation that his countrymen were alive and well. He had been more concerned with the mysterious missive. To feed and house an entire crew in secret seems improbable at best. Perhaps it is telling of Naahui, that she cared enough to keep them all this time. As Runa bathes away the grime of the jungle in an open roofed villa deep in the shadow city, she pauses and smirks. From what she saw of the queen, the care of the crew is and always will be secondary to the Queen's motives. At times, she wishes that she could be so singular in her focus. She wicks the water from her eyes to look out over the dimly lit city. There it is, or at least, a part of the quandary. To the south and over the dark cityscape hang twinkling stars. The sight draws her back over a year ago, to those last candid moments with Amil before her world had been turned upside-down. The nine stars that form the constellation of the heretic are rising.

Joining the others in the simple but comfortable silken garments in the dark and mottled fashion of the Uxians, Runa lets out an exasperated sigh. "What did it say?" she says, barging into the communal room. The others stare at her in confusion. She is being direct, but after the events of the day, her poise is lacking. "The letter Adanon received from the queen," she says. The Oma's face betrays that they do not know. "Where is he?" Runa presses. "He hasn't been himself, Runa," Oma admits. Runa scoffs "Good! We came all this way and he sat down. Maybe what the Commander said is true. At times I have seen him driven but meek. Nurturing but ruthless. Which is real? Do any of you know?" She turns to Turios who is lounging on a hammock. He stirs, noticeably affected by her line of questioning. "I understand your frustration. But I think it's best that the Akroates and the Queen of Ux did not meet," he says. Runa finds his response purposefully misleading. She throws her hands up and shouts, "Why?!" Turios takes off his glasses. As he cleans them against his silken shirt he says, "I thought you might have figured it out by now. The Akroates is a listener, a hunter of those outside the fold. It is a job reserved for the darkest, most skilled, but tainted among us. The evil you know, I guess." Thand sits up and hisses through her teeth at Turios. "She deserves to know," he says, "Why do you think it was he that first met you aboard your family ship? He and Talin were sent to kill you if you chose to stay with your family." Runa's heart skips a beat. Rather than arguing or rebuffing the accusation, she turns for the door. "I'll find him," she says as she closes the thin door behind herself.

It's easy enough for her to find Adanon. There seems to be an unspoken bond between them. She plods down the hall her, her face burning. She stops, grabs the handle to the nearest door. After her inexplicable conjuring of the blade just a few nights before, the manipulation of the physical has become easier. She isn't certain that Adanon is on the other side of this door, she only gets a feeling. Clutching the metallic knob, she wills the mechanism to corrode away. The lock makes a tinging, delaminating sound. It's enough. As she shoves, the lock yields like brittle timber.

"Good evening," Adanon says, sitting hunched at the end of a bed. Runa had been rash to come here, she knows, but she had been spurred on by frustration and exhaustion. "You lied," she says before Adanon looks at her. He sets down the letter in his hands on the bed. "I've lied a lot, but never to you," he says, casting his eyes to the floor. Runa takes a step into the room, saying, "You deny it then? That you would have killed me if I took your offer to stay among the flotilla?" Adanon sighs. "I have no doubt that many things were said about me when you met the queen, but I don't think that was one of them. Who told you that?" Runa is beginning to reconsider confronting him. Despite the anger in her belly, she says "Turios," sheepishly. Adanon looks at her for the first time since entering. "That's an entirely different discussion. He bears a weight of expectation, being blood to a councilor... not that blood counts for much for succession." He is steering the conversation away from her question, but Runa takes the bait. "Care to elaborate?" Adanon clasps his knees and looks at her curiously. "I wonder how much she played up the nine lives motif," he says with a cocked brow. Runa fails to bluff, her cheeks dimpling. Adanon speaks lower, "A fair amount then. It's not levity or play. I don't know if it's wise for you to learn such things. "Ad, if I waited until I was ready, I'd never accomplish anything," she says. "There may be some truth to that," Adanon admits with a sigh, "Runa, do you know why the Council was created?" he says. Shrugging, Runa says "They were following the decrees of Agrios." Adanon cracks a wry smile. "That is how they justify their existence, not the reason." Runa says, "Control." Adanon smiles, saying, "Correct. The control of information, people. It's why the dredgers mistrust us and our enemies hate us." Runa paces the room. "Enemies?" she says. "Many and varied, but sharing a singular hatred. Somewhere along the way the paradigm flipped. We were once an oddity to be subdued, enslaved. The past thousand years have seen us rise to become the masters. On the surface their grievances would be with stripping families of their gifted children. Underneath, they blame us for the diaschisms. In a 'schism the balance fractures, creating unimaginable fluctuations in elemental forces similar to praxis but many magnitudes greater. So, their assumptions are not wholly unjustified." Runa flops on the bed. "But there have been 'schisms within the Federation. Your home ..." Adanon pinches the bridge of his nose. "You can't apply logic to malice, Runa. We are different and different is always the opposition." "Then why the friction between Ux and Esoptria?" Runa says. "Because, The Council, your new friend the queen, they truly remember. Each councilor spans centuries of collective memory. They remember centuries of conflict and grievances that don't die with their wielders. Do you understand the gravity of this information?" "I understand," she says softly, "but you've also avoided my initial question. Would you have killed me? I want to know." Adanon flips the paper off the bed and. "Enough. I can't say what I may or may not have done," he says, anger in his voice, "The Akroates must make heavy choices. That is my burden. Not everyone can undo their mistakes as easily as you." He arches his shoulders and presses his head in his hands. So, he does know about her feat amid the mortal struggle with the wreather. Runa's lip quivers. After a time Adanon says, "Pick up the paper. Read it but show me the blade." She sniffles and fishes the knife from her nightclothes. Adanon takes the blade. Runa slowly stoops to pick up the letter. She can't be certain, but a glimpse of fear seems to cross Adanon as he inspects the blade. Locality is claimed to be fundamental to praxis. The importance of contact cannot be understated. In certain instances, great focus and willpower may expand the sphere of influence, but seldom beyond the perception of the praxiat. "You told me that you cast this into the sea. I wonder... is this an incarnation spun from your remembering, or have you actually done the miraculous?" Runa sits beside him. She can't bring herself to bring up the peculiar dreams she has been having. "Which is more concerning?" she says as she turns over the folded letter. Adanon smirks and sets the heirloom between them on the bed. "The latter, by far. You were right to lie about this," he admits. Runa reads over the singular line several times. "This is cryptic," she says before doing her best impression of Naahui, "The hounds eat the leader that fails the hunt."

CHAPTER 42

Runa sleeps until the first cerulean wisps kiss the southern sky. Morning dew clings to her face, taking her mind back to countless sunrises on the deck of the Shyena. For a moment she wonders where Amil is before returning to lucidity. As she looks again over the moss-laden half of the Gibbous city she pines for meaning. An intruder to her room cuts short her ponderous morning moment. The Uxian child smiles at her without a mask. It's Oti. Runa had never thought to see him again. She covers her mouth and addresses him by name. "Is fine- I earn a new face today. Let me help, h'Laksima zoqui," he says with cheer as he gathers up her discarded garments from the floor. Runa, mildly affronted, holds up a finger in protest. "Firstly, what does that mean?" Oti scratches his head, saying, "Erm, how do you say? She who tinkers- No, it's a sculptor of clay, but not 'of clay,' as you say," he gets visibly frustrated. Runa stoops to meet his eye, saying, "Describe it as best you can." "Things—" he waves his arms, "that happen." "Time?" Runa posits. There is a knock at the door, then Adanon peers in. He clearly had been listening through the thin door. He addresses Oti in Uxian. Then, after a short exchange, Adanon says, "Fate." He closes the door as abruptly as he had entered, leaving Runa and Oti to continue their conversation.

The city is in a frenzy as Runa and the others set out into the street. People greet them all by name, or in some cases, dubious Uxian phrases which go unelaborated. At some point Runa loses track of Oti and her pack he insisted on carrying. As they pass by the western base of the arch, Runa deduces that they are taking a different route back to New Astoraph. Soon after, a concealed entrance to a manmade canal is revealed. There, the few members of the crew that chose to return, await them. Out of the hundreds of initial members, only eighty-two sailors and three praxiats remain. A dozen wide wooden boats load up the departing Esoptrians with little fanfare as Oti returns.

Shortly later, amid the verdant thicket through which the muddy water flows, everyone makes light banter. Even Adanon, who seems in better spirits, tells a tale about his youth. It piques Runa's interest, how the Anvilites live most of their lives in the domes. That strikes a particular chord with her. There are similarities between them she had never considered. As an aside to his story, Adanon points out that they had been disproportionately chosen to flush out Uxian tunnels in the war. Runa would like to see the Anvil someday despite how bleak it sounds in recounting. After an hour of travel the tributary joins the mighty Seprinos river. Runa sighs with relief, no longer watching for a glint of crystal through the foliage. No one else had spoken on the wreather but as they leave the shade of the jungle all four acolytes exchange knowing glances. Runa questions the pilot of the wooden ship as to when they should arrive. When he tells her it will be before sunset she looks incredulously at Adanon. "We could have traveled by water the entire time," she says with a sneer. Adanon thumbs over his shoulder at the other nearby boats. "Could have been worse," he says before reclining and resting his eyes.

As the shadows grow long to the east and as sure as rain in Ux, Medon's castle appears around a bend. It isn't as imposing from the water. Given time the river too will erode the stone along with all the triumphs and tears that built this place. Runa is in raptured the sight straight ahead. As if orchestrated, dark clouds speed westward, closing the band of blue between a pincer of dark sky and dark stone. An uneasy feeling settles over her despite the throngs of people gathered on the terraces of Medon's home. Somehow he had known they were returning at this place and time. As they draw closer, the extent of their reception becomes clear. The same fine trappings decorate the large black stairs which rise to the landing on which Medon waits in grand attire. The purple and gold streamers strand proud, contrasting, to that dark edifice upon which the opulent and sad man stands in finery. Above Medon and his attendants hangs a royal shade against the elements. In his fashion, the shelter is held up by Uxian servants bent by shame or wear. Runa looks from the formal display to Oti who is staring blankly into the murky waters beside the boat. As the attendants on the angular shore begin receiving the first boats to arrive the first spits on warm rain spatter waters around them. "Ominous," Turios says as the boat grinds against the stone berth.

Climbing the steps, servants shade the ascending party of wayward Esoptrians against the rain with great fans of fern leaves. In their climb a swell of jaunty music from the apex terrace assails them. The melody contrasts heavily with the odious atmosphere. Adanon approaches first upon reaching the landing, followed by Runa and Turios. The view offends Runa more than the noise. Under the dribbling canopy rests a menagerie of strange animals and Medon standing, arms outstretched in reception. The music stops with a gesture. "What a joyous day," he proclaims, his jowls quivering as he speaks, "To think you would return from that vile place with a flock of the lost. You are as great as they say, Akroates." Adanon stops short of the tent and gives a slight bow. "Medon. I can't claim the praise for their return. She secured their and our passage," he says, turning slightly to Runa. Medon seats himself and turns to the obese tree hound to his right. The chalk white animal sniffs at his master's grub-like fingers, licks them, then rests its head at his bloated feet. "I see," Medon says, resting his chins on his hand, "Your sharp tongue served you well it seems. But the future is bleak if we leave matters or state to girls in dark places. Come, come, tell me how you managed this." Runa hesitates. Oti, who has been close to her side since leaving the boat nudges her knee from behind, forcing her to take a step. She greets the man with an equally short bow. "Kyr, I only had something which the Queen wanted." Medon hums then runs his eyes over the group again. "Did she woo you with lies? Half-truths of peace? Let me guess, masked sighs of tribute to a cloistered queen. No- Mithragen wouldn't mince worse so. Where is he?" Adanon interjects, "He was giving a proper burial. Short but proper." Medon's face turns a startling shade of red, followed by a guffaw. "Oh sweet Mithragen. I curse the day that Lykios forced me to this forsaken land, but he made it bearable dealing with these savages... How did this happen?" Oti presses past Runa and Adanon and proclaims in perfect Esopt, "I killed him and the jungle is too fine a place for his bones." He punctuates his proclamation by spitting on the still dry stones under the tent. Medon heaves himself over his would-be throne. "What is the meaning of this?" he shouts. Oti lets out an unsettling chuckle. "We'll meet again, Runa. Thank you for this gift," he says, as he bolts forward, brandishing her blade. Runa pats at her pocket in disbelief. It's gone. Before anyone can react, Oti closes the several paces toward Medon. But the beast at his side swats down the boy assassin, crushing him to the coarse black stones. Runa's blade clatters to the rain-slick ground. The hound flexes its hooked claws into Oti's back, pressing him ever harder. He makes a sound, but it isn't as it should be. It is a wheezing laugh, then silence. Runa turns her eyes back to the knife, It's still sheathed. She lets out a gasp. "Ad! It's her!" Medon's look of pleasure at Oti's pain quickly turns to fear as the animal that had just defended him, turns its gaze upon him. It lacks the ability to smile, but it cuts a jagged grin across its maw, then swiftly rakes its daggered paw across Medon's mounded, fleshy belly.

The next few moments are chaos. Servants scream. The tent collapses. Shapes roll beneath the fabric. Adanon produces an aster as Runa scoops up the knife. The sound of squelching and tearing is nearly inaudible over the tumult of panic and torrential rain. In a flurry of claws, the hound frees itself from its moist prison. Its white fur is stained and matted with crimson and gore. It glances at Runa, lets out an almost human laugh, then buckles into a seizing heap just as Adanon brings the aster to bear. The myriad blades sing through the rain but fall impotently atop the jerking and slathering heap of a beast. "She's gone," Adanon says flatly before turning to the others. Thand and Turios are both poised for action but Oma seems to be in a state of shock. Potzl climbs the steps holding an oar. He looks over them and says, "You should leave now," as a concussive boom comes from the direction of the colony.

CHAPTER 43

More blasts rock the city as the praxiats make their way through the recently departed's fortress. No one had bothered to check under the fallen tent. Bright blood had pooled from under that makeshift burial cloth, mixing with the rain in a frothy mortal slurry. Runa shakes the image from her mind as they exit into the courtyard where they had first arrived. Thand kisses her hand and holds it to the sky, reciting a hasty devotion as they round corner to see several out wheels waiting. Adanon climbs to the hatch and slides into the driver's seat as the others funnel in behind him. Thand takes the seat beside him. The others sit in the back. "Is anyone going to talk about what just happened?" Turios says, shaking the rain from his glasses. "Not now," Adanon barks, "Thand get on the horn with the Nurval- Runa, how do you start this thing?" Above him is a panel of switches. Several buttons line the console beside the steering column. He presses several of them to no avail. Runa kneels between the seats and flips up a shielded panel revealing placarded positions for starting the motor, but it's missing a knob. "Military's finest," Runa sighs as she drops to the deck and rolls on her back. She slides up headfirst against the foot board to see the access panel. She pulls out her knife and begins backing out the bottommost screws. It is fiddly at best, but she gets one screw loose. "Move," Thand says, reaching her hand down by Runa's face. "Aye," she says, pressing herself toward the rear of the vehicle. As if no great labor, Thand wrenches the panel upward bending the brackets and panel while divorcing the remaining screws of any remaining thread. Runa returns to her position. Only being able to fit her head and one shoulder into the space, she runs her hand along the braided cables. If anything, her years among the Janamudra had prepared her for this. A few moments later the machine hums to life.

The transit back to the coast is a treacherous muddy venture. Outside the armored skin of the out wheel the sounds of explosions can still be heard. "I've got them," Thand says, "They say... they are leaving. The whole fleet." Adanon snaps a look at Thand that makes Runa shudder. "Put me through to the Commander," he says in a measured tone. Thand relays the message. She tenses, saying "They say it's Admiral now." Adanon punches the panel. Thand offers him the headset without prompting. They are nearing the coastline. Adanon clears his throat and says, "This is the Akroates. I need to speak to Admiral Lamphros... please." Oma speaks for the first time since Medon's insides met the outside world, "What are we going to do about all those people? You don't think—" she looks at Runa. "I don't know. I only met Naahui for a short time, but I think she's true to her word. Her grievance was with Medon, so I-I don't know," Runa says delicately. Adanon is speaking to someone on the headset, but Runa can't make it out over the whine and vibrations. Then he yells, "What do you mean vanished? Then what about the Janamudra?" Runa moves to hear better. There is a prolonged pause from Adanon. "Why would they head here? Comma-Admiral, the situation ashore is... I'm sure you can," he says, clearly being interrupted, "No, listen. We are returning. Stop the Nurval or I will!" He throws the headset off. They have arrived at the beach. Runa secures the overhead hatch and hopes dearly that this out wheel is seaworthy. They hit the water with a wall of dark spray which lurches everyone forward violently. Once the vessel is soundly afloat, Adanon stands and says, "Runa, you pilot. Get us close." After some awkward shuffling, Runa finds herself steering the cumbersome craft over the wine-dark waters. The storm and the fading light make for poor visibility. Nevertheless, Runa can make out lights in the distance.

"Is that it there?" Runa asks, pointing at the silhouette against the rising dark. Turios moves alongside her. He leans against the control panel, gazing out of the forward viewport. A wave overtakes the out wheel, bobbing them like a cork. "Maybe. It's them or the Rushan—" Turios cuts short with a retch. The rough seas are taking their toll. Thand lets out a frustrated grunt as she takes off the headset. "No use. They are no longer answering hails," she says. "Light then. Here," she flips an overhead switch, sending out a beam of focused light from a lamp between the two viewscreens. She pulses the light, "M-A-Y-D-A-Y." Turios pushes her hand away. "You focus. Rather not become a submarine," he says. They are drawing closer to the warship. Despite his pallid and sickly look, Turios continues the distress signal. They are close enough for the lamp to illuminate the port quarter of the large vessel, but no response comes. Runa looks back at Adanon who is leaning against the rear bulkhead with his eyes closed. She reasons that he must be projecting but is unsure what he intends to accomplish. Past the wall of flickering rain and the swell of waves she sees the powerful churn of the warship. Her heart sinks as it won't take long for the ship to be out of reach of their tiny amphibious vehicle. Adanon places a hand on her shoulder. "Wait for it," he says with an assuring squeeze. The deck of the Nurval lights up like a mantle on Aneletide. Soon several searchlights fall upon them. Runa steers the out wheel alongside the ship, saying, "I don't know what you did but it worked." Wet ropes and ladders rain down on the armored roof, thumping loudly.

Moments later, after braving the beating rain and temperamental seas, the praxiats slump on the deck of the Nurval. A sailor offers a hand to Runa, helping her to her feet. "Seems the Admiral had a change of heart. I think we're gonna need y'all real soon," he says in a thick Anvilite accent. Adanon helps himself up and addresses the sailor, "Ensign, I'd like a brief of what we've missed, as I'm sure everyone would like to know what's happening over there." He points ashore. Another flash of light from the battlements is followed seconds later by thump. "No worries there, Kyr, the Admiral is on his way down in a tizzy," the ensign remarks, "Jannies are heading north. Said them Orin boys up and left two days ago." Adanon pats the young man on his poncho ladened shoulder. "Thank you, son. Which dome?" he asks in almost a whisper. The ensign holds up four fingers just as a bellowing command for attention comes from his superior. He then falls in line as the newly pinned Admiral Lamphros hurriedly makes his way past the sentinel sailors. The Admiral is accompanied by an attendant holding an umbrella while everyone else on the deck is battered by the rain and wind. The stern-faced man with bushy brows stares down Adanon. "Clear the deck. Everyone to their stations," he says, snatching the umbrella from his attending officer. Adanon raises his chin to the man. "Akroates, if you ever intrude on my mind like that again I will see that you council puts you down," he says with venom. Adanon smiles, the rain streaming off his brow as he says, "If I had to spend another minute in your skin, Admiral, I'd welcome it."

CHAPTER 44

Talin slinks through the courtyard of the Lykios estate at midnight. She peers over the stone railing at the approaching ferry. Cutting a devious smile, she recognizes Zidero's silhouette preparing to disembark. She watches intently from the shadows. She must maintain a visual to remain unseen. Masking her presence and being invisible are entirely different. She scoffs at the thought of bending light. As if such a thing is possible through praxis. Even the greatest praxiats need time and focus to impose their consciousness over the physical world. Her mind turns to the diaschism that consumed Rhygell. She can't imagine what it had been like as the forces that bind the universe together had faltered. "Probably hurt," she mutters to herself as Zidero climbs the steps.

The estate has been empty for weeks. Talin and Ade had argued often, wavering between the certainty of Zidero returning and the foolishness of the entire endeavor. Ultimately they had always decided to stay because they needed surety. Talin's memories of her time in Gaerdan would be poor balm to the wound she had created in leaving. If she can deliver Zidero to the council perhaps they will overlook her dereliction. "Ade," she says into the transmitter in her ear, "send out the call." Then, mindful of her footsteps, Talin follows the industrialist as he shambles into the estate.

Zidero passes through the main dining area, lifting a decanter of spirits and places it to his lips without breaking stride. He continues, pausing for a moment to knock on Razmu's door before groaning and continuing. Talin skirts the outer wall, moonlight drawing thick lines through the dust suspended in this mirthless abode. Zidero comes to a stop at a boarded door on the lowest floor. Setting down the decanter, he proceeds to yank at the aged wood barring his entry. After exerting himself he presses his sweating forehead against the door, panting. Then he forces the stuck door open with a crack. Talin follows to just outside the room, the floor groaning slightly. Zidero shuffles in, flipping switches as the machines strewn about the room hum to life. The long abandoned biolume fixtures fail to illuminate, the light giving organisms long dead. Stooping to light a dust laden hearth, Zidero says, "Come in. I know you're there."

Placing a fist sized crystal on the desk, Zidero groans into a creaky chair. The milky crystal crackles with silent fire in the presence of praxis. A very useful piece of contraband from Uxkukul. Letting herself be perceived, Talin steps in. Then lithely steps over cables, paper, and discarded machinery before she sitting across from Zidero with a smirk. "Of course it's you," he says after another draw from the decanter, "Don't look so smug." Talin rests her head against the fingers and stares at him. He will say anything to diminish her success here. "Ready to tell me everything? Or should we go to the Council first?" she says, narrowing her eyes at him. "No, this is where I want to be. I know we left on poor terms but... care for a drink?" he says, pulling a coilgun from his pocket and placing it on the desk. He thumbs off the safety, the nearly inaudible whine ringing past the crackle of the fire.

Talin is unfazed by the threat. At this distance she could be upon him before he even reached for the gun. "I'll abstain," she says. "That's a pity. I know you think you've won some great victory in finding me here, Talin. But I want to be here, much to the annoyance of Darian," Zidero says, rapping his fingers beside the gun. "Why come at all? The life of a traitor and insurrectionist not to your liking?" Talin quips, rocking back in her seat. Zidero feigns a smile, takes another swallow of the punchy liquid, and says, "Funny coming from you. No, because I'm tired."

"So you admit it. You willingly colluded—" "Tell me, Talin. Do you think a man should be held responsible for what he can't even remember?" he interrupts. "Then Darian forced you?" Zidero chuckles, "I did nothing outside the law." Talin looks around. The equipment is dated but something about the setup reminds her of the collapsed cenobium in Gaerdan. The thought of that place sends a shiver down her spine. "What is this place?" she asks with a tone of sincerity. "Ah, this was Shwari's study. Haven't been here since she... left," Zidero says, slurring slightly. "What was she researching?" Talin says, wiping a line in the dust on the desk. "She could never accept that praxis was random. She wanted to understand the mechanism. I think a part of her could never accept that Razmus was a dredger." Talin smiles, thinking "Finally, some useful information." She says, "Would you say Darian continued her research? I saw his handwork in Gaerdan." Past furrowed brow, Zidero says, "Something like that."

Ade's voice crackles in Talin' earpiece. A vessel is approaching the island. Zidero takes another gurgling pull from the bottle. "Let's talk about something else," he says, now visibly intoxicated. Talin shrugs. "You and me. We are the same, Talin. We are both cowards," he says, pointing between them with the sloshing container. Talin bristles, spitting, "I forsook everything to find Darian for Adanon. I'm no coward." Zidero thumps his hand on the desk in approval. "Aha, there it is- for Adanon. He has no idea how much you crave his approval. You'd run to the ends of the world rather than confronting your love for that man. You see? You're here with me, not with him." "You have it wrong. I have—" "Do you even know where he is?" Zidero interrupts. Talin looks away. "I'll save you the trouble. He's off wrangling snakes in Ux, with Runa no less." Talin doesn't understand Adanon's preoccupation with the Jana girl. She had seen firsthand how soft he was around her. "She's just a girl," Talin forces herself to say. "That's where we differ. You lie to yourself and act like everything is fine," Zidero says. "I couldn't, so I asked Darian to take the memories away." "It doesn't matter. I'm taking you to the Council. They will shred your synapses looking for Darian." "Oh scary," Zidero mocks. She is getting nowhere. Clearly the threat of psychic distress is nothing to him. They could trade insults and quips until he passes out, but she won't get what she wants. "I have a wager. For every drink I take of that poison, you'll tell me a truth," she says. It's shrewd enough to work on the tycoon. For each drink she takes, her praxic ability wanes, making her less threatening. Zidero is a glass on the edge just waiting for a curious paw. "S-sounds fair," he says rolling his head back, "Drink up."

She takes the decanter and swallows deep. It burns its way down, notes of wood and bitterant leaving her mouth dry. She knows this foul taste. It's Anvilite bark liquor, meant to be mixed with water. Trying not to grimace, she places the decanter back on the desk. "Did Darian compel you to help him?" she says. "No, Talin. You were the only praxiat to ever compel me. Truth be told, I kind of liked it. Very bold," he says with a smile. Crossing her arms and legs, Talin says, "Very cute. We know I'm not your type." She holds up the bottle high, ensuring Zidero sees her next drink. "I've never heard of your wife's research. Why?" she hisses through the burn. "Because they don't want you to know-oh-oh," Zidero replies in a singsong fashion. Talin feels ill. Her eyes float over to the gun on the desk.

She drinks again. "Know what?" Zidero giddily rocks in the chair. "That they don't care about Darian at all. They want the secrets for themselves but aren't willing to search for them," he says. "Why?" Talin asks. "Aht-aht. You didn't drink," Zidero stammers. Talin's stomach turns in knots. She is going to be ill. Just one more. "Fine," she says, downing the last swallow, "Agh- why won't they search for them?" "Because Darian made off with the one thing that can sever them from the cycle. And they are afraid," Zidero says with a flourish. Talin doesn't understand. The members of the Council give up metempsychosis to have recall of their past lives. In the end, they are sacrificed in an ancient ritual which keeps their secrets well beyond the grave. "Being removed from the cycle is their duty. That can't be why..." Talin whispers to herself. She clasps her hand over her mouth, saying, "Unless they are trying to escape that fate." Zidero claps. "A fun game, Talin. Ah, the bottle runs dry. S-suppose our time is up," he says, struggling to his feet, "You're not as terrible as he says."

"I'll come with you, just... hands off," Zidero says. In a moment of uncharacteristic understanding, Talin stands. She is certain they are both too inebriated to do much. "Pardon me," Zidero says, turning to relieve himself in the corner of the room. It almost coaxes a chuckle from Talin, if not for the missing weapon. "I want you to know I asked him to give them back. Oh how I regret it. Raz, forgive me," Zidero says in a somber tone, turning out of the corner with the coilgun held under his chin. "Wait!" Talin shouts, as Zidero closes his eyes then he pulls the trigger. Of all the thoughts lost to eternity, the last to pass through Zidero's mind are of neither life nor love. As violence ushers in the dark, he thinks of his legacy, then nothing ever more.

His body folds beside the hearth, spilling a dark pool which seeps under the tangle of cables. Talin lets out a primal screech, but not for the loss of the man; for herself. Her one avenue to vindication is now a gurgling corpse. She drops to her knees before the hearth and does the only thing her mind can muster to gain some semblance of control. She strikes the dead man. "How dare you," she growls as her fists slam into Zidero's lifeless husk. She repeats this over and over until the words lose meaning and her hands tremble. Tears dry on her face as footsteps approach from behind her. "Talin Argyra, by order of the Council you are being detained," a gruff voice says from the doorway.

CHAPTER 45

"What do you mean, 'evacuating Esoptrians isn't a priority?'" Adanon asks Lamphros on the helm of the Nurval in the early morning hours. "I have my orders," the Admiral replies, peering through a pair of binoculars at a wall of fog. After the rain had abated, the heavy fog rolled over the southbound fleet from the west. Near the two men, a communications officer pulls off his headset. "Kyr, something strange out there. Low gain- it's everywhere," he says, offering the device to Lamphros. He refuses with the wave of his hand. "Kyr, it's artificial. Maybe it's the Janamudra?" Adanon takes the headset and presses it to one ear. All he hears is static with interspersed pops. Now keenly interested in niggling Adanon, the Admiral pulls away the headset and says, "That's unnecessary, Akroates. Tend to your children. We have work to do here." Adanon glares at the man. "My children, are none of your concern. You've already overstepped your authority moving Holfnir to the Rushander- I need a direct line to the council," he says rapping his fingers on the communication console.

Adanon wipes sweat from his brow as the communications officer hands him the headset. "Cryptography paused running that signal for this," Adanon sighs. "Alright, I'll take it here," he says. Moments later the garbled but familiar voice of councilor Aoifia greets him. "Potentate, things in Uxkukul are... tenuous. The good news first, we no longer have to deal with Medon." Several of the eavesdropping sailors glance about nervously. "Dead?" Aoifia asks pointedly. "Correct." A distorted sigh comes across the line. "You have a strange notion of good news, Akroates. What of the queen?" There is a protracted silence. "Emboldened," Adanon says after a time. Aoifia mirrors his silence for a time. "Tenuous indeed. I also have good news, your wayward protégé has returned. Safe journeys to rendezvous with the Janamudra, Akroates. I have an interrogation to conduct," she says before the signal falls silent. Adanon sits for a time at the console with his head pressed into his hands. Talin has returned, as if he doesn't have enough to worry about. From the printer a cursory decryption of the transmission begins to print, "DA-RI—"

A bleary-eyed Turios shares a glance with Runa, who is sat upon the table within the Stanchion. "I can't see anything out there," Runa says, rubbing her eyes. That's not entirely true. While projecting, she can make out the lights and masts of the Rushander, Ereshkin, and what she assumes is the Uruun trailing far behind; all warships of the same class as the Nurval. The smaller ships within the fleet are lost among the heavy haze. Turios pinches the bridge of his nose as listens to the disordered transmission. "Go look again, Runa. Something is off," he says. With a frustrated groan, Runa opens a sachet of goldcap then downs the contents as she lies back. The console printer begins printing a decrypted message. "DA- RI- AN- S- EN- D- S- HI- S- RE- GA- RD- S—" From her vantage far above, Runa can make out the shapes of ships in the distance. They are only dark smudges against the southern horizon but an unexpected joy wells up. She recognizes the three large cylinders rolling their way through the mist as the Sabitum of the Janamudra. She turns back to the north for just a moment.

A shockwave ripples through the fleet followed by a flash and a thump that resounds through the hull of the Nurval, rattling her body in the Stanchion. A rolling plume of smoke ascends, pulling fog and flame skyward. The yellow-orange flames are snuffed out in a gasp as a second bloom of radiance washes through her incorporeality. Long shadows cast far through the haze from the cyan sun burning through the hull of the Uruun. Writhing bands of blue twist through the blackened superstructure of the Uruun unabated, before snapping and sending plasma whipping into the roiling sea. The faint odor of sodium hypochlorite washes over her as she returns to the Nurval and sits up. Turning to the wide-eyed Turios and Thand, she mutters "The Uruun is... gone." A second, much closer, explosion shudders through the superstructure of the Nurval. "God in heaven," Thand mutters as Oma rushes to the chamber that controls of the ship's defenses. Runa shakes off the shock. Everyone aboard the Uruun is gone. Something had ruptured the reactor containment, but how? Runa lies back, intending to find out.

Down, down through bulkheads, past the writhing reactor and through the belly of the ship Runa descends. It's a synesthetic assault on her would be senses. The taste of steel. The smell of ozone. The chill of water. Far below and behind her the burning sphere of the core of the Uruun sinks through the murky water. It's beautiful in its intensity, a peerless, gleaming pearl plunging toward the abyss. Runa lets herself drift downward. The ships above churn the luminous waters as she observes. There are far too many ships, far too close. One vessel, with a wide and shallow hull bucks broadside to an Esoptrian frigate. The latter ruptures in a downspout of bubbles. The enemy is interspersed with the fleet. They slipped in with the fog, right under their noses. Another ship erupts. Its bulbous bow lifts out of the water from the detonation. As it returns to the sea the buckled keel sheers under the ship's weight, sending everything aft of midship below the waterline. Then Runa sees them, the people in the water. Some are swimming, some still. The vessel near the flotsam of the Uruum powers ahead, its posturing aggressive. Runa returns to her body.

"Quarter mille south-southwest of the Uruun's last position. Enemy vessel," she slurs. Thand shouts, "You have direct to the bridge." The Nurval shudders as the port propeller churns in reverse and the rudder lunches over hard. A volley of missiles leaves the Sophir, piercing the fog in a symphony of skyward screams. After a leisurely turn, they turn their pointed gaze back slapping the sea in a soggy staccato. From below, Runa watches as they cavitate around the ship. One finds its mark, tearing a gaping hole in the ship's side. In a matter of moments, it lists heavily and rolls its bow toward the seafloor never to reemerge. It's an ugly feeling; she had sent all those people to their watery graves. She has a dark thought: The Deep Father will be greatly pleased. Then she turns her attention toward another vessel. It becomes clear to her how the enemies had infiltrated the fleet under the cover fog. Without the advantage of visual detection from praxiats, the angular structure of the maligned ships had evaded detection by fleet sensors. It seems they were prepared and keenly aware of Esoptrian capabilities. The pearl of light that was the core of the Uruun's reactor impacts the sea floor with a shuddering pulse below. Outside the shallow sea, beyond the Straits of Mulsyn the core may have fallen forever. For more is known about the topography of Fengari than the lightless abyss of the Southern Kitaine ocean. It is the Deep Father's domain, and the ostensive reasoning for the yearly migration of the Janamudra.

"Runa," Turios' voice echoes. He need say nothing more. She understands that he is by her side back on the Nurval. "Relay as best you can but you have to calm down," he says. She is calm. She darts above the surface. The area around the ship is clearing either from the rising sun or an erstwhile errant wind. There is an abstract beauty to the unpredictable movements of the defensive plates orbiting the Nurval. They quiver at Runa's notice. Beyond, the ships in the distance are drawing closer to the battle. Runa is conflicted. The joy at seeing her people is fleeting. It's easy for her to hate them for how she was treated. Finding the courage to forgive them is difficult. She returns to the Nurval, sits up, and lets out a desperate sigh. Turios blinks at her as she places her face in her hands. It is a pivotal moment for her. On one hand she has come to understand that fear of the unknown binds humanity in its ubiquity. On the other, she is still hurting. She turns to Turios, saying, "I think the Jana are heading toward the battle." Thand strolls over accompanied by more muted detonations. She pats Runa hard on the back and says, "Ship-to-ship combat it is then—" She checks her boot knife, aster, and coilgun, "Hope they are as good as you with a knife." Runa smirks. They will need to be, having no weapons of war. Then she returns to her work.

The ships above burn. No matter the outcome of the battle, it will be a pyrrhic victory by the magnitude of loss. To the south, the Sabitum rams an Oringian aggressor. The groan of steel fills the air as the gargantuan ship from a bygone age brings its heft to bear. Runa is so caught up in the sight that she fails to see the prowler. A low-lying vessel approaches the Nurval from the northeast on a broadside intercept. It is only as the malicious barrel of the ship slaps against the orbital armor that she makes the call. The metallic plates ping noisily as Oma brings them around to defend the portside. It's too late. The mass of the ship is too great to shrug off. Runa must do something. She understands now what happened to the Uruun. The Oringian vessels are targeting the reactors. The reactor is two levels directly beneath the stanchion. The Nurval swivels its fore and aft railguns but they can't take aim at a ship so close and low. They fire over the top of the aggressor vessel. The concussion bends antennae and masts of the Oringian ship and sends countless defensive plates pinwheeling through the sky. Runa slides off the table, moving unsteadily toward to port bulkhead. Her heart leaps within. She must get there in time.

Time dilates as she reaches the port most wall. It takes a dozen milliseconds for a human to perceive outside stimuli. She knows her senses will fail in the face of the forces at work. So, she won't use them. She clutches the blade at her hip, recalling her improbable feat that night with the wreather. Preempting the ship-killer weapon firing, she holds her hand against the clammy steel bulkhead. In this moment of utmost gravity, she casts aside her thoughts, the strength of stars coursing through her veins. Through her, an accretion of consciousness coalesces in a moment that breaks parity. Then the Oringians fire.

The heat piercing the bulkhead kisses Runa's flesh followed by the vengeful mass. She grasps it with the care of a priceless instrument. An instrument on which she plays a final chord, the notes of which resolve the dissonance in the design. The gout of destruction collapses at her touch, arresting every inextricable unit of matter into that place beyond and letting the infinitesimal remainder pass through. But not before leaving its mark.

Adanon bursts into the Stanchion as thunderous report on the starboard side rocks the ship. Smoke and sunlight greet him through a cavernous hole in the port bulkhead. He is dumbfounded. Everyone on the ship, much less this room, should be dead. Near the mangled steel, illuminated by the hazy daylight, Runa writhes on the floor. Like a newborn, she struggles to crawl. Shouting and movement echo about the room, but heedless of the commotion Adanon rushes to her side. He cradles her as a return volley rumbles the ship. Runa's thoughts are erratic. He doesn't mean to breach that barrier of trust, but her delirious eyes are asking him, "Why?" Shakily she says, "I thought I could fix it." Adanon lets out an incongruous chuckle, wishing he had some way to soothe her. He searches for a pleasant moment in recent memory, but he comes up short. Then he thinks back to his youth. Not to the blustery years among the domes, but the last time he can remember being content.

It's an evening in a tavern in Stenandra, on the Esoptrian side of the lift. The air is thick with the scent of maple liqueur on the lips of boisterous youths. Laughter fills this place. Gathered around are the members of his cohort. Darian, the brash but empathetic. Jaxa, the quiet, pensive; Turios will one day favor his father in this regard. Shwari, the Jana exile who had always been too clever for her own good. Her cunning, only outweighed by her care for her future son Razmus. Their waitress is Diba, Adanon's future wife. But for now, she is just the buxom dredger with the raven hair. As the drinks flow and the youths speak of changing the world, Adanon is happy to be in such fine company.

This is how he likes to remember them. He focuses on that feeling of conciliation, imparting it to Runa as she lies bleeding in his arms.

THE END

ΞPILOGUΞ

Runa checks the fit of the full-length leather glove on her arm, or rather, what had once been. She flexes the similitude of a hand, testing her control. Biomed has made many advancements but it cannot regrow a limb. The fragments of metal secreted within the dark hide frame clink against one another. The aster will have to stay on permanent assignment. She winces. The pain is still very real and probably always will be. At least that's what the physicians say. She feels different now, not just physically. She has had time to think and to grieve. There have been many dark nights thinking about loss. Perhaps her younger, less seasoned self would have been broken by the loss of her limb. But praxis has given her an unwavering focus. She scoffs as she shoulders her pack. For now, she takes it one day a time. Relearning a lifetime of tasks with an appendage of her own imagining. What is it that Naahui had said? "We all have to give up a piece of ourselves to be the person we're meant to be." A cruel joke if she had known. Then again, the queen didn't seem predisposed toward jest. Runa has since given up understanding the queen's motives. Naahui had orchestrated an assassination with Runa's unwitting assistance. The cackles of the treehound as the Queen possessed it still rattle her dreams. After the catastrophe orchestrated by Orin on the southern reaches of the shallow sea, the queen of a freshly liberated Uxkukul boldly, or foolishly rendered aid to Esoptria. An unlikely allegiance in a time when allies are fleeting.

After a time, she makes her way out of the room, making her way through the sterile white halls of the hospital at the heart of Esoptria. She frowns stepping out onto the quiet streets of the capitol. Adanon and the members of her cohort had visited her in those long days after her injury. He had told her to keep quiet about what happened that day aboard the Nurval. 'A critical failure of enemy munition,' read the official report. Anyone who had surveilled the damage would know that was a fabrication. "Avoid the attention of the Council. I can only do so much," Adanon had said after his first visit. Only time will tell what he had meant by that. Presently, Runa crosses back through the city toward the harbor, away from the Grand Cenobium where she and her cohort will be assigned a tour of duty. It seems Adanon's attempts to spare the younger generations of praxiats from war have fallen short. Stopping to rest her hands on a railing near a canal, she looks up. Upon what had once been the pristine glass edifice of the Lycorp building a banner hangs. Emblazoned in red across the banner are the words, "Know thy enemy," above the billowing image of a one-eyed man. The sight gives her pause. There is a difference of decades, but the likeness is true to the visage in her dreams. His single gleaming eye emerald pierces her with its intensity. She stands there for a time, transfixed by the likeness of a man she has never truly seen. The groan of the metal yielding under her grasp brings her back. Thinking of the small satchel gifted from Naahui still secreted away in her pack, she turns away from the imposing canvas of the enigmatic Darian.

She winces at a phantom pain in her arm. It urges her to carry on. "One mystery at a time," she mutters to herself. She is on her way to see something she can't believe. During the time limping back to Esoptria, Runa had spent time projecting over the fleet, searching. Presently, she is drawing nearer the harbor, the smells of the lagoon driving out the stench of the mire. Her mind turns to home, and for good reason. Home is here. At the end of the pier, she looks out over the shimmering lagoon upon which bobs the Janamudra flotilla. It's hard to make out the individual vessels from this distance, but Runa knows one ship is missing. She had confirmed that beforehand a dozen times. The Shyena hadn't been among those lost running the blockade, nor was it damaged in the battle. Her family's ship is simply gone, and she intends to find out why.

ABOUT THE AUTHOR

Eric Miltner lives in Warner Robins, Georgia with his wife and two daughters. An alumni of Mount de Sales Academy, he continued his education at Mercer University and Macon State University. He currently works with the Department of Defense and enjoys playing video games and tabletop games. When Eric is not writing or painting, he can be found studying psychology, anthropology, and astronomy. He plans to complete his first series of novels while spending time with his children.

DEAR READER

I hope you enjoyed Accretion. I am truly grateful that you took the time to read this book.

I would really appreciate it if you could take a few minutes and leave me a positive review on Amazon.com and Goodreads.com. Your feedback is very important to me and it helps spread the word about my new series. Join me on my social media channels and website to keep up with all of my adventures.

Thank you again for believing in my words. I have been working on this for a very long time and I am so thankful that I found a way to do it. I look forward to working on the next book in this series.

Made in the USA
Columbia, SC
27 March 2024

33710117R00147